Gold Miner's Daughter
Cold Justice on the Last Frontier

Rick Steeby

Table of Contents

Copyright

Acknowledgements

This book exists because of John and Dee Steeby, my parents who shaped all my experiences. Mom helped edit my first novel attempt before cancer took her, and Dad, who read this manuscript, left us last summer.

Key influences include Mr. Kirk, who taught me to truly live; my military and career experiences—from Army MP to Alaska Pipeline security to the Anchorage Police Department; and my first wife Sherry, who blessed me with daughters Heather and DeAnna.

My APD colleagues and friend Wayne Vance inspired my writing journey. Most importantly, my wife Linda has supported me for over twenty-five years, bringing stepdaughters Shelley, Jennifer (RIP), and Nickie into my life.

I'm grateful to editors Mellissa Swenka and Cayce Berryman, and mentors John Battaglia and Dan Mills, who encouraged me throughout this journey. Thanks to Gloria Peoples Elam for her Texas Ranger insights, and to Vicki Sanders-Riendl, whose expertise on Alaskan placer mining kept this story authentic.

To Dan S. Mills, my friend since our days at Chugiak High School and somehow we survived our wild years and made it to the good ones. Thank you for giving visual form to my imagination. The star on this cover is his gift to my story.

Chapter 1

For a drifting, Parker County Texan, after surviving my second winter in the Klondike, spring in Chicken, Alaska, didn't impress me as warm. After months of isolation, reading books and reciting poetry to fill my time, it was a welcome sight.

The sun in May shines brightly for sixteen hours a day. Back home, it would be in the eighties. I watched the snow dwindle. Mud and standing water filled most open areas, waiting for the ground to thaw enough to soak in.

After the mosquitos appear, the next sure sign of spring is when the Yukon River breaks up in Dawson City. Due any day, unofficially, it marks the start of the 1960 mining season. The Fortymile area was part of the 1898 gold rush that reached Alaska in 1900. On the Alaska side of the border, it included the communities of Boundary, Eagle, and Chicken.

I pushed my well-worn brown Stetson back and took in an enormous sky stretching from north to south, east to west, without a single cloud. Fifty-degree daytime temps thawed out the mosquitoes. They froze in midair last September, and as if resurrected from the snow by Jesus himself, they shook off the cold like a layer of trail dust and formed vampiric swarms of gray fog searching for blood.

Swatting at the bugs, I saw scrub brush half buried in the snow, already sprouting leaves. The pussy willows line the banks of Davis Creek, and water peeked through and gurgled in open patches in the ice. Spring signaled a fresh beginning and change in the course of my life.

It started almost a year ago. After leaving Korea, I never intended to live in the cold again. Years of drifting with no plan but to be gone from Texas, fate changed my opinion of the frozen north in a choking breath of dust and a blink of a blue eye.

My dirt-stained white T-shirt had holes in it, and my jeans too. My slip-on rubber boots completed my uniform for the summer in the mining camp. The rest of my gear fit inside a surplus duffle bag from the Army I got after leaving the service. This morning, I pushed back a two-year growth of dark hair on my head and face.

Being a thinking man, I contemplated my sudden desire for substance and surveyed my new gold claim. It wasn't much, but more than I held title to since the war ended. The previous succession of owners all gave up because the price of gold offered by the government didn't pay for the cost of operations required to hold the claim. Having worked on the claim downstream, I believe there is gold on this patch. Where and how much — those were the questions.

Making a living above expenses had proven impossible for Rosenburg, and the same was true for those before him. I figured on a low overhead operation to try and not go broke. My ambition was sparked by Amy Crockett, more than making a living mining.

Before freeze-up last winter, Dottie, the bartender up at Chicken, told me Rosenberg quit his mine, and it would be available. The place appealed to me for several reasons. First, I could walk to my current employer's claim. More importantly, it put me a short hike to Amy Crockett's claim.

Acquiring this place was important enough for me to fly white-knuckled in a Super Cub with the pilot who brought in our mail. Chicken being his last stop, I bummed a ride to Fairbanks. I don't care for airplanes; the smaller they are, the less I like them. In the Army, I always felt safer after jumping out of them.

I arrived in Fairbanks the night before I could file, and I submitted the paperwork for the claim the following day. Like that, I became a mine owner. A huge step up from drifting laborer in my mind, and —I hoped— in Amy's.

Standing on the creek bank, over the constant hum of emerging insects, I heard the growling rumble of an approaching swamp buggy. The rig belonged to the proprietor of the Chicken General Store, the town's unofficial mayor. Most everything qualified as unofficial when it came to Chicken. Visiting often with Gene at his store helped me survive the winter as a caretaker on the Barnes claim. The rolling icebreaker bounced along the creek bed, sending water and ice flying onto the banks kicked from under the huge surplus tires made for a World War II bomber. They stood six feet high, mounted on a same era, five-quarter ton, carryall Army Dodge still painted splotchy, drab olive green.

It was not pretty, but Gene's rig served as the most reliable off-road, year-round transportation and taxi service in the greater Chicken area.

The mayor I counted as a friend and one of those quirky citizens a place like Chicken attracts. Dottie said, sometime back, on an extended winter stay after too much booze, Ol' Gene saw apparitions in the sky—things that scared him to his core.

Nowadays, Gene listened to the Russians on his amateur licensed ham radio but told me he couldn't decide if the Communists flew the spaceships or aliens. Whichever, it put him to watching the subarctic sky and listening intently to his radio.

Seeing the buggy surprised me, but Gene driving a passenger surprised me more. The blue uniform and the Smoky Bear campaign hat, with a grizzly bear emblem emblazed on a gold badge, marked him as an Alaska State Police officer.

Gene's beast blew a puff of black smoke, spewing from a vertical exhaust pipe. His buggy hummed along in granny low as it scratched onto a gravel bench near the school bus abandoned by someone before Rosenburg, and then he squealed to a halt.

With a tinny screech of the door hinges, the state cop, a big fella, stepped out on the running board, held his hat, and jumped. He hit where it looked dry on top. The officer stood taller than my six-two and thirty pounds heavier than me. I ate better and weighed more before arriving in Chicken; it's been a year or so since I consumed regular meals.

He landed, squishing mud and water up around his rubber boots. The controlled smile told me two things. First, it was a friendly visit, and second, business.. Besides, no one made the trip from Chicken up Davis Creek sightseeing.

"Officer Robertson, folks call me Robbie." He extended his hand to shake, showing a lot of trust for a lawman.

I figured Gene filled him in on my character and what little I shared about my past. Taking the offered hand, I looked him in the eye, gave it a pump, and stepped back. A proper greeting the way Pa taught me.

"Wyatt Peoples, sir. I don't have the deed for this property yet, but I have the stamped paperwork saying I filed on the claim."

The creases around his eyes suggested a man more prone to smile than frown but remained neutral because business came first. "I'm here to see you, but not about your claim. You know the Crocketts over on Poker Creek?"

I glanced at Gene, who surely had told him that much.

"I've bumped into them a time or two up at Chicken, Boundary, and a couple of times in Dawson. Following the creek banks, their place is a few miles south and east of here. When I first came into this country a year ago, I went by their place and asked for work." Unsure where this conversation might lead, I understated how well I knew them.

Robbie nodded. The shadow from his hat moved across his face, and he swiped at the bloodthirsty insects. "Is that where you met Tim?"

A chill in his voice made me aware there was more to the question. Tim Crockett, the mine owner's oldest son, rated my best friend in Chicken, which topped a short list of folks. The least ambitious of the kids, he found any excuse to make a trip to town. I ran into him at Dottie's Bar and Grill when I first arrived. He liked to talk, so when I said I needed work, he took me to the claim to meet his dad.

I never got to speak to Tim's dad or get a job, but I did see Amy. It wasn't much of a meeting, and after shaking her hand, I developed the damnedest speech impediment.

I cleared the memory. "No, sir, up to Chicken, hunting a job."

"Word is you're friendly with him."

I tried to think of anyone who wasn't. "Did you ever meet the guy?"

Robbie nodded his head.

"So, you know he's outgoing, and most everyone is friends with him."

"Information we received is he had his eye on this place."

The officer barely let me finish before making his statement.

I wondered who said so. Tim told me how to acquire a claim if the owner didn't do his prove-up work. Besides, it was hard to believe Tim was hunting for the kind of work owning a mine requires.

"Miss Dottie told me several folks hankered for this place and said to get to the claims office opening day. I didn't ask who." I held the state cop's stare. "What's this about?"

Robbie's eyes twitched at the mention of Dottie's name. He pulled his head back and puffed up, showing me his authority before answering.

"Tim flew into Chicken a week ago to prepare the family claim. Gene said he dropped him off near their place soon after arriving at Chicken. No one has seen him since. His brother Ricky came in two days ago, and it appears Tim never reached their mine."

"Officer, I didn't know he was in the area, and I haven't seen hide nor hair of him here or where I stayed at Barnes's place. Which is odd because he's a social kind of guy."

"Gene," Robbie tipped his head toward the buggy, "drove him up the road to the trailhead for Poker Creek and said he walked in."

The highway curved north of Davis Creek, then turned southeast toward the Canadian border and crossed the upper reaches of Poker Creek. A trail ran from their place on the south side of the river, a shortcut to the Crocketts' mine rather than the creek road, and a much easier path to walk.

A thought occurred I didn't like. "Bear popping season and a Toklat grizzly passed by here a couple of times in the last week." Hibernation ended a few weeks earlier for the brown bears, and black bears would soon appear.

Robertson stared upstream considering my words. "It's a thought we have to consider. I'll be around for a while hunting any sign of Tim."

The winter season is hard on the wildlife, and many don't make it.

I gestured to the wilderness surrounding us. "Guessing between wolf and spring bear kills and the usual dead moose and caribou defrosting, it won't be an easy spot."

After some discussion, the mayor and officer departed the way they came, planning to visit Crocketts' next. In my limited experience in the north country, a man missing for a week, with below-freezing nighttime temps, encounters with bears, moose, or an accidental fall, could be fatal.

Chapter 2

When I drifted into Fortymile country by way of Dawson City, Alaska still hunted statehood in the summer of '58. Last year, I survived four seasons in the Klondike, and although considered a newcomer, but not a *cheechako*, I was promoted by longevity to a "sourdough." The joke was that sourdoughs were sour on the Yukon but lacked the dough to get out.

In '59, Alaska became a state. Law enforcement duties changed from federal Territorial Police to State Police. The same people, but they were still dealing with the change. Bill Egan got elected governor and took a tight grip on guiding the new government.

While hunting a job, my first encounter with Amy Crockett caught me off guard. First, she operated a Cat bulldozer, pushing a load of gravel into the header. The earth mover crept forward and filled the air with diesel exhaust and a cloud of dust.

The header swirled full of water, and the family crew washed the dirt into the chute. The water separates the raw minerals from the clay and flushes all the material over the riffles. The Crocketts diverted a water supply from a tributary spilling off the bluff for sluicing the gold-bearing soils. From there, it flows into a settling pond where the silty sediments drop out before the water filters into the stream.

Late in the season of '59, laid off from the dredge I worked on near Dawson, I went hunting for a job. I stopped at Chicken, the second place I came to, seeking employment. The day I met the family, it was hot by Alaska standards, in the mid-eighties. Amy materialized out of the dust, standing on the giant machine's track, one hand holding the engine cover.

She barked orders at Tim and Ricky, her brothers, before turning her sparkling blue eyes on me. Her hair hung around a freckled face, dirty blonde, or maybe just dirty, matching the smudges on her jeans and denim shirt with cuffs rolled up to her elbows. A black leather belt pulled tight at the waist accented her figure. In the dust and sunlight, she was the most attractive gal I ever set eyes on.

She jumped to the ground and landed with a solid thump I heard over the idling dozer and splashing water. She walked the rim of the tank like a tightrope, hopped across the chute, and lit in front of me. The top of her wavy hair came to my chin.

Amy jerked off a leather glove, slapped her bare hand against her leg, and shook hands like the boss, not a hired hand.

"Hi, I'm Amy, and I'm afraid we don't have any work for you. I assume my brother brought you along to cut back on what little he does already."

Tim protested, and Ricky smiled and kept a close eye on the water as he mucked dirt into the current. I tried to say howdy, but came out, "Ugh."

The words hung up around my paralyzed tongue. A speech impediment developed right on the spot.

Embarrassed, my stomach rolled its eyes so hard I contemplated throwing up. Not that my gut had eyes, but my whole being felt confused. Tim laughed, and I hunted for a suitable rock to throw at him. Unable to speak, choked up, and humiliated, I turned and started walking to Chicken, kicking at the dirt and stomping through the creek.

I faced a bayonet charge of a thousand men on a frozen hill in Korea with less fear and more grace than standing in front of a woman I had never met before. I hiked up the trail, kicked rocks, and smacked myself on the back of my head. The Barnes mine sat a few miles downstream on Poker Creek toward Chicken. I chatted with the line boss, Chet Robarts, and went to work for them. Chicken, Alaska, felt like home after meeting Tim's sister.

The only explanation—love. A different breed than any I experienced elsewhere. With the short summer season, mining camp didn't leave time for socializing or romance. After meeting Amy, I couldn't leave Chicken.

Amy rarely left their camp except after cleaning the sluice every other Friday. Then, the family gathered their guitars and headed to Dottie's place or Action Jackson's bar in Boundary, and, sometimes, in Eagle. On rare occasions, they trekked to Dawson to perform on stage at a gambling saloon there. Doug, Ricky, Tim, and Amy played as musical siblings. They sang folk and country tunes from memory and drew a crowd wherever they played.

My schedule seldom meshed with theirs since my employer, Barnes, preferred his people to work daylight hours, which started early and ran almost all night in the summer. Folks say that I have a fine baritone voice when my mouth functions, but it fails me if I stand in sight of Amy.

I stood by the bus smiling, staring off where Gene's 4x4 slung mud and muck up on the bank, and listened to the flathead six-cylinder engine rumble toward the Barnes claim. My mind wandered elsewhere.

On Dad's ranch, near Weatherford, I picked up reciting cowboy poetry memorized while mucking out barns and on the back of a nag horse chasing cow critters. When I hit Dawson in '58, I worked on a gold dredge south and east of town. I bought a book of Robert Service poems. They came in a pocket-sized hardback. The poetry I found similar to the cowboy variety. Before long, I added "The Spell of the Yukon" and other Service poems to my memorized repertoire. After hours, the dredge crew hounded me to entertain them while they ate or in the bunkhouse before the lights went out.

When Dottie overheard me spout a few lines from "The Cremation of Sam McGee" to Tim in her bar, she hired me to fill in during band breaks. Live entertainment reigned supreme since no radio, TV, or movie houses existed there. Gene owned a phonograph but not too many records.

Dottie, I guessed to be old enough to be my mother but still a striking woman, and one I'm never too sure of. With a sharp mind for business and a curvy figure, Dottie used her intelligence and looks to her advantage. I swung my hat around, scattering the skeeters, and jammed it over an excess accumulation of hair. I reckon Dot's wit and charms swayed me as much as the next guy.

Don't get the wrong idea. Miss Dottie never hired traveling bands, either. Miners or laborers with musical instruments would join others and play during their free time; often, the entertainment amounted to nothing more than a jam session.

I learned from Tim and Dottie that the Crocketts were special since they performed as a family from childhood. The four members qualified as the closest thing nearer than Dawson City to being a professional group. Like everyone at Dottie's, they played for tips and one complimentary drink each.

Being a fan of rustic architecture from being around ranch houses, barns, and mining camps, I marveled at the roughhewn nature of Dot's bar. She was proud of the post and frame construction. Someone canceled an order for twelve by twenty-four inch, rough-cut timbers in Dawson. She bought the whole lot at a bargain price, trucked them in, and designed the building around using them.

She made the floor, posts, and rafters from the beams and used them as the bones of the bar. The ceiling someone built from varnished shiplap boards with steel roofing tacked on top. The walls matched the ceiling, covered with sawmill slabs on the outside to look like logs.

In spring, summer, and fall, the wood stove in the kitchen remained in use. The one in the dining, dancing, drinking, and eating room Dottie fired up on chilly days. It reminded me of a hunting lodge atmosphere and smelled of cooking, pinewood smoke, cigarettes, and dirty miners. Dottie had an eye for décor and framed the windows and bar with diamond willow. Chicken's chief and only paid mechanic, Boyd, carved it for her.

Her entertainers used the stage in the corner, which she constructed a foot higher than the floor and made from oak boards salvaged from shipping pallets. In the summer, additional lighting was optional during the day, but they lit oil lanterns on the walls when it got dark. Each one Dottie had strapped on a shelf in case of earthquakes. A shake in '55 knocked over a light and caused a fire that burned the previous owner out.

One Friday night during my first season in Alaska, Dottie asked me to open the entertainment covering for a late band. Since everyone's first job was mining, playing came second, so Dottie accepted delays as inevitable.

Running through a rendition of poetry, I stalled for the band. I opened with "Bessy's Boil." Followed them with a couple of cowboy poems I knew, and then I finished with "The Spell of the Yukon."

Over the past winter, I have practiced it often and felt a dual meaning in Service's words. Bowing to my audience at the bar, I realized most of my ovation came from behind me. I turned and spotted the Crocketts, instruments in hand, waiting their turn on stage.

As Amy passed, she said, "And here I thought you couldn't speak."

I croaked, "Hi," and in the bar mirror, I saw I turned red as a beet.

Tim shook his head, grinning, and said, "You're a regular Shakespeare," and then, "Well done."

Their father didn't come with them. He went to Anchorage early, Tim told me later, for a doctor's appointment.

Late last summer, I found my voice while performing around Amy, but in conversation, I still fumbled with words like *the, but,* and *hello.*

Some patrons started calling me the Red-Faced Poet, and it stuck.

Amy and her brothers worked at the area bars a few times with me over the rest of the summer. By the season's end, I could form simple sentences in her presence. If she had any feelings for me, I couldn't tell. All business at work or play, she didn't want or require a dance partner. Tim said she had recently divorced and that I should not bring it up with her.

Over the winter, I practiced my poetic delivery while shadowboxing or punching a bag of sand—homemade boxing gear like Dad set up in the barn. Even my sister learned to box. We boys all fought Golden Gloves in school. I tried to pen a love poem for Amy, but I ran out of paper. Punching the bag took out frustration for having no more luck writing lyrics than trying to talk to her.

After slapping a skeeter on my arm, I pulled the Stetson down tight and stared as the swamp buggy bounced over gravel bars and around the bend. Quiet returned, and a few magpies fussed in the distance. A lone raven passed, heading east toward Canada.

Before walking to the Barnes mine, I kept a wary eye on the brush along the creek banks for bears or moose. While busy outdoors, I recited poetry to prevent startling either one.

Tim worried me. I liked the guy, but didn't care for his odds. I studied the leftover junk strewn across the claim by the three or four failed attempts to make it pay since the rush of '98. An old shot-up gold pan half buried in the sand and a broken hand rocker thrown in the willows. Along the bank, rusty piping brought water from upstream to wash gravel through an old sluice that needed repair or replacement.

It's been a long road with lots of bumps to end up in this spot. I left Fort Worth with my tail tucked because I brought shame to the family name.

Dad and two uncles were lawmen. One uncle on Mom's side got elected sheriff in Parker County, Dad retired from the Texas Rangers, and Grandpap's youngest son rated as a legend in the Rangers.

As a name, Wyatt pointed to the importance Pa put in law enforcement. My older brother William Hickock Peoples serves in the Texas State Police in Austin and is destined to be a Ranger, too. He served in the Navy at the end of WWII.

History, I can't change; but this claim is a fresh start. The mystery school bus rolled out of the factory in the early '50s, and a near genius had converted it into a mobile residence that was safer to sleep in than a tent.. For added comfort, someone glued Styrene foam insulation inside to hold the heat generated in a homemade stove for heating and indoor cooking. The foam boards gave it an igloo look from the inside, only with windows.

When I moved in, about when Tim went missing, I cleaned the bus and made a proper place for my sleeping bag and duffle. Over the winter, another miner called it quits. He sold me his two-wheel drive motorcycle. It came with garden tractor tires front and back and ran on a small gas engine. One previous owner painted it black, but I saw the factory orange where the paint wore through.

Walking the gravel path, I crossed the stream in a shallow spot, stumping my way to Barnes's mine, wishing my motorbike was reliable. It worked any time I didn't need to go somewhere. The last time I took it to Barnes's; I pushed and carried it back. I ordered a tune-up kit from Sears and Roebuck.

The big Barnes operation was to be up and running in another week, and several chores needed to be completed as part of my agreement to winter on the claim. Barnes provided grub and a small cabin with a wood stove. I split wood, cooked for myself, and stayed all winter in Chicken with a dozen other permanent residents. Turning over another new leaf, I took the caretaker's position to avoid trouble with booze and save money. I didn't consider myself an alcoholic, but God blessed me with an excellent memory and cursed me with too few good ones.

Walking the creek bank to work, I swung wide of a family of porcupines, ducked under a birch tree limb, and wondered about Tim. I decided to visit Ricky after my chores. If asked, I would help search for

Tim's body. I lived in this wilderness long enough to guess he stood little chance of being alive.

~~~

At the day's end, I walked upstream on Poker Creek, following a road in the water almost as much as out. I spotted Ricky sitting at the campfire, roasting a hot dog. A can of pork and beans sat on a hot rock beside the fire.

One glance at their operation with several acres of bulldozed land made me aware of what it took to create a working claim. It required laborers and equipment like their big D8 Cat, which I can't afford. I'm five or six years away from matching their operation. A guy could pick up most of that stuff from quitters, who outnumbered start-ups.

Ricky favored Amy's looks, taller and without her shape, sporting a beard and a mustache. The wavy hair and color, an easy smile, and gleaming blue eyes marked them as siblings.

He jumped from the camp chair and grabbed a shotgun when I hollered, "Howdy."

He recognized me, leaned the gun against a barrel, and welcomed me to camp.

"Pull up a stump. Have you had a bite?"

"Nothing since breakfast." I dropped on a stump stool.

Ricky dug into a canvas bag and came out with a blue-speckled enamel plate and a spoon. He handed them over. "Cut you a willow stick and toast yourself a dog. There's bread in the sack and cold beer in the creek."

"I'll drink water, but thanks." My host used a gloved hand to pick up the hot beans and poured some on a plate. I walked to the spring with a coffee cup, dipped some water, and cut a willow branch with my knife.

Ricky stared into the fire. After I took a seat, he said, "I guess you heard about Tim going missing."

Build-wise, Tim looked a lot like Ricky, only with dark hair, and his facial features chiseled with harder lines, Tim taking after his father. Amy, and Doug, I assumed, favored their Ma, someone not as slim, with a rounder face and freckles.

"Yes, sir. Gene brought the lawman up to my place, checking for him." I replied.

"They came by here also, and Officer Robbie walked up to the road on the trail."

On foot, the shortest distance to Chicken was to hike to the highway and take it back. A wide spot in the road made a place to park a car.

From my claim, I could take a shortcut trail southeast over a rise to Crocketts'. Most walking paths started as game trails, which tended to wander and not take the most direct route.

Stabbing a hotdog on a stick, I shoved it in the fire. Being hungry, I preferred charred over slow roasted.

"You know of any trouble Tim had with anyone?"

Ricky sipped on his Olympia beer and turned his head. "Wyatt, you're sounding like a cop."

"Sorry, an old habit."

"How's that?" Ricky put his empty plate on another stump serving as an end table. I scooped a spoonful of beans while keeping an eye on my wiener. I talked little about my past.

In the bush, people considered it impolite to inquire about a person's history. Laboring in a mining camp, folks found how hard and smart you worked more important. Everyone expected peculiarities, and lord knows, I arrived in Alaska with my fair share.

"Before the war in Korea, my uncle hired me out of high school to serve and protect the good people of Parker County as a deputy sheriff. As the sheriff, it was his prerogative. I turned eighteen during my training. I quit a year later and joined the Army. They sent me to Fort Benning to learn how to jump out of airplanes. The wrong time for me to discover I didn't like to fly. Then, the war broke out in Korea.

"After I mustered out, I hired on with the Fort Worth PD. Being a veteran, tall, born in Texas, and with a famous Texas Ranger relative or two, they took me on. I guess cop work is in my blood and background."

Ricky watched me sort of sideways. "I didn't know you were ever in that line of work. All you ever talk about is growing up on the ranch and working around mines. You went to war, too?"

"Back home, I had a name to live up to, a legend, and I didn't measure up. While at Fort Worth, the war was still fresh on my mind. I had danged few memories worth hav'n from Korea. Drank too much whiskey trying to forget."

It's been difficult for me to forget anything since I learned to walk. My siblings and I were taught to see details and remember them. Pa asked questions about our day and wanted details. A serious lesson, he made it sound like life or death. Seeing and remembering things helped keep me and my fellow Rangers alive. Details are important, and memorization, Dad ingrained into my soul.

Ricky stood, strolled to the water, and pulled out another cold beer. He walked as if asleep.

Dropping into his seat, he used a can opener on a string tied to a post. He glanced at me while I wrapped a slice of white bread around the cooked dog and took a bite.

He said, "Tell you the truth, when I got here, I was pissed thinking my brother ran off to Dawson or something, leaving me all the work to do."

I swallowed and said, "Then."

He nodded. "Then, I realized he never made it to the camp. I searched the trail from Chicken along the creek with the Jeep Boyd lent me, and alongside the road from his shop to the trail, but no sign of Tim. I sent word out with Gene by radio, and they pointed Robbie here from Tok to investigate. He flew into town yesterday."

"So, Tim had no trouble with anyone?"

"Nothing I'm aware of until the cop said something about Tim wanting your claim, which is pure BS. Gold claims are hard work. My brother is okay, but he had plenty to do here. No way he went hunting for extra."

"I thought it out of character for him, when Robbie asked me about it. Dottie told me someone wanted the bus mine. She would have told Tim before me if he wanted it."

Ricky poked at the fire with his hot dog stick, and I finished eating. Hungry enough to eat way more, I refused when Ricky offered. My ma would have whipped me had I imposed. Not taking advantage was more than being polite. It was law at the Peoples' Ranch.

We talked about Tim and things I needed to prioritize to get my claim running. An hour or so before it was pitch dark, in the long twilight of spring, I said goodbye and started for the cut-through trail.

Ricky said, "Where's your gun?"

"I don't like packing the shotgun, and I don't own a pistol or a rifle."

Ricky's eyebrows raised. "Not worried about the bears?"

I smiled, hitched my foot on a boulder, and an elbow on my knee. "We've come to an agreement. I stay out of their way, and they won't eat me."

Turning, I walked to the trail. Darker among the trees, in less than a hundred yards tramping through the shadows, I wished for my shotgun.

The dark triggered memories of Chinese regulars who came screaming out of the night. The brutal, ruthless drive to survive left me alive, earned me a medal or two, and gave me dreams no one wanted.

The chaplain in Japan asked if I believed in God. Sitting in a hospital bed, I told him, "I'm not a good Christian by Bible Belt standards. However, I'm sure God exists because I served my time in hell and looked the devil in the eye. If hell is real, then God and heaven must be too."

The trail merged with Davis Creek northeast of the claim. Out of the woods, I took a breath and turned downstream. Nearing total darkness, I splashed through a shallow channel and stepped onto a low cutbank. Gravel broke away underfoot, and I lunged forward, swearing a blue streak. The commotion startled a flock of roosting ravens and magpies.

I froze, wary of the birds. A winter kill, I suspected they found a dead caribou. Judging by the odor, Mister Grizzle E. Bear would be here soon. I could think of no reason to investigate without a gun and some light.

Birds give a bear room, so I thought it unlikely one hung out nearby. Still, the better plan was to leave it be.

Chapter 3

Early the next morning, I built a fire to cook some sourdough pancakes and take some chill out of the air. Frost lined the creek bank and the outside of the bus. The sun peeked over the trees, and I heard movement upstream on the trail I walked last night.

I reached for the shotgun when someone called.

"Hello, the camp."

Relaxing when I saw Officer Robertson, I said, "Come on in and take a load off."

Robbie, dressed in his uniform, kept it in military neatness. He watched me lean the gun against the bus but close at hand. He hiked on in and held his hands out toward the fire.

"Care for a pancake?"

It meant splitting my breakfast, but etiquette was to share with visitors.

"No thanks, Mr. Peoples, but a cup of coffee would be good." Robbie replied.

That made me grin. "Just Wyatt, mister sounds too uppity. Your stomach strong? I made it fresh the day before yesterday. When I woke up, I added some water and grounds this morning. Fixing for myself and being poor, I don't throw it out until I can't choke it down."

I found a half dozen tin cups in the bus, and with a clean rag I wiped one out for the officer to pour his own. "I'd say pull up a chair, but I'm fresh out, so sit on the log."

Robbie considered it a second and folded down in a squat, keeping his feet under him, holding his cup left-handed. "I stayed in the guest house at Dottie's last night."

Her guest house amounted to a converted wooden crate that a giant diesel pump came in. She put a canvas over it and made a door in the front. It came with room for an Army cot. You could stand up in it if you stood five feet, six inches tall, or less. I stayed there a few times, but lodging in Chicken was always in short supply, and a night's rental was steep for my wages.

"Better than on the ground, I suppose." I offered, and free until she gets into town.

He held his coffee up, and I noted an indent around his ring finger, but he wore no ring. It's a curious thing, none of my business, but as dad said, details are important. The officer eyed me as I flipped almost burnt pancakes.

"Any line on where Tim disappeared to?"

Robertson started to speak, nodded, "Someone suggested places I ought to look."

I slid my pancakes off the griddle onto a plate, poured syrup from a can, and took a bite.

The cop sipped his coffee, made a face, and waited for me. It didn't take long. In Korea, we ate in a hurry when we had food. When I swallowed my last bite, I walked to the stream, dipped the plate in the water, scrubbed it with sand, and hung it in a tree to dry. As I reached the fire, Robbie gulped what remained in his mug and scrunched up his face again.

I chuckled. "Gave you fair warning."

He stood. "I've drank worse, but not many times."

"Look, sir, I don't mean to be rude, but I have things to do here and down to Poker Creek to earn my keep."

Robbie put up a hand, indicating more to the visit than bumming lousy coffee. "I won't hold you long. I want to show you something."

He marched toward where he came from.

"Leave the gun." He stopped and looked over his shoulder, his hand close to his gun.

I wondered at his tone. I took it as an order, not a suggestion.

"I'm not sure how far we're going, but up yonder, I ran into a bunch of ravens sitting on a winter kill last night in the dark. A shotgun might come in handy." I suggested.

Robbie stood still eyeing me over his shoulder. He meant it to appear casual, but his stance indicated concern, which confused me.

"I have a gun. Leave yours and come along."

Robbie walked along the path, staying to one side. I noted he followed over his tracks and avoided mine from last evening. At a wet spot, he stopped and examined a footprint in the mud.

He placed his right hand on his hip and pointed with his left hand. "Would you mind stepping alongside that print for me?"

"Not much point. It's my print from last night." I wondered about what those birds found.

"I don't doubt it none, humor me." His smile appeared friendly enough, but Robbie stayed careful.

I stepped in the mud, and then back.

Officer Robertson inspected the prints. "A dead certain match. You have a chunk missing out of the heel right there." He pointed a finger at the spot. "You must have caught it on something."

Turning back down the trail, he stepped off at a marching cadence. We reached the squawking birds fighting over scraps. There, Robertson turned toward the woods, pulled his pistol, a blued six-shot .38 Smith and Wesson, and fired a round into the woods, scattering feathered critters in every direction.

He opened his cylinder, removed the spent round, put it in his jacket pocket, loaded a new one, and holstered his weapon.

"Come here." Robbie motioned me to follow, keeping me on his left side.

By then, I knew what I would find and wasn't too excited by the prospects.

Nothing prepares you for what you experience in war or as a cop. The sight of the body in the alder brush rated among the top bad things I ever saw, and I saw a lot of awful stuff. I expected it to be Tim, but whoever lay there was unrecognizable as human other than by exposed bones.

The birds and other four-footed scavengers had ripped the clothing to shreds and eaten everything they could reach other than bone or parts they hadn't gotten around to yet.

"You recognize him?" Robbie asked.

Resting on his back, ribs and skull exposed by scavenging, I saw a hole just off-center through his breastbone. I recalled the dead I helped pick up. Yeah, I laid eyes on worse.

"No, sir, but my guess is Tim. The size and hair color are about right." Obviously, Robbie discovered the remains before coming to camp and why he wanted me unarmed.

A gaunt, emotionless stare from the officer. "You don't look too shocked."

Robbie anticipated a different response. I swallowed and stood taller. I kept my hands down and visible and returned his gaze.

"I reckon from how you carry yourself, you were in the service and, by age, either World War II or Korea, maybe both. You march and wear a uniform like a veteran. If you saw action in either place, you've seen worse or as bad."

"You were in the Army?"

I nodded. "Yes, sir."

"Where?"

Stepping away from the scene and the stench, I turned my back to Tim, glad Amy and her family would never have to live with this memory. For me, it's another to add to my nightmares I lived with.

Birds squawked and flitted from tree to tree, waiting to return to their prize. I pushed my hat back. "Korea."

Robbie spun around in a stiff about-face and stepped closer to me and away from the body. "And you saw worse than this?"

He turned a shoulder toward the corpse.

"Unfortunately, yes." I replied.

From an arm's length away, he crowded me, but I stood my ground.

"Where, exactly, in Korea?" Robbie asked.

Sighing, I gazed over the trees at the bright blue sky. My mind's eye returned to the place I never expected to leave alive.

"Chosen Reservoir was the worst of it, I guess." I lowered my eyes to the officer's face. "What does Korea have to do with this?"

"Nothing, I served as a reserve officer in the Air Force. We maintained and loaded arms on the planes, trying to give you guys air cover. I didn't see a lot of combat. You're lucky to be alive." Robbie replied.

Lucky, maybe, but if so, it only made the guilt worse, thinking of those whose luck ran out. Even for the men I killed, following orders to kill me. But it was senseless for me to go down that rabbit hole again. It caused me to drink too much in the past.

"Yes, sir, Tim's lucky streak ended."

"I thought you didn't recognize him."

I grunted a bit, put off that he thought me an idiot.

"Not much left to go by other than what I mentioned, but, sir, let's be realistic. There aren't more than two dozen people inside fifty miles of here. By now, you've likely accounted for twenty-three, and unless someone else is missing, it narrows the chances to one."

Robbie aimed a finger at me. "I suppose I should arrest you then."

"Why?" I asked.

"Suspicion of murder?"

"Nope." I shook my head and figured Robbie had decided as much.

"Why should I take your word?"

"I would go with the evidence." I said.

He looked back toward the corpse as a couple of ravens hopped closer to the carnage. "And what evidence would that be?"

"First, you followed my tracks from here to my place. I didn't carry the body in there and walk back without leaving tracks. Second, the body was shot with a pistol or a rifle, smaller than a .45 caliber and larger than a .22."

"My guess is a .38 like yours, making you a more likely suspect than me. I own one gun, a shotgun loaded with double ought buckshot." I thought for a second. "Until yesterday, the last time I walked up here, I placed my corner markers. I didn't come up this far. At the time, everything was covered with hard-packed snow in and near the brush before Tim arrived.

"But he got dumped here before it melted. Snow is still under the body, blocked from sunlight. Unless he fell from the sky, there would be no tracks because they would have been in the snow, which is gone now. So, whoever killed him came from Crocketts' camp trail or the one from the highway, which hasn't officially opened for traffic yet."

"Why from the road or Crocketts' and not up from your claim?"

"I'm observant, and no one passed through other than the grizzly I mentioned, and it makes me wonder why he isn't here."

Robbie shrugged. "They generally won't eat humans; we must taste bad to them. Polar bears are the only ones that hunt people. The others might sample a body but generally look elsewhere for food." The tall officer looked puzzled. "Where did you get your training?"

"Fort Benning."

"Military Police?"

"No, sir, Rangers School."

He smiled. "I meant your crime scene training."

"Deputy sheriff once, and after the war, an officer for a short stint with the Fort Worth Police."

Robbie frowned and glanced at Tim, then at me. "Something is up here I'm not seeing yet, but this scene bothers me. I can't leave you here. Despite your convincing argument, you're still a suspect. On the other hand, I need to go to Chicken and send word to the coroner and send someone to transport a body to Anchorage for autopsy."

"Okay, I'll hike to Chicken for you and call for your reinforcements, but it's a long hike, so you can plan on being here for a while."

"Out in the bush, it's one murder, one officer, and no backup. We serve a big state. Have Gene guide whoever comes from Fairbanks and stand by to transport us and the body back to the airport. Tell him Alaska will pay for his time."

~~~

I made the trip down Davis Creek to the Barnes mine, then along Poker Creek to the highway west of Chicken. At a double-time march, I took it to Gene's in a little over two hours, and I arrived around lunchtime at the general store.

The proprietor called on his ham radio and contacted the State Police in Fairbanks. Word came back that their Cessna 180 would be enroute with the doctor and a body bag. A doctor seemed a bit late to my thinking, but he gave us an ETA of four hours. Gene told them about the sloppy airfield conditions and asked them to land a little long where it was better packed.

The wait left me with time to drink good coffee and contemplate who would or could have killed Tim and why.

Chapter 4

I considered the situation while I cooled my heels in the back of Gene's single-story rough plank building, home to the Chicken General Store and Café. People unfamiliar with Alaskan bush communities might think the residents of Chicken would have to be insane to live there.

Granted, being crazy probably didn't hurt. Some eccentric people indeed lived there, and as such, I'm as qualified as any Chickenite. Since meeting Amy at Chicken, I felt at home lost in the wilderness— a place where folks tolerated civilization only to the degree it was inescapable.

A local legend I heard from Gene was a group of miners— the founding fathers—wanted to name the community Ptarmigan, taking the name of a local grouse and main ingredient in homemade soups or stews and occasionally broiled or grilled over a fire.

Among the naming committee's combined intellect, no one could spell *ptarmigan* for sure. So, instead, they chose the next-best eating foul and called the town Chicken.

I pictured the scene, having attended meetings in mining camps from Colorado to the Klondike, including Chicken. A group of guys who might not have graduated sixth grade but could build a bridge, a dam, or dig a mine tunnel but couldn't spell crap with a mouth full. I see them sitting in makeshift chairs in a log cabin surrounding a woodstove, voting for a town name they could agree on the spelling.

Gene said Chicken became the second incorporated community in the territory of Alaska, but after the gold rush died, they lost their status. Since then, the population wavered between as few as eight permanent residents and as many as forty-one.

I made no effort to meet all the full-time residents. If we had a dozen, I had met over half of them.

A few people, for whatever reason, listed their residence in Chicken, but like Dottie, they owned a home elsewhere in Fairbanks or Anchorage, too. Dottie said she spent several months each winter with family in Florida.

Observing people and details was a habit my pa beat into my head as a kid, committing what I learned to memory. Dad could quote chapter and book from the Bible. He taught us to know our surroundings, understand what motivates people, and pay attention to small things. Like Robbie wore a ring for a long time and doesn't now.

Gene qualified as a genuine full-time resident by default. Literally every asset he owned in the world resided there with him. His favorite pastime was to take off-colored ethnic jokes and change them to tourist or *cheechako* jokes. A *cheechako* being someone with less than one whole year in the Klondike or Alaska. The jokes didn't always translate well, and he delivered them so poorly as not to offend anyone seriously, but everyone a little.

After freeze-up, when the roads closed and the Yukon River iced over, for entertainment, Gene monitored the Commies on his ham radio. He powered it with a WWII vintage Signal Corps portable generator. The generator provided a constant drone in the background unless down for maintenance or refueling.

Sometimes, Gene caught a Finnish AM station playing American country music on skip. He couldn't understand the disc jockey, but Hank Williams sounded the same from halfway around the world as on a radio station in Fairbanks. During the long polar nights, the radio waves bounced off a layer of atmosphere and happened to land back in Chicken.

Aside from concerns about Russians, UFOs, and green men, Gene fit ordinary by bush expectations and reigned as unofficial mayor and postmaster.

Gail Richner makes me smile. She reminded me of Mom's older sister, a sweet old gal and a year-round resident. Not a miner, Gail was a bit eccentric and, of course, fit right in. She might tip the scale at over a hundred pounds, but not by much. Her hair was a thinning silver blonde that came with age, cut short below her ears and above her shoulders.

Gene said she came up the Alcan from Santa Fe, New Mexico, and left an artist commune because there were too many weird people to suit her. Chicken came with its share, but not so many, total. Gail owned one of the nicest cabins, and she qualified as our most senior resident.

Gene sold some of her art painted on canvas, rocks, tree shelf fungus, antique saw blades, and gold pans. She also made silver and gold jewelry, rings, and pendants. Some mystery surrounded her. Everyone acknowledged Gail as the wealthiest citizen of Chicken, but no one knew where her money came from.

Staunchly independent, she sold her artworks at Gene's store and hung paintings in Dottie's establishment. Gene told me she did it because she ran out of room at her place and never needed the cash. Whenever the mayor took her a check for sales through his store, in all those years, she never cashed one. I don't see her often, but I'm fond of her.

Notorious for being tight with his dough as bark on a birch tree, Gene was a rarity among mayors—honest. He tracked how much Gail was due and maintained it as his minimum balance, even when he borrowed during a slow year. Traits I liked in a man, and I considered Gene a friend. I saw no fault in any man who could survive running a business in this wilderness for years.

Then I thought of ol' Boyd Harrison, the only person of African descent nearer than Tok, or more likely, Fairbanks. He would argue he came from Louisiana, not Africa, because all his people were Cajun from the bayous. A genial, lanky man, he came into the country during WWII as a member of an all-Black engineering battalion that built most of the Alcan Highway.

After the construction ended, he went home, but the spell of the Yukon gripped his soul. He returned at the war's end. Another unexplained but noted mystery is that Dottie and Chicken's chief mechanic knew each other from the highway construction era before she came to town.

The ol' boy owned a gold claim but hardly worked it. Boyd's mine ownership came the same way I procured the Davis Creek claim. Originally, Boyd started to work in the goldfields as a seasonal laborer. Later, he gained a reputation as a mechanic fixing mining equipment, dozers, scoop shovels, dredges, pumps, or anything with a motor, tracks, or wheels. He made a living doing those things and worked on his claim only as much as needed to keep it and his year-round home.

The slow-talking man retained more than a little accent, and his ways inspired me to take a similar path. Boyd's good nature found quiet ways to even the score with people who slighted him financially, for his difficulties with English, or for his race.

Those needing a talented mechanic stayed on speaking terms with him. Word is, Gene started converting his favorite racist jokes to *cheechakoes* to stay on Boyd's easygoing side or do without his swamp buggy or generator. Now, the best of friends, they argued like a pair of old biddies over the price Mayor Gene charged Boyd for goods and the cost of mechanical work, but they refused to buy from anyone else.

Boyd lacked book learning, but he understood figures and what it cost to get a mechanic out of Fairbanks. How much he charged above or below that number was based on his assessment of your character, ability to pay, and need. He was free with his time for good folks down on their luck.

I counted Boyd as another friend, not just because my motorcycle needed work.

After a short review of the remaining residents and possible suspects, I found none fit my idea of a killer. From my limited time as a cop, I know a person inclined to commit murder preferred to live in big cities like Dallas or L.A.—easier places for a killer to be overlooked by the police. I couldn't believe Tim's killer would remain a mystery for long.

In Chicken, everyone knew each other, and in the summer, when the temporary residents arrived for mining season, the population reached somewhere south of fifty people. It didn't take long to find out the skinny on everyone. You learned about those you never set eyes on because, at Dottie's, the primary entertainment aside from booze, came from gossip about who arrived new into the country.

Dottie, my favorite part-time citizen— next to Amy— owned and operated the area's most popular and largest saloon. The best known of the seasonal residents, she came to the Klondike and Territory of Alaska during early WWII. Dottie arrived in Chicken a few years before statehood, paying cash for the burned-out building and lot.

Boyd knew her background but stayed closed mouth when it came to her. He respected Dot's business knowledge, and everyone knew of her influence in Alaskan politics even though she rarely participated in the mining camp pastime of arguing politics—an intelligent businesswoman.

My mind wandered. I sipped coffee and kept it warm by setting the tin cup on Gene's wood stove, a cast iron pot belly with claw feet nailed to the floor. I supposed that eccentric would best describe a Texas cowboy who reads poetry in the Alaskan wilderness.

Some around Chicken might think I ran away from something, and mostly, they would be right, but what exactly, I couldn't say. When I arrived, having money wasn't any motivation beyond not starving to death. Being unhappy is a sight easier when you don't need to work so hard. I generally enjoyed living here. Physical labor suits me, and I like most people, especially Amy.

The reason I took the job with Barnes and stayed in Chicken revolved around her. The gold miner's daughter caused a sudden urge to better myself. Those folks around I didn't care for, I avoided.

So, why kill Tim? It had been a long time since I thought about solving crime and never a murder, which exceeded my pay grade. Although neither Robbie nor I mentioned it, Tim died somewhere else. From the small amount of blood that soaked in the snow, he bled out somewhere else. The remaining snow stood out as white in contrast to the body. Hopefully, whoever did the autopsy would narrow the time of death.

Dottie's bar hadn't opened yet, so I sat at Gene's store and tourist trap. I read all of Gene's magazines over the winter and learned Chicken gained popularity recently due to *Look*, *Life*, and *Time* articles. Thanks to an adventure writer who passed through before statehood, they even included Chicken in the *Milepost* book travelers bought to navigate the Alcan.

The coffee tasted much better than my camp coffee. I planned to return to the claim with whomever arrived, and ride along with Gene in his buggy. As the sole representative on the Barnes claim with work to do, and their crew was due this week. That fact kept any of them off the list of suspects.

"Hey, Gene," I hollered.

The mayor listened to his ham radio through Army green earphones. A pudgy man, a rarity in the bush where most folks possessed little to eat that a person could get fat on, perched on a military surplus office chair on rollers—one of four rollers was missing.

He pulled the headphones off his balding head and draped them around his neck. Gene combed his side hair straight back and plastered it down with Brylcreem. He swiveled around, careful not to lean over the missing wheel.

"What?" Gene blinked and pinched his dark eyebrows together over a prominent red nose.

"No, forget it; you're busy."

"No, just keeping an ear out for them reds. I wish I knew how to speak Russian. I considered getting one of them home study courses on a record album. Only afraid if I did, the FBI would be looking for me as a Commie spy."

Gene owned a wind-up phonograph on a stand next to his chair and a handful of records he liked to play.

I winked. "Yeah, it could happen."

He caught the sarcasm. "So, what did you want?"

I slurped some coffee and eased it back on the stove. "I've been wondering if any strangers or new people are coming around."

"None since you hit town last year. You're beginning to sound like the cop dressed up as a drill sergeant or something."

"Robbie's okay."

He watched me from his chair. "You on a first-name basis with our law dog nowadays?"

I sat my empty cup on the table. "Naw, his name is easy to remember, and besides, I used to be a cop not so long ago. Got an uncle who is plumb famous, lawman down in Texas."

"Humph." Gene puffed, "Well, since we're a state now, Texas is the second biggest."

Where did that fit into our conversation? I let it alone.

"Did you see Tim hanging around with anyone?"

Gene sat with his hands in his lap, twiddling his thumbs. "Can't say as I did. Not many folks around. Tim did mention running into your boss in Anchorage."

"Barnes?" That piqued my interest.

"Yep. Tim called him an asshole." Gene said.

"I haven't met Barnes but once or twice, he seemed reasonable, but a hard man."

Tim liked to talk too much. He worked hard so long as Amy kept her eye on him. Tim was much more at home playing and enjoying singing and drinking. I believed him a fair judge of character.

"Did he give a reason?"

"No, just drinking his Jim Beam and Coke and stating it as fact. Those of us at the poker table didn't feel inclined to disagree with his assessment. Tim looked sour about it. Barnes is full of himself and thinks his big foreman scares people. Folks out here don't scare worth a tinker's damn."

Chet Robarts, the Barnes foreman, ran their operation and was the only man kept on the payroll year-round. What he did the other eight to nine months, I didn't know.

Until Tim got killed, I didn't much care. I understood from talk that Robarts came from the Ozarks near the Missouri and Arkansas border. With dark curly hair, he stood as tall as Robbie. Thick as a side of beef, Chet's the kind of guy who likes to show off his strength. I saw him grip the ends of a full fifty-five-gallon fuel barrel and pick it up.

"Who played in your game besides Tim?" I wondered.

Gene's eyes wandered, considering what he should say. "Old lady Richner and Boyd; penny ante, and Gail cleaned up."

"What did you mean folks around here don't scare?"

Having grown up on a Texas ranch, I had an idea. Texans took pride in independence, and it ran deep in Alaska, too.

The topic made Gene grin.

"Take Miss Gail." Gene said. "She's a sweet gal in her late sixties, I would guess. She totes a .45-long Colt single-action Peacemaker in her bag. I understand she can haul it out and shoot birds on the fly. She ain't scared of no one."

"Most people in this country carry a gun, I pack that old shotgun you sold me, and I'm the least armed man in the territory."

It made me think. Tim carried a gun, a short-barreled revolver, a Colt double action, and he kept a shotgun handy at their mine. Scatter guns topped the list of preferred weapons at close range with a bear. I didn't see either one near his body.

"Gene, when was the last time anyone got murdered in this general area?"

As mayor, and the unofficial historian with lots of time to read, he maintained the records back to the town's founding.

"I'd have to look it up in the archives. I'm not sure anyone ever killed someone that counted as murder. Gold rush miners and claim jumpers being what they are, most likely happened at some point."

"What do you mean, counted?"

Gene put a fat finger on his chin. "Like a while back, shortly after the Alcan was finished, a pretty-looking fellow owned a claim about halfway to Eagle. The few ladies who came to Chicken without a man and short on good sense found him attractive."

He took a sip of his coffee, then continued. "Story goes they would go to his place after leaving the bar, the one that burned down in the earthquake of '55."

With little else to do, I listened, waiting for Gene to answer. I felt warm, —close to hot—by the stove, and thankful for the slight breeze blowing through an open window.

"The story goes, a couple of gals got beat up and shot at a few times before getting away from him. Then he picked up the wrong woman. She untied herself, but didn't make a run for it. Instead, she found his gun, and it turns out she shot better sober than he did drunk.

"The investigating officer asked her why she shot him six times. The gal said she couldn't find the bullets to reload. Ha!" Gene slapped his knee and nearly tipped the chair over.

I surmised, it to be a clear case of self-defense or justifiable homicide by territorial, bush-accepted conduct.

"You hear of anyone who wanted the mine I filed on?"

Gene shook his head. "I didn't know old Rosenberg decided to quit the country. Why are you asking?"

"The cop, Robbie, when he came out looking for Tim, said he had his eyes on the place. Ricky said his brother wasn't interested in owning anything he would have to work at, and God knows the claim will require lots of work."

The airport radio frequency squawked. I glanced toward it as Gene carefully swung his chair around to repeat his earlier instructions about landing.

The pilot replied, "Roger."

Chapter 5

Gene provided taxi service for the new state coroner out of Anchorage visiting the police detachment in Fairbanks and decided to ride out with the pilot to pick up the body. After meeting the coroner, a tall, skinny kid, not old enough to be a doctor to my thinking.

We talked while bouncing around in the converted Army rig Gene said may have served as an ambulance during World War II.

When not holding on for dear life, Dr. Rogers said, "Besides being the coroner, I'm also a flight surgeon for the FAA. I started medicine as a new Navy doctor in Korea stationed on a hospital ship."

"I knew guys who went to the hospital ship. Considered ambulatory, they sent me to a hospital in Yokosuka and treated me for frostbite. Doctors took off my little toe. The frostbite crippled two others, but they saved my right foot." *Yep, one of the lucky ones.*

When we arrived at my bus, the ugly green buggy came to a noisy halt. Gene decided he wasn't interested in seeing anything so gruesome and elected to stay by the fire.

I grabbed my shotgun and led Rogers off on foot. The earlier frost melted off, and the muddy spot with the boot prints dried up and cracked. We skirted alders. And I jumped at the sound of a shot. My Remington came to the ready, and crouching, I moved to cover. "Officer Robbie, are you okay?"

"I'm fine, but I'm getting tired of playing cat and mouse with Yogi. The furball ran off somewhere nearby. Your curious bear wanted to know who or what died, I guess. Come on in."

I lowered the gun.

Doc Rogers let out a sigh of relief. "Never a dull moment in this this job."

On the way, he said he planned to change procedures and travel to crime scenes to view the bodies. He used his camera and took pictures.

"As Coroner, I want to document why it is important to see the body before it is disturbed. The birds beat me to this one, but even that has teaching value."

Doc spread a sheet on the ground, and with Robbie's help, he rolled the body over and on it.

Robbie pulled a wallet from the back pocket of the tattered jeans. Inside, a paper driver's license belonged to Timothy Crockett, but the doctor would have to ID him by his dental records. Next to his license, the officer took out some pictures. One photo of his family band, and another was of Tim with his wife—a wedding picture.

Tim talked for hours and never mentioned being married. Therefore, I suspected, also divorced. It's funny how little you know about people. I suppose Tim knew no more about me, maybe less.

Robbie also found money and a few business cards. "I don't see any evidence in the wallet. Think I will detour over to visit Ricky on the way to the airport. I'll send the doc along with the body to Fairbanks and hop on a ride with them to Tok."

I frowned. "You're finished investigating?"

"Not by a long shot, but I haven't been into the office in three days, and I have a lot of territory to cover. I'll be back when the road is open, and I can drive in and out."

Understandable, it was part of remote policing.

Robbie tipped his head down to look me in the eye. "You know, there are things a person could follow up on. Like, where is his gear? He didn't get to camp with it, so there is a duffle or a backpack somewhere."

"He always carried a Colt pistol with him and kept a shotgun handy at camp, too," I said.

Tim never went without it and told me he kept the shotgun in camp. I couldn't imagine he planned to stay in a tent without it.

Rogers interrupted, "Through and through bullet path, exit out the back. The lack of blood under him in the snow indicates he died somewhere else and was dumped here."

But why here, and shot where?

The officer made some notes. Rogers placed Tim in a new body bag. Doc lifted him at the feet, and Robbie and I grabbed the handles on the other end.

~~~

After a rough hike to the bus, we loaded Tim's body in the buggy. I dug into my supplies for some moose jerky Gene made to feed Robbie.

The big cop hadn't eaten, and likely, it would be several hours before he got another chance.

Robertson took a handful. He cocked his head slightly, and his eyes narrowed for a second. "Thanks. I will see you soon."

Shortly after, they departed. I watched through the glare as the sun neared the horizon. Gene's buggy rumbled off in the distance, spewing grey smoke with Tim's remains bouncing around in the back. Although it was possible to cut through the woods and beat them to Ricky's, death notifications were Robbie's duty.

I grabbed some things and headed to Barnes's claim; finding Tim put me a day behind schedule. Although Robarts didn't scare me much, it was easier to meet expectations. Besides, I never shirked a job I agreed to do. Barnes's crew would arrive when the road opened. His men, a big truckload of supplies, and smaller vehicles would drive in to run their operation. Robarts would take over the cabin I used over the winter and make it his office.

Robbie's remarks about having plenty to do with Tim's case sounded like he wanted me to do the State's work. Not my job, but given some time to hunt around, I might find Tim's gear. Maybe his guns, too. I suspected whoever killed Tim took his Colt before or after and may have shot him with it.

Robbie made a point of telling me I'm still a suspect. He probably hoped it would motivate me to help solve the case when Robbie couldn't be everywhere or devote the time immediately.

Then it hit me. Robertson couldn't come out and ask for help because I would be an agent for the police and restrict what I could do. Anything I did on my own couldn't damage his case. *Sneaky.*

~~~

Gene came by the Barnes mine the next day with the latest gossip on his way to take a casserole Miss Gail baked to Ricky. Rumors he heard focused on the killing having something to do with my claim.

For a place with limited communications, rumors spread faster than mosquitoes bred. From my days at Fort Worth PD, I knew in most cases of murder, the victim knows his killer. In Chicken, it was a cinch that would be the case.

A nice day to get Barnes's water system and sluice ready to work. Warm enough, I worked in a T-shirt and soaked my exposed skin in Army surplus bug dope left from Korea. The skeeters still bit me but didn't hang on as long.

I got the notion anyone coming in from outside Chicken flew in. The snow at the time Tim disappeared had melted into corn slush during the day, making sled dogs unusable. From the sixty-mile trek I made with Gearhart on the highway to Chicken through the muck, it made for a tough slog.

I partially avoided the hike by catching Gearhart walking in his backhoe. The German had a claim up near Boundary. It might have been possible to get a four-wheel drive truck in behind us if it looked like Gene's. Otherwise, it's iffy fording some of those washouts. Backhoes have big tires, hydraulic buckets, and arms to drag them over boulders and build ramps that probably washed away ten minutes after our passing.

Unlikely anyone flew in unnoticed during the transitional time between landing on skis and using wheels. Tim chartered a flight out of Gakona on skis, and since his arrival, the mail plane was the only aircraft in or out until the State Police, the first to land on wheels. Nothing made sense.

~~~

The next day after work, I walked up Poker Creek, wading part of the time and ducking overhanging willows or alders when the trail climbed the bank.

Earlier, Gene dropped my weekly food supplies and mail at Barnes's. He told me the mail flight arrived with the news that Doc Rogers identified Tim by dental records. I planned to help Ricky through the motions, and a man ought not to be left alone for so long after the bad news.

At his camp that afternoon, Ricky told me, "Tim left home with an old surplus Army duffle bag. It came with straps to carry like a backpack. During the last few years, he packed it with extra clothes, magazines, and paperback westerns he liked to read in camp.

It was Army green and had the name SANDERS stenciled on the side, presumably the name of the guy who owned it in the service."

"Gene told me the doctor identified Tim for sure."

Ricky stared into the fire, slapped his knee a few times, and said, "Wasn't much chance anyone else had his wallet."

It frustrated me having spent the day taking mental laps around the evidence only to end up where I started. No suspects. I hung out with Ricky, helping prepare their camp until he ran me off near dark.

~~~

Over the next three days, temperatures climbed to the sixties, and the forest greened up but became tinder dry. Any spark might start a fire. Everyone hoped for rain, but the central part of Alaska was deceivingly green in a place where annual precipitation rivaled Alamogordo, New Mexico.

Gene let me know the day before the road opened to Chicken. I hiked into town ahead of the road commission grader, making his first pass the length of the Taylor Highway to Canada. A parade of vehicles followed him to town. Chet Robarts led the way with a big diesel 6x6 deuce-and-a-half loaded with gear.

I met them in the parking lot in front of Gene's store to let the foreman know the claim was ready to work.

The big guy walked up to me. "I got a word for you from Barnes."

Surly like always, Chet wore a ball cap, bib overalls, and a T-shirt two sizes too small to show off his muscles.

"We're all set to go to work. So, what's the word from the boss?"

"Two words. You're fired. Pack any of your stuff off our property, and don't set foot on it again." Chet growled.

The beefy foreman reached into his back pocket and slapped an envelope with a loud smack on my chest. He wanted it to hurt, and it stung a bit. After spending a winter keeping up the camp and preparing it for service, his attitude set me off.

Careful to control my temper, I ignored the envelope, snatched the meaty hand away, sidestepped, and jerked it into a wristlock. Robarts flailed with his other arm. It knocked my hat off, but I ducked the blow and slipped under the extended arm, making a half-turn. The Army Rangers' move caught him off guard and forced Robarts to dive forward or let me break his arm. He hit with a thud.

Ticked off, I held his face in the dust. "Why?"

Chet tried to free his hand under him, but I kept his face and chest tight to the ground. He twisted his head to get his nose and mouth out of the dirt. He spat a mixture of blood and mud and curled his lips back.

"Barnes planned to buy Rosenberg's mine, and then the guy disappeared," he tried to twist out, but I pulled his arm higher, and he stopped, "and you jumped the claim."

Odd way to word what happened. "I hear he went home, wherever he lived, and I filed legal." I emphasized my point with a shove on the wrist, pushing him harder to the ground.

Robarts wouldn't call uncle or show pain. "Maybe legal, but you jumped it."

"Did he have Tim killed?" I asked.

I glanced back and saw Boyd, Gene, Gail, and some of Chet's new crew facing off behind me.

Chet's face frowned. "Tim Crockett? Hell no, I hadn't heard anything about it. You after his claim too— or maybe his sister."

That did it. I wanted to knock his crooked teeth out on the ground. I put my boot right on his ass, turned loose of his arm, and kicked. It shoved his face into the dust and gravel.

The foreman pushed up quick, face scraped up, ready for a fight, but he stopped. Boyd held a wrench as long as a ball bat over his shoulder. Gene carried his pride and joy, a Stevens double barrel 10-gauge express gun tucked casually under his arm.

A slim fellow from Chet's crew with scars, pale skin, and the sunken eyes of prison time started forward.

Miss Gail asked him, "Which of them big toes is your favorite?"

The thug in a sleeveless shirt and dirty jeans checked his heavy work boots and glanced back at the older woman. "Why?"

She flipped her Colt out of her bag like Annie Oakley, giving it a twirl, and pointed it at his feet.

"Because you take one step further, young man, and you can carry it in your pocket as a good luck charm."

Robarts turned to leave. The rest of his boys followed his lead, back to their vehicles and ready to drive off in a cloud of dust and diesel fumes.

He yelled out the window, "This ain't over, Peoples."

I didn't figure otherwise. I caught Robarts unaware. No doubt I would have to fight him again. It wouldn't be so easy next time.

A poke in my back, and I spun around, fists up.

"Hold on, Wyatt." Amy held her finger and thumb cocked like a gun.

She dropped her hand, standing in her usual mining get-up, rubber boots, jeans, and long-sleeved blue canvas shirt. Her hair was tied back with a ribbon, and Amy looked as cute as a pup. She picked up my hat and handed it to me with my final check and a pink slip from Barnes.

"Cowboy, I hear you're out of a job." Amy grinned.

Then, she choked up, and her eyes watered. "Dad says we're shorthanded. He can't work this year, and with my brother, Tim..." She swallowed hard and fought back tears. "If you can work as well as you fight, we can use a good man."

After an eight-month remission, my laryngitis returned in spades. I nodded.

I felt my face heat up, and she said, "Good, the way things are shaping up, we may need a fighter, too." Amy turned on Gene and slapped him on the shoulder. "Is Dottie open?"

He pointed down the road with the shotgun. The sun hung a bright orange over the mountains. "I expect her anytime."

Ricky walked up. "Well, my brothers and I are hungry, and based on the excess belt hanging loose, our new guy hasn't had a decent meal since freeze-up last fall. What do you have to eat?"

I fingered my belt and remembered only adding two holes over the winter. Not bad by Texas standards.

Chapter 6

Mayor Gene received advanced word the road would be open and prepared his outdoor smoker and grill. Anticipating hungry travelers with dollars to spend, he pulled some moose and caribou out of the icehouse, sliced off some steaks, and mixed up some fancy new powdered mashed potatoes and canned beans. He threw in some canned peaches for dessert.

After Amy provided payment for dinner, the assembled residents of Chicken included late arrivals like Dottie. The saloon owner arrived, hands down the best dressed, and wearing a dress. In fairness, Gail also wore one, but Dottie's garb appeared shiny and new.

Everyone stood in front of Gene's store drinking beer, including many family members who would return home after helping set up operations. Latecomers chewed dried smoked salmon sweet as candy— Gene's secret recipe. As the default mayor because he owned the ham radio, the only year-round business, and acted as postmaster, Gene called a town meeting and declared a forum present. Gail volunteered to take down the minutes.

After a joke about how many *cheechakoes* it took to change a tire that garnered groans from the crowd, Gene opened the meeting with a prepared speech.

"Fellow citizens of Chicken, I come to you with a heavy heart. I wish to first pay respect to Tim and his family for their loss of a brother and a son."

He bowed his head, and the crowd went silent for twenty seconds.

"After this evening's run-in with the Barnes outfit, I foresee trouble maintaining the peace. Further, having spoken to the State Police Commander in Fairbanks, he informed me Officer Robertson is our State Policeman. He is stationed ninety miles away in Tok and will respond as needed. He might be delayed for days by weather or attending to other duties in his patrol area."

The crowd groaned again, and some mumbled swear words under their breath as women were present.

Gene said, "I motion we elect a town sheriff. Do I have a second?"

Boyd said, "Second," without hesitation.

"All in favor, say aye."

A majority of the group said, "Aye."

"Having heard no nays, the motion carries."

Dottie inquired about how they would pay for a sheriff, and some discussion occurred. The mayor tabled the discussion on wages for a later meeting. He followed by asking for nominations.

Things happened fast. It appeared the mayor, Boyd, Gail, and some others planned the proceedings. It looked like Dottie was now informed and in agreement. I remained left out.

"Do we have any nominations?" Gene asked again.

Dottie said, "I nominate Wyatt Peoples; he has law experience and handled things well today."

Me? Before I objected, Amy's little brother Doug Crockett said, "I second."

I turned to look at him and Amy. Her face showed concern, but Doug's showed resolve.

"All in favor of electing Wyatt as sheriff, say aye."

Trying to protest but caught off guard, I abstained. Amy, too, but the mayor declared me sheriff by unanimous vote.

Gail stepped forward. "I designed and made a new five-point star badge from gold mined right in this area."

She accepted the honor of pinning it on my shirt. It had taken time to make the badge, proving Gene planned this election without my knowledge. They bestowed an honor and duty on me. I left Texas to put both behind me.

It amounted to a vote of no confidence in the State Police as much as an affirmation the citizens didn't see me as a suspect in Tim's murder. I stared at Amy. She walked up, shook my hand, and gave me a devilish grin. Turning, she yelled,

"Speech!"

The crowd chanted, "Speech, speech!"

Amy stood at my arm while my stomach quivered, and my tongue almost lost all function.

With concentrated effort, I mumbled, "I-I-I was railroaded," which was true.

Later, I sat beside Dottie at the bar, watching the bartender unpacking liquor and contemplating events. Happy about my new employer, but being sheriff didn't fit my plans. The Crocketts broke out a guitar, moved onto Dottie's stage, and gave a command performance for the new sheriff.

I stared at a lukewarm Coke and the badge sitting on the bar. "This can't be legal."

"Wyatt, I'm not sure it is, Hun, but the good residents voted for you. I did specify the good ones. Legal or not, you have their faith and backing." Dottie sounded concerned.

"What do I do? I mean, as sheriff." I spun the shiny badge, tapping my finger on the bar as it twirled.

Dottie smiled and leaned an elbow on the bar. She looked me in the eyes.

"First, don't ever expect to get paid. You may rate a free meal here, or Gene's, maybe some mechanic work at Boyd's, and Ms. Gail can give you shooting lessons, if needed."

Dottie spoke fluent sarcasm, and it made me grin.

"Second, it's a part-time, limited appointment. When the season ends and everyone who voted goes home alive, you've done your job. The voters know you have a claim to prove up. Miss Amy will take fourteen to sixteen hours a day from you for your real wages."

I picked up my hat, as nervous about the job as when I led the Lord's Prayer at church as a kid. The star stopped turning, and I flipped it over– *Sheriff.* The irony hadn't escaped me. I didn't want the responsibility before the war and proved unworthy afterward. I never wanted the job my uncle sought and revered, and here I am, toting a badge I hadn't asked for. "I'm not sure how well this is going to work."

"Simple, Sheriff," humor saturated her tone, "when Amy says something, nod your head, or if you can manage, say yes, and go do it."

Dottie laughed at her joke, and I saw in the mirror my face turned red. This had been caused by girls since grammar school. "Thanks."

Then again, what she advised worked for my folks. Pa was in charge because Mom said so. When it came to life or death or holding the ranch, no doubt, Pa took charge.

"Granted, you won't be able to respond to emergencies right off, but maybe we can get a radio out at the Crocketts'. Poker Creek is much closer than Tok, and waiting two or three days, the State all but said it's up to us, and we elected you."

Amy sang a Patsy Cline tune. The mayor and constituents danced while drinking Dottie's beer.

The town didn't tolerate criminal behavior or bullies. According to Gene, until now, it was not recognized as having a qualified murder either. I scanned the assembled residents, both permanent and seasonal, like the Eddin brothers Frick and Frack, who drank their beer and listened to Amy with rapt attention.

"My experience is," I poked lightly at the badge, "once you pin this on, you're the law and not a friend or neighbor."

"Don't be too full of yourself. Step in only when you must— otherwise, keep it part-time." She tapped a well-manicured finger on her chin. "I have friends in Juneau. Maybe we can arrange a special peace officer's appointment, like a posse member for the State Police."

"I think I would rather pretend than have real authority." I picked up the badge and slipped it into my shirt pocket.

She chuckled at my discomfort. "I'll check into it. Legal status may protect you civilly and those, like me, who elected you."

Dottie's grasp of civil law and business outshined what I remembered of civics class. "Could be."

Amy ended her bluesy love song. It felt appropriate, considering the circumstances and my unspoken feelings.

Leaving the stage, she said, "It's after midnight, and we are headed to the claim. While we pack up, let's call our sheriff to the stage to close with an acceptance speech or something from Robert Service."

I glanced at Dottie, shaking my head. "That's my cue."

Taking the platform, Amy brushed my arm.

I stood on stage. "Mayor, I demand a recount."

Gene climbed on a chair and whistled through two fingers loud enough to pierce ear drums. "All in favor of Wyatt for sheriff, say aye."

I gained at least one more vote as Amy yelled, "Aye," with the crowd. Alcohol only fueled their enthusiasm.

On a base level, I found it hard to turn away from service. A cop twice before, and I served in war. Some might call it a family tradition, but refusing the job meant not investigating Tim's murder. If I read it right, Amy pinned hope on me being sheriff. Careful not to look at her, I said, "I humbly accept your faith in me, but as Miss Dottie pointed out, I have my claim and a full-time job to do for Miss Amy. Please feel free to fire me at any time."

Gail stepped forward. "You don't get out of your duty so easily, Red Face. Now let's hear some of your mesmerizing voice and give us some poetry."

I opened with a poem by Baxter Black, a young cowboy poet I met in a bar in Fort Worth after the war. I closed out with one fitting for the occasion, "The Shooting of Dan McGrew," by Robert Service.

It ends with these closing lines:

"These are the simple facts of the case, and I guess I ought to know.

They say that the stranger was crazed with "hooch," and I'm not denying it's so.

I'm not so wise as the lawyer guys, but strictly between us two —

The woman that kissed him and — pinched his poke — was the lady that's known as Lou."

Tipping my hat to applause, I stepped off the stage. I ran to catch a ride with Amy. My boss allowed me to sit on top of the gear in the back of the flatbed pickup. Being the last hired, sheriff or not, I rode where space was available.

Chapter 7

Two days later, Robbie visited the Crocketts' mine to talk specifically with me. Amy stopped pushing dirt with the big Cat, idled it back, and threw up her hands. The season was short, and to hear her say so, any hold-up costs money on a claim, barely paying the cost of operation to hold it. A premise I believed she exaggerated.

Her scowl said we would work an extra hour. The state cop took me aside, and we discussed Tim's case at length.

It puzzled me. The open exchange on an active case where some details Robbie kept from the Crocketts concerned me.

"Why are you giving me this information?"

His face wrinkled like he bit into something sour. "Wyatt, you have a friend with influence in Juneau; the word is, you are sheriff."

"I guess, Dottie. She planned to do something, but how and so fast?"

Robbie nodded. "The mayor and his radio. Dot, knowing the governor and his past, comes in handy. No matter, I received orders to type this memo and notarize it."

His use of *Dot* instead of Dottie or Miss, I'm sure she has a last name, and I wondered about both. Robbie reached into his jacket pocket, hesitated momentarily, and handed me an envelope.

"You're to keep this arrangement to yourself for now, or maybe forever if nothing comes of it."

"What's it say?" I stuffed the letter in my back pocket.

Robbie raised his right hand, placing himself between me and Tim's family. "You swear to uphold the laws of the USA and the State of Alaska?"

"Huh?"

Robbie spoke like someone held a gun to his head. Clearly, this went against his better judgment. "Hold up your hand and say yes."

I raised my arm. "Yes."

Robbie rolled his eyes and shook his head. "I'm deputizing you as an agent of the Attorney General of the State of Alaska to investigate the murder of Tim Crockett in the southeast district of Fairbanks."

I peeked around his head at Amy and her brothers, watching the odd ceremony. "This is official?"

"The citation says: authorized by the Governor, the AG, and the Commissioner of Public Safety. But keep it to yourself unless someone else in law enforcement questions your authority. Then, and only then, show them the letter."

Robbie turned to housekeeping. "To be legal, you must track your time spent investigating and what you were doing, and thinking about it doesn't count. If you incur expenses, save your receipts.

"You will be paid for your hours upon receipt of your reports. At the closing of this commission, if unsolved at the time, you are no longer a state investigator. Do you understand?"

"Yes, sir."

"I'm not your boss. You don't have one below the governor, but feel free to report to me as the closest state contact."

It sounded a little thin and left me as off-balance as the election in Chicken. Unsure how to proceed, I shook Robbie's hand. "Thanks, I guess. If anything breaks, I can have Gene call on the radio."

His face turned grim, and he offered some advice. "Sheriff, keep in mind, unless I'm here, your backup is only days away, so don't do anything stupid. Make friends, because it is up to them to cover your backside."

Frustrated, he left, kicking rocks into the stream, and crossed the area already mined and cleared. He went to search in the alders for Tim's duffle along the trail to the highway.

Ricky and I combed the heavy brush and trees around Crocketts' claim earlier. The woods thick with underbrush made finding a green bag no easy task.

~~~

The next night, Doug and his brother spent a few hours helping me set up a sluice at my place. The claim would be a pick-and-shovel operation this season.

I would run dirt to the sluice in a wooden, rickety wheelbarrow with a steel wheel. So, after examining where Rosenburg dug his workings downstream from the bus, Ricky dismissed it and suggested a bench he thought held better potential. It made sense to pick a place higher than the river. It was less work for me to haul dirt downhill than across level ground. Also, it was easier to push an empty wheelbarrow uphill.

Standing on the high ground, Ricky said, "This bench was river bottom a thousand years ago. It is tight to the bluff and probably in a bend back then. Gold would have collected in the bend and left behind when the river cut a deeper course."

The bank sluffed off, covering much of the outcrop, and required digging through it to reach broken bedrock. To verify Ricky's theory, we dug down to bare rock, where it was easier to reach. We carried a couple of pans to the creek. After I soaked the gravel, I swirled the pan in the stream to wash off the excess material. In the evening, light gleamed a small nugget and some fine gold. Not much to celebrate, but it proved digging there wouldn't be a total waste of time.

~~~

Days went by, working hard and having no luck finding clues to identify Tim's killer after work. Soon, with two weeks gone, I felt the pain of burning the candle at both ends. Boyd worked on my motorcycle, improving its reliability. After cutting back the brush, I could ride the bike over the path to Crocketts' and the one from my claim to the highway without crossing Barnes's claim.

That Friday, the Crocketts shut down operations early to clean up their sluice. They removed high-grade paydirt, and Amy almost smiled, meaning it met her expectations. On a warm June night, we wanted to celebrate and were on tap to play at Dottie's.

I slapped some drying mud off my pant leg. The evening sun shimmered off the water. "I'm going to my place to clean up. Meet y'all at Dottie's."

Ricky pointed me to the trail. "We'll see you there. We're on our way as soon as Doug and Amy are ready."

~~~

After a short, bumpy ride on my Tote Goat, I was back on my claim and aimed for the tub. Once the snow melted, I painted a galvanized tub black for bathing. By propping the tub off the ground on rocks and filling it with water in the morning, the sun heated it, and by afternoon, I could take a warm bath.

All clean, I pulled on a pair of jeans, a white T-shirt, and my best denim shirt. I used leather chaps to fend off brush and stickers. My cowboy boots required a shoe brush to buff them off, and I gave the ol' Stetson a shot with it, too. Jamming the hat tight on my head, I aimed the two-wheeler for town.

I tried not to get down over how little progress I made on my claim or Tim's killing.

Riding the motorcycle through the woods reminded me of riding a half-broke horse through the buck brush and live oak while chasing cows. Any lapse in concentration was bound to hurt.

Topping the bank with a spray of gravel, I hit the highway. Calling the Taylor Highway a highway was a generous description of a potholed dirt road. It wound through a wilderness from Chicken, only broken once by the community of Boundary. That place consisted of cabins, sled dog huts, one drinking bar, and a short airstrip.

After stopping to pick it up twice, I tied my hat to the cargo rack, then cranked the hillbilly Harley up to all-out top speed. Ricky clocked me with their truck once at about thirty-five miles an hour. Alders flew by thick and leafed out up to the shoulders on both sides of the road.

A flash of tan and brown bolted from the brush. I jammed on the brakes, the tractor tires hopped, and gravel flew as I slid sideways. Bouncing, I maintained balance by hopping on one leg. Stopping upright, I leaned on my foot and came short of colliding with a high-speed grizzly dragging something white.

The maneuver resembled a matador missing a fighting bull by inches. Instead of horns, this guy sported five-inch-long claws and a set of teeth capable of crushing a moose femur. I watched the bruin busting alders for fifty yards. About then, it dawned on me that the bear fled with a set of long underwear dangling from his mouth.

Where did he get underwear?

Scanning the direction of the departing bear, I caught a glimpse of him crossing an open patch of swamp half a mile away. The young grizzly lost the underwear somewhere in between. I kicked the stand down and rocked the two-wheeler up on it.

The bear tracks I spotted coming up the bank, scratching with those long toenails to hit full speed.

Gene told me bears were a lot like humans. "If they kill something, they'll fight for it. If they find it, like meat hanging in a hunting camp, they know they are stealing and will generally chase away without a fight.

"Young grizzlies aren't too sharp at hunting," he said. "Once the momma leaves them, they receive a butt whoopin' from every bigger bear he crosses paths with. It makes them wary of getting caught by surprise. After several lickin's, they tend to run first and ask questions later."

"However," Gene warned, "if a man walks up on one and the youngster isn't startled, he might be the most dangerous animal in the wilderness. A feller alone is smaller, with no claws and few teeth. It makes them the right size to take some frustration out on."

I couldn't make the bear out after crossing a bog and disappearing into the woods. I returned to his trail. Six feet into the thick brush, buzzing and alive with mosquitos, I found a patch of ground packed down, and with scattered articles of clothing.

Some pieces were little more than shredded strips about the width of the gap between the animal's claws. While busy ripping up the clothing, the grizzly, caught unaware by my sudden noisy approach, bolted for someplace safe.

BVDs, socks, empty snack bags, and other debris were tossed around and hung in the underbrush near a green duffle with the side torn out. So, food attracted him. I glanced toward my camp, the closest place other than Boundary, but it's not my duffle. The bag caked up with settled road dust that turned to mud by melting frost and clung as it dried.

The air was still, and gray dust covered most of the trees. The bag was waterproof at one time, and what remained inside stayed dry. A lump came to my throat; stenciled on the side: SANDERS. I had packed up more than a few such bags with the personal belongings of dead soldiers. Searching through the litter left by Smokey's cousin, I spotted a red spiral notebook, the kind that fits in a shirt pocket.

I hesitated when the notebook sparked a memory of Amy issuing Tim instructions at the store in Chicken last year. He planned to go to Fairbanks, and she insisted he write what they needed. Tim pulled a pad like it from his pocket.

Thinking back on Tim's body when Officer Robertson took me up there, I didn't recall seeing or hearing Robbie say anything about one. He habitually carried one.

I picked it up. A business card dropped out. It was Byron Lovell's card, the hardware store's outside salesman. An Anchorage office with another in Fairbanks was listed at the bottom. On the back, a phone number and the word CALL was handwritten in blue ink.

I slipped the card and the notebook into my shirt pocket. I grabbed a red bandana handkerchief and tied it to a tree limb near the road to find this spot.

~~~

Driving over the rough road, I entered the parking lot late at Dottie's. Tracking Gene down, we went to call Robbie about my discovery and waited for instructions.

The dispatcher replied, "Robbie said to take pictures, dry everything out, and put it in a sealed box. He thinks he might get to Chicken late tomorrow."

A problem for me was I didn't have a camera, but Amy did. Already late for Dottie's, I waited for the Crocketts to end their session—the first scheduled performance without Tim. Smoke hung like a low ceiling in the bar. The place smelled like a mix of cigars, cigarettes, beer, and faintly of puke. I went to catch Amy when Dottie grabbed my sleeve.

"You missed your opener, bud. What do you have for us?"

"Trouble." I reached to catch Amy's arm before she got away.

She looked at me. "What?"

Dottie stepped in closer. "He says trouble."

"I've got bad news for the bar, but a break in Tim's case. Amy, I need to borrow your camera. I found your brother's bag. Robbie wants me to collect it, take pictures, and mark the place for him."

Her eyes clouded, and she took a sharp breath. It caught for a second. "The camera is in the truck. Where did you find it? How?"

Dottie interrupted, "This means you aren't going to spout poetry for us?"

"Yes, ma'am, sorry, but you helped elect me as sheriff."

She peeked over at the stage where some gray-bearded miner set up to play a little fiddle music during intermission. "If I realized it would interfere with my entertainment…"

Amy cut in. "Hold your thoughts. It's about to get worse. I want to go with you."

"Not a good idea." Telling my boss what to do was odd, but she never hesitated.

"You ever take pictures with a thirty-five millimeter camera, mister?"

I shook my head.

"Okay, so you need me to do it and get it right."

"Ah, heck, you're gonna take my lead singer too." Dottie looked ready to punch me.

I"No."

"Yes, he is." Amy turned, walking toward the truck.

I attempted to follow with Dottie pulling on my sleeve. Doug and Ricky blocked my way, not knowing the situation. By the time I explained, and the boys agreed to stay and sing, Amy waited in their Dodge behind the wheel, engine running and in gear.

I worked for her long enough to know not to argue.

To make matters worse for Dottie, several truckloads of looky-loos followed Amy as word spread. Later, at the scene, I threatened them all with arrest if they picked up or touched anything I thought might be evidence.

Amy fetched a hammer and a timber spike out of her toolbox. In front of witnesses, I drove the spike into the road as a durable marker for Robbie and left the hanky.

I made sure everyone else stayed put while she took pictures with color film. They showed the bag, the debris, and the bear prints.

She went pale and sucked in air like being punched in the gut upon seeing his bag. I noticed Amy reached for Tim's clothes, stopped, and closed her hand inches away. As my photographer, I had told her not to touch anything.

Earlier, Gene gave me a new pair of cotton gloves and a handful of paper grocery bags. I showed Amy each piece of evidence and dropped all the evidence into three bags. I left the remaining contents inside the duffle to go through with Robbie when he arrived. Several volunteers searched for the long underwear the bear departed with, but no luck. While unarmed, following a bear wasn't high on anyone's agenda, so they lost enthusiasm quickly.

Robbie could find it if he thought it necessary. The last items photographed were the notebook and business card. Amy said she gave the series of lists to Tim to take care of, including meeting Byron before leaving Anchorage.

"The meeting occurred because the store pulled the items from the shelves or ordered them in time for me to pick them up. Byron is my sales rep at the hardware store."

The salesman I didn't know, but instinctively didn't like, nor how she said *my sales rep*. I tried to speak his name without stuttering.

"Your-r-r sales rep?"

"Well, Dad's— ours, I guess— but I often deal with him." The corners of her mouth lifted a bit. "He has a site visit scheduled for next week."

Closing the notebook, I tucked it back in my shirt. I tossed the evidence in the seat and climbed in her truck.

I said, "If we hurry, we might make last call."

"No rush. Dottie's closes when the last paying customer leaves. You have your sheriff duties tonight, but we start work at eight. Be sure to be there and work until Robbie shows up. I'll let you work late on Monday to earn your hours. Gold doesn't crawl out of the ground on its own."

Amy dropped the truck into first gear, popped the clutch with a spurt of gravel, and made a three-point turn to head us back to Chicken.

I sniffed at the dust as we rattled down the road no faster than on my motorbike. I pulled on the brim of my hat. *My rep— ha; I don't like him.*

Chapter 8

Amy's truck screeched to a halt in front of Gene's store, dust rolled over us, and the cloud grew thicker as the rest of the convoy found parking spots. The air tasted stale, and the sun spread blood-red across the northern horizon. Doug, Ricky, and someone with a banjo played "Foggy Mountain Breakdown," keeping the beer flowing. Dottie's crowd was about to double.

I picked up all the evidence bags in one armload. Amy found Gene, and he opened a surplus Army storage locker after I assured him the State would pay him the standard daily rate, a minimum of two days. Plus, the cost of a padlock. I tucked the key in my pocket.

Walking out, I spotted Barnes's blue and white Chevy 4x4 carryall as I moseyed toward the bar. Amy was already inside belting out "Walking After Midnight." A dog tied to a truck outside either attempted to sing along or howled in protest. A critic or kindred soul—I wasn't sure.

Doors and windows open at the bar poured smoke from cigarettes and cigars like a house fire. The first person visible through the haze, Dottie, sat at the register near the door. Dressed like the proprietor of the Long Branch Saloon on the TV program *Gunsmoke*, she had a few years on Miss Kitty, but Dottie shaped up well for her age.

Chet Robarts glanced at me when I walked in. He wore an old plaid shirt with the arms torn off, a set of wide red suspenders, and heavy boots. His footwear looked right for hard work but not dancing. Rib busters, I thought, and he plans to use them. Chet stood near the stage and kept reaching for Amy. She slapped his hand away and started in on a Kitty Wells hit, "It Wasn't God Who Made Honky Tonk Angels."

I stepped toward the stage, but my foreman shook her head no. It wouldn't stop Robarts, only delay him.

Robbie told me after the first run-in with Chet that the State Police got notified by the Army that the skinny felon, Slim Parsons, did time in Leavenworth prison for a stabbing and robbery before they released him to go home to Alaska. Recently, he spent time in jail in Anchorage.

Slim eased through the crowd, trying to reach my blindside. Korea sharpened my wits and observation skills to where Amy was my only blind spot.

A third man moved in— a short, stocky feller thick in the shoulders, stubby arms, his legs stout as oak trees. Shorty didn't have much reach, but he sized up as a grappler. He sneaked around to my other side. Boyd eased over, blocking Shorty's view, and bumped me with an elbow.

Still dressed in green coveralls, the mechanic slipped his hand-carved diamond willow walking stick into my hand and stepped away. The old mechanic carved several canes over the winter to sell through Gene's place, also at a tourist shop on Fourth Avenue in Anchorage. This one looked well-worn and substantial.

Dottie nodded toward Shorty. Nothing much got past her. My pa said there's a time for talking and a time for doing. When the time comes, be decisive. I didn't see much point in conversation.

Chet would make a play for Amy to get my attention. Once I started forward, the two thugs would jump me from behind and let Robarts work me over.

Amy sang the final chorus: "Too many times married men, Think they're still single, That has caused many a good girl to go wrong."

As expected, Chet grabbed her arm. Two things happened. Sitting in the back of Amy on a tall stool, Ricky planted his bootheel hard on Chet's elbow. The Crocketts played rowdy bars, worked hard at the mine, and weren't greenhorns. The other, I started forward fast before Chet moved, gaining two steps on Slim and his stubby pal. The skinny one's scars on his face identified him as a scrapper.

Turning, I put the peeled-bark spruce post in the center of the bar between me and Slim. It forced him to push past Boyd. He expected to catch me unaware. Instead, I pivoted and lunged a long step while he rounded the post. Swinging my other foot with full force, I saw his eyes grow wide, and he reached to protect his crotch. If the convict ever intended to father children, his chances narrowed. My boot lifted him a foot off the floor, and he coughed and doubled over.

I twisted around the pole to slow Stubby and caught the mobile fire plug closing fast. Faking a left jab at his head. He grabbed my fist and never saw the swinging club. My backhand swing caught him across the right knee and sounded like the cane snapped, but it remained whole. He rolled, writhing on the floor.

A meaty arm reached around my neck. I dropped the cane and grabbed an elbow, clamping it hard to my chest. I planted my feet and drove us backward, shoving Chet off balance, back peddling him across the room clear into Dottie's bar. Solid wood and well anchored, it weighed a ton or more and didn't budge or rattle glasses when we slammed into it.

Chet lost his hold, and I ducked out while he leaned back against the bar. I spun, hooked a heel behind his ankles, and swept his feet from under him. He went down hard, banging his thick skull on the bar and the brass footrail. Turning away, I suckered him into a mistake. Seeing a chance to push himself up, I watched from the corner of my eye until he shoved up hard.

Turning, throwing a roundhouse punch dragged from the back forty, I landed my fist square on his cleft chin. The blow caught him with his mouth open, leaning in with both hands behind him. His eyes rolled back, and his head bounced like a bowling ball off the boot rail and hit the floor. He didn't move.

Ricky bumped into me. I straightened up, shaking my sore hand. "Damned dumb cowboy."

"What?" I rubbed my knuckles.

"Kick him when he's down. Now your hand ain't in any condition for working, and any guitar player knows that."

~~~

Gene proudly owned an imitation totem pole Boyd carved him. Buried at the corner of his building, it sat in the center of a section of mowed weeds passing for a lawn. The three men were tied to the pole and informed that the state policeman would decide their fate when he got to town.

Amy gave me the day off thanks to a swollen hand and the prisoners who needed watching, but I owed her a make-up day. She tried to act disgruntled about the fight, but I saw through her.

~~~

Around seven o'clock the following morning, while I leaned against the wall of Gene's store, a red, rusted Ford pickup truck rolled and rattled to a cautious stop in the sunny parking lot.

A native man in a tan canvas shirt, blue jeans, and ball cap carefully eyed the three men tied to the totem. His wife stepped out the passenger's side in a one-piece dress, white with little flowers, and wearing PF Flyer tennis shoes. The doors slammed shut, and three wide eyed kids varying in size from knee to hip high followed their parents like a row of ducklings past me and into Gene's General Store.

A few minutes later, after purchases and a potty break at the outhouse, the family passed by again, each youngster with a Tootsie Pop in hand. They loaded into the truck, and all five stared over the dash, the father shaking his head like he encountered an alien, put it in gear, and backed out. He turned toward Dawson and drove away.

Gene appeared in his summer attire, the same as his winter outfit except for short sleeves. He carried a Colt revolver stuck in his belt, having assisted in guard duty. He handed me a cup of coffee. I felt sure the cost was listed on a running tab for the State of Alaska to pay.

"Butch Nelson and family." Gene nodded down the road. "They have kin folks on the other side of the border down on the Yukon. They think white people are a little strange."

I turned from watching the disappearing truck. "You have some breakfast and coffee for these three?"

"Is the State paying?" Gene wanted clarification.

"I guess so."

"You're running up a good-sized bill for Governor Egan."

"Well, Mayor, you were the one who put me up for sheriff."

Chet looked up, his eyes flicking back and forth between us. "You the law? When did that happen?"

A raven landed on the top of the totem and cawed at the morning sky. I hitched a thumb at Gene. "They took a vote and railroaded me into the job. Assaulting the town sheriff is the charge, and except for you three, the witnesses all see it my way."

I dug out the gold star from my pants pocket, gingerly pinned it on my shirt, and rubbed my aching hand. Chet worked his jaw around, and it irked me. The foreman's chin looked better than my hand.

"You didn't have no badge on last night."

Boyd and a couple of boys from a mine on Arkansas Creek held the two thugs, skinny and shorty, down and out of the fight with Chet.

"True, I just came off duty." I stared at the burly miner. "Can you behave long enough to eat and go to the outhouse?"

"We won't give you no trouble. We need to get back to our mine."

"That's up to Robertson when he gets here. Might have to take you to Tok to see a judge."

The shorter man whined. "I need a doctor; I've got to have my knee checked. I think it's busted."

"Play stupid games; you win stupid prizes. How and when you visit a doctor is between you and the officer, but I ain't able to transport you anywhere."

I saw to it the prisoners were fed and watered. Seeing the mechanic, I returned Boyd's fancy walking stick. Shorty wanted to buy it, but Boyd surmised bad intentions and refused to sell.

The mechanic pushed my motorbike to his shop and installed the new tune-up kit for something to do. Still early in the season for Boyd, and equipment hadn't started breaking down yet. Later, he would likely be working day and night for several weeks when he made his wages for a year.

Amy told me Dottie hooked ol' Boyd up with an investment broker in Anchorage who made him money funding startup companies. He recently put money into the hardware outfit Byron worked for and expected a sizeable return on his cash.

I ought to consult with her and maybe check into investing. *Investing?* That might be the first time such a thought crossed my mind.

Chet and the boys behaved, and I left them untied until Officer Robertson showed up around 2:00 p.m. His dispatcher warned him. He touched base with the magistrate who authorized Robbie to release the men based on their promise to show up for court.

The officer made them take a solemn oath I'm sure he made up. He issued each of them a ticket with the appearance date in Fairbanks court. The other option was to mail the ticket in, plead guilty, and pay a minimal fine.

After dispensing with them, we examined Tim's belongings. My police mentor gave me a begrudging attaboy for properly bagged evidence. After reviewing it, Robbie decided nothing there was tied to a suspect. He suggested giving it back to the Crocketts.

"I'll hold on to it for the time being." Some evidence might be there we weren't seeing. Possibly something that should have been inside and was missing other than the sidearm.

"Your call, Sheriff, but the State isn't paying for storage after right now." He stood and moved away from the table in Gene's back room. "Show me where you found this stuff."

~~~

I led the way on my motorbike, dodging potholes more effectively than the State's pickup, and slowed down so he could keep up. Following the bear's trail, Robbie spent two hours locating the missing underwear.

The partly ripped clothing showed streaks of peanut butter on it. It looked like Tim rolled them around a jar to prevent breakage—apparently not enough padding. At least not when thrown from a vehicle. The bear ate a good bit of chow, as Tim would have planned to be in camp for a while before Ricky arrived.

"Your bear tore it up, and with the snow gone, it is hard to say which way the suspect traveled when he tossed the bag," Robbie said.

"I agree, but the highway wasn't open then."

No one passed the whole time we investigated. The sun warmed me, still high, backlighting a pair of ravens flying toward Tok ninety miles west-southwest.

"Had to be someone local. It's hard to say if it was dumped here at the time of Tim's death, before, or sometime later." I waited for Robbie to respond.

The state officer tipped his head down the road toward the border. "Could have driven up from the Canadian side. The border station was still closed for the winter, but the highway was passable into Canada. After we found Tim's body, I flew with our pilot along the boundary, and this road looked good for at least ten miles further east we could see."

I rubbed my neck, a habit I started as a kid whenever I got confused. "You knew Tim?"

Robbie sighed and hitched his gun belt. "Yes, a little bit. He talked his way out of a ticket he dearly deserved the first time we met. I worked for the Territorial Police near Delta. I've seen the family up at Dottie's and Boundary several times. Tim was an easy guy to like." Robbie stooped over and pulled a stem of grass to chew on.

His tone said he knew Tim but stayed vague about how well, so I nodded. "I guess he never met anyone he didn't consider a friend."

Robbie peered from under his hat, squinting with one eye. "Which means someone he thought was a friend killed him," the tall cop winked, "that's why you're still on the suspect list."

"I didn't have a running vehicle at the time and couldn't have reached a road with all the snow if I had one." I read the amusement on his face.

"All the same, anyone big enough to carry him is still on my list."

"Narrows it down some, eliminates Miss Gail."

Robbie pulled his sunglasses out of his pocket, slipped them on, and tipped his head for me to follow. We reached the door of the State's truck. He leaned an elbow on the roof and spoke.

"That's the part that bothers me the most. I can't believe any of the full-time residents are killers. You're the best qualified and latest arriving resident in the suspect pool. Saying so, you make a better cop than a killer."

I flexed my sore hand, and Robertson saw it. "Thanks for your confidence, as I'm none too sure of myself."

"Where did you learn to fight? I know Korea, but that bruiser for Barnes didn't fail twice to separate your head from your shoulders on Army training."

"Boxed some in high school and spent time with a martial arts instructor as part of my frostbite rehab in Japan."

"The Army sent you?"

"No. I met a guy who owned a bar, about half my size. After a few drinks and angry about the war, I got loud, and he said I had to leave. I disagreed and threw a short left jab that should have knocked the squirt off his feet but missed.

"Then he quite expertly kicked my ass all over the bar and threw me out. I had to learn how he did it. I paid a man named Tanaka, and he showed me how easy it was to do. He spent a few months showing me the ropes."

What I didn't say was I trained more in Fort Worth and met others in mining camps to spar with to keep in shape.

Robbie smiled. "Learn from your mistakes. That's good." He gave me a two-fingered, halfhearted Cub Scout salute. I took it as a reference to my rookie status. He loaded up and drove on toward the border station.

I wondered what, besides a summer village for the natives, was over on the Canadian side. I never stopped between the border and Dawson. No doubt small mines like ours existed.

Looking southeast, then I stared directly east around the sweeping curve leading to the trail going to my camp. All the evidence, I tied on the back of the motorbike in a milk crate that Boyd fastened on it so I could haul gear. Mostly, I used it to carry my hat. I kicked the bike into life. It sputtered, backfired, and settled down into a steady idle.

"You piece of junk, I can walk from here with no problem." The threat coaxed it into not quitting before I reached the yellow bus at the claim. I reexamined every item and found a shot glass souvenir from another local watering hole.

Action Jackson's Bar took its name from the eighty-some-year-old owner, one of the original Klondike gold rush miners. The tiny community we considered a suburb of Chicken, called Boundary, sat on this side of the border between my trailhead and downtown Chicken. A closer drinking bar for some of the miners on other drainages of the Fortymile to use.

Without money to spend, I rarely stopped there, but Tim may have. Jackson's bar sat halfway between where Robbie found Tim's body and where I found his gear. The old prospector lived alone at that time of year, other than his team of dogs. He rented spare cabins to tourists or families visiting miners in the summer. Like Dottie's, the bar opened officially when the highway did. Ol' Action was reputedly his own best customer.

No new answers in the evidence for me, but one new question about the number on the card. I struck off to Amy's to try and work some before dinner.

Chapter 9

Days went by with no new leads, and we reached midseason for mining.

The screeching tracks and steady chugging of the bulldozer's engine mixed with the rattle of rocks on steel as we scraped paydirt into the chute. I watched the water rushing down the sluice riffles, pushing rocks clunking along until they spilled into the pond.

The dozer stopped, and Amy bolted, heading for the road. A white three-quarter-ton pickup with orange lettering and the hardware store logo lurched out of the creek bed onto the bank.

A young guy with dark hair, clean-shaven, wearing starched Levi jeans and a white shirt, climbed out of the cab. The salesman sported spotless black rubber boots.

I fought the urge to throw a shovel of mud on him. He didn't have chin whiskers. Hell, the kid wasn't old enough to shave. I stroked the beard hanging halfway to my navel.

Thankfully, Amy pulled off her gloves and shook his hand rather than hugging him. Byron waved to Ricky and Doug. Amy waved me to come over. Byron— bless his little pea pickin' heart— brought supplies and groceries with the delivery. As the low man, I received a nod to carry those supplies to camp while babyface spoke to her.

When the sales rep started to climb in his truck to leave. Friend or not, Amy made no allowances for holding up progress. I heard her tell Byron we would be at Dottie's on the Fourth of July.

He replied, "I will be doing site visits all over this area and will see you on the Fourth."

Byron pulled on the door, but I caught it. Amy's eyes flared, and the muscles in her cheeks twitched.

"Hold up a minute, *sir*," I went with politeness and professionalism, fitting for a sheriff.

The boy pointed a chin at me and asked her, "Who's this?"

I resisted an urge to backhand the little turd, and Amy hastily said, "Wyatt Peoples is filling in for Tim this season and doing more actual work. What's the problem?" She looked up at me. I saw the concern in her eyes.

"Sheriff Wyatt Peoples, and I have some questions to ask you."

"Chicken has a sheriff?"

I considered breaking the kid's knee by shoving the door closed on it, but Amy would fire me, so instead, I pulled the gold star from my pocket and extended the other one to shake. With clenched teeth, I put the badge up. It felt good, and I hadn't expected that. I wiped a sleeve across my face, smearing sweat and mud on it. Reckon I didn't much look like an officer of the law.

"I wanted to ask you about this card." I dug it out of my shirt pocket, wrapped in plastic and inside the notebook. "Is this your card?"

The kid grinned. "You're pretty sharp for a lawman; my name is on it."

Amy giggled, and Ricky smirked.

I swallowed more than a little pride. "Okay, did you give it to Tim?"

"I believe I did hand him one at the store in Anchorage, and he put it in a notebook like that one."

The engine and exhaust pipe on the D8 made ticking noises as it cooled, and letting it sit idle in the middle of the day didn't suit Amy. I needed to make it quick.

"Did you write this number on the back?"

Byron glanced at it. "No, and I don't know the number." He looked at Amy instead of me. The answer came too quickly and too confidently.

I smiled. "Sorry to hold you up."

I pulled the door open and slapped Byron on the back a little rougher than polite, leaving a dirty handprint on his white shirt.

The truck pulled out, and I walked past Amy, who stood with her mouth open, unable to form words— her problem for a change. I picked up the invoice from the grocery store with the food items listed. Byron hand-wrote several items on a list. He didn't use all the numbers from the card. The twos, fours, sixes, and the C and A on the bill matched. *He lied.*

Taking the invoice, I folded it with the card, wrapped it back in plastic, and stuffed it in my pocket. Amy needed the bill to track expenses but ignored me and climbed back into the Cat's driver's seat. I pulled the hand crank to turn over the gas-powered pony motor to start the big diesel engine. We went back to work.

A clue, but proved what? I suspected the number belonged to someone involved in something, but what? Otherwise, why lie? I needed to check in with Robbie. Amy shoved a pile of dirt against my leg. A not-so-subtle hint that I needed to pay attention. Otherwise, she might drop a two-ton dozer blade on my foot.

~~~

With three jobs, Crocketts' mine took priority, my claim second, and the law job came in a distant last. I sent a message to Officer Robertson, and the trip to Chicken cut into time for me to work on my claim. The sky clouded over before I got back from Gene's, making it darker, but on the first day of July, the sun barely reached the horizon before coming back up. The temperature dropped into the sixties and made working comfortable.

I built a flume from scrap wood and made a movable gate to divert water from upstream into the sluice. My operation was archaic compared to Crocketts' and way behind Barnes's.

While working I considered Tim's case. I visited Action Jackson's after finding Tim's bag. The proprietor remembered Tim stopping in and spoke to Robbie about it. He didn't remember any conversation with Tim because Action recalled being drunk that month. Robbie said nothing about talking to AJ, but then he said he spoke to everyone.

The diggings Ricky guided me to turned out to be an excellent location. I suspected Amy's brother knew more about mining than he realized. Working alone with a pick and shovel, I dug to bedrock, watching the undermined permafrost bank above. Once you disturb the insulating soil, it starts to melt. Stream-cut bluffs caused whole banks to break loose with little or no warning.

The pay dirt residing near the bedrock glittered in the sunlight, most of it being too fine to pick up and separate with my fingers. During my limited time working, I picked out half a dozen tiny nuggets, one big, and one nearly the size of an acorn. Nuggets, the government considered jewelry gold, and it was legal to sell it directly to jewelers. For the rest, Uncle Sam required miners to sell to him.

Standing at the base of the bluff, I glanced at the sun. It looked like the moon, shining through the overcast. A stiff breeze blew in from the northwest and carried the smell of the tundra mixed with the odor of wet gravel. Dropping the shovel, I grabbed the wheelbarrow's handles, lifted two hundred pounds of gold-bearing gravel, and started to the sluice.

Motion on the trail caught my eye. I stopped until I saw Robbie— 10:00 p.m. and late for him to be out and about and on foot. The road into my claim ended at Barnes's place, but past there required the swamp buggy or tracked rig like a Cat dozer to reach it. I glanced at the bus. It added to the mystery of how it got there.

I lifted the handles and pushed on downhill.

"Hello, camp," Robbie yelled over the sound of the water and gravel sliding over the riffles as I emptied the load into the wash.

"Come and sit if you're a mind to." Picking up my muck stick, I stirred the gravel until the pay dirt soaked through, then pushed it into the stream.

Robbie walked in wearing his police outfit and looking official. He took a seat on my log bench.

"You can try some coffee if you are brave enough. Hold on a minute while I wash this down the sluice."

"No thanks, Robarts downstream set me up with a cup of fresh-brewed and a decent meal to go with it."

I raked the muck back and forth. It took time without the water pressure the Crocketts engineered, or the diesel pump Barnes ran, but it worked. "I figured not to meet with you until tomorrow sometime."

Robbie said, "I'm supposed to drive in the parade in Tok on the Fourth, so I'm making a fast trip in and out. Dispatch called while I happened to be out near the Junction."

The water swirled around and washed the pay dirt across the tiny rapids created by the sluice board. I dropped the rake and walked to Robbie, and we shared the same drift log.

"I ran down the number, and it is for a law firm in Anchorage." Robbie glanced at me and pulled his four-cell flashlight from a belt loop. "Let me look at the card and supply note."

I went to the bus and grabbed them off the table. Robbie eyed them under the light and nodded his head. "Huh. A close match, so I guess the salesman lied, but why?"

"Well, sir, if we knew, we wouldn't need to investigate anything. To tell you the truth, I prodded him pretty hard because I don't like slick salesmen."

Robbie chuckled. "I would venture to guess jealousy might interfere with your investigation, too." He stated it as a fact.

"I don't have no call to get myself in a pickle over a gal who could have her pick of guys anywhere, let alone in Chicken."

"True, but you didn't deny it."

I stared at the ground, kicked the dirt, and flopped down on the dead tree. "Back to our investigation. What's this law firm do? Why would Byron want Tim to call them?"

Robbie looked amused at the change of subject and went into training mode. "You're jumping to conclusions."

"How so?"

"Tim may have picked up the card, and the number was written for someone else who left it behind. Or someone wanted Tim to call them. Byron wrote the number on one of his cards and gave it to him. I could think of other possibilities, but it is easy to see he may not know who the number goes to and will claim so regardless."

I gazed at the dying campfire inside a double ring of boulders. Being fire season, everything above the permafrost was tinder dry. "You're right; my feelings aside, he lied to me. Folks in Texas set store in honesty and a handshake. What little time I spent as a cop, I'm a fair hand at spotting liars."

"Well, you take your unnatural abilities to a superior court judge and find out how much it's worth." Robbie stretched out his legs, rattling the rubber boots. "I talked to the lawyer, Bilko's receptionist, a long-distance call from Tok. She politely told me to go to hell by saying it involved a client, and they were under no obligation to answer any of my questions."

Some legal procedures started returning to me from my days at Fort Worth. In an eight-hour day in Cowtown, I did more police work than a week in Parker County. My training officer at FWPD was a wet-behind-the-ears kid, like Byron. I witnessed more carnage in the Army in five years than I could ever explain to my young trainer. Those five years amounted to the difference in our ages. The kid believed I was a good cop, but I wondered if he thought so because of my family's reputation rather than my abilities.

I let that thought go. "Maybe if you snatched the lawyer up by the scruff of his neck and shook him, he might come around to our way of thinking. We're investigating a murder."

"The law is still the law, and you've burned up about half your investigation time. Those three yahoos you arrested pled guilty to disturbing the peace, and Barnes paid their fines."

"He ought to since the rumor is he sent Robarts to rough me up. I don't care for people who hide behind skirts or send hired help to make their fights. Anyway, I haven't had any truck with any of them since. I stay away from them; they do me the same way."

Robbie nodded. "From what I heard about the fight when he fired you, it wouldn't have taken much to talk him into it. You saved up any money?"

"I guess I expected the fight. Money is an odd question. Everything I own is in sight of where you're sitting. You fixin' to rob me?"

"Nope. I know a guy in Anchorage, a private detective for high-powered lawyers. He's a Texan, too, but I try not to hold it against him. He grew up on the King ranch. The name he uses is Darrell Johnson. You ever heard of him?"

"Not that I recall, and even at half the size of Alaska, Texas is a big place. Why not ask the Anchorage cops to run it down?"

"Number one reason is Bilko, the mayor, and the chief play poker together at the local furrier's backroom on Saturday nights." Robbie pulled out his notebook, tore a piece off the back page, and wrote a phone number.

"Word is, Darrell is related to the vice president. He denies it. I'll keep the note and business card and put it into evidence. When you get a chance, have Gene call Darrell for you." .

"Gene doesn't have a phone."

"It's a ham radio call. He calls a friend in town who calls on the phone, and you tell Gene what to say; he tells his friend, and the friend relays it to Darrell."

"I heard sometimes the Red Cross did that in Korea. I will give it a try."

Robbie stood and shook my dirty hand.

"You may make a bush cop yet. By the by, I dropped a used CB radio over at Crocketts'. I left another with Gene so he can monitor the frequency. Our dispatcher had them and recently upgraded to a new one he built from kits. Ricky and Doug were figuring out how to hook it up in their old Dodge." Robbie looked downstream. "I better hit the trail."

Where would I find money for a private detective, and what would he look for? Besides, nothing I told the guy would be secret. Anyone could listen in, and the radio operators would know for sure.

Something to ponder, but first, I need four hours of sleep if I hurry.

Chapter 10

The next day ended with me exhausted at quitting time. Every day, I'm amazed by how long and hard Amy and her brothers worked. We finished two weeks of labor by cleaning the sluice.

They shut off the water valve and began collecting the gold. The recovered gold was their payoff before the Independence Day celebration, Chicken style.

Collecting their fortune was a chore for the family. So, I hiked to my claim to clean up before trekking to Dottie's.

Keeping an eye on the wandering path, I dodged alder limbs on the trail to Davis Creek. My operation required a cleanup every day I ran paydirt. Otherwise, it made it too easy for someone to collect my gold while away.

Carrying any significant amount of gold posed problems and was a great way to end up robbed. I found a hiding spot away from camp to keep my haul.

Ricky's suggestion of where I ought to dig, either from experience or by accident, put me on an excellent deposit. I had already met my requirements to keep the claim, and a bit more. Enough that I dreamed of picking up a backhoe like Gearhart's and a 4x4 truck.

At camp, I stripped down to a full-course mosquito smorgasbord and climbed into the lukewarm tub of water with a bar of Lava soap. Sitting in the tub, a splash and rattling of rocks from upstream signaled something coming at a run. I grabbed the shotgun as two caribou loped by, frothing at the mouth. They were closely followed by a pair of wolves who barely glanced at me. If I saw two, then out of sight, at least a half dozen more wolves closed in from both sides. Life in the wilderness teeters at the bleeding edge of death.

I needed to find out from Darrell Johnson who Tim talked to, or if someone wanted him to talk to someone at the lawyer's office and why. Not much for him to go on, but a good detective might discover who.

Scrubbing the dirt off my hands and arms, I grabbed my knife and scraped the crud under my nails. What motive would someone have to murder Tim? Possibly a random killing, and the killer got scared and left.

I slapped a skeeter and noticed a thundercloud out east, north of Dawson, and it would, as usual, head southeast, away with the prevailing wind.

The idea of a random killer crossed my mind, but not likely. Robbie had alibied everyone around at the time. Same for the salesman. Any other people Tim associated with lived in Anchorage, where he spent the late fall, winter, and early spring.

A blur of grey fur blew between me and the creek before I could move for the gun. The two wolves disappeared upstream. I finished my bath and grabbed a moth-eaten beach towel.

Walking barefoot to the clothesline where my cleanest outfit hung, I heard Gene's swamp buggy. The mayor drove faster than his usual careful grind and pulled up with Boyd riding shotgun. I stood wrapped in a towel, still feeding dozens of winged bloodsuckers.

Gene dismounted and walked over. "Sorry to intrude, Sheriff, but we have an emergency."

"I'm Wyatt right now, and I'm off duty, as you can tell."

"I've seen more than I care to, and Miss Dottie will want a full report, but for now, you're on duty. Some people are dead. I contacted Robbie, and he's down on Ruby Creek near Nabesna on a possible murder-suicide. Some guy got word he had lung cancer and was going to die. Went home, got drunk, and killed his old lady and then himself."

"Okay, he isn't available. What's the situation? You said someone died."

"Two someone's, maybe— a mining accident—maybe. The Eddin brothers, Frick and Frack, at their place on Arkansas Creek."

"Frick and Frack?" The boys had stepped in on my side of the bar fight. "They're a bit out of my jurisdiction."

I had never visited their mine, but I knew where to find the Arkansas Creek drainage.

Gene shrugged, "I told Robbie, and Boyd heard me. Ain't that right, Boyd?"

Boyd nodded from the cab. "But he said you are to investigate until they dispatched a state cop from Fairbanks. Robertson said it might tie into Tim's death."

"How?"

"He didn't say. Only to get you there on the pronto."

After some swearing and misgivings, I pulled my dirty work clothes back on and grabbed my shotgun and some shells. Gene decided my path to the road saved ten miles, and he drove the green beast up the slope, knocking over trees as big around as my forearm.

The F & F Mine sat about eight miles north by the compass. Using his buggy and his knowledge of the area, we made a right turn on the Taylor Highway. Driving a mile or so, he went off-road and ducked into the headwaters of Arkansas Creek.

Gene hollered over the sound of the engine and the snapping spruce trees. "Reaching the mine in the winter is a sight easier when the swamps are frozen."

We arrived after three hours of bouncing over hummocks of tundra and murdering a forest worth of small trees.

Concerned about Gene flipping over his buggy, I fought to stay seated for most of the trip until he stopped. Boyd opened the door. I pushed past him and stumbled out of the 4x4 into the fresh air, suffering from carbon monoxide poisoning and seasickness. After a few deep breaths, I straightened up, pushed through the willows to the stream bank, and washed my face in the cold water until the dizziness cleared.

Gene stopped when the campsite came into view. "I'll stay with the truck. Seeing dead folks makes me puke."

Boyd said, "You stay here then. We'll find 'em."

He followed me across the tundra a few paces back. We followed a game trail near the creek.

The Eddin brothers' camp sat near a bend in the stream. A surplus military pole tent served as their HQ, large enough for two of them to sleep and keep a kitchen in. Based on the fire pit and a makeshift outdoor counter, they ate cowboy-style in the open air, weather permitting.

On the ride in, when not holding on for dear life, Boyd said, "A wife expected to meet the brothers in Chicken four days ago. After waiting, she hitched a ride to the Walker Creek mine and hiked to her husband's place. She saw where the bluff the brothers were working under collapsed in a landslide, exposing a hunk of ice."

I guessed the slab of ice sticking out of the mud would measure in the millions of gallons of water once it melted. Thinking about my mine, I didn't know what in a few feet of digging might start a catastrophe like this.

Scrub spruce and tundra from up top stopped in a half-milelong wavy pile of rubble blocking the creek. It started to back up a small lake before the stream found a path around the end. The mass of soil and rock missed their camp by twenty yards. It stretched farther than several football fields and twice as wide as one.

Glancing at the buried iceberg looming overhead, I worried it might be holding back another avalanche of rocks and clay, depending on the thickness of the ice. The ground around it was frozen, but it started melting the instant warm air and sunlight hit it. Water streamed off the face, forming puddles and small streams soaking into the loose gravel piled at the back against the bluff.

Boyd pointed. "The wife said to look over yonder." He indicated by tipping his head. "She come up from the trail what follows the creek."

We crossed to the north side of the slide, tripping and stumbling over the jumble of muck, frozen dirt, gravel, and tundra. We reached the far side, where the two evenly spaced trails led north toward Walker Creek. It looked like Gene's buggy trail.

Boyd helped me hunt for signs along the edge. He pointed. "There."

I spotted a leg sticking out of the rubble with a black rubber boot and blue jeans. No way for us to ID the owner from what we could see. The rest of him lay buried under tons of dirt.

"But for the grace of God—" I mumbled and looked to heaven.

"What's the plan, Sheriff?"

"Well, there's thousands of cubic yards of dirt. If two bodies are here, there is no telling where we will find the other." I considered a minute and said, "Have Gene tell the State Police what we are looking at. You worked the highway construction and must have seen stuff like this before."

"Yes, sir, we dug through these things on occasion. It happens out here all the time, but nobody sees them. In twenty years, this ugly slide will be overgrown in berries and fireweed and look pretty."

"I have to stay here to keep the animals away." I glanced at the foot once more. "If they have a search and rescue dog they can bring, it might help."

Boyd left. I had my shotgun and half a box of shells. I swatted at flies and mosquitos and eyed where the slide started. A loud boom sounded behind me and shook the ground. I turned toward Walker Creek. The Arkansas Creek ran into it a mile or so downstream. Turning, I watched a plume of smoke rise over the trees in a small mushroom cloud.

Dynamite. *Did the brothers set off this slide accidentally with explosives?*

Clamoring over the rubble to their camp, I saw Gene cross the creek, swing wide around the new lake and the end of the slide. He saved miles and time returning to Chicken by taking the established trail.

Once in camp, I searched their tent and supplies stacked in open cartons or under canvas tarps. No sign of dynamite blasting caps or fuse material in or around their camp.

Guns—one, a .44 Magnum pistol, under a rumpled pillow, and a bolt-action .30-06 rifle were rolled in a wool blanket under that bed. Both weapons were newer and well cared for. A lever-operated 30-30 showed wear and tear, but was in good condition, was sitting beneath the other cot in the tent. An older, single action Colt .45 one brother left was tucked under the pillow of his cot.

An accident? The slide might have been natural, or maybe they undermined the bank, but such a catastrophic slide didn't sit right on my stomach, so I chewed on possibilities.

Stepping out of the hot, stinky tent, I studied the escarpment. At the highest point, maybe three hundred feet up, water dripped off exposed tree roots onto a dirt-streaked blue-green chunk of ice as large as Weatherford's Parker County Courthouse. As a kid, the huge rock building looked impressive. The runoff formed a grim, greasy mudpuddle pond at the base of the ice.

I jerked my hat down tight and started to hike along the edge of the broken bluff, partly out of curiosity, and a hunch something wasn't right.

The south side of the bluff sat behind the camp. A mountain goat or a climber with ropes might make it up, but not me. I hiked a couple hundred yards further south and found a runoff gully choked with scrub spruce and broken rock to hold on to. It occurred to me that the gully probably formed from a similar slide many years ago.

Twenty minutes later, I topped out and spied the mine on Walker Creek past a swampy area west of the slide. After a quick visual survey, it looked like the bottom of the bluff fell out, and everything above it followed. I saw places near Dawson where melting permafrost weakened the bank close to the bottom. An all-gravel bank tended to slough off a little at a time.

But sometimes chunks of ice formed or possibly were left by glaciers, creating a weak boundary. When destabilized enough, the whole bank collapses. Some of those slides I saw in Canada came off slopes and ran across the valley floor for a mile before stopping.

Concerned about further collapsing, I walked well back of the edge. Climbing toward the crest, I spotted many deadfalls and weathered dead spruce looking like burned-out match sticks.

Some years back, a forest fire had come through. The new growth looked to be forty years old or older. Gene may have a record of the fire since it would have happened during the heyday of the Klondike rush. On the horizon, small puffy clouds tinged with pink and orange lingered as the sun dropped and the camp below fell under the shadow.

Reaching the crest, huffing and out of breath, proved a stiff workout after a long day on the job. Dottie will be ticked because I didn't show, but she voted to make me sheriff. By rights, I shouldn't be here, but sheriff or not, if asked, I would have come along anyway.

Stepping out to peer over, I saw a thirty-foot drop to the visible part of the iceberg almost straight down. Reaching back, I grabbed a small spruce to hold onto and felt the sticky sap. The stuff gets on your skin and eventually turns black. It takes a bar of Lava soap to remove it or wait for it to wear off. The dang stuff stuck better than anything Elmer's invented.

Wiping my hands in the weeds, I discovered the sap came from peeled bark. Porcupines chew on the bark, but no teeth marks. Checking the area, I spied other fresh scars and broken limbs.

Stepping farther away from the bluff, I found pieces of tundra hanging in trees or clumped with soil-side up here and there in the woods. It's funny, but I didn't notice any of it until I grabbed the tree. From farther back, it became obvious an explosion occurred on the part of the bluff currently at the bottom.

After making notes, I hiked down the north side of the slide to where Frick's— or maybe Frack's— leg stuck out of the dirt.

I ambled up on the slide at the base of the slope near the new pool of water. When I got a whiff of the lingering order of dynamite, I stopped. We used it in Korea, as well as in the Colorado and Klondike mining camps. It leaves a fruity smell in the air, like bananas.

Twisting, I picked out landmarks and marked my location mentally. I continued walking to the camp and found an empty, rusted Blazo can from years ago, and I snatched a wool blanket off one of the cots. I returned to the body with my seat and some defense against mosquitoes to wait for the recovery team.

The Eddins boys stepped in and helped keep Chet's pals off my back. I needed to talk with Skinny and Shorty.

Chapter 11

A small company of four-wheel drive vehicles arrived around noon the next day, led by Gene's swamp thing. They came up the almost-dry creek bottom since most of the water was held back behind the dam caused by the slide. A state cop, a runt by Texas Police standards, about five foot ten, named Stuart, came with a dog handler and German Shepard. Also, a half-dozen volunteers from Chicken and the claims along Walker Creek came to assist.

James and Bobby Eddin went by Frick and Frack, something a family member started calling them as kids and stuck. They made a sign declaring their holdings as the Frick and Frack mine and referred to it as the F & F for short. The cascading dirt swept away their marker.

The exposed boot belonged to Bobby and was the first body they recovered. From a description Nora gave Stuart, he identified the victim by a tattoo on his arm that Eddin had picked up in the Navy somewhere in the South Pacific during World War II. It appeared he made a run for it and almost escaped.

I discussed my theory with Stuart.

"Might be he was going to the creek for something and had a bit of a start," Stuart suggested.

I thought about the evidence of an explosion up above them. "Or Bobby had some warning and made a run for it. They had a good path from the tent to go to the water. I think he heard or saw something— like the explosion— and took the angle where he stood the best chance of getting clear. No way to try and reach their camp."

James's wife Nora gave the State Police pictures taken at the start of the mining season showing what it looked like before the slide. A larger version of the bank I worked on my claim, the two men operated with wheelbarrows carrying dirt to the stream from above an outcropping of bedrock. In the picture, you could distinguish where the men cleared away small slides before they set to work for this season.

We examined her pictures and picked out landmarks still visible to determine where their workings had been, hoping to narrow the search for James.

"Something is bothering me, Officer Stuart."

"What?"

I pointed to the top. "Up yonder, I found signs of a dynamite blast."

Old Boyd quietly walked up and joined us. "Wouldn't make no sense to blast up there Mr Wyaatt. No matter what, all you gonna do is dump a lot of dirt to take off to be where you started."

Boyd just stated the obvious in my way of thinking. Stuart wasn't a mining man or an engineer but looked to be a fine investigator.

He stared up, then turned and scanned the devastation around us. Taking off his campaign hat, he scratched his head. "So why?"

"When I walked up there, I wondered the same thing." I waved for the other two to follow, and we walked to where I picked up the odor of spent explosives.

"You smell anything?"

Boyd nodded. "Nitro, alright."

Stuart stood on a lump of frozen dirt and visually searched the broken tundra for evidence. He climbed over a clump the size of my bathtub and examined the ground. "I got some charring on this piece of tundra. Everything is so broken up it is hard to say what might be from an explosion and what came from the slide."

Taking out his knife, the state officer cut out the charred moss and later put it in a tin can that paint came in and where the brothers had later stored spare nails.

Using the picture, we located a high spot in the debris we thought matched the bench outcrop before the slide. The canine named Barron found a place he thought they should dig a few feet from the outcrop.

The mass of gravel mixed with ice was packed rock hard, and it took until midnight for the crew to locate what remained of James. It appeared he jumped down and pinned himself against the face of the rock. Tons of griding ice and stone left only pieces of bone, tissue, and clothing streaked down the slope like a bug hitting a car window.

During the time the volunteer crews worked in shifts to dig out his body parts, Stuart searched the camp and spoke to anyone who knew the brothers. They were quiet, stuck to themselves, and generally were well-liked. Both had family in Palmer. James taught school over the winter, and Bobby worked for the Alaska Railroad.

The one thing that stuck out was their lack of any history of using explosives. With no experience and no evidence otherwise, why would they suddenly start?

We decided maybe it was not an intentional murder, but it wasn't an accident either. Most likely, an act of sabotage had gone wrong. But, like murder, what motive would someone have for disrupting the Eddins' operation?

Anyone who planted the dynamite would have no idea a chunk of ice sat below them or the eventual outcome. Someone wanted to scare them off their claim, but again, why? To my knowledge, these small outfits made no real money, and the government regulated their profits. The bigger the operation, like Barnes's, the higher the overhead, so the profit percentages were nearly equal.

We searched up top again but found nothing usable as evidence to identify who set off the blast. With easy access everywhere to dynamite, it would be impossible to pinpoint who bought it or where it came from. Stuart's evidence would go to the FBI lab in Washington, D.C., but the Klondike gold fields would be deep in the middle of winter before we saw a report.

~~~

Back at the Crocketts' mine, after Gene dropped me at the trailhead the following day. Amy, in a rare fit of sympathy, decided to return to production after the Independence Day and memorial service for Frick and Frack on Monday. She gave the whole crew eight hours' wages for today, Sunday. We didn't work Monday, the official holiday, and no one expected to get paid for another day off.

I missed their cleanup, but suspected it turned out better than expected. Being a bit cynical from experience, I knew Amy's nature to forge ahead through everything to meet expectations. However, she had recently lost her brother, and there was no question about his death being a murder.

After missing the Friday show, I promised Dottie a makeup performance, having become almost as popular as the Crocketts. Or maybe I thought so because we always performed together. I'm lucky to be a part of their show.

Things moved slowly at Chicken on the Fourth, and it suited me. I needed sleep, but my mind stayed up, trying to understand what I saw. Gene called Darrell Johnson for me, and the PI promised to find out what he could. It was a favor for Robbie, and he said we could work out something on payment if he ran into expenses.

Nora Eddin agreed to return to Chicken on the Fourth to represent the families at the short memorial for Frick and Frack before the singing of the national anthem to kick off the Independence Day festivities. I spotted Nora after the service in the parking lot of Gene's store. A short woman wearing a blue blouse and blue jeans. Her rolling walk and demeanor reminded me of a momma bear.

I caught her heading for her car near the totem pole. "Ma'am, sorry to bother, but I wanted to pass on my condolences in person."

She sniffed, glanced at my badge, took out a pack of Salems, tapped one out of the cardboard box, and lit it. Nora glared at me, and I saw little trails still damp on her cheeks from tears. "Why? You want to buy the mine, too?"

That surprised me. "No, I can't find time to work the one I got." My hat felt clumsy in my hand. I heard the celebration starting to kick off with the national anthem before Gail began her trick-shooting show. "Does someone want to buy it, ma'am?"

"Ain't worth nothing now— have to move a dirt mountain to reach any paying gold. The place is worthless to me." She sucked hard on the cigarette, and nearly a half inch turned to ash. She blew it out the side of her mouth away from me.

She stared for a solid minute, then let out a sigh. "I got a letter at home from some land holdings company in Anchorage. I never liked this dang mine. It looked like a death trap to me.

"James and his brother always had to do things together, and Bobby staked this claim a couple of years ago. He came back from the big war with some demons. You know what I mean?" She turned her eyes on me.

Staying silent, I owned a few of those demons, too. I nodded. Not talking helped keep someone else carrying the conversation. Mrs. Eddin took another long drag on the cigarette, threw it on the ground, and crushed the butt under her bootheel.

"I got word to Gene to tell James I was coming up to discuss selling their claim, but I knew he wouldn't be happy about it."

I tipped my head for her to continue.

She shifted her weight to one side and drooped her shoulders. "I thought he was mad when he didn't show. I waited and figured my old man would come to town soon, and we would talk about it. He didn't, and I had enough of waiting and rode to the Walker claim with one of their people. I hiked up Arkansas Creek, and I found Bobby, only I—"

Tears streamed down her face. I took out a clean handkerchief and passed it to her. She wiped her tears, blew her nose, and went to hand it back.

"No, keep it."

"When I walked back to the Walker camp, they said they heard the boys blasting and the sound of the bank coming down but thought it was on purpose. They use dynamite on their claim on Walker Creek to break up the overburden, scoop it off the top, and reach paydirt." she said.

"I guess you know the rest." She wiped her nose again. "When did they hire a sheriff in Chicken?"

I said, "Part-time and after Tim got killed."

Her red eyes widened. "Tim Crockett got killed?"

"Yes, ma'am, this spring."

"How? I hadn't heard." she replied.

"It was murder, and someone—Officer Robertson—thought the two cases might be related. He asked me to go up there because he was stuck on Ruby Creek."

"I heard the news on the Glennallen radio station– a terrible, senseless thing."

"Likely alcohol was involved, ma'am." I shrugged and flopped my arms. "I don't want to pry into your affairs, but do you have the letter, and did you need the money?"

"It's in my Jeep, and not really. This mine was like a hobby farm, the Alaskan adventure James and his brother wanted to experience and tell the grandkids about." She sniffed and started to cry again. "They couldn't wait to get back up here."

Nora coughed, blew her nose, and walked towards a tan Willys Jeep. She reached behind the visor and pulled out the envelope. It had seen some wear and tear.

"I debated bringing this up with James and fumbled with it many times before getting the nerve to call him."

Postmarked in May, the return address listed Auroara Land Holdings, LLC, in Seattle, but originated from the Anchorage post office and went to Palmer.

"Do you mind?" I asked.

"Read it, but we may need the money if we can sell after this. James didn't have a lot of insurance and without his winter income… I guess everyone figures to live forever."

The offer to buy the claim sight unseen was a fair price. At the bottom of the page, an attorney's name, Bilko, with an address in Anchorage as the firm's legal representative in Alaska.

"Was Bobby aware?"

She said, "I saw he was CC'd as half owner, but his letter is probably at the post office. It came when they were up in Tok waiting for the road to open before going to their mine."

My attention strayed to two truckloads of men from the Barnes mine arriving late. Chet Robarts looked over, waved, and smiled like we were pals. I didn't see the two sidekicks.

"Ma'am, may I keep this envelope? I want to find out if anyone else around received an offer."

"Sure." She removed the letter and shoved it behind the visor.

Nora started the Jeep, slammed a door, dropped the clutch with a scratch of the tires in the gravel, and drove away. I watched the dust and smelled it as it drifted off in the light breeze.

Boyd came up and asked, "What's going on?"

I explained and showed him the envelope.

"I got one of those for my claim, too, but I think from a different company." Boyd said.

"Do you have it?"

"No, siree, Sheriff, I done throwed it in the trash the day I got it." Boyd pulled my arm. "You need to come along; Miss Gail needs your help."

I pondered the letters and followed along with Boyd. When I stepped out behind Gene's store, where they had erected a small set of bleachers, I saw Gail dressed in a Western outfit.

She hollered uncharacteristically loudly, "Here's my cowboy assistant now."

I stopped like I walked into a pole.

Gail stood before the bleachers, armed to the teeth in her Annie Oakley attire. "Sheriff, close that pie hole before you choke on skeeters and loosen up your arm. You have work to do."

It was the kind of show I attended at rodeos across Texas but never participated in. She shot rifles, pistols, and shotguns. I wore my arm plumb out, throwing targets for half an hour. Mostly, I tossed rocks of different sizes while the lady sharpshooter popped two or three at a time while telling the crowd stories of the Wild West.

The temporary bleachers sagged with rough-looking miners sporting beards and wearing denim of some variety— coveralls, jeans, and shirts. Visitors, wives and girlfriends in dresses, and children in bright shirts sprinkled bits of color into the audience. Robarts sat alone front and center, calling out advice and good-natured questioning of the strength of my throwing arm.

After an extended run of shooting a shotgun at clay pigeons, Gail parked the long gun and loosened the long Colt .45 in her holster. The rhinestone sparkling belt slung around narrow hips, held up by her skirt more than anything, with the holster a little left of center.

She hollered to the spectators in a voice like Minnie Pearl that I heard on the *Grand Ole Opry* radio show. "Alright, everyone, only two more tricks to go."

The crowd groaned in disappointment.

"But they are my big finale and require someone bigger and stronger than our tired sheriff." She rubbed her chin with her hand. "Who can we get to volunteer?"

Throwing up his arms, Chet couldn't get out of his seat quickly enough.

"Now, Wyatt, sit here," she pointed to the seat the big foreman just vacated, "and rest a spell while this over-growed man shows us how to do it."

The burly *segundo* smiled wide enough to see every one of his crooked teeth.

She counted out five white Jawbreaker candies Gene supplied into Chet's fat paw.

"Mr. Robarts, you are exceptionally strong." Gail used both hands to squeeze a bicep. Chet bulged it out with a flex of his bare arm. "I need you to throw these candies as high as possible because I need time to aim and shoot all five before they hit the ground."

He nodded. Gail adjusted her wire-rim glasses and tugged the old Colt Peacemaker out of her holster. She made a show of checking each round. As the sharpshooter inspected them, she asked, "Mister Chet, you aren't afraid of guns, are you?"

"Hel—Heck no."

She smiled, and I saw the mischief in her eyes. "Are you scared of women-folks?"

Robarts grinned. "Not at all. I kind of find them fun."

"I bet a man your size could go hunting grizzlies with only a switch and give the old brute the switch."

He nodded again. "I might, at that."

"Well, it takes nerves of steel, like Wyatt's. Right, Sheriff?"

"Sure," but I wondered where her act was going. The longer she dragged it out, the less sure Chet seemed about what he got into. She spun the cylinder and then dropped the gun into her holster.

She yelled, "Throw 'em high, Chet."

He turned and flung the candy way into the air.

Gail swung around, her dress fanning out, turned to the crowd with her mouth open wide, and said, "Wow, he is strong."

Swinging back, she drew the Colt, fired five times so close together it sounded like one drawn-out shot, and each candy ball exploded; the last one, a few inches above the ground.

"Whew," she sighed dramatically, "that was close. I must be slipping in my old age." Gail dragged a sleeve across her forehead.

The crowd clapped and laughed. It looked like Miss Gail aged twenty years while shooting that last round. She ejected the five empties with two very shaky hands. Carefully, Gail reloaded and dropped one cartridge, missing the chamber. Picking it up, she blew the dust off, seated the round in the cylinder, and snapped it closed. Gail removed her glasses and wiped them with a lace hanky before putting them back on. Chet started for his seat in the stand.

"Hold on there, young man, we have one more act before we finish, but as an old lady, I tire a lot easier these days." She surveyed the crowd and appeared exhausted.

Chet stopped and stared, waiting for instructions.

"Mr. Robarts, are you a smoker?"

He nodded.

"Well, light one up." she encouraged.

He pulled a pack of Camels from his pocket and lit one with a flip-top lighter.

Gail turned to the crowd and put the back of her hand to the side of her mouth. She winked and stage whispered, "It might have been a good time to quit."

Chet let the smoking cigarette droop, and his eyes widened.

"Now this young bear wrestler here is going to hold that cigarette between his lips and," she pointed with a shaky hand holding her heavy Colt, "I'm going to shoot it off right at the filter."

He spit the cigarette on the ground.

"It ain't got no filter," he said, and ran for the bleachers.

"Hold on, I've done this trick a million times and only missed once. You can ask him about it because he's fine." She held her hand with her fingers about half an inch apart. "Missed by that much."

Someone in the crowd yelled, "Ask who?"

"A feller runs the car dealership in Omaha. Folks around those parts call him No-Lips McPherson."

The crowd laughed again.

Then Gail said, "Okay, Red Face, let's finish up and head over to the barbecue Gene cooked up for us."

I put my hand on my chest and glanced around. People started pushing me, including all three Crocketts at my back.

Amy said in my ear, "Double dog dare ya."

I turned red, I'm sure, but managed to walk out. Boyd handed me a cigarette with a filter and lit it.

"I don't smoke."

Boyd smiled. "Okay, so this will be your first and last."

I considered his words as the mechanic turned and walked a safe distance away. Gail came up and faced me sideways towards the crowd. When I started to turn, she squared my shoulder and pulled my ears, so I stood with my profile to the crowd.

"Stay put." Speaking to be heard by everyone, she said, "Now, hon, you want to hold real still; this isn't supposed to be a moving target."

Gail spoke over her shoulder to the audience, "I figured out where I slipped up with Mr. McPherson. I counted the paces wrong." She steadied me with her hands on my shoulders. "Don't move."

She turned, faced the crowd, and made the sign of the cross. Everyone laughed.

Gail planted her heel and started pacing. "One, two, three, four, five, six..." She halted and looked confused. "Ah, what did I say last?"

The spectators yelled, "Six."

"Yes, Six, Seven—"

"No, seven, start with seven," the spectators hollered.

Blinking in the hot sun, I started to sweat as my nerves began to fail, but at least the crowd took up for me. Gail stopped, came back, and pointed at the audience.

"You count out ten steps, I will turn, and on three, I'll shoot. You got it?"

They all nodded.

After she went over the instructions one more time, I started to feel light-headed from the cigarette. They counted to ten. Gail turned with a flourish and pulled her pistol. Sweat trickled down my forehead, and my eyes watered from the smoke. The cigarette got shorter by the second and made my insides quiver. I tried not to shake, but by then, my knees had turned to spaghetti and were as strong as my nerves.

"One!"

My hands curled up into fists on their own.

"Two—" Boom!

Chapter 12

Darkness cleared, and I heard murmuring in the crowd. Someone asked, "Is he okay?"

Amy sat on my chest, slapping me. "Wyatt, wake up."

I stared up into the face of an angel. "Am I shot?"

"No, you big goof, she shot the cigarette off, and you fainted."

Well, maybe not such an angel. She seemed awfully amused.

No doubt Miss Gail's show was the hit of the celebration, and I took slightly less ribbing than Chet. The beefy foreman walked by later in the bar and said, out the side of his mouth, "Wyatt, that took some balls."

The celebration ended with a dance at Dottie's. Amy turned the show over to the boys and a fiddle player from Barnes's outfit who sat in, and they played, "Waltzing Across Texas." She pulled me away from the wall I held up, and we danced.

Amy wore a simple, western-style blue cotton dress that may have been homemade. I sensed an ulterior motive as we danced when she inquired about what happened at the F & F Mine. We hadn't talked about it. Primarily, it concerned her because it appeared to be sabotage, which worried most of the mine owners. Amy seemed worried by my response to it. Raised as a cowboy, I learned to contain my emotions. After the war, it didn't make me easy to read on matters of life and death.

The band, at her signal, played an extra-long version, and I ended my report with Nora's letter. The music stopped, and Amy went pale.

Ricky called from the stage.

"Amy, let's have one of those Patsy Cline songs you do so well."

The dancers whooped and hollered until she took the stage, lost her shocked expression, and managed a tight smile.

On my way to the wall, I considered Amy's reaction. Miss Gail hooked an arm and took me back to the floor, and we danced to "Walking After Midnight."

She smiled and said, "Who knew you could dance?"

I recovered some from concerns about Amy's reaction to Nora's letter. "Well, ma'am, I kept it a secret." I took her hand, stepped back to the floor. "I thought you said on three?"

"I did, but amateurs always flinch on three, so I shoot on two, and it makes us both look better."

"Until I fell like a pole-axed steer." I two-stepped her around in a circle.

She laughed out loud. "Unexpected outcome. I didn't think of you as faint of heart, but the crowd loved it. Your lack of sleep for two days and recovering those boys likely contributed. You dance fine, but you need some sleep."

Only, after our dance, I didn't get any rest. Mom thought every cowboy should know how to waltz and two-step. She taught us all to dance. Later, I learned some of the more modern dances Mom would have called spasms or something distasteful, but the ladies thought I did okay.

Once word got out the Chicken sheriff could dance, I danced with Dottie and about every miner's wife or girlfriend who came to join the Independence Day party. The look on Amy's face nagged at the back of my mind.

Through it all and two sessions reciting poetry, even though everyone had heard them before, the crowd sat mesmerized and quiet as a fart in church, but Amy's reaction to the letter required follow-up.

I closed out and rushed to catch up with her and bummed a ride to their place. From there, I could cut back through the woods and put on work clothes for morning. Amy let Doug drive, and Ricky rode shotgun. My boss chose to rough it in the bed of the old Power Wagon with me.

"What's with the letter?" I asked.

The truck rattled and bounced down the rutted road. Amy blinked and took a deep breath. "We all got one. See, we are partners in Dad's claim. Dad and all of us kids got a letter that sounded exactly like the one the Eddins received. We all threw them away."

She didn't sound confident.

"Are you positive?"

"No, because they came in the mail about when Tim was leaving for Tok. But we were all in agreement. There has been talk of lifting the gold restrictions, and if we hold out, the value of our claim could triple. It would make us all millionaires, or close, anyway. Something to leave the kids and grandkids someday. Our legacy or our folly."

The truck lurched and bounced over potholes and ruts, raising dust as it beat us up, following the way to the Crockett mine.

I ventured a question I considered asking about for a while. "You have kids?"

"No." She moved away and got quiet for the rest of the trip.

Note, in the future, ask no personal questions.

~~~

I slept outside with a wool blanket and fifty thousand blood-sucking close friends for a few hours. Come morning, I quietly slipped out of camp waded bare foot across the creek and hit the trail to my claim at a fast trot. The jeans, cowboy boots, and denim snap-button shirt were the closest things I owned to dress up. I intended to be back at work before everyone else finished their breakfast.

Dodging branches, I listened to birds quietly chirping in the trees and caught an owl's hoot, probably the last for the day. At four in the morning and daylight, the sun still hovered low in the sky, and the branches soaked my shirtsleeves and pantlegs with dew.

Breaking into the open on Davis Creek, I spotted the tracks of Gene's swamp buggy on the route out to the highway. A glance at where we found Tim, and I cursed under my breath at the lack of progress on his case.

Some progress, but slow. This offer to buy, for instance. Were outside operators in competition to buy out the small miners? Or was it a big company using fake purchasers, so no one realized it came from the same outfit?

In Texas and Colorado, many commercial farms bought small family operations and used in-betweens because families refused to sell to the conglomerates. When straw buyers didn't work, their tactics got more forceful, often ruining markets, drying up water, or buying debt or tax liens to compel the sales– and sometimes— violence.

Stumbling to a stop at camp, the hair on my arms raised. At first, I thought, a bear. Second sense, some folks call it, or a subconscious awareness. I trusted my feelings.

Scanning my sluicing operation, I studied the dig site. Everything as I left it. The towel hung on the clothesline, and my plate and fork sat on the rock by the fire pit. The pit sat on an old sand bar I stripped of vegetation to keep the fire danger to a minimum. Indistinct footprints tracked over mine. I made out where I talked to Gene before getting dressed and loaded into his buggy.

Other footprints crossed over mine coming up from downstream—two pairs, one larger boot than mine, and the other smaller. I followed them to the creek, where they disappeared into the water. One faint print remained in the wet sand from the smaller rubber boot. I dropped to my knee for a better look. It's the same as a green BF Goodrich brand boot.

Dad encouraged tracking as a hobby on the range in Texas, and I learned to identify boot tracks, horseshoe styles, and tire tracks by the manufacturer. It wasn't long in a mining camp in the north country before I memorized the rubber boot patterns.

Probably fifty percent of locals bought from Sears Robuck or Montgomery Ward's catalogs, and half of them in Chicken wore BF Goodrich. The boot tread was well-worn, and the owner tended to walk on the outside edge of his shoe. Being slightly bowlegged, my boots wore down in a similar fashion.

Getting up, I walked around camp and found the prints followed Gene's rig until he started busting trees, and there I lost the trail. I thought it curious that the bigger boots took a shorter stride and seemed unsteady. Possibly the guy was crippled or injured.

Circling back, I noticed the warmer air and the sun was higher. I needed to hurry but took time to check around the bus. The big-footed guy peeked into the windows. Inside, things looked nearly like how I left them, but not exactly. Someone searched the bus.

Knowing miners, it looked like they took the opportunity to hunt for my stash of gold when I went to Chicken. On the off chance one of them watched me with field glasses, I didn't go to my hiding spot. No tracks in that direction indicated the two men never went there. I checked under the bus and the hood around the engine. I thought about dynamite and glanced to the top of the embankment over the diggings.

Changing to work attire, with rubber boots clunking, I jogged back to Crocketts' camp. I arrived in time to grab a plate of hot cakes, bacon, and a cup of coffee. I pulled Ricky over to the side after eating.

"Someone searched my camp yesterday. You might want to check things and keep a careful eye out for strangers."

He nodded. "What did you say to sis last night?"

I stopped, thinking. "We talked about the offer letter. Why?"

Ricky lifted his fork slightly above the cakes on his plate, held it, and looked over his shoulder at Amy.

"Sister woke up like a she-grizzly with a sore tooth this morning. I recommend you mind your Ps and Qs, and if she says to jump, ask how high on your way up?"

"Darn, good advice." I agreed.

Amy came up, the sound of her steps covered by the idling D8 dozer and the low roar from the creek.

"O-oh, mamma bear is back." Ricky stepped away.

"Eat and get to work, both of you. And, you," Amy aimed a finger at her brother, "stay out of my personal life, or I will make yours miserable."

"Worse than usual—"

She grabbed a cast iron skillet, and Ricky dove out of reach. It was going to be a long week today.

Chapter 13

The difficulty of being sheriff and conducting an investigation while working a full-time job felt like an excuse to me. With no leads to follow or evidence pointing me to a suspect, work helped to pass the time. Tim's murder still gnawed at my conscience. Amy's attitude always improved with making headway and the amount of dirt we washed over the riffles. Her demeanor only improved over the following days. Doug figured out the CB radio installation for the truck and established a connection with Gene. My habit became to check in with the mayor on the radio before supper.

Gene told me on the radio Robbie would be waiting with news at my claim. Amy listened from the creek, preparing to wash up. Her forehead wrinkled a little.

Earlier, she had mud up to her elbows from repairing a section of separated pipe supplying water to wash the gravel in the header. Covered in grime, she looked perfect, and I wanted to say so. As usual, words failed me, and when they didn't, they came out wrong.

Hanging up the radio, I said, "Officer Robertson wants to meet me at my camp."

She leaned her head towards the trail, dismissing me.

~~~

On arrival at my claim, I found Robbie had built a fire and filled the coffee pot with water, waiting for me to show up and refill the grounds.

"I took the liberty to throw out the old dregs since you boiled them so many times that they turned yellow."

I said, "I figured to squeeze two more pots out of those."

"Yeah, well, I'll add another quarter to your paycheck, skinflint." Robbie pulled off his hat and carefully hung it on a tree limb secure enough not to get blown off by the light breeze swaying the willows along Davis Creek.

"Do you think I earned one?" I pulled out my can of coffee from under the bus's dash. "I've been feeling pretty useless as a lawman."

He picked up a burned-off stick, poked at the flames, and looked up. "I spoke to Officer Stuart in Fairbanks on the phone. He says you earned your keep up at the F & F."

I filled the basket with fresh grounds and set the pot on the heat. I tried to decide if it was disappointment or surprise in his voice.

"You did a fine job up there, and Stuart might have found the same evidence, but you saved him a load of time he didn't have." He tossed the stick on the fire and sat up. "The coroner's inquest says the blast was deliberately set and therefore a double homicide investigation."

"I never believed it was an accident." I peeled out of my dirty work shirt, dropped it in a wash basin, pulled off my boots, and added my jeans and socks. I slipped on a T-shirt and a dry pair of work jeans off the clothesline. When I returned, the coffee sat off to the side to settle before pouring a cup.

"Darrell said he couldn't reach you, so he sent word with me. The law firm sending out those letters is run by a big-time Anchorage lawyer named Bilko. He helped get statehood and has political pals like Dottie, well, maybe not as many. I'm sure they know each other."

"You think Dot has some ties to what's going on here?"

Robbie shook his head. "I said they knew each other, and I don't think Dottie would cross the street to pee on his grave."

"So, Bilko works for this Auroara company?"

"Johnson says it's a convoluted relationship. He has someone in the office who might get fired for talking about Bilko's business. The lawyer sent the letters for someone, but they are sending the same offers from four companies, of which Auroara is one. Although the claim is they were hired, the source hasn't seen paperwork yet."

I poured coffee and handed Robbie a cup. "I've seen similar things done. Big operators buying land through proxy buyers, so no one knew who was behind it."

Robbie sipped his coffee, blew on it some, and took another sip. "All four companies are out of Seattle. Darrell says he has a PI friend who owes him a favor and lives in Tacoma. If need be, he can dig into business records at the courthouse or over in the capital to find who owns them."

A camp robber jay landed within arm's reach of Robbie on my sitting log, decided nothing there interested him, and flew off to perch on the bus.

I pulled up a stump and took a seat. "Was that all?"

"No. The number on the business card Tim had is a backline number for Bilko's office. It doesn't go through the switchboard at the reception desk and isn't listed in the yellow pages."

"Why would Byron have it? And why give it to Tim?"

"Sheriff," Robbie made out to gag some at the title, "curiosity is a strange animal, and when you give a detective a lead, that turns up a new lead; naturally, he follows it. Darrell will contact you if he finds answers to those questions."

"I don't have the budget to pay for his investigation."

"He's a good guy and will work it out with you." Robbie grinned.

"Someone searched my camp."

He looked up at the bluff above us, and he turned his head to make a visual estimate of how far it might slide beyond the creek.

"The top at the F & F Mine reaches twice as high," I said. "But I have the same thoughts."

The officer got up, washed his cup, and hung it on a tree limb.

"I have to cross the mess Gene made of your trail. I left my state truck up on the road." He smiled. "I spoke to Gail about you quitting smoking."

He laughed, pulled his hat off the tree, and screwed it down tight on his head.

"First Red Face and now fainting. I'll have to leave the country to get my reputation back."

He turned serious. "Son, you're building a reputation here as the kind of solid citizen we need and a fair hand as a detective, too." Robbie hesitated, puzzled.

He shook his head, waved, and started up the trail. Curious and unexpected praise, it sounded like Robbie took a poll, and the results surprised him. In his eyes, I remained suspect because he reminded me of it at each visit. He must have a reason, but he didn't share it.

Glancing at the top of the bluff, I decided to make the climb for peace of mind. Those footprints went toward the road, but they also took the easiest access up top.

~~~

My last cleanup showed the best so far, and I picked up one odd-shaped nugget an inch and a half long and three-quarters of an inch wide. A shiny chunk of gold I spotted in the dirt with bits of quartz crystals in crevices and rounded on the edges.

The growing stash of gold, I hid under a boulder in the thick underbrush of alders between the bus and the bluff. Careful, I used a different path each time I went to the boulder. Dried leaves covered the hole and the ground all around. It's not exactly a bank vault.

The patch of woods served as the outhouse at the mine ever since it existed, so trips to and from, an observer would attribute to a nature call. On the third night after Robbie's visit, I hiked downstream. Still, there was a steep bluff, but a feeder stream also came down, making it possible to reach the top out of sight of anyone watching.

Moldy leaves gave the place an earthy smell where water trickled over mossy rocks. Alders choked the little gully but provided hand grips and solid footholds for the climb.

Breaking out of the alders, on top the underbrush thinned, and the tundra got spongy. It would be swampy in the spring, and the odd angled spruce trees indicated the ground stayed frozen less than two feet down. The thick, soggy tundra moss acts as insulation and protects the permafrost from the summer sun but does not provide much stability for tall trees.

I walked carefully and didn't expect to find anyone, but a hunter and soldier's way to move quietly. Keeping the bluff in view, I stayed back from the lip because of the potential for it to break off and form a new talus slide.

Reaching the point above my dig, I looked around for signs of disturbance. The first indication—weeds were pressed down near the edge. Something or somebody laid down there. The mossy undergrowth the weeds grew in didn't leave tracks, but also didn't have cigarette butts either.

I spotted field-stripped cigarettes. The spies had carefully stubbed them to prevent possible forest fires. The military insisted on it, indicating ex-service members spied on me. No filters left, but paper and grains of tobacco. I thought of Chet's Camels. No signs of anyone burying explosives; still, someone had recently spent time there, and it irked me.

I couldn't spot my diggings from directly above, but I had a clear view of the camp and to where Robbie found Tim. The trail to Crocketts' hid in the trees, but if someone walked the trail, it would be possible to spot them.

A game trail took the easy route off the bluff, and I emerged about halfway from the camp to the path to Crocketts' place. I wondered what the spying meant and decided to find out.

~~~

Nothing much happened over the following week. While working, I mulled over my investigation. Calling the F & F Mine disaster a murder and proving it was two different things. The Eddin brothers landed high on my list of unsolved murders, and the newly formed State Police wanted a reputation for solving them instead of not.

Robbie and Stuart worked together on all three local murders, but physics got in their way. Time and distance made for constant adversaries, and why the two state boys happily let me run errands.

One such errand meant going to the different camps and seeing who received letters to buy them out. Two camps along Walker Creek were abandoned with signs indicating they sold out to someone. The corner cans still showed the old owner's information.

The big claim on Walker Creek rivaled Barnes's operation and sat closest to the dead brothers' mine. Frick and Frack received an offer and ignored it. With jobs in town, the boys made enough money without their mine income to survive. It likely produced enough to fund their operation until the government lifted their restrictions. It appeared all the old timers felt the drop in restrictions was coming soon. After deregulation, their claims would gross twice yearly, which Bilko offered.

Those who saved the offer letters gave them, or the envelope they came in, to me. I gave them to Robbie or Stuart, whoever came to Chicken first.

Shortly after the Fourth of July celebration, Gene sent word Stuart and Robertson wanted to meet with me. The police Cessna 180 flew to Tok for Robbie, and they expected to be in town at 10:00 p.m. They asked to meet me at Gene's store to discuss the case. It seemed odd with their area of coverage to have both officers in Chicken at the same time.

Amy weathered her pout and appeared happy with the recent cleanup. We were invited to travel to Dawson and play Diamond Tooth Gertie's Saloon and Gambling Hall.

For the Crocketts, it was a paying gig, and due to the popularity of my poetry, Gertie booked us as a single act. The trip to Dawson boosted everyone's spirit. The lack of progress on Tim's case, notwithstanding the pain of loss for the family, dropped to a dull ache instead of an open wound.

After the CB call, Amy sent me on my way. The meeting didn't take away from the good feelings for the upcoming trip. As I hiked along, I practiced a cowboy poem about a lonely line shack, an evil cat, and a stick of dynamite from an abandoned mine. Current circumstances may have brought it to mind.

Pulling up to my camp out of habit, I glanced at my workings. On one of those talus slides, it looked like someone painted a bright red exclamation mark starting near the top and extending forty feet down.

"Gotcha." I pointed at the splash of color and an empty paint can.

After finding the cigarette butts, I set a trap. Using a toppled spruce, I lodged the base into a forked tree. Tying some green nylon parachute cord, I pulled the top around like a horizontal catapult or a sweeper. I placed a gallon can of red oil-based paint Rosenburg left on the bus in the branches.

Loosening the lid, I laid a trip line about ankle-high on the game trail.

Below the exclamation point, a trail streaked with paint and stumbling tracks left by a two-legged critter, a man. Checking the path, I tracked drops of paint back as far as Gene's new path of destruction. There, the sign dried up, and the trail went cold. With my trap, I intended to douse the spy in paint and make him easy to identify.

I climbed up the bluff to check what happened. I assumed the unsuspecting man turned and caught the can splashing paint over his face.

It sent him stumbling blindly over the bank, emptying the remaining material in one long line and the ending dot where his body hit the bank and rolled.

A guy with bloodshot eyes, red paint and sand in every wrinkle in his skin and matted up in his hair should be easy to spot up to two months from now. I might have felt bad, except the culprit dropped a paint-stained dynamite stick near the can.

Chapter 14

Thanks to Gene's handy work, I walked to the highway and hitched a ride with a Canadian couple. They wanted to visit our town because it was their first trip to Alaska. Driving from Edmonton to Dawson, they wanted to say they went to the new state, and Chicken was the closest settlement.

They gave me the rundown on their adventure during the bumpy ride in the couple's International Harvester Travelall. The nearly new truck rode like a lumber wagon over the potholes and washboard road at a safe twenty-five miles an hour.

I talked up Gene's store, Dottie's bar, and Gail's artwork on the road for something to say and finished up with our planned appearance at Diamond Tooth Gertie's over the upcoming weekend.

After saying goodbye, I left the couple in Gene's hands and stepped into the back room, where Robbie and Stuart sat at the table examining photos.

"I like this shot of the body. It has a view of the victim's face and the witnesses," he said.

Stuart made a furtive glance my way and smiled. "I sort of like this one best with the shooter in the picture."

"What are you guys looking at?"

"Crime scene photos. I picked them up at Stewart's Photo Shop in Fairbanks," the shorter policeman said.

"Mind if I look?"

Robbie grinned. "Not at all."

He laid out twelve, four by four color pictures of me face down in the dirt and one last photo on my back and Amy slapping my face.

Stuart said, "You should hire Dottie to photograph all your crime scenes. These came out great." He practically fell out of the chair while the other lawman stomped his foot and slapped his knee.

"I thought you guys called a meeting for something serious." Thinking they spent good state money flying to Chicken to harass me and get a good laugh.

"We did," Stuart said, giggling again. "No, really, wait."

Robbie wiped his eyes and regained his composure first. "I talked to Darrell. He thought it was better than a radio message and figured you would tell me anyway."

I pulled out a handmade kitchen chair matching the rough-hewn kitchen table. The wear on both indicated the strength and longevity of Gene's furniture, which I found to be durable, if not fancy. "What did our PI find out?"

Rob worked at not grinning about their prank. "First, Tim called Bilko, and the lawyer wasn't happy about how the conversation went."

"Someone heard the call?"

Stuart listened to Robbie also. "Darrell said his contact heard it but didn't make the connection until Darrell asked about Tim calling. It went in on the private line, but the lawyer buzzed the reception desk and had her ring long distance to Seattle."

"To Auroara," I said before getting up and helping myself to Gene's coffee because the smell was killing me, and no one offered to pour me a cup.

Robbie scrunched up his lip and dipped his head. "Well, to the conglomerate, a holding company. Each of the listed companies is part of the group. According to his friend in Tacoma, they are all on paper but have no hard assets, making it possible for them to do business in the States.

"On top of that, the head outfit is part of an international conglomerate with their headquarters in Vancouver, BC, Canada." He added.

I put my coffee mug on the table. "Let me guess, they are owned by someone else."

"Correct, a British LTD mining giant doing most of their business in Africa, China, South America, Australia, and Canada." Robbie replied.

I sat back in the chair. "Hard to tie them to Tim's murder."

Robbie nodded his agreement. "Yes, but Darrell's pal has connections across the border, and they made some calls. The top brass in jolly old England were unaware of what was happening. He said it wasn't unusual for individual companies to make those decisions unless it commits the parent company to more than a set limit."

"Sounds like sales haven't been too brisk. Two claims sold out but looked no bigger than my place." I glanced at the pictures and chuckled. "They would look funny if it wasn't me."

Stuart laughed out loud. "That's why I ordered one of each."

"Ordered?"

Robbie nodded. "Dottie requested four copies for each picture, and she posted one set behind the cash register. She has been taking orders all day with a pretty good margin. Amy Crockett reserved a complete set over the radio without ever seeing a picture."

"You're pulling my leg now."

Robbie put up his hand like being sworn in before a judge. "No, sir, Sheriff, your pictures are the hottest commodity in Chicken, Alaska."

I flipped my hat off, dropped it top down on the table, and ran my fingers through my shaggy hair to push it out of my eyes. "Is that legal?"

"I don't know, but Miss Gail ordered a blowup of this one with Amy slapping you." Robbie stopped giggling, wiped another tear from his eye, and tried to get serious again.

"Darrell talked it over with his friend, and they think this is being cooked up between Vancouver and Seattle with someone besides the lawyer involved in Anchorage. He doesn't have a clear lead to follow but has some sticks in the fire and will give you a heads-up, probably through me."

We talked over the cases and still believed there was a tie to Tim's death. The idea brought up the trap I set, and I told them.

"You could have killed the guy," Stuart said and slapped his hand on the table, laughing as hard as he did at Dottie's pictures.

"Should be easy to spot if he comes into Chicken." Robbie added, "Likely he will bypass town and see a doctor in Tok or Fairbanks. Either way, we can send out the word and receive a notification."

"I reckon all I could charge him for is trespassing, but because of the F & F case, the dynamite he left behind would make whoever it is a suspect for murder."

Stuart said, "I ran down everything I could find on the Eddins, and they never bought or borrowed dynamite for their claim. Someone blew it up knowing full well those boys were down there somewhere and a cinch to get caught in a slide, even a minor one."

After the meeting, I talked Boyd into a ride to the trailhead to my place.

As we passed Action Jackson's, I asked him, "You in on the pictures?"

"Yes, sir, Mister Wyatt, I bought me an original set. So did Miss Gail and Gene, too."

"Whose pictures were those two cops flashing around?"

The ol' boy kept his hand tight on the wheel to keep us on the road but peeked at me out of the corner of his eye. "I 'spec, them belonged to Gene and probably why he steered clear of your meetin'."

In my mind, I plotted revenge, but I wasn't sure when, what, or how.

~~~

I landed hard in bed on the bus, thinking about how to find the fellow who got painted. I couldn't do much in Anchorage or anything at all in Seattle or Vancouver. My best lead was finding who skulked around on my claim.

In the morning, I made up no trespassing signs and a few notices there may be traps on the property. I jogged to reach Crocketts' in time for breakfast and coffee. They planned to hit the road early enough to make it to Dawson and set up. I intended to buy a new pair of jeans and have my boots shined before the show.

~~~

After hot dusty sixty-mile road trip, we crossed the Yukon River and rolled off the ferry at the outskirts of town. A Royal Canadian Mountie in a red and black uniform flagged us over to the side of the road. He wanted to talk to the sheriff of Chicken.

Ricky hitched his thumb back at me, riding with Doug and the instruments in the back of the Dodge. Taking me off the truck, he waved the rest of them to Dawson. Amy rolled the window down and asked how I would get to Gertie's. The RCMP officer said he would drive me downtown.

The hat color and badge were different, but looked like Robbie's, or an Army drill sergeant's, headgear. The red tunic and black leather gear was clean and polished.

"What can I do for the RCMP?"

The Mountie stood about my height. He turned, sweeping his arm toward a truck and not a horse. I would have preferred a horse after a dust-choked ride from Chicken. The Ford looked clean, so I slapped some dirt off before climbing aboard.

"What's this about?" I pulled the door shut and rolled the window down.

Having worked in Dawson two years back, I couldn't recall doing anything to land me in trouble with Canadian law.

"Mountie Carter, at your service, sir."

"Thanks, but…"

"Alaska State Police Officer Robertson and I are friends, and we compete in the annual pistol contest between the RCMP and the Territorial, and now State Police, eh."

Carter ended the sentence with an *eh*, which I often heard in Canada while working on the dredge. "And?"

"Robertson called last night and described someone wearing red paint and seeking medical attention."

"So?"

"This morning, I inquired at the hospital and doctors in Dawson. A doctor who is better renowned for his drinking and gambling skills than as a physician, eh. He told me he treated James Smith, an American, and removed the paint and all the hair on his patient's head, including eyelashes and eyebrows." Catching my anticipation, he hesitated and left off the eh. "He required stitches and said a friend threw a can full of paint and hit him in the chin. The top came off, doused him, and he fell."

"I expect it was a hell of a fall." I couldn't help but smile.

"Our doctor confirmed it was, resulting in many abrasions on his extremities."

"Do you know where Mr. Smith is?"

The Canadian cop pointed his chin at the departing ferry. "I spoke with the ferry captain and confirmed Smith went across last night back toward Chicken, but the border guards said they did not see him leaving or returning through the border checkpoint, e—" Catching himself, it might be a verbal habit he intended to break, at least around Americans.

"I assume crossing elsewhere wouldn't be too difficult."

"Not at all, and it happens all the time." Carter provided a description I recognized as Slim Parsons, the skinny ex-con working for Robarts on the Barnes claim. I planned to meet with Robbie and go to the Poker Creek mine to talk with Robarts and his pal.

After giving him Slim's real particulars, the Mountie offered to call ahead to Robbie and would catch up with me at Diamond Tooth Gertie's later.

~~~

I made my first stop at the general store. I bought and changed into a black canvas shirt with two button-down pockets and a pair of jeans, off-the-shelf Sears brand. They were the only pair fitting me an inch or two too big because they would shrink once I washed them.

The jeans were stiff and creased, but I made my way to the Emporium Hotel and Restaurant and met the Crocketts. They bought my first meal in such a place since I left Dawson going on three years ago.

"What did the police want with you?" Ricky spoke for the table.

Amy looked gorgeous in a white blouse and some gaberdine slacks. She brought other clothes for the show. My boss paid close attention to the conversation.

"We talked about the F & F case. Robbie told him I was on the way. Carter, the Mountie, wanted details since some less desirable Alaskan citizens frequently enter Canada without permission."

The explanation satisfied them, and the conversation turned to the sights around town. After lunch, Amy and I strolled up the hill overlooking Dawson to Robert Service's cabin, where the poet once lived. He wrote most of his prose while at the bank. He worked there, and besides being warmer, it had better lighting at night in the winter.

Her brothers wanted to see the sights downtown, where women walked around.

Bees hummed, moving around the wildflowers. We enjoyed the evening view downtown and the river. "I was married once," she said.

My knee started to give, and I considered the possibility of fainting. "It's your private life, I had no call—"

"I'm your boss at the mine, and when we return, I will be again. Your question caught me by surprise."

"I heard it mentioned."

She glanced up at me. "Were you concerned I might still be?"

"No, Tim told me you divorced."

Amy fell quiet, staring off into the distance. We walked down the hill toward downtown, and I spotted three sternwheel paddle boats drydocked near the river. She hooked her hand around my elbow. "Tim tended to talk too much."

Amy looked at me, and my throat dried up. The paralysis of my tongue started as soon as she touched my arm.

"I miss Tim a lot."

It lit my verbal fuse. "I, ah, I, well, dang it, Tim was a friend, and I miss him and feel hopeless to solve his murder, and I know you are depending—"

"Wyatt." She stopped and pointed her finger at my nose. I quit rambling. Amy motioned with her hand to bend down, reaching her left hand behind my head, and I expected to get popped behind my ear. Instead, she whispered, "Shut up," and kissed me.

~~~

Mostly, I forgot what happened afterward, but two hours later, I worried my being mute turned permanent. If lunch hadn't cost so much, I would have puked. It might happen yet because my ol' heart chased my stomach, stomping around in my guts. No woman ever affected me in such a way.

We prepared for the first session in the dressing room at Gertie's with Doug and Ricky. My job was to open with a poem. When finished, I would introduce the Crocketts. Later, I would join them in ending their first set, with the boys strumming a cadence for "The Cremation of Sam McGee."

After their break, I would welcome them back for the second session. I would end the set with "Dangerous Dan McGrew." Doug would accompany me on the house piano. After the Crocketts' final set, I would close the night with a crowd favorite, "The Spell of the Yukon."

All those plans depended on one thing—Being able to talk.

"Did you just climb off a roller coaster?" Doug asked.

I shook my head.

"Something you ate make you sick?" Ricky looked genuinely concerned, as this gig meant spending money.

"I, it was—"

Doug smacked his forehead with his hand. "Sis," he laughed, "she admitted she likes you, Red Face."

"It's an ugly green color right now," Ricky said, "about how she looked all last fall and winter back home."

"She was sick?" I managed to spit out.

"Lovesick and wouldn't admit it under torture. Several guys, mostly Byron, came around, but she stayed home looking pitiful as a lost puppy,"

Doug added, "She couldn't wait to head back to Chicken, and if she thought Tim could have organized everything, she would've come up here first instead of him."

"Why?"

Ricky slapped my back. "Regarding our sister, you are slower than Moses in the desert."

"She's in love, and I seen it the day she set eyes on you," Doug said.

Maybe they were funnin' me, but it worsened my vocal problem.

~~~

A short time later, Amy and the boys waited backstage, and Gertie introduced me as a former resident of Dawson who had come home.

I managed a quick joke about a doctor, and it went well. So, after recovering, I told the story of Bessy's Boil, which kept them laughing and loosened them up for the Crocketts.

Introducing the brothers, I did okay, but when Amy stepped out, I stammered. "Have you ever, I mean, have you ever seen an angel so, so, quite so beautiful as to leave a poet without words?" The audience held their breath with me. "Miss Amy Crockett, come sing me, us, a song."

I may have imagined it; a teardrop glistened in her eye.

I finished our last session with "The Spell of the Yukon" two hours later. The crowd demanded the Crocketts play two encores before Gertie pushed them off stage to get the audience back at the bar and on the gaming tables.

Unsure what to expect, I rode in back with Doug when we headed home. He said, "She's the boss and must keep up appearances."

Then Doug saw my reaction and laughed all the way across the Yukon.

Chapter 15

The distance from Dawson to Chicken measures 108 miles, but time-wise, it's as few as three hours when the road is dry and freshly graded. Maintenance on the Canadian side is usually poor at best, and better than the job the State Highway Department did on the Alaskan side of the boundary.

At 3:30 a.m., Amy pulled into the border checkpoint. The sun peeked over the horizon, but everyone's eyes were barely open. Ours, in the back, were closed out of necessity because of the fine dust coating us head to foot.

We climbed out and off the truck, beat the dirt off ourselves, and accepted the coffee the US and Canadian border agents offered. Both shared the same facility during the months the road stayed open. Located in Yukon Territory, US Customs paid rent on their side of the facility. All the officials were friends with the Crocketts, and most had heard of the Red-Faced Sheriff of Chicken, at least by reputation.

The US Customs officer, Sam Henderson, who attended the Independence Day festivities in Chicken, asked, "Wyatt, I ordered a blowup of one of those pictures from Dottie. When it comes in, could you sign it for me?"

I shook my head and turned red around the gills again. "Sure, Sam. If you could keep an eye out for that skinny felon. He should be easy to spot."

"We got the word from Robbie, and the Canadians got one from RCMP. But the trails north and south of here cross the border and have for hundreds of years. A man on foot or horseback can go where he wants, and we only set eyes on the honest folks and the dummies, not the smarter criminals."

"Sam, the skinny one, now bald with no eyebrows, doesn't strike me as too bright. He already spent time in prison."

~~~

Amy dropped me at the trailhead before heading to their claim. By the time they went almost to Chicken, made their U-turn, and took the mine road back to the claim, I would be home and in bed.

As I hiked, climbing over the broken trees Gene mowed down, I considered getting my axe out to start clearing them away from my trail after a nap.

Walking past the shortcut to Crocketts'. I spotted tracks coming and going to my camp. The warning sign I made lay on the ground. Someone had pushed it over. I smiled.

Standing it back up, I looked around, scanning the wood line on the bluff and the far bank of Davis Creek. A creepy spider-like feeling crawled up my spine as I edged into the brush until I could eyeball the camp. Except no camp existed.

Pieces of the bus were scattered on the ground and up in the forest. The clothesline, campfire, and my sitting log were gone, and a crater slowly filled with water. Someone blew the place to bits, and my diggings collapsed under a fifteen-foot-deep dirt slide from off the bluff.

I counted three blasts, one to take out the bus, the second, all of my gear. and the last explosion to cave in the mine. Slim and his partner were pissed about the paint job.

"Amy!"

Hitting the trail at a dead run, I bounded across Davis Creek onto the shortcut. I ignored tree limbs slapping my face and scrambled onto the sand bar at Poker Creek. Amy, Doug, and Ricky stood in devastation.

Their D8 Cat with a broken track leaned precariously over a ten-foot-deep divot in the gravel. The six-inch diameter water supply pipe twisted forty-five degrees in the air with a fifty-foot section missing. Water spewed from the broken end like a fire hose, washing away the bank and half of their campsite.

The header and riffles of the sluice, scattered, twisted fragments, were littered across the scene. A twenty-foot wide and six-foot deep chasm in the gravel marked where it used to be. Their wall tent was gone. A small crater marked the spot. All their gear was demolished and hung in bits and pieces in the trees.

The scene reminded me of Korea, and the Crockett family wore the same shocked appearance as refugees of war. It was the proper term. Someone had declared war on us. Maybe I didn't shape up as such a great cop, but I'm one hell of a soldier when necessary. I didn't know who to fight other than the skinny guy, Slim.

Amy didn't run to me for sympathy or comfort. Instead, she asked, "Hit you too?"

"Yes."

She made a quick left face toward Ricky. "Take the truck and head to Chicken. Send Boyd out here and have Gene call the State Police. You've worked here long enough to know what we require. Go to Anchorage, pick up everything, put it on credit, and have Byron deliver it as soon as possible.

"Doug, we're going to need guns. Go with Ricky and grab whatever you can find in Chicken." She added.

"Hold on, I will go with Ricky. Keep Doug here and start preparing shelter and making a camp again. I'll pick up the arms and be back." I glanced around. "I need to talk to Robbie, now."

No one stuck around to take credit for the damage, which opened a window of opportunity to regroup. The Canadians didn't care for Americans carrying weapons across the border, and all ours we left in camp. My Remington, I hid on the bus and Crocketts guns stayed in the tent and were blown to pieces. It left us defenseless.

~~~

We drove into Barnes's camp right as their crew started work. Robarts spotted me and waved for Ricky to stop.

Chet wore a shit-eating grin. "You're trespassing."

I wasn't smiling. "You're lucky I don't have time to deal with you, and I'm on official sheriff business. If you try and stop me, I will put you in a hospital first and jail when you get out."

"What business?" Chet didn't look worried.

Ricky said, "Someone blew up both our camps, and if you didn't have anything to do with it, you better stay the hell out of our way."

Chet's face and demeanor changed as curiosity and concern creased his face. "We heard the explosions and wondered what you were up to."

I hitched my thumb over my shoulder. "We were in Dawson. What time did you hear the blasting?"

"Ten o'clock up to your place, an hour later at Crocketts'."

"Where is your skinny friend?"

"Sheriff, he ain't my friend—someone the boss hired. Slim walked off the job after the old man paid our fines. I haven't seen him or his buddy in two weeks."

"If you do, he's wanted for murder. Let me know where to find him. Let's go."

I had little evidence beyond the paint trap and the RCMP identifying the trespasser as Skinny. Add to that the attacks on our camps, so out of fear for the Crocketts, I believed anything bad about the ex-con.

I pointed down the road. Robarts backed away, and we drove to Chicken.

Ricky radioed ahead and raised Gene on the CB before we reached town. Gene and Boyd waited for us. Gail drove her black '59 Rambler station wagon up as we arrived.

"I heard from Mr. Boyd what happened, and you needed arms." Gail opened the back of her car and displayed a small armory of weapons and ammunition. "Pick what you need. Brushy country up that way. For close-range shooting, I recommend shotguns and double-ought buckshot. My moose gun is a bolt action Remington .30-06 with the scope and is accurate out to four hundred yards."

I selected the long guns, two over and under 12-gauge open choke skeet guns Gail used in her show, and the .30-06 for longer-range stuff.

Boyd said, "I brung along my M1 Garand. It shoots ought-six rounds, so you can use the same box of ammo, and I have an Army canister of surplus full metal jacket bullets I use for target shootin'."

Gail pulled a Colt 1911 from a wooden display box, polished and engraved. "This is my protection gun at home and traveling. It shoots dead on and never misfires. Keep it on you, and when you find the bastards who did this, you shoot them for me." Her words shocked me as much as the sabotage. "We had a nice town here, and someone is trying to ruin it. Killing Tim, murdering Frick and Frack, and attacking you and the Crocketts is an attack on all of us."

Ricky jumped in the truck with a Smith and Wesson .44 Gail supplied and headed to Anchorage. Gene loaded his Swamp Thing with groceries, cooking supplies, and blankets. Boyd threw in an old Army tent like the one at the F & F Mine and lent it for use at the Crocketts'.

The atmosphere felt 180 degrees out of sync from the Fourth of July, even though the weather turned out much the same and the day would be hot.

Boyd said, "My joints be telling me we're due for a storm the next day or so."

I looked around at a cloudless sky. This time of year, storms are usually summer afternoon thunderstorms and short-lived. Later in August, storms pushed over the Wrangel Mountains out of Prince William Sound could be dangerous with rain, floods, or sometimes early-season blizzards. Preparing for it was best because no one questioned Boyd's achy knee in Chicken.

Gene said, "Robbie is on the way from Tok and could be at Crocketts' by noon," which meant as fast as road conditions allowed.

~~~

On the way back, Robarts waved as we drove through. I remembered the second set of tracks, big boots like the ones Robarts wore. He said Skinny left two weeks ago, which may or may not be true. Since the fight at Dottie's, Chet settled down and acted content to mind his work. Over the Fourth, he had been almost friendly, at least not confrontational.

Back at camp, Amy kept busy making things right. She took the tent with Doug and started to set up. I mentioned Boyd's weather prediction. Amy moved it to higher ground, a place better protected from the wind. An hour later, the weatherman arrived in his one-ton Chevy with a toolbox built into the bed. Without asking, he went to the broken Cat track.

"Takes a sight of dynamite to bust up a Cat dozer." The mechanic checked it all over and set out some tools. "Miss Amy, I knows you will be needin' of tools to get your water runnin' and rebuild your works. You use what you want. I'll be comin' back here soon. I can find parts around my place to put your dozer back in runnin' condition."

Doug helped me and Boyd. We lifted the heavy box off the truck.

"How long, Mister Boyd?" Amy stood with her fists against her hips.

"Well, ma'am, by this time tomorrow, or I'll give up on mechanic-in' altogether."

She said, "Bless you. We have a bunch of work to do."

The mechanic disappeared, driving around the trees and through the creek bottom, and the three of us got the tent up. Doug found the shutoff valve in one piece, but we needed to remove the broken pipe. He climbed the bluff and diverted the water to shut off the flow through the pipe.

Amy located scrap pipe lengths they stored onsite in the underbrush. She cleaned the threads and joined the pieces. Last, the three of us put the valve back in place.

We turned at the roar of a big engine, the crash of dragging equipment, and a splash of water downstream. I spotted Barnes's deuce-and-a-half coming up the road. With Boyd's M1, I went to meet them.

Chet rode the running board with an arm hooked on the mirror. When the truck slowed, he jumped down. "No need for a rifle."

"What do you want?"

"Settle down, Sheriff. I stopped our operations today, and we are here to help, no charge."

Charity from Chet?

"Why?"

He shrugged. "Might be because Boyd said he wasn't doing a lick of work for us unless we did or because it's the neighborly thing to do."

"Where's your fire plug?" I asked.

Confused, Chet said, "What?"

"The short, stocky fellow."

Amy walked up and stood beside me.

Chet said, "Like I told you this morning, he walked, well, hobbled, thanks to you, with Slim."

"Two weeks ago, and you haven't seen them since?"

"That's a fact." The foreman shrugged it off, working on not taking offense.

"You know where they went?"

Chet looked me in the eye. "No, but they talked about going to Dawson and finding work on the river. Seems Shorty had ties in town. Let it go, Sheriff, and we will get to work."

That information RCMP Carter could use, and Robbie could send to him.

Amy looked past the truck. "What did you bring on the truck?"

"Materials to build a header, and we dragged our spare sluice behind the truck. With our crew, we should have you ready to operate before Boyd fixes that Cat. If he can't fix it, we can lend you a smaller Allis Chalmers dozer."

"Thanks, we can use the help, and we owe you if you need a favor someday." Amy extended her hand that all but disappeared in Chet's paw and shook on it.

And we all went to work.

Chapter 16

For now, my duties as sheriff superseded working my claim. Regardless of how well the Crocketts did before the sabotage, any significant delay before reaching normal production might lead to a costly loss for the season.

The expenses to rebuild and replace damaged equipment would eat up profits. Replacing the supplies and materials from Barnes's outfit, Amy made her second priority.

A friend who isn't so friendly, you don't want to delay setting things right. She wanted to be square with Chet soon as possible. If in a reverse situation, she would have done the same. People in Alaska took pride in being self-sufficient. When you needed and got help from neighbors without asking, folks assumed you would do the same. Gene called in her order to the hardware store for Ricky to add to his list.

Chet floored me by showing up, and whether it was because of Boyd's threat or him being neighborly, he made good on his promise, and we worked side by side. I gained a lot of respect for the man as nothing seemed too heavy for him to pick up. Amy got her working sluice operation in eight hours, well ahead of Boyd's repairs on the dozer. Up to their elbows in grease, come-alongs, hydraulic jacks, and broken or spare track links, the mechanic and Doug worked without breaks.

We set the tent up and built a functional outdoor kitchen.

Robbie arrived and complained about messing up his crime scene. So, armed with the M1 and Gail's Colt, I took him to my undisturbed camp's devastation.

He busted my chops because there wasn't much to gather from the wreckage. Someone used dynamite, probably with a fuse, because we found no trace of wire or blasting caps at any of the craters.

"I estimate it took more than six sticks to blow the bus. My gear and sluice wouldn't have taken much, or blasting my works." I used explosives in the Army for demolition, and I'm a fair judge of what it took to get a result.

"What are you trying to work out, Wyatt?"

Standing near the crater where the bus used to be, I saw the half-buried left front tire sticking out of the sand at the rim of the largest crater, not far from where the bus started.

I looked at the state cop near where the fire ring used to sit.

"At least two suspects. Because, between the dynamite used here and over at Crocketts', it must have been half a case. They wouldn't know what they would need ahead of time. I guess they brought a whole case with them because Slim was pissed. Too much weight with fuse and tape and carrying guns for one man."

Robbie nodded. I noted clouds building behind him over the mountains to the south.

"Let's hike up to where you were digging."

"Hold up." I stared at the overhanging tundra and trees at the top of the bluff.

Robbie turned with a blank look on his face.

"You didn't see the other slide. We ought to check the topside first and make sure no one is there."

He dipped his head. "Show me the way."

We took the gut I used before, where alders covered us. Bushwacking all the way, the police uniform and gun belt didn't make it easy on Robbie. Once on top, I followed a game trail roughly thirty feet away from and parallel to the edge.

Stalking dangerous game, enemy soldiers, or criminals requires stealth, and plays on your nerves. I crept around, keeping trees or brush in front of me. A hundred yards ahead, through an open patch of woods, I caught a flash of movement. Moving closer, I made out two men kneeling near the bluff, peaking over the edge. I recognized Shorty when he turned and looked right at me. His lips moved, talking to the bald guy with his back to me.

I pointed, showing two fingers. Robertson nodded and moved away from me to gain a line of sight on the suspects.

Shorty jumped up, yelled, "Run," raised his arm, and fired two pistol shots whizzing past my head into the woods. Turning, he followed Skinny, who limped along worse than his shorter sidekick.

I dodged right, then ran ahead, hurdling over bushes and dead trees. I almost reached where the two men were spying. Shorty stopped running, turned, aimed, and fired again. I dodged left behind a small tree as bullets zinged by. Further to my left, Robbie shot three times before I got my rifle up.

Shorty dropped to one knee, held for a few seconds, and slowly tipped over to his side. Out of the corner of my eye, sparks spurted from the ground where the two bandits had hidden in the bushes. A burning fuse!

"Run!" I yelled, pointing away from the bluff.

Without knowing how much explosives or fuse they set, I sprinted for safety, driving my body between scrub spruce, fighting for every inch of distance. I covered twenty yards in five seconds before diving to the ground. The earth seemed to jump and hit me on my way down. I didn't hear the explosion. The shock sent me cartwheeling another twenty feet, tumbling through the underbrush.

I glimpsed Robbie flying with his arms and legs spread out, flailing as he swam through the air.

Stopped against a dead tree stump, I blinked my eyes and shook my head before pushing up on my knees. Blood dripped from my nose on the mossy tundra, and I wiped my face with a sleeve. Ringing so intense— I couldn't hear anything else. Bits of dirt, rocks, sticks, and tree bark rained from the sky, landing all around.

Crawling over, I located Robbie, unconscious and struggling to breathe, jammed in a tree fork. He hung with his feet and legs off the ground on one side of the tree with his head and shoulders suspended on the other.

Ducking under his waist, I grabbed the tree trunk and pushed up, lifting Robbie on my back and out of the jam. I laid him on his back in the tundra and rolled over beside him. A hand grabbed my sleeve. Conscious, Robbie tried to sit up.

I turned and got to my knees. Rob took my hand and used my shoulder to push himself to his feet, then holding on to a leaning tree, pulled me up. Stumbling around, I snagged a handkerchief from my back pocket and wiped blood off Robbie's swollen face. He pointed at me. A touch told me I was bloody also.

Why I laughed, I'm not sure. Then we both did. Robbie gestured to his ears and shook his head no. I nodded, flipped my ear with a finger, and we giggled some more.

The bloody cop stumbled through the underbrush and found his pistol. Swaying like a fireweed in a stiff breeze, he ejected, pocketed three spent rounds, and reloaded the gun from his belt loops.

I picked up the M1, cleared the chamber, jammed the cartridge into the magazine, ensured the barrel was unobstructed, and chambered another round. The .45 stayed in my waistband.

We stumbled around, locating our headgear, and went to Shorty. Dead. Robbie had shot him twice an inch below the sternum and once at the base of the throat. Impressive shooting, considering the range and conditions.

The ghostly banana-smelling haze hung in the trees. I squeezed my eyes closed and pinched at the bridge of my nose. My head throbbed like a beating tom-tom drum. Carefully, I staggered to the edge and peered over the bluff. Through blurry eyes, I spotted Doug, Amy, and Boyd coming at a run out of the trees at the trailhead.

No ice lens under the blast, so it blew a small crescent-shaped notch out of the bluff, scattering debris across Davis Creek. The explosion started several new but small talus slides, including one that erased the red paint.

I raised and fired the M1 three times into the woods and barely heard the discharge, but I did hear something. Boyd pointed at me, and I waved, unsure what I looked like.

~~~

It took us a while to get off the bluff. Boyd helped carry Shorty to the State Police truck. I made Amy and Doug stay at their mine. Robbie drove us like a drunk, but six hours later, we got to a doctor in Tok. The ringing still bothered me, but I could hear it if people talked loudly enough.

We sat in the exam room on a plastic-covered cushioned gurney table in a tiny, eight by ten room stuffed with doctorin' gear.

Robbie said, "I got to ask you something, Sheriff."

"What?"

"I got to ask you something?" he yelled.

"I heard you the first time. What did you want?"

We sat together in our underpants on an exam table, waiting for the doctor to clear us to go back to work.

"Did you notice Shorty's shoes?"

I nodded my head. "Yeah, I figure the punk, and his pal tried to frame Robarts by wearing a pair of the big foreman's old boots over his shoes. I saw the tracks before I set the paint trap and suspected Skinny and Robarts. I didn't have any clear tracks to go by."

Boom! The building shook, and we dove for cover on the floor as the door opened and the doctor entered. He stared at us. "Thunderstorm. Looks like we will have some needed rain."

Once we recovered our composure, Doc Simpson said, "You two take it easy for a week and rest. Likely, both of you have concussions and should be around someone to monitor you if you start acting loopy." He would have put us in a hospital, but they didn't have one in Tok.

Robbie spoke for us. "We aren't going to Fairbanks to check into one either."

~~~

The storm raged for hours. I followed Robbie to his office, and we took turns sleeping on a cot. When the storm let up, we loaded into his pickup and headed back to Chicken. Doctor Simpson took custody of Shorty's body and waited for the state pathologist to come to Tok or for an order to send the body to Anchorage for an autopsy, which seemed senseless because we knew what killed him.

After turning on the gravel road at the Junction, we forded several washouts. It looked like the area received the entire summer's rainfall in four hours. The average rain in a summer amounted to less than an inch a month. Poker Creek ran twice as wide as usual and raged down the valley and over the road to Barnes's and Crocketts' mines. So, Robbie dropped me at the trailhead nearer Crocketts' mine.

It put me on the correct side of the stream. The trail flooded, and in places, I waded waist-deep into ice-cold feeder springs but made it to camp soaking wet.

The sun dipped low in the sky, peeking over the mountains under dark grey clouds. It created a rainbow that spanned the river.

By the time I arrived, the creek returned inside its banks but ran full, at double the average volume.

Doug said, "The water came over the new header we built, but it didn't wash it away."

Amy set a cot up in the tent and built a fire in a little barrel stove designed by the Army to use in the tent. The stove pipe ran through an insulated hole, and baling wire kept it from blowing away. She took my wet clothes and shoved me into a sleeping bag to rest. Boyd and Doug continued working on the D8, but it looked like the big Cat would be operational by morning.

~~~

I didn't recall falling asleep. Dreams of artillery fire in the war woke me with a start. I sat up, hearing the cranking of the pony motor, which fired, backfired, and eventually began to idle. Easing my aching head back onto the pillow, I closed my eyes. In a few minutes, the big diesel engine turned over slowly. The compression relief valves stayed open until the oil pressure gauge indicated it reached the normal range.

Amy showed me how to start it when I began working for them, creating redundancy in skills she deemed essential. Ricky was the next best operator to Amy, but they all could run every piece of equipment at the mine in case someone got hurt or had to leave in an emergency. Life went on, but in Amy's world, production halts were unacceptable.

I lay there with all the throbbing body aches. Thoughts of Amy ran through my sore head, and the big engine fired pop, pop, pop in the slow cadence of pistons the size of buckets.

"Gears and low-end torque," Boyd told me once, "create the force to push ten tons of dirt in front of a two-ton blade."

A squeal of cables and clutches assaulted my ears, and I pictured her lifting the plow, followed by the rumble of tracks as it backed away from camp. In my mind, I saw her on the seat. One arm draped over the cable control bar that raised and lowered the blade, and the other operated a steering brake to make turns.

Amy, the angel I first saw through a cloud of dust. In Dawson—*She kissed me.*

My eyes opened, and as the tractor kept backing away, Amy stood, arms crossed in the door of the tent.

116

"Who is driving?"

"Boyd, he needed to run the track through and take some slack out before we can return to work. Are you hungry?"

"Yeah, I could eat."

"I don't know what you are smiling about. You missed breakfast." She waited, and I stared back, wondering if that kiss was my imagination.

"Doug felt sorry for you and saved some bacon, beans, and bread to make a sandwich. Are you fit to work?"

I wiggled my toes and fingers. Neither hurt, but everything else did.

"I'll hold up my end of a shovel until Robbie comes for me. I might have to make a trip to Fairbanks for a coroner's inquest for the guy he shot."

She asked the obvious question. "Where is the other one?"

"Hard to say where Skinny set off to, but he wasn't running too fast. Carter, the RCMP in Dawson, and Robbie have a theory. They think he might have a place on the Canadian side near Little Gold Creek. Close enough and yet legally far away."

Amy said, "The Mounties have a low tolerance for American criminals and will gladly run him back across the border." She moved my feet over and sat on the cot. "What happened to your foot?"

"A personal question from my boss?"

"Doug and I voted to adopt you last night, and you're family now, but I'm still in charge."

"Frostbite in Korea. I'm lucky I didn't lose my foot or leg. A lot of men did. I lost a toe, and frost crippled a couple of others After a long day on my feet, it makes me walk funny, with a little hitch, like John Wayne in the Westerns."

"I noticed." Amy cocked her head, "Does the tattoo on your back come with a good story?"

"It must, but to tell the truth, ma'am, I was drunk in Japan, out partying with my Ranger friends before shipping home. It must have been a good time because I don't remember any of it."

"That would explain the Ranger banner, parachute, and the skull, I suppose." She slapped my hip.

"Up and at 'em. This is the last time I wake you other than with a bucket of ice water."

She threw my dry clothes at me and walked out. I liked waking up to Amy, even when being tough as nails.

Chapter 17

After a week, our borrowed food supplies dwindled to a few cans of oddities like Spam and Vienna sausages. When Ricky drove in, we were all happy to see him and the gear that would replace what the Crocketts borrowed. It would restock Dottie and Gene's supplies.

"How was the trip?" Amy asked.

"Rough. The storm caused a slide near the Gulkana River over the road and took out a section of pavement. The highway department opened one lane and alternating traffic using a pilot truck. I almost ended up going the long way to Delta."

Doug asked, "How's Dad?"

Ricky eyed me suspiciously as I leaned on my shovel handle, where work stopped on his arrival.

"Don't mind him; sis and I adopted him into the family after you left. 'Lot's went on since then," Doug said.

"I heard Robbie killed someone. It made the news in Anchorage." Ricky looked at Amy, and she nodded her head. "Pop's been a handful for Mom. He's cantankerous and wanted to come here and hunt down whoever did this."

"He was pretty worked up." Ricky ducked his head down and shifted his eyes towards me. "I told Dad we had a sheriff in Chicken who could handle it."

"And that satisfied him?" Her hands locked on her hips, and she leaned his way. "I don't buy it." Amy bored her eyes into him.

"What did you say, exactly?"

Ricky kept his eyes down. "Not important, let's unload and start work. I'm sure we are well behind schedule."

"Stop right there." She grabbed his sleeve and jerked him back around. "You told Dad something, and it must have been a big lie because I expected to have him bullying around camp."

"Well, Byron disappeared."

I dropped the shovel and joined everyone at the front of the truck. The smell of steam still came off the engine from fording the creek as the exhaust pinged in the sudden quiet.

Creases deepened around Amy's eyes and lips. "What, he quit the company?"

Ricky shook his head. "No, after he came up to the Fortymile for site visits, he never returned. No sign of him or the truck."

She turned on me, hands back on her hips.

"Did you and Robbie know about this?"

It hit me that Byron never showed up at the Fourth of July party. "First I heard of it." I blinked. "If Robbie knew, he may have forgotten to tell me."

She turned back to Ricky, and he squinted his eyes and drew his head back.

"I'm not done with you. You dodged my question, and you better fess up because I'm worried about Dad and Mom."

"I think we should discuss—"

Amy stomped her foot like a two-year-old. "Now!"

Ricky jumped and put his hands out to protect his face.

I saw her go fist-city with her brothers for teasing her. She couldn't hurt them without a club, but a foot stomp meant she was finished talking.

"Well, I told Dad we all liked Wyatt, and he was doing a good job of hunting Tim's killer."

Amy started for him with both fists, and I stepped in front of her. She threw one punch under my arm, hitting Ricky in the gut. It made him laugh—the wrong thing to do. I held back a feral cat who intended to scratch Ricky's eyes out.

"You start talking, or I'm firing you and this bum."

She shoved my chest. I smiled, no way she could fire Ricky, and she needed my help. I considered her stress since the sabotage, and being mad enough right then, she might fire me. My smile didn't help matters.

Ricky stepped around me and said, "You can beat on me if you want to, but it isn't Wyatt's fault. He may want to thump me also, and he scares me almost as much as you do."

I considered turning her loose and did when she quit trying to hit him.

"What...?" She caught her breath. "What did you tell Dad?"

"Pop was mad and didn't have a lot of faith in this guy. So, he started packing to come up and find out for himself. Mom worried something awful and told me to do something."

"So?"

"Sis, you know how he's been since the old timers started."

She increased her volume and stepped closer. "So?" Amy bared her teeth and hunted for a likely place to bite him.

"I said he would meet Wyatt when we finished the season—" Amy lunged and grabbed his arm. "—because I said you were going to marry him."

"What?" She stopped, her mouth opened wide enough to swallow a baseball.

"All I could think of."

Doug slapped Ricky behind his head. Stunned, I stood still, and the boss shook so hard it rattled her teeth. One look, and Ricky took off around the bulldozer. Amy picked up a hammer and went after him. Last I saw, the hammer flew off in Ricky's direction of travel.

Her brother's last words before disappearing into the woods were, "You said he was family." She picked up rocks and threw them into the brush as he dodged them.

~~~

Later in the day, Amy went to the creek and dunked her head twice, cooling off enough to allow Ricky back in camp. Doug and I worked unloading the truck. One good thing Ricky did was borrow a big-tired trailer to haul the new sluice and materials for constructing a header.

Between the four of us, we unloaded the sluice and loaded the loaner to return to Barnes with the material to build a header, deciding it was easier than dismantling the one Barnes's crew built. It saved time, and that saved money.

By supper, Ricky got nervous anytime Amy walked close or picked up anything. She ghosted around uncharacteristically quietly. It was common to hear them sing songs and harmonize in the evenings while fixing meals or preparing for bed. I would recite a poem when requested, but tonight, everyone sat around the fire, fending off skeeters, and ate in silence. Afterward, I announced I would go to my camp to assess what I needed to start mining again.

The concussion left me with occasional dizzy spells, made my heart feel funny, and made it hard to breathe. Every so often, my brain gas-locked and lost a train of thought. It had happened often enough to concern me. Still sore all over, I was unsure if my pain came from working for Amy or was leftover from the blast.

Ricky stood and said, "I'll tag along and give you a hand. You have a lot of material to move besides fixing a sluice operation."

I shrugged and grabbed the M1, the .45, and a spade shovel. Ricky picked up the 30-30 Savage, a pick, and another shovel. We headed to the shortcut trail.

Arriving at camp, I noted it got darker earlier in the evening.

Ricky whistled. "That's a lot of dirt to relocate. Best if we start shoveling below and make a flat spot. Then, we have a place to put the dirt we take out from the diggings. Use some to build a wider ramp. Otherwise, we'll move the same material two or three times."

An hour later, we excavated a couple of yards of gravel out of the way. I estimated it would take me two weeks at four hours a day to reach where I started over a month ago.

A rumbling noise in the distance caught my attention. Ricky stared at the ground, and we listened to the low rumble of an engine, snapping trees, and the squeal of a track. We turned and watched trees topple. Amy's D8 backed up, stopped, and pushed forward again, scraping the roots up and out of her way.

Twenty minutes later, she cleared the beginning of an almost straight road through the woods to Crocketts' camp.

After fording Davis Creek, she moved all the dirt below the dig and back-bladed it flat. Doing so created a level spot above the flood waters and a place for me to build a camp eventually.

Then, Amy went to work on the mine pit. The explosion's one good outcome was it set the bluff back and stabilized the bank. After dark, she used the headlights to see and bulldozed an easier path for the wheelbarrow to roll on.

She idled back the engine, sitting on her iron throne like a queen. "We need to build you a sluice and a header and put a coffer dam up on the creek bend. Lay some pipe and put a valve on it to make cleanup easier for you. Friday, when we finish over at our mine, we can cancel at Dottie's and stay up late, making this place operational."

She jumped onto the tracks and down to the ground with the strength and grace of a big cat. I couldn't find words. It was the first time Amy had spoken to anyone since arriving. She saw what we needed and did it.

Ricky stepped over and hugged his sister. She pushed him away with both hands. "I'm still mad at both of you, but he's family, and we do what we can for our family."

She climbed back into the seat and aimed the D8 for home. We exchanged glances and followed along behind.

~~~

Friday came, and I insisted we not cancel on Dottie. We owed her too much, and besides, I ordered clothes through Gene and wanted a spare set since I only had my new clothes and the blood-stained clothes I wore home from Dawson.

Doug stayed behind, refusing to leave the camp exposed to another attack. His brother and sister grabbed their instruments, and we drove to town. At Barnes's claim, their crew also prepared to go to town. Robarts gave us a friendly wave.

Since Doug stayed, I rode between Ricky and Amy, who drove. We hardly spoke since she bulldozed the road to my camp. I hoped it wouldn't be awkward at Dottie's.

Ricky helped me build the coffer dam and lay pipe. He bought a spare valve while in Anchorage and lent it to me to use. Boyd was building my new sluice. He was busy, so it might take him a while. I found enough junk on my claim scattered in the underbrush to construct a new header. With the sluice and a few more hours of work, I'd be back in operation.

Riding in the middle, I wanted to stretch my arms out and hold the seat to keep from bumping against Ricky, but I couldn't bring myself to put an arm around Amy, whose touch made me tingly inside already. Putting one behind her brother didn't look right, so I bounced around.

Dottie's place was hopping, and it looked like folks came in from Eagle and Dawson. Ricky and Amy went in to set up, and a cheer erupted as they entered. I hiked to Gene's to pick up my mail-order clothes and changed inside the office while the proprietor cared for an unexpected influx of customers.

After I finished changing, Gene called Robbie on the radio, and the state cop said he knew Byron went missing and admitted he withheld the information. Curiously, he didn't say why. Robbie did say Skinny vanished, and the RCMP issued a locate for him on their side of the border. He added that a judge set an inquest on Shorty's death for the twenty-first. The court issued a subpoena for me to appear, and he would serve me on his next trip to Chicken.

~~~

Granted, a crowd in Chicken wouldn't fill the back room of a good-sized bar in Fort Worth or at Diamond Tooth Gertie's, but thirty people in Dottie's rated as a full house. Amy and Ricky stood at the bar when I got there, just not next to each other.

Someone yelled, "Red Face is here," and a cheer erupted.

Dressed in their finest Gold Rush-era dresses, Dottie and Gail hung out at the bar. Dottie's gown was a burgundy saloon style, shiny, fit to accent the low-cut front, and sported a slit almost to her hip on one side. Gail's, a pale blue satin, decorated with lots of frills in lace, formed a closed collar around her neck. Both ladies wore bonnets to match their outfits and held them in place with old-fashioned hat pins.

Boyd was absent, working at Walker Creek fixing a diesel pump.

Amy wandered over and pulled my arm. "We need to talk."

My face flushed. Everyone in the room watched us. Those four words my dad told me you never wanted to hear from a woman.

I swallowed. "About what?"

She held onto my elbow and scanned the crowd, eyeing Dottie and Gail. "I don't know, but those two old hens are cooking up something. Dot has her elbow on a rolled-up banner. She says it is a surprise announcement at our second break. She's tickled about something, and Miss Gail swallowed a feather, too."

"Okay." I watched all the stares and felt like Rudolf the reindeer.

"People are being nice," she said.

Grinning like an idiot, I said, "Everyone is always nice to you."

"No, not 'normal' nice."

Robarts and company came clomping in and pushed to the bar. Chet got a beer and started conversing with Dottie. She didn't like him, but they smiled and carried on like two schoolgirls.

I studied the room some and began to catch Amy's drift. "You want to leave? I'll back you up."

Amy said, "Déjà vu," and shook her head. "They came to hear us play, and the show must go on."

Gene entered, and the crowd cheered. He said, "Let's get this party started. Wyatt, the Red-Faced Poet and local sheriff hero, will open. Welcome him to the stage."

Amy yelled over the applause, "Break a leg."

And I did, in the showbiz sense of the word, and after the past week, I'm not sure she didn't mean it in the literal sense. People yelled requests as I walked to the stage. After warming them up, I introduced Ricky to polite clapping and his sister to cheers and whistling, Gene's being the loudest. I passed the mayor on the way to the bar for a beer.

He said, "Congratulations."

"Thanks, I thought I did okay."

Gene beamed. "You've done great. We couldn't be happier."

That unnerved me. It was a good opener, and the crowd got into it, but my performance didn't feel exceptional. The mayor acted as if he spoke on behalf of everyone present.

Amy, bolstered by the cheery audience, sounded better than ever. Her brother announced a break and told the audience to give him five minutes. Amy came over smiling and allowed Ricky to stand next to her without trying to bite him.

Amy nudged my arm. "I love this; I don't remember such a friendly crowd."

"It is weird," Ricky spoke over the jabbering and clinking of glasses, "I wish Mom, Dad, Doug, and Tim could see this."

At Tim's name, Amy teared up. "He should be here. I forgot. I'm a terrible sister."

We tried to cheer her up until Gene called me to the stage. "Dan McGrew" is a crowd favorite, so I opened my second set with it and, as always, closed with "The Spell of the Yukon." The first time I read the poem, I thought Service wrote it specifically for me.

Amy pushed me back on stage and handed me a tambourine. Someone gave me a stool behind Amy while they played their second set. Ricky led their last song and sang "Young Love" by Sonny James, and Amy sang back up and harmony.

I felt like a bump on a log. Robarts helped Dottie tack her rolled banner up above the bar. The brother and sister act wrapped up to a standing ovation. Then again, Dottie's bar didn't have a lot of seats.

Dottie pushed us back on stage. Gene and Gail joined us on the crowded platform.

Dottie said, "We have a big surprise; most of you know it by now. You can't keep a secret in this town, can you, Amy?"

She nodded, but her face looked unsure.

"Amy and I go back to when she was knee-high to a malamute dog. Her mom and dad helped me acquire this place; of course, Tim, God rest his soul, was one of my better customers."

Gene loudly proclaimed, "We recently got a call over the ham radio from Anchorage letting the cat out of the bag."

Ricky looked puzzled and glanced at me and Amy.

Gail said, "Your father is so proud of you, and he wanted to let you know he supports you one hundred percent. Congratulations."

Someone pulled a string, and the banner unrolled: *Congratulations, Amy, and to my soon to be son-in-law, Wyatt—signed Daddy.*

Amy swiveled at the hips and punched Ricky in the gut. He doubled over as she ran out the door.

Gene turned to Ricky, who straightened up and said, "There's been a misunderstanding."

Chapter 18

Needless to say, Ricky's announcement hit, splat, like a wet rag on the barroom floor. Dottie's crowd evaporated within an hour of Amy's departure. She took the old Dodge, spraying gravel and dust out of the parking lot, but left us and the instruments. Dottie, Ricky, and I sat at the bar. Gene promised us a ride to their claim in the morning.

"It's my fault." Ricky leaned his head down, making a swirling motion with his Coke can on the bar.

"Yes, it is. Your father has trouble enough, and your sister is very popular. The idea she would marry this cowboy broke a lot of hearts."

"Miss Dottie, I'm sorry, I never imagined—"

"What? That your father would remember what you told him. She's his princess and does everything to make him happy. So, you can add another broken heart."

His pop can stopped moving. "She's closer to a psycho—"

Dottie threatened to knuckle-bump his head, and he drew it away. "Ricky, she didn't say anything to your dad. That's your doing." She cut him short.

I stared at and twirled the gold star on the bar and sipped my Coke. "I think—"

She turned on me. "Shut up, Sheriff. No one cares what you think."

Especially Amy. I didn't solve the murder and maybe brought the attack on the Crocketts. I glanced over. "Yes, ma'am."

Ricky sat up. "I care what he thinks. Go ahead."

After considering how all this would affect my relationship with Amy, I leaned toward him. "I think she should shoot you."

"I changed my mind. I don't care," Ricky thought a second, then added, "well, I do."

I fought an urge to backhand him. He seemed inclined to speak, even if not in his best interest.

"Wyatt might be one of my best friends, the most honest guy I ever met, and," Ricky held up a hand, "no one else appreciates my sis the way you do."

Ricky continued, "I told Pop you're marrying her because I wanted it to be true. I know she is lovesick, but she won't say anything until we close for the season, maybe a month and a half away at the longest. She's responsible for a lot of stuff, and ensuring our folks are okay tops her list."

Dottie sat, eyes wide, lips parted. It shocked me, too, thinking Ricky harbored such feelings. Well, he ran that train plum off the tracks.

He kept on. "Sister would love to have a day job and dress up with makeup and her hair styled, and she does every winter. Amy takes different jobs to be close by to help Mom. My sis might kill me for saying so, but I love her. I would die for her, but when she gets her feelings and pride hurt, she is more dangerous than a wounded grizzly."

Dottie blinked teary blue eyes. She dabbed them with a hankie. "Well, maybe you better stay here and leave the sheriff to face the music alone."

I gripped the bar and started to stand up. "I ain't scared of much, but that woman does something that leaves me with the backbone of a night crawler."

Dottie's face lit up. "You love her?"

"Yes, ma'am. From the moment I set eyes on her."

"Did you tell her?"

I picked up the badge, hefting its weight, and then slipped it into my pocket. "Miss Dottie, I can't say that to my boss. It ain't proper. I need to be on a sure enough date where I won't have to take orders from her the next day."

Ricky said, "I knew it. You both are in love, and both cowards."

Dottie rapped Ricky on his head. "Says the guy who lied to his dad."

"Ow. It wasn't a lie." He rubbed the newest knot. "It just isn't the truth yet, but I bet you fifty dollars those two are hitched before next spring."

"That's not a wager for a gambling woman. How about I put this place up against your share of the mine."

My neck snapped like a whip, turning from the bar mirror to Ricky. "Miss Dottie, it doesn't seem like equitable stakes."

"Darlin', let me tell you two a secret. The government isn't going to be regulating gold much longer."

"That rumor has been going around since FDR kicked off," Ricky said.

"I have sources, and those in D.C. tell me this new president has plans. Some of them don't sit right with the big banks. He's waiting for his next term and campaigning partly on deregulating gold."

I blinked a couple of times. "Wait, do you think that's true?"

"I bet my place if your big-mouth partner in crime isn't too scared to put up."

"I can't. Our mine is in a trust. I can't sell unless everyone else dies without my involvement. Dad set it up before he started getting old timers and forgetting things. The doctor says Dad may be that way for a while or turn worse awful fast. About the only thing he remembers for sure is music."

Dottie said, "That, and your sister is marrying him," tipping her head at me.

Ricky took a swallow of his Coke. "Let's drag Gene out of bed and head to work. If sis starts shooting, poor light might be to our advantage."

I considered Dottie's words and didn't doubt her connections. "How many folks know about this?"

"Enough to be dangerous." She stood up, stretched like a she-cat showing all her claws, and yawned. "I think it got four men around here killed so far."

Now, there's a thought to consider.

~~~

Ricky shook the mayor out of bed, and after a sickening trip in Gene's rig, we came to a safe stop away from camp. We climbed out, leaving the vehicle between us and an angry woman. I couldn't see how this was my fault, but I felt guilty anyway. Amy had breakfast on the grill and said nothing while we unloaded the gear from the buggy. Doug came out to help.

"What the heck happened last night?"

Ricky asked, "She didn't say?"

Doug shook his head. "I don't know what you did, but our sister's been up all night playing Jekyll and Hyde. Smiling and talking to herself, then screaming mad and punching things before smiling again. She shifted to neutral since we heard Gene's buggy coming."

Gene turned down an offer for breakfast, wanting to depart before gunfire broke out. Sitting down, I spooned some scrambled eggs and beans on a plate and snatched a couple of biscuits. I lacked an appetite until the smell of coffee and biscuits hit me.

Ricky kept his distance. Our boss's eyes twinkled with mischief as she sat silently on a stump, sipping a cup of Joe. The sun almost reached the valley, and the trees on the hill steamed, creating a haze as the dew evaporated. The D8 idled, warmed up, ready to go to work. The creek gurgled, running at normal levels, and the camp robber jays perched nearby, waiting to steal scraps once we went to work.

With the meal out of the way, work commenced with a vengeance. Lunch passed like an errant thought as Amy pushed dirt as fast as the header could clean it. Doug opened the water valve wide, and we spilled yards and yards of material over the riffles.

At supper time, Amy made sandwiches with peanut butter and jelly. Afterward, we watched her load up the truck with gear. She nodded, indicating Ricky and I should climb aboard, and then we mud-slogged over the new road to my place. Upon arrival, we found the new sluice Boyd left sometime during the day.

Without a word, she went to work putting my claim in order, and before Amy let us quit, well after dark, the mine was operational.

She started for the truck. I put out my hand and touched her shoulder. She whirled like a gunfighter, and I stepped back. "Thank you and your whole family."

She stared at me like she might cry. Ricky shook his head and started walking to their home camp, mumbling, "Darnedest thing I ever..." to himself.

"I'm sorry."

She began to say something but choked up.

"Talk to me, hit me, but I can't take watching you cry and not hearing your non-boss voice."

Ricky turned the corner and disappeared.

Amy cleared her throat carefully, put her hand to her neck, and tried to speak twice. She turned and held her hand up for me to wait, doing a little dance like a kid needing an outhouse. "I'm so used to your inability to talk. Now I get how hard it is to know what you want to say and..."

"You can't get the words out. Amy, you're the only person who affects me that way."

She gritted her teeth. "Shut your trap and don't interrupt. I want, I have to…" She stalled again, and I waited, hat in hand. "Oh, this is hard."

I looked around at all our work, and it dawned on me. "What, you're firing me? We did this to get me out of your camp. I don't—"

"I love you." She barely whispered it.

"I know you were embarrassed—" I stopped and grabbed her shoulders. "What did you say?"

"I said I love you. I hope you're planning to kiss me."

And I did, and then we crawled in the truck's cab to escape the hoard of bloodsuckers.

~~~

Doug knocked on the window.

I opened my eyes and rolled the window down. Amy lifted her head off my shoulder and rubbed the sleep out of her eyes.

"Did the truck break down?" He asked.

Amy frowned. "No, I got too tired to drive, so we decided to take a nap." She checked her watch. "Oh, shit."

We were three hours late for breakfast.

"We've been working shorthanded, and not going well. Ricky's too scared to come to look for you, and I don't blame him so—"

She elbowed me. "Drive, and, Doug, jump in. We got work to do."

~~~

That morning, the sky turned overcast and gloomy, and the temperature in July dropped into the fifties. Standing in ice water all day made it just plain cold. I needed to buy a coat, and probably the closest and least expensive would be a used clothing store in Dawson, where I purchased clothes before when I worked on the dredge.

Two things weighed on my mind—holding Amy while she slept; the other was Dottie's idea the president planned to drop gold trading restrictions, and that caused someone to kill Tim, Frick, and Frack. Then Robbie shot Shorty, also. Four men died over a rumor.

A guy might hire a couple of low-rent crooks like Shorty and Skinny for murder or sabotage, but they didn't have the combined brain cells or cash to consider buying up gold claims in the Fortymile District.

I lacked the mental power to understand what buying up the claims at the current market price would take. I didn't know anyone with that much money. There's a pretty good chance Miss Dottie would know.

Another thing is whether it would only affect the price in the States and not Canada. A flood of American gold on the international markets might drive prices down or up compared to currency. International economics confused me, but I suspect Dottie knew and understood the implications.

How would deregulation change Chicken or Dottie's business? A colossal conglomerate running self-contained floating dredges in the creek bottoms. Massive hydraulic mining equipment capable of scrubbing the bluffs above the streams, killing off ninety percent of the vegetation that sustained wildlife, and filling the streams with silt. I saw both operations.

Granted, it was a small part of Alaska and would eventually grow back, but it would never be the same. The animals would get out of the way, and ultimately, when the mines closed, they would return. The same way they did after floods or fires.

I waited for Amy to call it quits for the day. She ran long to make up for sleeping in and barely allowed us time for beanie weenies and bread. I watched her on the dozer, scraping dirt off the bedrock and pushing it into piles to feed into the header. She smiled a lot, whistled, or sang to herself. Her brothers remarked about it, too.

"What were you two doing all night?" Ricky asked.

"Sleeping, neither of us slept a wink in two days. Your sister said she wanted to talk before driving to camp and fell asleep on my shoulder. I was afraid to move, and the next I knew, Doug started knocking on the window."

I left out the kissing, and the talk about love. Once she started in, Amy could hardly stop until her eyes closed. Afraid, not wanting to break the spell, I waited.

She shoved one last load and called time for supper. I stood holding a plate when Robbie's truck scratched its way up the creek bank. The flood washed out much of what passed for a road between us and the Barnes outfit.

"Well, there goes my plans for the evening."

Ricky glanced down the road from building a fire. The other two rustled up something for the grill. "Wonder what he wants?"

"Robbie said he had to serve me with papers and may have news."

I walked to meet him. Doug and Amy spied on us but kept working.

Robbie stopped, shut his truck off, slid out, screwed on his hat, then shook hands. Ricky stayed on his seat, too bushed to push himself off the stump by the fire.

"As promised, here is your court appearance paperwork, but you won't need to worry. I'll get you there." He handed over the envelope containing the summons. "Inquests seldom are rescheduled, so you can expect to testify."

"You have any word from Darrell?" I leaned back on Robbie's fender.

The police uniform, a blue version of the RCMP, struck me as awful formal for the bush, but Robbie said it carried authority and, often as not, all that he required to restore peace. Shorty was an exception.

Robbie nodded his answer. "Let's visit some, and we can talk later." He sighed. "It's been a long day."

I rubbed some mud off my shirt. "Same here."

Amy hollered, "Hey, Officer, are you hungry?"

Robbie pulled his hat down tighter. "I could eat a horse."

"Well, the meat is a gift from an undisclosed source, so as far as I know, it's beef, but it might be a horse."

"Convenient since moose or caribou are not in season." He rubbed his tummy. "I'll eat it and not ask questions as long as it doesn't bite back."

She grinned. "We're not much on frills and condiments since someone blew up most of our stuff."

Robbie elbowed me before picking a stump out to sit on. "A birdy warned me to keep my head down, but she's in a good mood."

"Try not to mess it up. It's an emotional thing and changes rapidly."

"What does?" Amy threw down four slabs of meat on the grill, each an inch thick and the size of dinner plates. None of them showed any signs of fat marbling.

Rob examined the meat sizzling on the grill. "I guess the old cow starved to death."

Amy shook out generous amounts of salt and pepper, seared the bottom side, flipped it over, and browned the other. Doug helped her lift the grill higher to let the steaks roast. Amy set an open quart-sized can of kernel corn on the grill to heat and a skillet full of canned baked beans.

"Did those steaks try to nip you? If not, we can assume he was on a diet." She giggled and then turned serious. "Any word on our skinny killer?"

"I need to discuss crime with the sheriff after dinner. I'm not at liberty to talk with family members of a victim about developments. Which means I don't have much to make you feel better."

I caught the tone and figured Robbie might not have any leads on Skinny, but he had something.

Chapter 19

After supper, I rode with Robbie to my claim to look it over, but in truth, to discuss the case away from the Crocketts.

We sat on a driftwood log that floated down in the flood. Amy had pushed it up with her Cat to the new campsite. We slapped mosquitoes and watched the water.

"Darrell called. He says Bilko also represents the hardware store where Byron, our missing salesman, works." He shrugged. "Not sure what it means to our case or him being missing."

I nodded and asked, "Anything on Skinny?"

"No one has seen him since they tried to blow us up. Even here in Alaska, completely disappearing is nearly impossible. He isn't a woodsman and must eat." Robbie glanced over. "If he were on this side of the line, we would receive word of thefts, break-ins, or robberies. We haven't, and I have checked every unoccupied building in the area."

"He may have stolen everything from the Crocketts, but it would have been too much to carry. Judging from the debris, the blast blew their food supply to smithereens. So, what's it tell us?"

"What does it tell you, Sheriff?"

"Canada?"

"I talked to RCMP Carter. They are checking, but they had a bank robbery in Dawson. None of the suspects match Skinny, who is relatively distinct in appearance these days. However, the RCMP followed bank robbing clues south of Dawson since crossing the river north wasn't possible in a hurry. The Mounties are preoccupied for the moment.

"Carter agrees our fugitive is likely holed up in Canada, but someone supports him because he hasn't been spotted in town, and there are no reports of petty crimes near the border."

I picked up a rock and tossed it, bouncing with a tinny ping into the header.

"What about the salesman and his truck?"

"Same—same as Skinny, no sign of him or the truck. We have an APB for the pickup and locate for Byron. It didn't go through the border checkpoint, which is the best we have. Not many roads here for him to hide, but long ones with lots of places to ditch a truck. Darrell's pal in Seattle is getting word from the Canadian corporate headquarters, and they are denying any plan to buy up mines in Alaska. It doesn't mean one of their smaller companies might be. They are checking into it."

I tried keeping my mind off Amy but right here she said love. "Dottie thought that might be the case, or at least, it might give them deniability."

"Darrell thinks it originates in Seattle, but he can't find a person to tie to a company there yet. At least no one admits they are buying claims on a grand scale. They operate out of Anchorage, but who is responsible besides the lawyer? He can't say, and the attorney isn't required to tell us who hired him."

Robbie aged since the shooting. Lines on his forehead and around his eyes were deeper. "I'm a small-town country boy. Big business isn't my calling, but it feels like someone rustling them a starter herd."

Robbie scrunched his face up. "Lost me on that one."

"Darrell would know. Lots of ranches started in less than honorable ways. Steal a few head of the boss's cattle where the loss wouldn't hurt the big ranch, maybe a few from neighbors too. Push those cows onto a starter ranch three to six hundred miles away and build up your herd."

I continued. "I feel like someone low down in the corporate structure is using the company's name to represent the buying power of the conglomerate to build their mining empire on the sly. Several mines sold. I wonder if they appear on the books of any companies making the offers?"

Robbie continued to frown. "I'll have Darrell check on that. I guess you are implying no one knows about it because when the deal closes, it isn't with any of the companies sending the offers in the mail."

"Bait and switch is what we called it in Texas. It's a possibility."

"I'll pass your theory on to Darrell. When I worked in Fairbanks a few years ago, we helped the US Postal Inspectors with a mail fraud scheme. I know a guy who might look into it and tell us if their letters are legal or if they fit mail fraud."

I picked up a broken piece of alder Amy ran over, opened my pocketknife, and started to whittle the end. "If it isn't, then Bilko's firm may be committing a federal mail fraud, a felony. You or the Post Office Inspectors could serve search warrants on his office."

"Don't expect a Christmas miracle because my experience with the Feds and the Post Office are both slow and thorough. Nothing will happen before next spring at the earliest."

~~~

Robbie gave me a ride back to Crocketts' camp and then drove towards Barnes's operation. Nothing more than work happened until, true to his word, he came to get me on the twentieth.

In Fairbanks, I testified at the inquest on the twenty-first. The proceedings are generally informal as court cases go. I stated the circumstances of the shooting as I recalled them. The coroner and the jury asked me questions.

Later, they voted the death was a justifiable homicide and sent it to the State Attorney General, who agreed with them and declined prosecution. The only unexpected part of the trip was Robbie flew into Chicken with the State's pilot to pick me up.

After the trial, Stuart dropped us off at the airport, and we walked out to the blue and gold Cessna 180. The sun was still high at four in the afternoon. Pink tops of fireweed popped up in the gravel next to the runways and taxiways. We swatted at swarming mosquitos, which, besides getting back to Amy, gave me more incentive to board the airplane.

"If I had any idea you would fly, I would've ridden my motorbike."

Robbie laughed. "It isn't legal to drive on state highways."

"Well, I would hitchhike back, but I promised Dottie I would show up to make up for the disaster Ricky caused. Right now, I want a way to escape these flying menaces." I jumped in the backseat.

Robbie and the pilot rode up front.

Robbie spoke over his shoulder. "Where did you wander off to last night?"

I hoped no noticed I left the hotel. "I haven't been in a big town since, well, three years at least, back in Edmonton on my way to Dawson City. Other than filing on my claim, I didn't stay in town and needed to get back to Barnes's. I wanted to take in the sights."

The pilot cranked the engine, and after the prop blast blew as many mosquitos out as possible, we closed the windows and finished off the survivors.

I wrapped my hand tight around the seat handle and closed my eyes on takeoff. I didn't want to see the crash coming. The night before, I searched for a reputable jewelry store for two reasons. The first reason was to sell nuggets deemed jewelry quality directly to the shop owner, and the second was a surprise.

Mr. Brown struck a fair deal for my gold and promised to have the custom made piece I ordered sent to me before the freeze-up. My eyes opened when the pilot backed off the engine speed, and the plane leveled off. To the south, I spotted Mount McKinley, Brooks, and Foraker sparkling pinkish orange off the white slopes of the Alaska Range.

The nearer mountains to the south and east were the Wrangles, and to the northern horizon, the Brooks Range. The immense beauty of Alaska almost made the flight bearable until the bottom fell out. The Cessna dropped a couple hundred feet, shuddered, and started back up like a roller coaster. My stomach took a wrong turn and got lost somewhere in between. I also don't care for amusement parks. The ride reminded me of my courting Amy—an exciting experience but hard on my guts.

Our pilot shouted out the side of his mouth over his shoulder, "This turbulence is normal and will calm as the sun goes down." I held a death grip on the seat, clamped my eyes shut, and mumbled, "Our father who art in Heaven…" Most of my stronger religious beliefs developed in war zones and airplanes.

~~~

After a sickening, long ride, I swore off ever flying again. Robbie borrowed Boyd's jeep and dropped me off at the highway trail. I headed to my claim. The state cop went to the border checkpoint for patrol purposes and would return to Tok by air late in the evening. I wore my best clothes from the Dawson trip, so after a quick check at my work, I aimed for Crocketts' and my regular work duds.

"Hey, slacker," Ricky greeted me as I walked up the new road. "Two days off, and show up in time for dinner."

"Well, I did a fine job of testifying, and they decided Robbie murdered Shorty."

Amy's jaw popped open. "What?"

"Yep, they say shooting a guy who dies is homicide. They also say it was justified because the dummy tried to shoot me."

Amy punched my shoulder. "Ouch."

"If you hurt your hand, it's your fault for working me so hard."

She glared at me. "I can find me an equalizer if I need one."

Doug said, "Don't shoot him. I'm tired enough from picking up his slack. Feed him something, and after his rest, he can work while Ricky and I—"

"Work, the way I figure what we lost, we all need to work hard and pray tomorrow's cleanup is profitable. Then you, *Ricky Dale Crockett*, can make a public apology for misleading the fair citizens of Chicken."

"I didn't; that was Dad's doing. I just misled him."

Amy pointed a wooden spoon at him she stirred beans with. "I rest my case."

"Are we going to eat them beans, or are you going to stir 'em into paste while us working men starve to death?" Doug asked.

Amy opened a Dutch oven with biscuits and passed them around, leaving the spoon in the beans for everyone to help themselves. Then she unwrapped foil from around a moose tenderloin she had roasted in the coals of the fire starting at lunchtime.

I waited until last, as would be proper since I didn't put in any work. Besides, Robbie gave me a genuine State of Alaska check in my pocket for my time. He told me to report my hours working on Tim's case and the F & F Mine case. That time was covered on the check in my pocket. I expected another one for the two days away to testify with per diem to pay for the room at the Travelers Inn. Sheriff's work began to pay off.

~~~

The following Friday, with nowhere else to go since my bus home blew up and my recent promotion to family status, I helped with the cleanup. Although shorthanded for two days, it amounted to more gold than I ever saw in one place. A good payoff by weight, but they wouldn't get rich at the current exchange rate.

Dottie told me what she thought was coming. Their take at three or four times the current exchange rate would make it a new baseball game. I started doing the math in my head, and although Amy pushed trying to make ends meet, if they averaged two-thirds of what we sacked up—? My math skills never impressed anyone, but something wasn't adding up.

Chapter 20

Amy, Ricky, and I climbed into their Dodge, but Doug stayed to guard camp since Ricky had a *mea culpa*, and I'm a separate act. We took the regular path to Dottie's since Chet's recent change of heart, so I moved him to the bottom of the suspect list for the time being. We arrived early, and I walked with Amy after setting up.

"I have a question."

A chill hung in the evening air. Amy wore a lightweight, waist-length, navy-colored wool jacket. She didn't look up. "Figured you might."

"I don't—"

She interrupted, unwilling to wait for me to beat around the bush or get tongue-tied. "We have an average take each year," she peered out in the shadows, making sure no one listened, "we figure to make that much and a bit more. This year, we need to make a lot more than average because of the damage and loss of gear."

Her eyes focused on the distant hills and a flock of honking geese preparing for the long trip south. "So, we take an average from each cleanup we report to the government. Enough to prove up and cover expenses. I believe every miner in the district is doing the same if they are smart and are finding gold on their claims."

"And the rest?"

She glanced up at me. "There isn't any rest. Keeping it from the ATF or Treasury Agents, they can take you to jail, so we leave the excess in the ground."

"But…"

She nodded. "When the restrictions disappear, let's say we know where to dig and a little closer to home." Amy popped her shoulders up. "It's why most of these miners hold on to their claims. The gold from the claims will be traceable by the general makeup of the deposits in their mines. Once the government lifts the ban, these mines will produce far more gold with less effort."

"And it's why no one is interested in selling a producing mine."

She stepped around a log used to separate the parking lot from the area where I fainted. "Correct, because it would be difficult to explain to a T-man where you came up with a bunch of new gold without owning a mine."

I walked close, rubbing the arm of my fleece-lined jacket against her shoulder. "So, my claim was not a producing mine?"

"Not the way Rosenburg ran it and those before him. He was one of many short-term hobby miners in the area. My brother pointed out a better opportunity than where they worked. It still is an inefficient operation. Many people sell off claims they think are worthless. Then someone who knows what they are doing hits a big pile of paydirt."

"Knowing where to dig."

Amy scoffed. "That helps, but there is more to it. This country has gold on all these claims, some more than others. Some years, we come out of pocket because we can't find enough gold to cover the expenses. This season has been a banner year. A certain amount of luck is also involved."

We strolled loops around town through patches of fireweed growing through the gravel. You could fit the business district of Chicken on one-half of a football field. "So, how do the big commercial outfits like in Dawson make it?"

"Simple," she said, "by taking luck out of the equation. You have a big claim for one guy to cover, and in fifty years, you might cover it all."

"Okay."

"The giant outfits with a floating dredge and hydraulic mining could strip the whole thing bare in a single season, scrape up all heavy minerals and gemstones on the property, and move down the creek. No luck involved. X number of yards of material moved produces X amount of profits." She explained.

"Gemstones? No, forget that part. If I understand you correctly, if the government lifted the restrictions and the price of gold doubled, it would be a boom for you and me. But for the commercial operations?"

She leaned into me steering me to the right. "In reference to gemstones, think garnets, topaz, and hematite are some of what we find, but up near Fairbanks, they found a huge jade mine everyone overlooked while hunting for gold."

142

Amy continued. "As for what an increase in gold price would mean for big operators, it's a bonanza. Only they would need this whole area. A single claim like yours or multiple claims together like ours is too small to start up one of those big dredges. They need to be able to operate efficiently for the next twenty years. It means all these river bottoms for four hundred square miles."

She stopped behind Dottie's rental room crate, out of view of the stores and the street. She grabbed my sleeves and smiled, facing me. "It's been a difficult time for me to get here. I didn't think I wanted a partner, and I have too many personal things on my plate with Dad, the mine, and past relationships."

"You changed your mind?"

"Not easily. It isn't as if I'm sure of who you are, either. I have questions, but I've decided they can wait."

"Oh, I see." Only I didn't, exactly.

"I'm off duty as your boss or mining professor, and I want a kiss."

"I thought—"

"There you are." Gene bounced around the end of the building. "Robbie wants to talk to you on the radio."

So much for romance.

We followed the mayor in and to the corner of the store where he kept his ham radio. I flopped into the rolling chair, and it tipped. I threw out my arms and landed with my knees and elbows on the floor.

Gene said, "I thought you knew about the missing wheel?"

I jumped up so fast most people wouldn't have realized I fell. "I forgot."

Amy busted a gut.

Red-faced, I sat in the chair, turning the leg with the missing wheel facing the front. Gene pushed a button and spoke into the microphone on the desk, spouting a call sign, KL7FKF. The dispatcher in Tok is another ham radio operator and part of an unofficial emergency network across the state. He answered, and Robbie called back.

"Skinny was spotted in the vicinity of Dawson. Over."

"When? Over," I responded.

Radio communications are about the same as we used in the service.

"Earlier today on the ferry on foot, leaving Dawson, he is possibly hitchhiking. The RCMP launched a second manhunt. With the bank robbery, they are shorthanded." Robbie ended with, "The Mounties intend to scour the border country and might flush him out into Alaska. Over."

"I understand and will be on the lookout for the fugitive," I said. "Thanks for the heads-up. Over."

"Tok, ASP, out."

I carefully swiveled the chair around and caught Amy's amusement.

We walked out, and I asked Amy, "Where were we?"

"Too late, Sheriff. It's time for me to slip into costume and for you and Ricky to hit the stage. I don't come out until my brother clears the air."

Ricky's confession, I hoped, was premature. She said love but doesn't mean I qualified as marrying material. Amy would be rich if the Feds lifted the gold ban. By my standards, the Crocketts were rich already. Mentally counting my assets, I owned an off-road motorbike, and a skimpy gold claim I acquired as an excuse to stay in Chicken. I credited Amy for that. I need warm clothes and a cabin before winter, or I'll freeze to death. Sixty below zero was a frequent winter temp around Chicken.

Hard enough being a part-time mine owner, a full-time mine laborer, and a hobby lawman. The heft of the badge in my shirt pocket weighed much more than on any scale. My family took the oath seriously, such as I remembered Robbie administering it. They prided themselves on honesty and fair play, a job and a promise I had failed at before.

This time, my neighbors picked me to do it. It meant I would patrol the border instead of working my claim in the morning. Well, if Amy loans me the truck.

My head jerked up from staring at the ground.

"Yo, Red Face, we are on. Get in here," Ricky yelled from Dottie's door. He didn't want to face the music alone.

~~~

After finishing his heartfelt confession for misleading his dad and, therefore, the good citizens of Chicken, Ricky took a lot of ribbing over his indiscretion. Later, after opening the second set, I sat next to Dottie at the bar and watched Amy sing in the mirror.

"It's a shame," Dottie said.

"Yes, ma'am." I glanced at her and nodded. "What is?"

"You big goof, that you aren't marrying her."

"It's not like the notion hasn't jumped the fence and crossed into the pasture of my imagination, Miss Dottie."

"Did you ask her?"

"About what?"

"I know you're a smart man, Wyatt, but when you are around her, your IQ is about equal to a toad." She shook her head. "To marry you, dum-dum?"

"Well, I ain't much more than a broke cowboy with a claim three or four others gave up on. Amy has payin' jobs in Anchorage all winter and a nice house to live in. I'll be lucky to make it to spring without starving or freezing to death."

Dot mumbled loud enough to hear over the music. "A waste of time, money, and talent."

"What, my sheriff's wages?" I slapped my hand on the bar. "No one is going broke paying me."

"The ring, Mr. Brown, at Brown's Jewelers, you commissioned."

I twisted in the chair to spot Amy on stage, turned back, and whispered, "How?"

"We go way back. Your jeweler heard rumors Amy was getting hitched, and Mr. Brown came out to buy nuggets from some of the mines. He stopped by to see me."

I leaned toward her ear. "Does everyone know you?"

"No," she flipped her hair back with a little flourish, "but it's more important I know everybody. And I do, at least the ones who count."

That struck a memory from a conversation with Robbie. "You know a lawyer in Anchorage named Bilko?"

It looked like Dot bit a green persimmon, her eyes squinting, her mouth pouting, and the cords in her neck stood out. "Way better than the snake likes, and I know your pal Darrell Johnson, too. He's a good guy. Given time and some help from friends of mine, he'll figure out who killed Tim or paid for it. It'll be up to you to catch whoever pulled the trigger."

My mouth stood open, and I sat on the stool with one elbow on the bar. "I don't understand where you pick up your information."

"Well, Gene is one source, but Robbie and I have known each other since he pinned on a badge for the Territory. Back then, I struggled as a working businesswoman earning a dollar in essential enterprises.

"I don't speak of this with many people, so I trust you to keep it to yourself." She added.

Shocked and honored by her trust, I nodded.

"My company provided needed services. Maybe those services were less than the written law allowed. I kept things peaceful and fair. You might say he overlooked my portfolio."

Dottie watched me until she knew I understood. "I prospered and occasionally whispered in his ear." She smiled, and I raised an eyebrow. "He took evil men away to jail. It helped his career and my business, then statehood reset the clock for both of us."

I frowned and wondered at the intimacy implied.

"Don't feel sad for Robbie, Sheriff. He's on the fast track. Before Bill leaves office in eight years, Rob will be Commissioner of Public Safety."

I watched Amy in the middle of a Kitty Wells song, then Dot's reflection in the bar mirror. "Okay, I believe you because you're never wrong and know everything. So, where is Skinny?"

"Gene says it sounds like Canada, but you know from talking to Robbie earlier. You know as much as I do. If that changes, I'll let you know."

"Will she say yes if I ask?" Suddenly, I felt like I was begging my mom for a puppy.

Dottie's face lit up with a bright red lipstick smile. She didn't answer; she just turned away and talked to Baker, the bartender.

~~~

We ended the show and packed up. On the way home, Amy told Ricky to drive, but she waited on deciding to let me borrow the truck for patrol. It beat my motorbike, and Boyd said there was a chance for snow.

"It doesn't happen often," Amy said. "Some years, we get late summer snowfalls. Blizzards, and might drop a foot of blowing snow. It always melts off. After August twentieth, all bets are off whether new snow melts or stays till spring. I plan to be packed on the twentieth and unpacking in Anchorage the next day."

In early September, the road commission closes the highway except at your own risk and stops maintaining the road until May.

We rolled into Barnes's camp, and Robarts stepped out into the headlight beams and flagged us down. I aimed to argue about trespassing but didn't get the chance.

"Who is up to your mine?" Chet asked.

"Doug. Why?" Amy said past Ricky.

"We got back, and our guy says he heard shooting. We planned to go up and check but decided you would be along, and we could follow you. I don't need to get my head blown off. If Doug's in a fight, he might not look to us for help."

A right reasonable assumption.

Chapter 21

After a fast, bumpy ride in and out of Poker Creek, Ricky eased up to the last curve before crossing the stream and entering camp. I handed him Gail's Colt, and he fired three close-spaced shots out the window. Three rifle shots sounded from the mine, a signal it was safe to advance.

Amy wondered aloud what her brother shot at as she banned target practice in camp. Ricky dove into the main channel, and water rushed over the bumper and high on the driver's door upstream. The old Dodge crabbed sideways, bouncing over submerged boulders until it clawed up the gravel bank.

The headlights fell on Doug. Sitting, he leaned back against the blade of the D8. Blood drenched him from the top of his head to his knees.

Amy screamed, "Doug!" and pushed her way out over me.

Grabbing the Colt back, I went for extra bullets in the tent. Doug's position indicated the attack came from across the water and upstream.

Amy ran to Doug. Robarts and company pulled the deuce-and-a-half alongside the Dodge, and four armed men spread out to give us cover.

I grabbed a spare magazine and traded the full one for the one in the gun. Reloading the spare, I slipped it into my pocket before checking Doug.

"I'm okay. He only nicked me."

"Hell of a lot of blood for a nick," I said, standing behind Amy.

Doug spoke to me, maybe because I carried the badge. "They gave me no warning, shot my hat off." His eyes wandered around, dizzy. "It might have knocked me out."

"When I opened my eyes, I played dead and got the pistol out of my waistband. I went down away from the fire over there," he pointed toward the creek bank, "and in the dark, so they didn't know where I fell."

"I heard them splashing in the deep water, crossing the creek. I'm sure one was Ol' Skinny, but I couldn't see. The other, I'd heard his voice before but couldn't place it. Over the creek noise, I couldn't make out their words."

Doug put his hand on the rag Amy placed on his head and pushed her arm down. He handed the .30-30 to Ricky.

"In case they came back, I reloaded it."

"What happened after that?"

Doug turned to me. "When they almost reached this side of the creek, I figured twenty feet away standing in moving water was my best chance to make a play. I rolled over and emptied the gun at them. They shot back a few times, but I scared them enough they didn't score any hits." He grinned. "From the howling and cussing, I must have at least burned one."

He aimed a finger across his body with his free hand. "They set up across the river and started shooting again. I made it to the tent and fetched the rifle. I fired back several times. Later, I heard the shots and Barnes's truck coming, and they took off upstream for the highway trail. Didn't hear our Power Wagon over the sound of the diesel rig."

Amy found a flashlight and examined Doug's head. I saw a streak of pinkish-white bone that didn't look broken. A three-inch-long gash ran from his hairline above his nose, up and over toward his left ear. Head wounds bleed something awful, but unless Doug had a concussion or fractured skull, he was probably not in danger of dying.

Once everyone decided the battle was over, Amy and Ricky loaded Doug in the Dodge and started for Tok. Unable to raise the mayor on the CB radio, Amy promised to stop and have Gene call Robbie and tell him what happened. Robarts sent his crew off to bed and volunteered to stay and guard the camp. Clouds thick and sooty blocked the rising sun, and it appeared Boyd's weather forecast was accurate.

It reminded me of guard duty in Korea, a memory triggered by the surprise attack.

At five in the morning, enough sunlight penetrated the overcast sky to see. The wind blew out of the northwest as if straight off a glacier.

Robarts huddled on a stump in a borrowed wool blanket. Ricky's oversized parka kept me warm on a stump.

Chet glanced at the sky and said, "Sheriff, I have a crew to put to work, and those lazy bums won't turn a lick if I ain't there to kick them in the ass."

"Go on, I've got this but keep your head up and watch your back."

"I don't get the boss's idea about you, but you're a fair man, Peoples, and tough enough when Gail isn't shooting at you." Chet gave me a casual punch on the shoulder with a fist the size of a ham. It nearly knocked me off the stump.

"I could make excuses about why I fainted, but I never got shot in Korea. I earned some stitches the medical corpsman gave me for bayonet cuts but no bullets. Gail's shaky hand when she pointed her gun, I don't blame you for runnin'. Prudence over valor."

"No one on the ship ever tried stab me, benefits of going in the Navy. Yeah, I took a lot of grief over skedaddling and required knocking some heads to get my respect back. But no one took a picture of me leaving." He grinned. "See you around, Sheriff."

The walking side of beef rocked stiff-legged back and forth, stepped into the creek, holding his shotgun over his shoulder, and worked his way across, facing into the flow. Poker Creek ran deeper, wider, and faster than Davis. Upstream, it spread out, shallower, and easier to cross.

Amy plowed the new road over the ridge and down into Davis to my camp, and where Robbie found Tim. Who would have guessed all this? If we—well, the thing to do was to catch who did it and clear Tim's case.

What motivated the killers? In gold mining territory, the apparent motivation is gold, but with regulated prices, claims didn't produce enough wealth to get rich no matter how many a man owned. At least by Amy's ratio, the cost of dirt moved to gold found, times the price paid.

A wind gust flapped the blanket I wrapped over my parka after Robarts left. No one shot at Chet—a good sign. Walking to the outdoor kitchen, I shook the coffee pot and heard slushy ice scraping. The creek and the ground remained too warm to freeze. The air fell below freezing, and the windchill made it feel much colder. I wished Chet luck working them boys in weather like this.

It took ten minutes and one fire starter tablet to bring a fire to life. I added another row of rocks on the north side of the ring to protect it from the wind. Hefting the pot, I judged two cups of coffee slushed inside, and I sat it in the flames. Something hot to drink and a fire, it was all the caveman in me needed. The war instilled the notion we hadn't progressed far from the caves.

Skinny knew from the past, or may have heard, we would be at Dottie's. Possibly, he came to hunt for their gold or to sabotage the camp again. Doug caught them unaware, but someone murdered Tim, so killing his brother wasn't a leap. The skinny felon picked up a new partner, but Doug said someone with a familiar voice. From around here or a voice he knew in Anchorage?

After coffee, the clouds swirled like liquid steel wool, and sleet began to pelt me with each gust of wind. Any evidence left on the other side of the creek would soon be covered with snow and lost when it melted. Waiting for Robbie wasn't possible.

Keeping gloves on, I pocketed the pistol in the parka, tucked the Savage under my arm, and hiked to the crossing. I waded the creek carefully, and no water spilled into my rubber boots.

On the far gravel bank, I turned downstream, searching for signs. Across from where Doug said the shootout occurred, I found blood, bright red and recently frozen on the rocks. Judging where Amy's brother holed up behind the dozer and fired with the rifle, I picked out the nearest cover and located large bloody splotches on the ground.

Doug hit an artery. It looked like the first spurts happened in the creek, and the shooter held a hand on the wound for a few steps before he decided finding cover took priority.

The wounded man went down, leaving a puddle of blood. Tracks indicated the other shooter held long enough to return fire but fled, leaving his pal behind. Tracks and blood left over the shoeprints proved the coward abandoned his partner. *No honor among thieves.*

After ten minutes of working through the spruce and alders, my search for Skinny ended. Based on blood loss, the felon hit empty and tangled himself in the underbrush, probably lost in the dark.

The uninjured partner ran across the shallows above, where I crossed, and went up the trail to the Taylor Highway. I tracked the fleeing suspect, who came to the road only minutes from the border. I lost the tracks of the same type of rubber boots I wore, and that Ricky recently procured at Byron's store in Anchorage.

Acceleration marks at the side of the road indicated a four-wheel drive truck left in a hurry toward Canada. The suspect didn't dare go through the checkpoint, so he turned off and crossed the border nearby. Weather dictated my theory would have to wait.

Sleet turned into big wet snowflakes as I made notes estimating the truck's size from the tire marks. The roiling clouds promised a lot more snow.

Working out on the plains, a man could see the weather coming and have time to size it up. In the Fortymile area, it popped over the mountains and could change from sunny and warm to a blizzard in an hour.

Bushwhacking my way down the trail at a jog is tricky in rubber boots. Limbs slapped against my arms and shins. I stopped when I reached Skinny's body.

Searching him, I found a pistol under the jacket tucked behind his belt. I couldn't say for sure it was Tim's. It looked like his, the same make and model.

Folks told Tim it wouldn't kill a bear. He always asked if it could cripple a man. When they said yes, Tim said, "Okay, then I should never travel alone."

I wiped tears from my eyes and blamed the icy wind.

Snow gathered in pockets out of the wind, and it began to settle around the brush. I gave up my blanket and used it to cover Skinny's corpse. I weighed the corners down with driftwood and rocks from the creek bank. Freezing, I faced a cutting wind returning to camp when I broke out at the shallows. By then, snow came down so thick I could barely see across the stream.

Wading, I reached the far bank without filling my boots with water, which could be fatal in this weather. Walking from alder patch to alder patch, I arrived back at camp, where embers barely glowed in the fire pit. I carried two armloads of wood inside the tent and lit a fire in the stove. Closing the door flap, I tied it tight.

Setting up, we buried the tent walls in the gravel at the bottom and backfilled it to keep the wind from getting underneath. The guy ropes we tied to steel stakes four feet long that we drove in with sledgehammers. Long since, we had pulled all the slack from the lines. The tent would hold up through worse than this, and I experienced worse on *the hill* in Korea.

I tried sleeping for ten hours while the storm tore at the tent. Images of battles holding the high ground ran through my head until I craved whiskey. I wanted anything except to be alone. My dreams were haunted by frozen and dead soldiers scattered over hundreds of acres of tundra.

Time felt endless, but eventually, the wind let up. It did not stop but slowed, based on how the tent billowed. Earlier, the wind gusts reached sixty miles per hour or more. At that speed, the flapping canvas sounds like the constant popping of bullwhips overhead.

Lying down on the cot, I peeked at Amy's partition. A piece of rope ran from the wall to the center pole and another spot on the wall with blankets hung on them for privacy. I smiled. *She kissed me and said love.*

Chapter 22

Two hours later, I poked wood into a two-foot-high oval-shaped tin can, complete with little ridges around it. The Army stove was a multicolored, blue-and-gray splotched metal from the heat. It warmed the tent but stayed comfortably chilly. Opening the door, on a gray morning sky that showed patches of blue. The wind settled to a light breeze at ground level, but aloft, clouds screamed south across the sky.

Ice formed around the rocks sticking up out of the creek. All the snow came down sideways and collected in drifts behind the tent, the bulldozer, and trees.

Surface ice on the ground formed from melting precipitation when the storm started and had already begun to thaw. According to the thermometer tacked to a four-by-four post outside the tent door, the air temperature read thirty-six degrees.

As sheriff, it was my duty to preserve evidence, so I hiked to the shallows and waded across. The water level dropped with the cooler temps, making the crossing easier. Skinny, due to weather, was not yet food for critters. One corner of the blanket had pulled off, and I brushed the snow away and covered his feet back up.

The gun I took off him smelled freshly fired, all six rounds, and left the empties in the cylinder. In Tim's bag, I found no spare bullets. Either he didn't bring any, or someone took them. The second possibility I rated the most likely. However, Skinny didn't carry any spares in his pocket. He hadn't anticipated a shootout. Robbie recovered several slugs in the trees after Shorty shot at me, but I didn't recall his partner shooting.

The snow reached a slushy condition, ideal for snowballs. Caught in the leaves protected from the wind, it collected in the branches and fell in soft plops onto lower branches or the ground. The far northern sky spread azure on the horizon. If it kept clearing, the sun would be out by lunchtime.

Returning to the camp, I started a cooking fire and made a pot of coffee. I brushed away a layer of slush and opened the fridge. It exposed a hole in the ground with a sheet of plywood and two inches of blue rigid styrene insulation glued on it for a door.

The permafrost kept the hole at a steady thirty-eight degrees all summer long. I grabbed the butter and a carton of eggs. I took the skillet off the post, which served as a combination weather station and pan tree. Shortly, the coffee, toast, and scrambled cackleberries—what Ma called eggs— looked ready.

I left them in the pan to keep them hot and poured a cup of Joe. Sticking a fork in the eggs—

"Hello, the camp."

I nearly threw my breakfast on the ground, reaching for my rifle as Robbie walked on the trail from the highway. The state officer wore a heavy parka, but the wolf-fur-fringed hood pulled back and the zipper open. The Smokey Bear hat was replaced with a blue fur-lined cap with ear flaps, and snaps that held the ear covers on top. He snuck through the woods because I heard no sound of someone coming.

"I dang near spilled my grub. I didn't expect you until evening, and the road must be closed."

"Our pilot flew me in as soon as the snow quit. Had us a pretty hairy landing."

I scraped the eggs onto a tin plate and handed it over to the officer with a cup of coffee. I laid slices of bread on the grill and cracked some more eggs.

"Thanks for breakfast. I haven't taken time to eat since Amy got to Tok." He shook his head. "Drove out to the junction and got halfway to Chicken before I got stuck in a drift. I turned around and got stuck again, driving out. We had a full-on blizzard when I hit the pavement and drove into Tok."

"I rousted the pilot this morning, and we checked the weather reports from the FAA. Once he was satisfied, we took off. Be glad you missed that ride." He said.

"I prefer being shot at over flying, anytime. How did you get here?"

"Chicken Taxi Service. The mayor was concerned with the ice in the creeks, so he dropped me at the trailhead."

I sipped coffee, stirred the eggs one last time, and took them and the toast off to eat. I buttered the slices and, in between bites, explained what I did other than think about whiskey, the war, and Amy. "You know this far-north cop stuff is getting into my blood. Does your agency have any openings?"

"Dottie said you considered settling down. There are openings. I might even recommend you, but the State does a thorough background investigation."

"Meaning they would check in with Fort Worth PD."

"No, meaning with every employer you ever worked for after the age of twelve and your police and juvie record. Talk to all your family members who are still alive and track down your superior officers in the service."

"Oh," my jaw felt stiff, "I admit having a hard time after getting home. Truth is, I drank too much and worked too little, but no one questioned my bravery, honesty, or loyalty. That's been a few years, and I'm not so crazy any longer."

"Honesty is good, but is the war in your head over?"

I cringed at the vision of snow and death that haunted my recent dreams. "No, sir, and I guess it won't ever be over, but I contained it. I can't say the happenings here haven't sparked bad memories, but I'm hopeful for my future."

Robbie forked some eggs and stared sideways at me. "Good, because whether you take another job in law enforcement or not, Amy and her family are my friends."

An odd statement, but I said, "I understand," and then I did. Dottie blabbed about the ring.

I took the plate, pan, and cups to the creek and washed them up. Robbie stored the butter and eggs away, apparently aware of the camp routine. With breakfast out of the way, I gave him the gun I took off Skinny. Robbie rolled it in his hands, examining it closely, then stuffed it in the parka's pocket. We walked out to see the body.

The sun reflected off dazzling white patches of snow that began melting in earnest. Robbie opened his coat to cool off and pulled back the soggy blanket. He lifted the dead man's knee. His leg was stiff, possibly from rigor, or Skinny was frozen.

I said, "Doug nearly shot his balls off. The bullet must have clipped the femoral artery. Leaked out the entry wound as there was more muscle around the exit side."

Noting the small hole through the jeans, I determined it took a while for the blood to run down the inside of the pant leg, and each heartbeat pumped a blob to the ground. Stubble covered his face, head, and eyebrows. Red paint was in the creases behind his ears and on the back of his neck.

"I guess Doug nailed Tim's killer."

I stared at Robbie. "Is this some sort of test?"

The tall cop kept his eyes on Skinny, checking his pockets and finding a leather wallet in the back pocket. The officer spoke over his shoulder. "You don't think so?"

"No, and neither do you." I stood to give my knees a break, half-mad. "You alibied him in Anchorage and not hired by Barnes yet."

"Yep, but it looks like he had Tim's gun."

"I don't know for sure—"

Robbie cut me off. "But I do. We went out plinking a few times to give Tim some practice. He worked about as hard at shooting as mining. He fell climbing on rocks and scratched the grip and metal at the bottom. As soon as I saw the pistol, I knew."

Robbie checked the shirt and jacket pockets. He found a receipt from a store in Dawson dated the same day Skinny got spotted on the ferry.

"If it wasn't Skinny who killed him," Robbie gestured at the body, "what does this tell you?"

Assuming he meant the situation, not the corpse. "There must be three of them involved, at least."

"And?" Robbie motioned with his hands for a quick answer. "Think, Sheriff, like your life and, more importantly, the Crocketts' lives depend on it."

I eyed him. "Field training?"

"Can't help it." He nodded. "I've been training rookies for years. Quit stalling. What's the answer?"

I lifted my hat and scratched my head for time to think.

"Take your time, Wyatt. Right now, no one is going to die. Later, it may be more pressing."

"Shorty and Skinny alibied out for Tim's murder but are prime suspects for the F & F Mine murders. Their attempted murder of me and nearly killing us both with plan B after we showed up and busted plan A wide open."

"The now two dead suspects, Shorty and Skinny; of those two, who was the ringleader?"

I looked up over the trees. "Neither of them. Those boys didn't have enough brain cells between them to operate a flush toilet."

Robbie nodded his agreement. "And?"

My mind worked better at battlefield logistics than criminal investigation. I was plum out of practice. "Our third man is the ringleader, the brains, and he ran out on a wounded partner. A coward, but he provided the hideout and transportation."

"And?" Robbie rolled his hand again, digging for more.

"And what?"

"You think the two of them hired on with Barnes, came to Chicken, and somehow bumped into this third man by chance after getting fired?"

"No." Then it dawned on me. "Hey, you're pretty good at this."

"Yeah, and we need to have the guy who taught me look into how Barnes hired them."

"Who taught you? You didn't learn that from no academy."

Shaking his head, "You're slower than I thought at connecting the dots—. Darrell."

Robbie covered up Skinny. He headed back to the road, having told Gene to meet him in three hours and not to leave without him. He ran late, but if Gene weren't waiting, Robbie, after a long walk to the lodge, would beat him silly. Drifts wouldn't melt fast enough for regular vehicle travel, and the highway department didn't consider our road a priority.

Robbie planned to have the coroner flown in again if Rogers wanted to see the scene but expected to get the order to fly Skinny to Anchorage. He would pass the info on to Darrell and check if the PI had anything to share with me. Once they recovered the body, Robbie would fly to Tok until the road opened.

The Crocketts would wait out the plows or the snow melting, whichever came first.

I had plenty of time to consider who the third man might be. The leader is someone more intelligent, but Skinny was hired help. Where would they obtain and stash a vehicle and maintain a hideout? I considered the possibility they murdered the salesman and took his truck. Possibly, Byron participated, but that might have been wishful thinking on my part because he didn't give the impression of being a leader.

Robbie and RCMP Carter suspected a hideout in Canada, but not on the main road with the checkpoint. Aside from the Alcan, no other marked roads crossed the border, according to Gene's office map.

I returned to camp, added wood to the fire, and returned the coffee to heat. All the thinking hurt my brain, so I recited "The Cremation of Sam McGee" to the newly assembled flock of Canadian jays. My audience got bored and flew off. When finished, I poured myself some brew and got an idea.

Skinny and his most recent partner hadn't planned on Doug being in camp. They walked in on the wrong side of the river for the trail from the road. Meaning they went to my place first. They may have shown up before dark and waited at my place until late to be sure everyone was gone.

Was killing Doug their intent? If they planned on murdering anyone or everyone in the camp, then a rifle or a shotgun would have been the weapons of choice. Instead, they brought pistols and no extra bullets. That's why they only wounded Doug. With any decent long gun at the distance they shot from, Skinny or his partner could have drilled Amy's little brother easily.

Likely, they aimed a pistol for his chest and missed by that much. Sixty to ninety feet with a revolver off hand in the dark for an expert would be a difficult shot. In low light and unexpected, it was a miracle they hit him. When Doug fired back from only twenty feet away with as few as eighteen shots between the three of them, only two bullets struck anyone.

They didn't carry dynamite or wrecking tools, so theft I rated as the primary motive. I needed to check my stash and wondered again if Frick and Frack had hidden gold on their claim.

It made sense. The brothers likely did. It kept any excess gold hidden from Uncle Sam and Nora. So, if they got caught, she wouldn't be charged.

Chapter 23

Being a force of nature nearly equal to a blizzard, Amy had the state highway crew on the job the day after the storm. The snow that was not piled several feet deep in drifts began to melt and raised water levels. Their Dodge showed signs of water halfway up the door as the truck huffed out of the creek bed and parked near the sluice.

She jumped out the driver's door wearing the same clothes she wore at Dottie's. Ricky stepped out the other door, and Doug slid to the ground last with his blood-stained jacket and shirt. The doctor wrapped his head like one of those Turks I met in Korea.

Amy explained their ordeal of getting Doug to the clinic, getting X-rays, and threatening to tie him down to get him to hold still for stitches.

"I ain't scared of most things, but I don't like needles," Doug said.

I hated needles, but the Army used me like a human pincushion.

Amy took my arm and walked toward the fire., "It was late morning, and we took a room at the lodge to rest before returning. When we woke, snow covered the ground, and wind howled." Frustration etched a few new wrinkles on Amy's face. "We followed the snowplow out when they finally got one going, but we already lost a day of work."

"Trust me, boss, no work happened in that blow."

She kicked at the dirt. "Regardless, we waited for the plow to break through to the border on the Alcan and come back to the junction. I thought we would fistfight when the operator said he was headed to Tok and would return in the morning."

"Sis indicated my head wound came from disagreeing with her. He asked what happened. I told him I got shot." Doug laughed. "With her revolver behind her belt, he saw it her way."

Amy punched Doug.

"That's not true. I convinced the driver it was an emergency. The guy called on his radio. His dispatcher talked to Robbie and confirmed it was an emergency, and Robbie was on his way."

Ricky said, "That began the real work. We hit one drift; it must have been a half-mile long and four feet deep. The operator struggled to get through. Sister rode his bumper and wouldn't let him back up or turn around.

"Looked like the Barnes outfit put a blade on their deuce-and-a-half six-by and broke a path out to Chicken. We didn't hit any big drifts until after their place."

I shook the boys' hands, and Amy hugged me. Ricky elbowed Doug, and they grinned.

~~~

Doug tended to camp the next day, nursing a concussion that earned him light duty. Amy took it out on the hired help and Ricky. She promised if we kept up, she would treat us at Dottie's after the next cleanup. At dinner, we sat around bushed. Everyone ate the meal Doug cooked, and we prepared for bed.

"I have an errand to run and would like to do it before Robbie returns."

She looked at me, her eyes narrowed. "Doing what?"

"Something you said about people stashing gold made me think those guys expected us to all be in town."

"So, it's here, and okay; I checked."

I believed her but wasn't aware of the location where they kept their gold. It was more than anyone could carry comfortably and unnoticed. I hadn't kept an eye on her to allow some privacy, which I found hard. She's prettier than a Texas sunset and cuter than a newborn filly. Amy was exactly the kind of gal I wanted to watch.

"I stayed here; other than to take Robbie up to the body, and when the coroner flew in, and they hauled Skinny out." I tipped my head in the direction of Davis Creek. "I need to check on my cache."

"Go ahead. It shouldn't take you long."

I wanted a second opinion on an idea. "Well, the thought struck me. Frick and Frack may have stashed gold. I'm guessing, because I'm new here and learning these things. There's a chance it got buried, but I expect, if they have a hideout, it would be closer to their camp."

Her eyes stared hard at me. "You planning to steal it?"

"No, ma'am, but I guess the thought may have occurred to Skinny and his compadres. If I search and find any, I want it to go to the widow, as it is rightfully hers and shouldn't go to whoever ends up with the claim."

"F & F is out of your jurisdiction," she bit her lower lip and said, "but it's what we hired you to do. To look out for us miners and our families." Her face wrinkled. "Don't get yourself killed. I don't like many guys—and Doug," she caught him eavesdropping, "I'm putting you back to work in the morning. Jump your nosy self in the sack and rest up. You're going to need it."

"I have to make plans for the winter. I don't have a place to stay."

"You're right," she said. "We should talk but away from eavesdroppers. Get in bed or so help me."

Doug said, "Amy made out she was in a hurry to start back to work, but really—"

"I aim to shoot you myself if you say one more word." Amy turned around, hunting for a weapon to use on him.

"I'm going."

I said, "I'm waiting for something before deciding where to go. So, there is time to talk. Hoping I'll find something out by our next gig at Dottie's."

"Ain't going to be this weekend. We are way behind."

"Yes, boss."

Amy went to the tent. I sat down next to the dying fire. I had another errand. Robbie couldn't do it, and RCMP Carter had looked already. With Skinny dead and no idea who his partner might be, Carter could walk up, say hi, and leave without any clue he spoke to a killer. Maybe one desperate enough to need a way out of the country and cash or sufficient gold to make it happen.

The F & F might be the place to get it. I grabbed a flashlight and the .30-30 and headed for my claim. I would lose more sleep wondering than if I checked my stash.

Chapter 24

That night, it didn't take but a second to check my gold. I couldn't make out any signs of a search, but the storm obliterated any evidence of anyone being there.

Amy gave me the next day to hike to the F & F Mine, following the path of Gene's rolling monster.

In the clear, late summer and early fall weather, the sky on the distant horizon was blue as glacier ice. The temperature was a comfortable seventy degrees. Patches of pink spread across the landscape, fireweeds budding better than halfway to the top. A natural calendar, when the last buds opened, fall began. I crossed raspberry patches to munch on and kept my eyes open for bears who were also fond of snacking on red berries.

Blueberries needed a couple of weeks to ripen, and the blizzard reduced the skeeter population to about half. Enough to be noticeable, but the starving survivors intended to eat me alive. The caribou all drifted east and began banding up.

Making the bend where Gene parked his swamp buggy, I stopped. From there, the valley spread out below, patches of tundra, willow-lined creeks, and stunted spruce, to the horizon. I unbuttoned the top of my shirt and extracted the binoculars. Through the glasses, I studied the crescent-shaped gash in the bluff. The ice was no longer visible. Mud and gravel covered the scar.

The hole where the rescuers collected the second brother's remains sat filled with water and gleamed in the sunlight. The creek found a new course around the end of the slide, and the temporary lake drained to nothing more than a memory and muddy brush left by the receding water.

The mine sat silent as a graveyard, sacred ground. The distant circling ravens were a chilling reminder of Tim's body. The tent, ragged, ripped to shreds by the storm. The door was left untied and faced into the gale. Their camp was occupied and worked a few weeks ago, but it appeared abandoned for years.

I assumed whoever killed the brothers searched for a cache but surely waited for the State Police to end their investigation.

Realizing that any hiding spot might be buried under the slide, I studied the acres of muck and decided *probably* was more accurate.

In camp, I tried to get into their heads as I hunted. Under the tent seemed too obvious, so I started there with no luck. The outhouse contained what a person expected, crap and a Sears catalog missing many pages.

Items around the camp and tents were left in disarray after the valuables were recovered. The storm might have further scattered trash, and the melting snow removed any sign of tracks if the men Doug encountered came from the F & F first.

I puzzled over the third man while I spent two hours of searching. I leaned against a fifty-five-gallon drum that fed the tent's oil heat stove. They mounted it on sawhorses, and the heater probably didn't see much use except in the early and late seasons. Full, it would have been impossible to pack in. So, they brought in the empty barrel and filled it from five-gallon cans with spouts. Dozens of empty blue and white fuel cans were piled near the tent. I rocked against the barrel. It moved.

The drum was nearly empty, and the valve shut off. Stepping back, I examined the metal sawhorses that sat on two pallets to keep the rusted angle iron legs from sinking into the permafrost. The copper tubing from the stove went into a reducer attached to the valve. The finger-tight fitting, I twisted and unscrewed the connector.

Lifting the barrel, I set it aside, straightened up, and scanned around. Nothing, no one in sight. The only things moving were a couple of floating mallards and an eagle circling off by the nearest neighbors on Walker Creek.

Something felt wrong, but there was no threat that I could see. After another minute, I listened to the nagging voice in my head. Sure, this was part of an investigation, but it was out of my jurisdiction unless it tied in with Tim's murder. A good chance existed that it did, but I had no solid evidence to connect them. I planned to do the right thing, but would anyone else see it that way? Without a warrant to search, technically, I was trespassing.

Would someone accuse me of skimming gold without a witness? Maybe a lot? If I found only a tiny amount, it would undoubtedly cause suspicion. Greedy people always believe everyone else is also. That line of reasoning led to me being a suspect in Tim's murder in the first place. Anyone suspecting me of killing a friend over a gold claim would have no qualms accusing me of being a thief.

Putting the barrel back in place, I hooked it up to the tubing and set out for the road.

Two hours later, I caught a ride to Chicken in the back of a pickup. Gene called in my reinforcements. Asking Robbie to come out but not saying exactly why. Now finding nothing was also a risk. The best solution was to gather volunteers to search the camp for a gold stash, with witnesses.

Gene said, "Robbie is on the way and wanted to talk to you first thing in the morning."

I rented Dottie's spare room to get some sleep before Robbie arrived.

~~~

The sun through the window felt warm on my face the next morning as I sat at Gene's backroom table. I sipped on coffee. When Robbie arrived, he ordered and drank a cup and then paid for both and a half dozen fresh cinnamon-and-sugar-coated cake donuts Gene made.

We walked to the state truck, and Robbie started the engine but left the brake on and in neutral.

He said, "Darrell is getting nowhere on the investigation, but between him and his pal in Seattle, they believe the players are in Anchorage and scamming the corporation. Bilko fired his receptionist, Darrell's inside connection."

Rolling the window down an inch or two for fresh air limited the number of mosquitoes entering. I said, "Not much news. I figured you had something more."

"I might. I expect to hear from our favorite PI again soon, so we'll both wait."

"How well do you know Dottie?" I watched for his reaction.

He cocked his head and eyed me from under the brim of his hat. The corners of his eyes crinkled with the grin on his face. "We've never dated."

I shook my head. "Not where I was going. Dot said something, and it made me believe you went way back. She's also taking an active role in your career."

He smiled. "If Dottie is, I'm not aware of it." Sobering his expression, he said, "And, yes, we go back a long way."

"I'm telling you she is. You're saying we, meaning you, Darrell, and Dottie?"

"Yes, but Darrell's connection predates my involvement. While I was in training, Darrell suggested knowing Dottie and keeping an open mind would enhance my career opportunities rather than harm them."

"His suggestion came in the form of 'if you know what's good for you.'" He added.

"How long has Darrell been acquainted with her?"

"Back when the Alcan was under construction, Darrell worked as a captain in the Army CID. I assume you know—"

"Yes, I know."

"Well, he ran Criminal Investigations in Alaska for the Army during the highway construction. You might say she played a role in the entertainment the USO didn't provide the troops."

I nodded.

Robbie's grip tightened on the wheel. "The Army had a dual policy, which sometimes conflicted. One regarded, ah, adult leisure activities, and the other of getting the road built ASAP."

"I saw the same things in Korea and Japan."

"Officially, his job was to put her out of business. When he tried, construction stopped or slowed to a crawl, and his commander told him to work on crimes and not—"

"Entertainment?" I finished the statement.

"Exactly. That established their relationship, and Dottie proved to be a valuable information resource and made his job easier."

I thought about it. "A confidential informant?"

"Much more, and even being years older than her, they did date some by the war's end. They had a close relationship, but Dottie stayed in Alaska. Darrell returned to Humble, Texas. He resigned his commission and left the Army. He flew to Alaska and landed in Fairbanks, where he hired on with the Territorial Police."

"I want to hear more, but we should pick up a couple of volunteers."

Robbie asked, "Why?"

"It occurred to me that if the brothers stashed gold on their claim, we need help finding it."

Robbie released the brake, dropped the truck in gear, backed up, and pointed it east on the road.

"What you really mean is you located their stash and need a witness or two."

"Maybe, and the thought crossed my mind."

"You're the law, Wyatt. Act like it. Let's see what you found."

~~~

On the way, Robbie explained, "Dottie, like many early settlers, her startup cash came from questionable origins. Now, the queen of Chicken is an upstanding business community leader."

"Many political deals that ultimately led to statehood, the politicians worked out in the backrooms of some of her less stellar establishments in Juneau and Fairbanks." Robbie frowned. "Her interest in Chicken has always been a bit of a mystery, even to me and Darrell."

"She bet her bar against Ricky's holdings in their Poker Creek mine."

Robbie jerked the wheel and nearly drove off the road, squealing to a stop.

"What did you say?"

"I think she was joking, but I would not call her on it nor Ricky."

Robbie pulled back onto the road, and I explained as we continued. Stopping at the Walker Creek Mine, we picked up two witnesses to go and help search. After making a show of hunting around camp, Robbie gave the high sign, and I went to the barrel.

Turning over the pallets, I found a foundation of river rocks, most about as big as grapefruits. The brothers were not trusting folks, and they buried their stash under eighteen inches of rock, undisturbed since they arrived this season. Meaning it came from years past.

Under the rocks, we uncovered frozen canvas bank bags full of gold dust. Frost covered the pit under a two-inch thick sheet of foam insulation. the same type the Crocketts used to cover their refrigerator.

"I reckon Miss Nora is going to find out her husband and brother-in-law had more than a hobby going here." We stared into the hole.

If the gold was only one layer deep, it could buy the City of Chicken and then some. Only the hole, thirty by sixty inches, turned out to be another three feet deeper beneath the rocks.

One of the Walker Creek guys said it was more than what they were hauling out. I mused it also beat what the Crocketts take. Frick and Frack hit a bonanza.

It caused me to wonder how much Amy and the boys were sitting on. Possibly years of hidden profits. The gold find would put a lot of claim owners at risk and did nothing towards solving Eddins' murders other than providing a motive.

The killers may have found this year's cache, or it may have been covered in the slide, but further searching yielded nothing.

Robbie drove the fortune to town in three trips because of the rough terrain and the weight. Gene put it on his antique scale, weighing over a thousand pounds of raw gold.

We decided the two boys hit an enormous placer deposit. Robbie guessed James and his brother kept the findings secret and held out until the government deregulated.

They would have been millionaires at ninety-six dollars an ounce, or three times what Uncle Sam paid. Whoever wanted to buy the claims realized the gold being extracted exceeded what the area miners reported. So, at least one of the people involved was an inside man. I had a notion who.

~~~

We delivered the fortune to Nora two days later in front of Gene's store. She would be well off after taxes, even at the regulated price. Also, the mine's value jumped in price exponentially as soon as the word got out. There would be a bidding war at the auction, with the Walker Creek Mine owners first in line, and an auction is what Dottie recommended Nora do. The claim would go for double or triple what the half-ton of gold would bring.

In the bar where we weighed the gold, Dottie pulled me aside with a grim look in her eyes. "You think my bet with Ricky was too lopsided now?"

"You're a smart woman. A lot brighter than this cowboy."

"Honey, if what Mr. Brown said about the nugget you brought him is true, then you may be sitting on a gold find as good as the F & F or the Crocketts." She closed her eyes, took a deep breath, and blew it out slowly.

I shivered. Dottie's assessment sent a chill down my back, and I told myself not to bet on it because many promising claims played out.

She said, "This will be great for Nora and her kids but bad for the rest of the miners, especially the smaller ones. The Treasury men will be suspicious folks around here have been holding out on them. It's late in the season, and the word will take a while to filter back to D.C. This year's freeze-up will happen before they have their shit, excuse me, stuff together, but next spring, we'll have government agents behind every tree."

Looking into Dottie's eyes, I saw a warning as dangerous as a diamondback's rattle. My popularity as sheriff would plummet come next spring. "Guessing re-election is out of the question."

"Some of us realized the true value of what is in the ground here, and the potential isn't in millions of dollars, Wyatt. It's in the billions, and Uncle Sam expects to get his share."

I said, "It's also why someone wants to buy all those claims. There is far more value than owners report, and if deregulation happens..."

Dottie nodded. "We'll have the potential for a single company sitting on billions in assets they can sell to that Canadian company or their owners in London."

"Meaning what?"

"Well, Sheriff, thanks to you, no one will sell out before getting top dollar. You exposed the reason for killing the Eddin brothers. You put someone's scheme out of business. They will lay low, and you're unlikely to find Tim's killer now."

I wondered about laying low. Miss Dottie miscalculated on one point —human nature and a desire for vengeance. I accidentally upset the inside man something awful. I couldn't see him taking it lying down.

Chapter 25

Dottie pegged the miners' reaction. Their first response was joy for Nora and the kids. Then came panic over government scrutiny. In the weeks before freeze-up, traffic to and from Chicken hit new heights.

Can't say I saw it exactly, but I assumed the extra traffic transported gold off the claims in small batches and into town and onto private property. The owners wanted it secured from the prying eyes of the T-Men and precluded parking it in a bank.

If distressed by the concerns over ATF intrusion, Amy didn't show it, and work progressed much as it did all summer. Time passed quicker the closer it got to freeze-up, and nights got colder. The need to construct a winter shelter became more pressing. Amy appeared determined to work me to death and keep me from building a cabin.

On the occasions when I did get to my place, I worked hard to make enough to see me through the winter. I met the requirements to keep the claim, but not enough to hide any from the government. I had little choice beyond living in town. Without a winter job, I would spend all my earnings and be broke by spring.

With time running short, the Crocketts did their regular cleanup before heading to Dottie's for our last planned show. After finding the F & F's gold, as sheriff, I made several excursions across the border on trails north and south of the Taylor Highway. I met many folks on small claims, some friendly, and a lot who were suspicious and warned me to leave.

Anywhere near the border, the trails were blocked by handmade barriers or gates. A fifty-foot-wide swath of brush and trees the governments kept cut marked the boundary. A straight line ran north and south from the air, visible to the horizon in both directions. Robbie was right—the ability existed for folks to cross back and forth even within sight of the official crossing.

Jurisdiction complicated my search since I had none in Canada and could probably be legally shot. Carter and the rest of the Canadians wouldn't have been terribly upset.

I didn't know who I was hunting for exactly, but I planned to let them know I kept looking. If I calculated correctly, someone would eventually identify themselves. Wherever I went, I told those I met about being at Dottie's, and I expected trouble to find me.

After cleanup, I took my motorbike over the new road to my claim. The Crocketts would meet me later in Chicken.

Before leaving, I called on the CB, and knew Mr. Brown had visited Dottie, and left my secret. Anxious to arrive before Amy, I hit the road, running full out on my motorbike.

Parking out front, I felt the chill, but the shiver came from anticipation. The bar doors stood open, and a few early arrivals sat at the bar. Miss Gail and Dottie occupied a table near the door. I strolled in and wiped mud off my boot on the doormat. It was almost dark, and thankfully, the drizzling rain stopped before my ride. I stopped by the wood stove and rubbed my hands together. The two women stared.

"Hello, ladies." I locked eyes with Dottie, and she gave a short nod.

"Come sit down. I already showed Gail. It's our secret, and we will keep it to ourselves."

"Thanks, ma'am." I sat and wanted to peek at it but froze when she placed the velvet-covered case on the table. Not much larger than a walnut. I couldn't open it.

"I'm sure glad Ricky didn't take my bet," Dottie said.

"Having this ring and getting married seems like a big jump for this Texas hop-toad."

"You're one fine Texan." Gail smiled wide. "I should know."

Dottie's eyes locked on Gail. "How's that?"

Gail slapped my knee. "I roped me one once, a long time ago, and married him."

"You were married?" Dot asked.

"Widowed. We married on July ninth, 1941. I said 'I do' to a cowboy with a college education, and we were both beyond what folks considered marrying age at the time. I earned a degree in fine arts, and he studied engineering." Gail recalled. "Shortly, the war broke out. Mr. Richner joined the Marines right after Pearl Harbor. He went to officer training in Virginia, then shipped off to San Diego and eventually to the South Pacific. It seemed he fought on every island out there. He won some medals and got himself a Silver Star on Okinawa, but they gave that one to me with a flag and the condolences of the Marines and the president."

Dottie put a hand to her mouth. "Well, I never—"

"I don't talk about it. Being a reasonably young widow, I never met his family before the funeral. Billy and I met in Durango, Colorado, and I never went to Texas. His father owned a place near Midland. There was oil on the ranch, and his folks did well selling beef and crude oil to the government—part of the war effort."

"I found out after Bill's funeral his share of the family trust went to his wife. Suddenly, I was rich and distraught." Miss Gail dabbed a tear with a lace hankie and continued, "I went crazy for a while. Bill always had money but never mentioned how he came by it, so it was never my priority. He fell out with the family before leaving for college."

She talked more about herself than I had ever heard, and from her look, Miss Dottie, too. "Being an excellent shot with a rifle, I took a job as a demonstrator with the Winchester Arms folks. Annie Oakley was a legend, and the company used my similarity to sell their firearms. I toured until offered a job in a traveling western show, which sounded more exciting. We hit all the big rodeos. I went to Europe and Japan to entertain the occupation troops."

Listening, I wondered if I had watched her perform somewhere, but the black velvet box held my eyes like a magnet.

"What brought you to Chicken?" Dottie asked. "Well, to Dawson first, where we met, you came here later for a visit and never left."

"I tell you, I made it to Calgary, Alberta, to do a show for the rodeo and heard about the Klondike Goldfields. An uncle— my mother's brother— went to the Klondike and never came back. He checked in at the border on the trail from Skagway and never heard from again. That's why I love Wyatt's poem about the cremation." She stopped, smiled, and looked at me. "Why don't you open it? You paid for it."

"I'm afraid to touch it. Afraid it might jinx me or something."

Dottie giggled, and my face burned. She grabbed the tiny case and started to open it.

"Wyatt?" Amy called from the door.

I snatched it faster than a card sharp can bottom deal. I slipped it into my pocket, nearly tipping over the chair and table.

Miss Gail lost all composure, let out a belly laugh, and slapped the table. The bar owner remained more poised but still grinned like the cat with a mouthful of feathers.

"What are you three up to? No more surprises like last time, I hope."

"Are you the boss or just Amy Crockett?" I choked a little. "Just being Amy is something like being an angel. I didn't mean it to sound like —"

She stood there, hands on her hips. "I think I liked it better when you said nothing."

Those words sparked laughter from the three women I held most dear, turning me redder than ever.

"What did you stuff in your pocket, Cowboy?"

"It's a gift I bought, but not for now or today or nothing."

"It's for me?" Amy asked.

"Hey, Wyatt?" Doug yelled from outside Gene's door. "Grab your badge and come running. You're on duty."

"What's the problem?" I walked to the door and recognized the Nelson family, Butch, his wife, and three kids in their pickup. Seeing me pin on the star, Butch climbed out of the truck.

"Sheriff, sir, I, well, what I found is pretty awful."

Doug said, "He told me he found a pickup truck with a body in the front seat."

I asked, "Is that right?" The man nodded. "Where?"

"A gravel pit about halfway to the border." His head twisted back and forth. Not saying no, he couldn't accept what he saw. "The boy needed to pee, so I pulled into the gravel pit and spotted a pickup. I went to see if they had trouble and saw blood on the back window. I looked closer, but he was dead."

The man glanced at his truck. "I'll go home now."

"No, not yet. Come in and talk to Gene. He has candy for the kids, my treat. You give him your address and phone number."

"We live in the village. No phone."

"Tell him the village and where we can find you so the policeman can ask questions. Okay?"

He nodded, but I saw it was not okay at all.

"Doug, take him to Gene, have the mayor call and let Robbie know what's happening. He may want the coroner with him. I'm assuming Butch knows what a dead man looks like."

Amy hollered, "Wyatt, wait."

"You're singing tonight. I got this."

I dropped my hat in the crate, hopped on the motorbike, and took off, running full out and dodging potholes, trying not to swallow any gnats or moths that survived the recent frost.

On the way, I started second-guessing my choice of transportation. The headlight lens was broken. This night would be the first time it turned dark before parking it.

Between where I found Tim's bag and the path Gene mowed through the woods to the road, a small gravel pit sat near the Boundary settlement. The highway department used it for major road repairs.

I slowed to a crawl before finding the turnoff and saw the general outline of a pickup in the dark sitting near the woods. The farthest place away from the road. Looking around, I could see no details below the tree line. A dark, gray, overcast sky promised it would be pitch black in minutes.

Kicking the bike up on the stand, I killed the engine and stepped off toward the truck, trying not to disturb possible evidence I couldn't see. *Why the hell didn't I think to bring a flashlight?*

I turned back toward the road. A vehicle banged and rattled, coming fast from Chicken. The noise and exhaust sounded familiar. The Crocketts' truck skidded to a stop short of running over my motorcycle.

The door opened, and as I ran back, I yelled, "Do you have a flashlight?"

A light beam appeared on the ground. "Of course. Don't you?"

I didn't need sarcasm, but I needed a flashlight and met Amy halfway.

"Please stay here long enough for me to check for evidence. If I don't find anything on the ground, I will call for you if you feel you must look. Did you bring your camera, and does it have a flash?"

"Yes, and yes."

"Please wait."

I started for the truck using the little two-cell with a magnet on it. I remembered seeing it hanging under the dash by the glove box. The weak bulb kept going out. I tapped it a few times to make it work again before reaching the truck.

Shell casings from people target practicing, cigarette butts, leaves, and other litter I saw scattered randomly around the gravel pit. Reaching the truck, I recognized it immediately—Byron's, white with the orange logo on the door. Covering the light to hide the door emblem from Amy, I pointed it in the cab before uncovering it.

A male adult sat behind the wheel, missing his face from the ears forward. Bone, teeth, and hair mixed with brain matter coated the ceiling and most of the truck's interior. I heard a step behind me.

"Is it Byron?"

"Amy, I can't tell. It's bad."

"Suicide?"

I turned and studied inside. On the seat, I spotted a note on an invoice pad. "Someone wants us to think so, but someone murdered this guy. Don't come any closer. Go back to town, have Gene update Robbie, and let him know I need reinforcements as soon as they can get here."

"Gene called. His dispatcher said he was out at a house fire in Nabesna, and they didn't have contact with him."

"Tell Gene to have Stuart from Fairbanks ride in with the coroner if they are available. Then come here, and we'll wait for daylight and the troops together."

Walking back with her, I tucked the flashlight under my armpit and blew on my fingers. The fog from my breath appeared in the dim light.

"Drive carefully, Amy. I might freeze to death if you don't come back."

"I have a parka behind the seat, Ricky's, you can put on."

No questions, and shell shocked, but she drove away determined and much slower than her arrival.

I slipped on the coat, and the sleeves were short. I walked back to the truck. Working in Fort Worth, I had responded to a suicide by shotgun. The victim sat in his easy chair near the fireplace. My backup happened to be a veteran officer of twenty years on the force. He spent time in the homicide unit as a detective but left, preferring to work in a uniform, where he wrote a report, which became someone else's problem.

He explained the evidence that made it a suicide, should I happen to draw another case. A likely probability in Texas I would. Also, he told me what to look for in a staged suicide. The memory returned much clearer than most of my time on the force.

The first thing visible through the window was a blood trail on his neck that had traveled front to back while the rest went down the front or blown into the overhead.

The buckshot pattern showed on the roof but hadn't penetrated. Next, the victim held the gun around the barrel with his left hand and a forked stick in his right. Presumably, to push on the trigger. His feet sat on the brake and the gas pedal with the gunstock between his legs.

The passenger's side window, the ceiling, the front seat, the dash, and the windshield were coated evenly with debris, but not the driver's side window, with only a minimal amount of gore. A quick scan with the flashlight showed debris on the ground outside the closed truck door.

What I observed added up to murder, not suicide.

I shut off the light to save the battery. The moon showed barely more than a dim white blob, the size of a dime on a black bedsheet shining through the thin overcast.

~~~

For two hours, I paced and thought about the case before Amy returned. She parked near the entrance, and I removed the coat before climbing in the warm truck. I shivered and held my hands out to the heater vent.

"Sorry it took so long. I waited for confirmation from Fairbanks State Police. They plan to be in Chicken at daybreak, weather permitting. Then I told Dottie what happened and bought gas from Gene so I would have a full tank, and we could run the truck to stay warm."

"That's why you're the boss. Always planning."

"Is it Byron?"

"I don't know if it is your salesman," the name still stuck in my craw, "but it's his truck, and saw some rough miles since we last laid eyes on it."

"How do you know it wasn't a suicide?"

I explained. Not the conversation I planned, but with Amy, talking about a murder was easier than talking about love. *Why?*

An hour before daylight, she fell asleep. We kept the window open a crack and assumed the idling truck would keep the predators in the woods. Why murder the salesman? Where did he stay? Where was he killed? The note might explain some of it, but nothing on it could be taken at face value, and with the dim flashlight, I couldn't read it.

I didn't see the truck on my way to Chicken. With only a short gap in the alders, even at the fastest I could go, I should've seen the pickup in daylight. So, it arrived between six and when the Nelsons stopped for a potty break.

Where did it come from? How did it end up here? If someone murdered him here, where did his killer go, and how did he leave?

These questions needed answers if I'm any kind of investigator at all.

Chapter 26

Darkness ebbed away as daylight crept over the eastern horizon. Although toasty in the truck, frost had covered my motorbike seat. Likely, it was the coldest night since spring. More autumn leaves turned to gold and trembled in the slightest breeze.

Awake and aware, I contemplated where this guy's killer went. The salesman's body, probably, but fingerprints and dental records would be needed for ID, providing the coroner could find enough of his teeth.

The sound of Gene's swamp thing rolling down the highway announced the Fairbanks party made it to Chicken as soon as there was light enough to land.

"Wake up. I have work to do."

Amy sat up, her cheek and forehead creased with red lines. She wiped her mouth, stretched, and yawned. Hearing the green beast, she turned and watched Gene roll to a halt.

Reaching across her, I grabbed the parka, stepped out, and slipped it on while walking to meet Doc Rogers and Officer Stuart.

"Howdy, glad you could make it." Puffs of condensation floated with each word.

Rogers said, "It's becoming a habit." He and Stuart shook my hand and started asking questions.

"Hold off on what I believe, and when you have a gander, you tell me if I'm right or wrong."

They agreed, and I led them as near as I could over the path I walked before. Stuart used his powerful four-cell flashlight to give us a brighter view inside from the passenger's window.

"My professional opinion as coroner is this is a murder staged as a suicide. What's your opinion, Stu?"

The officer pointed his light at the hand on the barrel. "Never saw a suicide still holding the gun they shot themselves with, let alone a stick used to push the trigger."

Playing the light on the driver's door, he said, "A cinch that door was open when the gun went off, and sure as hell, he didn't close it."

I pointed out, "There is blood on his neck, and it ran like he fell flat on his back after bleeding. Then someone sat him up before the blood dried."

Rogers nodded. "Good catch, Sheriff. It means he died before being put in the truck. The shotgun wound shows signs it occurred postmortem, but I can confirm better at the autopsy. Also, I can give you a closer time of death. When was the body discovered?"

"The Nelsons reported it sometime around seven last night, and I came by around six on my way to Chicken. It wasn't here then."

Amy walked up, placed her hand on my elbow, and stayed behind me.

"I got nervous." She pulled the coat zipper higher and shivered, maybe from the cold or the sight of the mess on the windows.

Rogers said, "I'll get my gear from the monster and be back."

"I'll give you a hand." Amy followed Doc.

"I want to look for tracks. Mr. Nelson said he stopped by where we parked. He spotted the vehicle and approached this side. Our witness never went to the driver's side."

Stuart glanced around with an experienced eye. "Pretty hard packed, probably won't find much on this gravel, but maybe scuff marks."

Stepping carefully a few feet away from the front of the truck, I detected a smudge on the front fender and pointed it out. The spot looked greasy with a dab of blood on it.

"Looks like the suspect got out and walked around before closing the door," Stuart said.

On the door, we found three sticky fingerprints. I saw some rocks turned over in the gravel near the door, showing sand stuck on them. Past the cab, a flat stone, roughly a three-inch oval shape, showed a dark pattern where a boot lifted dust and oxidation, leaving the pattern. Not enough for me to ID the manufacturer, but I suspected a hard-soled hiking or combat boot print.

On the truck bed, a palm print, greasy from the shotgun debris on the killer's hand. When the frost formed, it didn't freeze over.

"Was the engine cold when you got here?"

I looked at Stuart. "I couldn't make out a lot and didn't want to disturb evidence, which is the answer, but honestly, I didn't think to check."

"Honesty is a worthy trait in a rookie cop," Stuart said, and Rogers, who had returned with his gear, nodded in agreement.

Amy carried the doctor's camera gear. He brought a black satchel and a body bag under his arm. Stuart went over to point out the evidence we spotted on the outside. After showing the coroner, he went to get his evidence toolbox to try to lift prints and take pictures. The officer used his state-issued Cannon 35mm camera— the more pictures, the better.

Tracking people and animals is best if you know who you are tracking, how they think, and what they do instinctively. Are they attempting to hide, or are they unaware or unconcerned about being followed?

I took a knee by the smudges on the door. It was a lower grip than mine and higher than Amy's. About the right height for someone like Rogers or Stuart. It made the suspect five foot eight to six-foot tall. His walking step was an inch to two inches shorter than mine. At the back corner of the truck, the trail might go anywhere, but most likely back in the direction of the road.

A direct line would be to where Gene sat in the swamp buggy, mentally counting his taxi fee.

The sky turned bright but defused through the overcast, unsuitable for casting shadows. On my knees, I spotted a loose stone at about the expected placement of a heel, judging by stride, from the rock with the print on it. Two more paces in a sandy patch, I found an imprint but no definition. It established the apparent direction and not to the main road.

Taking a sighting from the truck bed corner through the two prints, I mentally marked a spot at the edge of the trees. I walked wide of that path, looking for any signs of shoe prints in the softer dirt along the edge of the pit. I found some old caribou tracks and trails into the woods. Most of the paths were covered by fallen leaves still wet from the previous drizzle.

Stuart watched, thinking I was confused, and maybe I was. The evidence indicated the trail ended in the gravel pit, but I spotted no signs of a second set of tire tracks like those left by the hardware store truck,

Amy's, or Nelson's. They all left faint tracks and were easy enough to make out. A second vehicle should have left some sign.

Stuart and Amy watched me from fifty yards away. Stepping one foot at a time, searching the ground, expecting to find a set of vehicle tire tracks somewhere between where I stood and the hardware store pickup.

Halfway back, there were no tire marks or dried puddles from an idling engine. Staging a suicide took time. The suspect would be in a hurry to escape unseen, if not into the bush, then in a vehicle. I pulled off my hat and scratched my head.

A broken flat rock became my first clue. It caught my eye, a thin, about a silver-dollar-sized gray stone with a fresh crack in the middle. I waved for Stuart. "Bring your flashlight."

With the officer's light to throw shadows, I found an impression of a straight, shallow depression on the rocky ground, and later, a matching one six feet away. The ground was so hard-packed that I walked over the impressions without seeing them. Other indications were black paint and some tiny metallic transfers to pieces of gravel. The indentions were deeper on one side and at one end.

"What do you make of it?" Stuart asked.

I held my finger up and closed my eyes. Mentally, I watched soldiers being medevacked and watched a helicopter touch down on the skids. The back left touched first, and then the right before rocking down flat. After loading the wounded men, the chopper shook and lifted off, tipping the nose forward and drifting to the left.

I scanned the area and saw for fifty feet around, there was not a leaf or shred of trash on the ground that littered the other two acres of bare gravel.

"Our suspect got into a helicopter."

Stuart glanced around and nodded. "You ever see one around here, Sheriff?"

"Nope, but a couple of years ago, down in Dawson, I saw some mining bigwigs fly one into Whitehorse, and I saw them in Korea."

Stuart drew a diagram in his notebook estimating the length and width of the skids and the distance apart. After giving up on finding other evidence, we picked up rocks with paint and metal transfers. I assisted in dragging the stiff corpse out of the front seat. We laid him on a sheet and emptied his pockets. Stuart collected business cards like the one I found in Tim's gear. The wallet in his back pocket contained a driver's license for Byron.

Coins, some of them Canadian, and lint in the front of his pant pockets. Stuart photographed the suicide note written in legible cursive and splattered with gore.

I killed my friend Tim Crockett. It was an accident during an argument. The three of us blew up the F and F mine. It was supposed to scare them, but the whole bank gave way and nearly took us down. Thomas got killed at the Sherriff's place, and then someone at the Crocketts' killed Slim. I ran out of food at the camp and nearly walked into the Sheriff in the Canadian woods. I knew I was caught, but I won't go to jail and wanted someone to find me.

Byron

"Convenient. He didn't mention the hideout location or if he worked for someone. His written confession wrapped up all the murders in a neat bow. Only, whoever killed him wasn't aware Robbie already verified Byron was in Anchorage at the time of Tim's murder," I said.

Stuart nodded. "Sounds right to me."

Amy looked sick, having seen the body when we pulled it from the truck. She identified the old single-shot Higgins 12 gauge as Tim's bear gun around camp.

~~~

Twenty minutes later, the swamp buggy took off with the State's people to return with the body to Fairbanks. Stuart took the film and the evidence with him. Rogers found further proof of staging, including body tissue under the victim's hand holding the gun barrel—some smudges and smearing on the shirt sleeve from moving the victim's arm.

Amy asked, "Wyatt, was Tim—"

"You don't want to know." I shook my head. "Best you remember the guy we all loved and not think about it."

"You saw him."

"I did." I turned her towards the truck. "I've seen worse. Let's go to your mine and do some work. It's going to freeze up real soon from the feel of it."

"What about Byron's truck?"

"Stuart said Robbie will send a wrecker from Tok and impound it there."

~~~

Only the weather, always fickle in the fall, turned warm. Robbie came to our camp late the following evening. Everyone sat around the fire and chatted. Amy's presence at the scene negated keeping the conversation limited to officers.

Robbie said, "Rogers's autopsy says Byron died several hours before someone blew his face off."

"He had been upright but not in that pickup when killed. Rogers recovered a twenty-two-caliber slug in the man's remaining brain. The killer intended for that evidence to get blown away with the rest of his face and forehead." He peeked at Amy. "Sorry, ma'am.

"Because of the dried blood trail on his neck Wyatt spotted, Rogers believed Byron got shot under the chin into the back of his skull, but with little evidence left to prove his theory."

Robbie stood to leave, and I said, "I had a thought about that helicopter."

He slipped on his hat and tugged it down tight. "What?"

"Remember when I said something like unless Tim fell from the sky…"

He nodded. "It would explain a lot, including where his bag landed when the road was still closed. I stopped by Action Jackson's. Several people there heard a helicopter fly close by the night you found Byron."

Afterward, Robbie departed on his way to meet the RCMP. They were searching their side for the hideout and possible murder scene in Canada.

~~~

The Crockett camp stayed somber every night for the next week. Darkness caught us earlier and earlier, losing close to ten minutes of daylight every day. Amy struggled with when to call it quits for the year and button-up operations. I fretted about the ring in my pocket. If I waited for spring, it terrified me to consider if I would need it.

Byron's death took the romance away, and Amy kept her distance. Working and sleeping took all our time. I worked on my claim as time allowed, figuring once the creek froze, I would go to town to cash out my gold and find a cheap apartment for the winter. I struggled with going to Anchorage to be near Amy. That might be a mistake. It seemed she held me responsible for the salesman's death.

One evening after work, Robertson came to camp in the dark and ate dinner with us. He faced the fire from his stump, leaning away from the smoke, and said, "Wyatt, are you even listening to me?"

I looked up. Amy, Doug, and Ricky all stared back.

"Sorry, lost in thought."

"I said, I've been working with Stuart and tracking down helicopters, which isn't an easy thing. There are more in Fairbanks, but I found only one in my jurisdiction that the Forest Service uses in Northway. It has an alibi, and the skid pattern isn't the same."

"Did Stuart have any better luck?"

"They have a variety at the airport and on the bases at Fairbanks. He thinks he has found a winner. Except the military keeps track of their helicopters and can account for all of them, the night Byron's body turned up."

"And the civilian?"

"Stuart says it's a Hiller, like those we flew for medivacs in Korea and the ones you are most likely to remember."

"I remember walking. The only time I recall wishing I could fly."

"Must have been bad as much as you hate flying." Robbie grinned when I nodded. Then he continued, "The tracks you spotted in the gravel pit match the size and spacing, but a pilot trainer uses the one he found, and another belongs to the State Fish and Game. In other words, it's one of ours, and they are both accounted for."

"What is the range on those machines?"

"Glad you asked. The military versions may differ, but the guy in Fairbanks says he might fly two hundred miles on a fill-up in perfect conditions. It depends on the weight; he can shorten the gas to carry more load. Also, in the bush, you better know where to find gas on an extended trip or plan a long walk home. He keeps trips to less than seventy-five miles to make a round trip, one hundred and fifty one way, and account for weather."

"Can you ask your pal Carter to check for choppers on his side of the border?" I thought for a minute, and Robbie waited. "And, if not from around here, anyone coming from Anchorage would need to fuel up somewhere along the way. Can the State Police check airports between Anchorage and here at seventy-five-mile to one-hundred-mile intervals? Not many pilots would chance flyin' cross country very far. So near roads."

"I like your thinking. That would be the Glenn Highway, the Richardson, the Tok Cut-Off, and the Alcan Highways. There are many minor airports at lodges, but I should be able to track them down next week. A lot of them don't have phone service. Our guy in Glennallen and I can cover the most likely spots."

"Are you planning to resign and move to town or stay as sheriff in Chicken all winter?" Robbie asked.

After staring into the fire, I looked at Robbie. Checking the faces around the circle, everyone had an interest.

"It may depend on my boss giving me time off to build a cabin on my place. She's been giving me a lot of working hours for wages and no time to dig gold or build a cabin at my place."

Amy dipped her chin down and grinned but kept her eyes on the fire. Doug's eyes lit up, and he glanced at his sister. "You devil."

"Shut up, or I'll switch you."

Robbie said, "Well, I brought it up because I talked to Dot on my way here, and she wondered about a bet she made, and your commission is about to expire."

Ricky shrugged and tried to look innocent, but Amy glared at him.

"I still intend to get Tim's killer," I said.

"We took over your case. I'm pretty sure no one near here is responsible. Also, a friend in Tok said he has a building you can put on your claim if you haul it off his property."

Amy's mouth pulled up in a tight line, and her glare bored into Robbie's head.

"How would I move a building in here?"

"Hell, man, how did they bring the bus in here? Determination, and in this case, it is in boxes. It's a surplus Army Quonset hut."

Amy's jaw twitched, and she ignored the state cop and aimed her gaze at me.

"I should look into it. If the weather catches us, I might have to wait until next year to move it up. I don't have any way to do it right now."

Doug said, "Guess we could load it on the old Dodge and get it as far as Chicken where Ol' Gene—ow!" Doug rubbed his shin.

"Oh," Amy said, "sorry, I didn't mean to kick you."

"It sure felt—" Doug glanced at her. "—like a bad idea."

Thinking over the idea of a Quonset, I said, "It's something to consider. I helped erect the tin huts in Korea and could put one up in less than a week. Finding a stove would be easy."

Cutting enough firewood for the winter would be nearly impossible. Besides, Amy acted like she wanted me off my claim and near her. If so, it suited me just fine.

Robbie pulled me aside before walking back to his truck.

"You're officially off the suspect list."

I glanced at Amy near the fire and then back at Rob.

"I thought I came off the list long ago."

"Well, it's official now. Our Anchorage office called me when Tim went missing. Someone called them saying you grabbed the claim Tim wanted. It cast a shadow over you, and after I found Tim's body, well…"

"Who called in the—"

"The dead guy," his head leaned toward me, "Byron. We don't know his involvement, but he fell into cahoots with Slim and Shorty. The Crocketts have alibied you at the time of the salesman's death."

"That and I don't own a helicopter."

Robertson left after dark, planning to stop at Chicken overnight. His comment referring to the bet was a dig to get under Ricky's skin. Robbie also knew about the ring burning a hole in my pocket.

Dottie pegged it. When it came to Amy, I had a yellow streak a foot wide up my back. I needed to be prosperous enough, with a real job and a home to offer a wife before asking her to marry me. I couldn't abide being a kept man.

A Quonset hut would not be much, but around Chicken, it would rank as upper middle class. If I took up with Amy and had no job, my brothers would never let me hear the end of it.

"Boss lady, I need to walk over to my place."

Doug said, "Want me to tag along?"

"No, he doesn't want you tagging along," she said.

"I hoped maybe Amy would go with me. I need some mining advice and decide where I will stay this winter."

Ricky started to say something, and she turned on him like a coyote on a rabbit, and he clammed up.

"I'm happy to go," Amy said, brushing some imaginary dirt off her jacket before grabbing a flashlight and two shotguns from the tent. Carrying the Colt had become a habit since Gail loaned it to me. The local sharpshooter said she trained Amy to shoot targets with it, and my boss hit what she aimed at. Hinting, I better not tick her off with a gun in her hand.

The walk was quiet. An autumn feeling filled the air with the tangy smell of overripe berries, and the leaves dropping so fast that no sooner than one hit the ground, another went airborne. Fall in Chicken usually happens on the weekend before winter. I knew the Crockett clan would be southbound any other year after their next cleanup, but Amy hadn't committed to it.

We splashed through Davis Creek and passed where Amy put a cross for Tim. His body waited in a mortuary in Anchorage for them to return home and bury him. I stopped at the drift log that served as the sitting bench. I grabbed some kindling and lit a fire.

While I fussed with the fire, Amy sat on the log, hands on her knees. Once I got it going, I sat next to her. She scooted closer and leaned against my shoulder. Alaskan romance isn't much like Texas in late August, where a jacket of any kind would be unnecessary, but in Chicken, heavy coats and long underwear were essential. On the bright side, the skeeters all froze to death.

"Wyatt."

"What?"

"I thought you wanted to talk."

I squirmed. "Yes."

"You aren't talking."

"Tell you the truth, I'm scared." I looked down and studied my hands.

"Of me?"

"No, ma'am, of me, my thoughts, my lack of means. Thanks to your family, I have something to show for the year. If I go to town, I guess I could be okay over the winter, but come spring, I'm broke with nothing but a gold mine and a lot of work to do. I can't even plan on money enough for supplies."

Her hand rested on my sleeve. "Think I don't worry about you and me? You could find a job in Anchorage, or maybe Doug can set you up on the railroad."

"Until recently, I planned to stay here and save my cash."

Amy stared into the little fire, a comfort fire. It didn't provide much warmth. "Alone?"

"Who would want to stay here with me?"

"If Dad wasn't in the shape he's in—"

I put my hand on her knee, which stopped a nervous bouncing. "You need to be in town and work. I'm a bum. I can survive this winter like last year."

She sat up straight and glared at me. The fire flickered in her eyes. "Last year, Barnes paid you, provided a place for you to stay, and firewood for the season. Why stay here, for what?"

I looked at her, struggling for an intelligent reply, and she stared back. "Ah, what's the correct answer?"

"Mr. Peoples." *Uh-oh, I'm in trouble.* "You better start thinking of something damned quick. I came here trying to decide what our future will look like, and it worries me."

My mind slammed closed like a heavy vault door. *Our future?*

"Just when I need you to talk, you turn mute again. Ever since Dottie's, you've kept a secret. I saw you snatch something off the table and stuff it in your pants. Every day since, I see you checking on it all day, making sure it's there."

My hand touched the lump in my pocket.

"Yeah," she pointed, "that secret."

"I don't know—"

"Dad-blame it. Dig the ring out and ask me before I get a piece of firewood and beat you silly."

"You know? Dottie said—"

Her eyes sparkled like a diamond backlit by fire. "She didn't say a thing. I guessed right! It is a ring, isn't it?"

I nodded numbly.

"Did you buy it for me?"

I gave her a blank stare. Who the heck else would I buy it for?

"Give me Gail's gun, Mister, 'cause I'm going to need to shoot you."

I started to reach for the gun, and she slapped my hand away.

"Well, show it to me."

"You slapped—"

"The ring!"

Kneeling, I shoved my hand in my pocket, and it got stuck. I stood to pull it out. Opening the little case, I stared at the tiny metal circle, a slim band of gold nuggets sparkling in the firelight. Mr. Brown topped it with a slender piece of jade and a small diamond set in the center. I turned it toward her.

"Is it an engagement ring?"

I nodded.

"You say something, Wyatt, or as God is my witness, I'll throw it in the creek."

I dropped to my knee like someone chopped off my leg.

"Miss Amy, would you marry me?"

She gazed at it and the firelight dancing in her blue eyes. "I need to think about it."

Chapter 27

Amy held the rest of my life in her fingers, twisting my beating heart around like a surgeon deciding if I live or die, and nodded. Yes.

~~~

Robbie had returned to the office in Tok to continue his investigation into the use of a helicopter to commit murder. In a few days, he struck crime-solving gold and relayed a message through Gene by CB radio at my evening check-in. Gene said he set up a relay, a talent where the mayor switched mics and speakers as the message went through his equipment.

"My State Police buddies in Glennallen checked local airports for a helicopter fitting the description. There were no filed FAA flight plans, but they confirmed one bought fuel in Gakona around the time Tim went missing, and again in the past week. So far, no return flight south was noted on this latest trip. Over."

Punching the key on the CB mic, I watched Amy pushing dirt and the boys mucking it into the header. Last night, she took the ring off and returned it. She said we could make it official at Dottie's before we called it quits for the season.

I said to Robbie, "Copy. Does the flight service have a registered owner? Over."

Back in Chicken, Gene listened in and held two microphones in front of the speakers, alternating between the CB and ham radios. Static and a squelch squawk sounded when he mistimed it.

Robbie replied, "The numbers are Canadian; the owners were a mining outfit that filed for bankruptcy and sold off the assets. Carter says it went to an unknown buyer in Whitehorse three years ago, about when you were in Dawson. Over."

"Maybe he never registered in the US, but he operates bandit and avoids airports and FAA controllers. Over."

"Based on travel distance, we are concentrating our search on airstrips north of Anchorage with light traffic. Somewhere with road access. Over."

Pushing my hat back, I frowned. I didn't have a clue how big of a job the search might be. "How many strips are we looking at? Over."

"There's the bug in the ointment. Most of the more popular ones are along the railroad, Birchwood, Palmer, Wasilla, and Willow. Like Gakona and Northway, the Army built them during WWII as emergency airfields. But a helicopter can sit down in someone's backyard. Most of the lots for houses are two and a half acres or bigger, and there are numerous homesteads out in the valleys with room for airstrips. The Anchorage area is the busiest place in the world for private airplanes. It may take a while. Over."

"We should be closing operations this weekend, and I need a home. Amy called for a semi-lowboy truck to haul the Cat back to Anchorage to tune it up or sell it. They may buy one of the newer hydraulic models. I'll stop by your office and visit on my way to Anchor Town. Over."

"You want that building? I can store it at my place until spring. Over."

I almost choked, closed my eyes, and pushed hard against the steering wheel. I considered Robbie a mentor on bush law enforcement but hadn't expected that. It surprised me how much it meant to have his respect and friendship.

"Yes, siree, it would be mighty neighborly of you. Over."

"Roger, ASP Tok, out."

It took a second to absorb what the gesture meant. Robbie offered to move the building to his place and protect it from the weather all winter, but it was much more. When I get to Tok, I'll have to help Robbie move the thing if time allows. The Crocketts would go on to Anchorage, and I would hitch a ride in later if need be.

Amy saying yes answered a prayer, but it required I find steady work in town. Outside of cowboying, mining, and a short stint in a logging camp, soldiering and law enforcement was about the extent of my skills.

A tapping at the window, I turned to see Doug smiling.

As the window opened, Doug said, "The boss has been in a good mood all day but says your lollygagging time is up, so get back on the end of a shovel. She plans to walk her Cat past your place sometime soon and make a shortcut to the road *we* can use next spring. The trailer should be there when she finishes. She plans to start road building this evening."

Jumping out of the Dodge, I shivered when the breeze hit me. Were the tremors from damp clothes or because Amy included me in her plans? It pleased me pink she did.

~~~

No news in the following days from Robbie or Anchorage, and there was little doubt Byron's, and likely Tim's, killer was long gone. Where? A reoccurring thought and being unfamiliar with Alaska as a whole, I planned on reviewing Gene's collection of maps.

Amy made Friday our last official day at the mine. That evening, the trailer hauling the Cat waited in Gene's parking lot. We buttoned up the mine and stacked their gear on the Dodge and Ricky's borrowed trailer.

There was little to do at my place besides picking up my sack of gold, which felt mighty light to me. It looked small compared to the chest-full carried by the Crocketts. I knew they cleaned out far more of the yellow mineral than they put in that chest. I wondered where it went.

This was a bonus day for Dottie. She anticipated closing earlier, but warm weather kept the clientele close. After Nelson reported his find, everyone looked forward to Crocketts' makeup performance for our hasty departures.

Dottie couldn't complain much. She helped make it my duty. Besides, the extra crowd stayed and drank her booze. Three guys jammed a session with Ricky for free drinks in our absence.

When we parked in front of Gene's store and Dottie's bar, Doug volunteered to stay with the gold, keeping a pump shotgun handy. He had bought it off Miss Gail when we returned the arsenal she had loaned us. Other trucks, like Barnes's outfit and the Walker Creek crew, also left armed guards on their rigs. Truthfully, gold leaving the Fortymile area in the next twenty-four hours would measure in tons. How much of it would reach government hands was hard to calculate.

Ricky and Amy carried in their instruments and got set up on the stage. Miners crowded the bar and tables when I walked in. I rode shotgun with the lowboy driver, a much warmer ride than on top of the gear in the back of the overloaded flatbed.

The number of customers surprised me, and everyone acted in fine spirits. Spotting Miss Gail, I stepped over to say hi. "Ma'am, I need to return this badge and your Colt."

She shrugged. "I don't want them, Sheriff."

"After tonight, I'll be a civilian again." I thought giving up the badge would be easier and relieving, but it held a particular pull I could feel.

"How much money has this town put up for your work? And you have done a sight of work, young man."

"The State—"

"The State didn't railroad you into the job. We did."

"Yes, ma'am."

"So total?"

"A couple of meals and a few beers is about all, I guess."

"Well, on behalf of the town, I ask you to accept the badge and gun in lieu of cash payment."

"I don't, I mean, well, you don't need—" I fought tears.

"I'm the first woman aside from Amy who made you stutter and turn red in the face." She smiled wide. "I love you too, Wyatt. Say thanks and leave it."

Robbie walked in with Stuart and Doc Rogers.

I rubbed my eyes. "Who died I don't know about yet?"

Gail patted me on the arm.

"Oh, sorry. Thank you."

"You are welcome. Now, go back to work."

She was the sweetest woman I think I ever met.

Doc Rogers and Stu walked to the bar. All three of the state officials were dressed in civilian clothes. Robbie could have passed for a miner or a lumberjack in a plaid wool shirt, blue jeans, and a thick leather belt holding a holster and his service weapon. Being off-duty was a fluid thing for a state policeman. Stuart wore black gaberdine wool pants, a white shirt, and a tweed jacket with leather sleeve patches. The gun he kept tucked into his pants, behind his back and under the coat.

"Did Stu take a job as a college professor?"

The tall cop lifted an eyebrow. "Yeah, he's all about education. No. The State promoted him to corporal and plain clothes investigator."

Doc went casual in a light suede coat over a blue shirt and jeans. He sat next to Dottie, and they talked like old friends.

"Is there anyone she doesn't know?"

Robbie smiled. "She knows the ones who count. Like many in the know, Rogers is an investor and seeks Dottie's counsel on such things. Same as those around Chicken, Alaska, and most states this side of St. Louis."

Dottie waved to me and Amy to come over.

"Excuse me? The boss wants me."

"Which one?" Robbie grinned.

"The bar owner tonight. Officially, I'm unemployed since we loaded Amy's Cat dozer."

Dottie stood and gave us both a hug. I couldn't recall her hugging anyone; even her favorite neighborhood dogs in town settled for a pat on the head.

"I'm going to miss you two over the winter. I can't wait for spring to see you again."

Amy said, "We'll be here."

"Me too, Miss Dottie."

"I thought I said so," Amy chided.

"Oh, I—"

Dot shook her head. "Hush, Red Face, before you embarrass yourself."

The crowd acted rowdy and celebratory. So, it must have been an exceptional year for everyone, or at least for those who didn't stay away. At the end of the night, I took my last request for the season, "The Spell of The Yukon," my usual choice to close with.

Coming to the poem's end, I dreamed of a new beginning.

"There's gold, and it's haunting and haunting;

　　　It's luring me on as of old;"

I held my arms wide, and it got so quiet you could hear the hiss and pop of the fire in the barrel stove.

"Yet it isn't the gold that I'm wanting

　　　So much as just finding the gold."

Amy was the gold I wanted. I closed my fists and drew them to my heart.

"It's the great, big, broad land 'way up yonder,'"

I swung an arm toward the window.

"It's the forests where silence has lease;

It's the beauty that thrills me with wonder,"

I clasped my hands in prayer.

"It's the stillness that fills me with peace."

The room went dead silent for a heartbeat, and then Gail jumped from her chair to applaud. I ended with a bow to a standing ovation and introduced Ricky and Amy back on stage.

Amy yelled, "Howdy!" imitating Mini Pearl from the *Grand Old Opry*. "I picked this song from a while back by Ray Price, called, 'I'll Be There If You Want Me.'"

I remembered the song but had never heard the Crocketts sing it. Everyone listened. Some who knew the words sang along quietly.

Amy sang the second verse.

"Love me, if you're ever gonna love me

> *I never have seen a road too ruff to ride*
> *There ain't no chains strong enough to hold me*
> *Ain't no breeze big enough to slow me*
> *I'll be there if you ever want me by your side"*

The music stopped. Amy stared at me, as did Gail, Robbie, Stuart, and Ricky.

Dottie elbowed me. "Ow!"

"Wyatt." Amy motioned for me to come to the stage.

"What?" I asked and started to step on stage, but she threw up her hand and stopped me.

I stood there getting red in the face, and everyone in the room held their breath.

"I believe you have a question to ask me."

Taking my hat off, I scratched my head, leaned in toward her, and whispered, "What?"

She stood tall on tiptoes. "Someone fetch me a stick of firewood so I can knock some sense into this dumb cowboy." While the crowd laughed, she said, "In your pocket; you brought it, right?"

The crowd went quiet and tried to hear.

I nodded. "Now?"

"Yes, now."

Slowly, I bent down on my knee and reached in my pocket. Then I stood again to get it out before returning to my knee. "Sorry, folks, it's my first time."

"Well?" She smiled.

I opened the little case and saw the velvet wore smoothly on the corners. "Miss Amy—ah— would you marry me?"

Dottie pulled a string, and a banner unrolled. It said: He asked!

The bar owner held two strings in her hand.

She said, "I need to think about it."

A collective groan came from the crowd, and then she nodded.

Dottie pulled the string, and another banner rolled out: She said yes!

Then they cheered, and I thought I might get beat to death by pats on my back. Chet delivered the most brutal blow.

Chapter 28

I only drank water. Generally, I like beer when I'm hot and thirsty and drink whiskey to forget. I wasn't thirsty and wanted to remember every second of the night. Amy and Ricky finished their session, packed their gear, and we went to the trucks.

It was a long drive to Anchorage, and time we got started. I pocketed enough gold to sell to the bank in Tok to have cash for meals, and I left the rest with Amy.

Robbie held a check for me and a notice that I was no longer an investigator. The State Police would solve Tim's case, if it ever got solved. My failure, but I provided them with leads and earned my keep. Dad and Uncle Max, both Texas Rangers, wouldn't see it so.

The state pilot took Robbie to Tok and flew Doc and Stuart to Fairbanks. Amy, Doug, and Ricky rode in the Dodge, towing the trailer ahead of us, acting as a pilot car for the wide load. The sixty miles to the Alcan Highway at Taylor Junction took four hours, averaging fifteen miles per hour.

I wanted to sleep, but it felt like the Christmas Dad gave me a horse. When we reached the pavement, frost heaves nearly high-centered the lowboy trailer twice. Road conditions slowed progress, but we pulled into Tok at 7:00 a.m.

Robbie joined us for breakfast. The café occupied an unpainted building with plywood siding and a metal roof. Two stacks emitted white smoke that drifted slowly across the highway. It shared a large frost-covered parking lot with a gas station and a general store. The eatery sat in view of the Tok Cut-Off Road, the way south to Anchorage or Valdez.

I ordered and ate a tall stack of sourdough pancakes, a slice of ham the size of a round steak, and too many biscuits to count. After breakfast, Doug and Ricky sacked out in the pickup truck and planned to take turns driving. I walked with Amy in circles around the two rigs, holding her hand.

"I need a job."

"No, you don't. You pulled enough gold from your claim to cover your expenses until spring," Amy said.

I kicked my heel down and cracked the ice in a water puddle. The temperature hovered in the twenties. The smell of grease and diesel fuel from the D8 mixed with the wood smoke from chimneys hanging in a layer slightly higher than the telephone poles. Someone went out to feed a sled dog team, and the howls could have raised the dead.

"I'm old-fashioned Texan, my whole family is too, and I won't step up to no altar without a job, and I don't want to wait until next fall to say I do."

"I'm planning on an April wedding before mining season. I want Dad to know what's happening. I'm afraid he doesn't have much time."

Tipping my head back, I took in the sky streaked with sunbeams spreading from behind the mountains like fingers from the hand of God. An omen? "I don't know how, but I'll have a job. I need to send word to Ma and the family. They likely won't be able to get here, but my folks will want the opportunity."

"We'll see about that. I want your family here, too."

"Not to change the subject, but what did you do with the, ah, the rest —"

She gave me a guilty smile. "It's difficult to get some things past you, not that we tried. It's mighty hard to hide something heavy and move it without people noticing, and since you found F & F's gold, the wrong people might notice."

"So, you hid it on the claim?"

"For a detective, you aren't too observant." She shook her head. "We loaded it on the bulldozer. An extra bit of load on a dozer weighing roughly 65,000 pounds, give or take, say a ton or more, no one notices. Boyd made some modifications last year when we pulled more gold out than expected. I anticipated needing a way to move it eventually."

After my mouth closed. "I'm not sure I'm smart enough for you."

"You're plenty smart about police stuff I don't understand."

"Maybe."

We arrived back at the front of the Dodge, and it was time for them to roll. Road construction on the Richardson Highway and more on the Glenn near Caribou Creek meant delays, so they needed to leave to reach Anchorage before dark.

With fogged-up windows on the trucks, I slapped the door on the semi and woke the driver. Amy rousted the boys, and they fired up the rigs to warm them enough to defrost the window.

Amy kissed me and rocked me to the soles of my boots.

"Don't make me wait long."

~~~

I watched as the two-vehicle convoy hit the junction and turned left. Robbie walked out of the café. He slapped me on the back and pointed to a bright red Chevy 4x4 pickup with an extended bed trailer hooked on.

"I told Bob we would be at his place early. He thinks early comes before daybreak. So we're running late."

We drove west of town three miles, turned on a dirt road, traveled another four hundred yards. We arrived at a sizeable log cabin, by community standards anyway. A pole barn sided in sawmill slabs and covered with a red tin roof sat off to one side. Mr. Parker worked for the road commission, operating heavy equipment in the summer and snowplows in the winter. Having a full-time job made him one of the wealthier residents.

My first impression was he stood somewhat taller than a fifty-five-gallon barrel and bigger around. He wore a green plaid jacket and matching cap with ear flaps pulled down to keep his bald head warm.

Bob adjusted his glasses and said, "I thought you said early."

"What can I say? I can't block love," Robbie replied.

"This the poor dumb sap who is marrying the Crockett gal."

"Actually, she's a Banks and has been for ten years."

I snapped my head around to look at Robbie.

Bob said, "I guess you never asked about her married name. Not sure Peoples is any improvement."

"Until I disgraced it, Peoples was a proud name in Parker County, Texas."

Robbie said, "Well, hitchin' up with that gal should help your status some."

Bob, Robbie told me was short for Robert Parker, said, "Amy may be the meanest woman I set eyes on. She didn't say so but implied she might shoot me back when we had the storm."

Bob looked me in the eye. "I made the landing at Normandy and wasn't any more scared than when she stood in the door of my plow grader and gave me the what for. You can have her, and good luck." He slapped his hands together. "I 'spect you're going to need a place to live soon, and the old Q-hut is in this mess of alder brush somewhere."

It turned out that Bob planned to build a kit house he ordered from a catalog. It would arrive in the spring. Electric power passed at the end of his road, and the power company would put a line to his new house. He needed to clear the brush and build a foundation in early spring.

"I got that two-story house coming in June. I bought this hut thinking of making it a workshop ten years ago and never put it up. Robbie said he was looking for something to use for a wood shop and told him he could have it. I didn't know he decided to give it away."

"You don't—" I began.

Robbie smiled. "It's an early wedding present."

"You're going to need a place to stay. That gal is a mean woman," Bob mumbled under his breath, but I caught him winking at Robbie.

We found the boxes containing all the parts for a sixteen foot by thirty-six foot half-round building. It's about six hundred square feet and roomy by Chicken standards. There were six boxes total, four by eight and two feet deep. The crates showed signs of rot in places.

Parker used his backhoe from his side business. He did digging jobs for neighbors. He lifted and slung the crates onto the trailer.

Bob's wife, Marge, came from the house to greet us and offered hot coffee and cake. She was much sweeter than the old buzzard she married, and the old grump minded his Ps and Qs around her. She congratulated me on our engagement, as she knew Amy. Marge worked at the general store, had served all the Crocketts there, and had even watched them perform.

Robbie gave me a shove for the door. "Well, let's get rolling. The day is wasting away, and it will be dark before you know it."

We thanked Marge for the goodies and waved goodbye on the way out. The trailer load pulled well on the tandem axles. Unlike the lowboy, it had higher ground clearance. Well east of town, Robbie drove steadily down the road.

"Where do you call home?"

He hitched his thumb back over his left shoulder. "Back there a couple miles."

I glanced back. "Where are we going?"

"I don't have any place to store these, and they are already starting to come apart. The weather's still holding, and Amy made a passable road into your place. Likely, it's frozen solid. Now is the best time to drag this onto your claim."

"I owe you a debt I don't know how to repay."

Robbie hooked his wrist over the steering wheel and kept an eye out on the road. "You could do me a favor."

"Name it."

"Did you ever work on a railroad?"

I gave a quick shake of my head. "No."

"Any objections to working on one?"

"No. I've ridden on trains, and I learn fast." I wadded up a pair of leather gloves. Labor, I figured, and I could handle whatever was needed.

"A friend of mine wants to quit his job, but he wants someone to replace him he trusts to do it right."

"I'm willing to try almost anything."

His expression changed, and I began to feel like when Gail started counting one and two. "Federal job, have to ride the train a lot to and from Fairbanks in all kinds of weather."

"I spent a winter in Chicken and one in Dawson; it couldn't be much worse."

Robbie braced himself and eased on the brake as we bounced over a frost heave. He glanced in the mirror.

"Still all there. I need to keep my eye on the road. Those bumps sneak up on you."

He looked content, like someone fitting the last puzzle piece on the table.

~~~

We reached the new turn-off to my claim and fought our way over Amy's new Cat trail. Once there, we used a cable come-along to drag the boxes off to the ground. Four hours after dark, we pulled into Chicken. Dottie stayed up late helping the bartender pack liquor to haul back to

Fairbanks and store for the winter. She gave us space on the floor near the fire to sleep for a few hours.

Before daylight, we woke Gene and bullied him into making coffee. The three of us sat around the table, trying to force our eyes open. A thumping sound came from out east, about to pass south of Chicken. I jumped to my feet, opened the door, and saw a flashing light in the distance.

"That's a helicopter." I pointed. "See it?"

Robbie said, "Sounds like it, but I can't see a thing but a blinking light."

"Those are the Commie spacemen. They fly around in the dark. I've seen them before over near the border."

"Gene, have you ever set eyes on a helicopter around here?"

"No, sir, Sheriff, I saw a picture in the newspaper once."

I said, "That ain't a spacecraft, and it might be a killer."

Robbie asked, "Do you have any ham radio operators near Gakona Airport?"

"One over by Gulkana and another in Glennallen."

"Try to send one over to the airport and put eyes on that chopper if he lands. Then tell my dispatch in Tok to try to reach Officer Tew at Glennallen to go over and obtain a description from the gas pump operator if no one else gets there first."

"Might not be the right guy."

"You ever seen a helicopter in Chicken since you landed in Alaska, Gene?"

"I said no. Well, only those spacemen."

Robby nodded. "When did you first see the spacemen?"

"Winter before last. Folks made out I was crazy, so I don't mention it much."

He spoke in radio shorthand with someone in Gulkana, then switched to the TOK ASP frequency, raised the dispatcher, and relayed the message to Glennallen dispatch in minutes.

~~~

Robbie didn't wait for a reply. We started on the two-hour-and-a-half drive to his office, slowed by the trailer and lack of a siren and red light. We switched to the State truck, which had a radio and emergency lights,

202

and headed for Gakona Airport as fast as possible while still staying on the road.

We lost radio contact in the mountains for a while. At Salina, Officer Tew radioed they missed the chopper but saw it fly away to the southwest.

Two men rode in the chopper, and he got the generic descriptions. The heavy-set white guy without an accent, and the other white guy —not heavyset and had an accent—the descriptions were of no real help. Robbie drove on and met the local officer at Chistochina.

He asked, "You have the letter I gave you?"

"The one taking back my police powers? Yeah, right here." I tapped my jacket pocket.

"Give it to me. I will mail it to you."

"I don't have a mailing address."

Amused, he smiled. "General delivery might take a while to catch up to you. Keep your other letter handy."

Robbie got out his wallet and handed me a business card.

"That's Darrell's card. Call him when you reach town."

"This is where I get out?" I looked dubiously at the State Police car, the only other vehicle.

"Yes, but it happens Officer Tew is patrolling down to Gunsight Mountain Lodge. He plans to have lunch with Officer Tandeske out of Palmer. Chances are, he will be on a run into Anchorage and can drop you at the Lucky Wishbone Café."

Robbie continued. "The owner of the café is a friend of mine and knows the Crocketts. He liked Tim and is a fan of the family band."

"Whatever you need, Robbie, name it. If I can, it's yours, no questions asked."

"I'll collect someday. Now, get going."

Chapter 29

Three hundred miles through the mountains and hours of riding in police cars, the last officer dropped me off at the Lucky Wishbone. It reminded me of the family-owned cafés in Parker County, a concrete block, flat-roofed building painted an almost white-tan color. I thanked Bill Tandeske for the ride and stretched, shaking out the kinks after getting out of his car.

Once I made it inside, I saw the counter bar with stools against one side and a few tables and chairs on the other. Behind the counter, the kitchen and the cash register sat by the door. Outside, the Glenn Highway became Fifth Avenue. The main road ran past Mountainview, near the airport, in front of the café.

I used a payphone near the door and called Darrell. After the call, from a seat at the bar, I ordered a basket of fried chicken and some fries , and enjoyed the quiet between late lunch and early supper.

When Darrell arrived, I wiped the grease off my fingers and face with a napkin. The PI didn't fit the mental image of a displaced Texas cowboy Robbie described. A bushy mustache fit, the weathered wrinkles and deep lines in his face, and a pair of piercing blue eyes felt right. Where things jumped the tracks, he wore a gray pinstriped suit, black tie, and fedora hat—more Mickey Spillane's Mike Hammer than Louis L'Amour's Chantry.

When he spotted my hat, he walked over and extended a hand. Standing, I took the offered hand.

"Darrell Johnson, at your service."

His voice sounded much clearer than over the phone, and the gravelly East Texas accent was far from a memory.

"Pull up a stool."

"I would, but I'm pushed for time. I have a meeting in the Anchorage Westward Hotel shortly." He nodded across the road. "I took it upon myself to rustle up a room for you at the Mush Inn over there as long as airplanes don't bother you."

"Only when I'm in one."

The PI smiled, my reputation proceeded me. "Good, let's talk over there."

I took it he wanted to talk privately. Taking my leftovers, we crossed Fifth Avenue under a gray overcast sky. It was warmer weather in Anchorage than Chicken, but still chilly, and snow dusted the peaks east of town. I checked in with the clerk and took the stairs to the second floor. The room key opened the fourth door on the right, and a single window looked towards downtown. A reasonably clean red carpet, cheap wood paneling, and a single bed left enough space for a small desk and a wood chair.

I sat on the bed and reached over to place my hat on the desk. Darrell took the chair.

"What do you know about the lawyer, Bilko?"

I scratched my head. "Nothing more than what you told me. Dottie seemed to have bumped into him sometime in the past but didn't offer much other than she didn't like him."

"Well, we all came here by different routes around the same time." He leaned his head toward downtown. "Anchorage is the little pond in which Bilko is a big fish, but he expects it to grow rapidly under statehood and plans to remain a whopper. To a degree, the mayor and local council are in his pocket."

The PI pulled a notepad from his shirt pocket and thumbed through the pages. "I never had any call to check his background, and I still don't know much. He joined the Army near the end of WWII and deployed to Japan during the occupation. He returned to the States, trained on experimental helicopters for the big green machine in 1947, and left the service as a warrant officer."

Darrell licked his thumb and flipped a page. "He graduated from college on deferment before joining the service. In '48, he went to law school on a VA loan in Philadelphia, came to Alaska by ship to Seward, and took the train to Anchorage."

Leaning forward, I waited for a break. "Helicopter training?"

"Thought that might interest you. I went to the only flight school here with a helicopter and instructor. And it is a Hiller but registered in the USA and painted bright red."

"And?"

"Oh yeah, about three years ago, Bilko started taking lessons and quit after soloing. The instructor noted his military experience and a natural ability with flying helicopters."

Traffic drove by outside as I mulled over the information. It didn't mean anything more than the lawyer flew choppers and went back and tried it out again with the only one available. He had the money to indulge.

Darrell said, "He owns a big house out in Turnagain near homes of other well-to-do residents in this city."

"Any connection to Barnes?"

Darrell put his notes down.

"Nothing directly, and it's strange. Barnes lives south of town in Oceanview on the bluff overlooking Turnagain Arm and Cook Inlet with a view of Sleeping Lady. A five-thousand-square-foot house on a ten-acre lot. Between Barnes's business and Bilko's financial wealth, they seem made for each other."

It made sense to me. "We know Byron was in contact with Bilko, and most likely Barnes, since the kid serviced all the mines around Chicken,"

Darrell coughed, clearing his throat. "Ahem. That's where things become interesting again." He smiled. "Not sure what it means, but three people loaned money to the hardware store's owner for his startup: Dottie, Barnes, and the shifty lawyer."

It made me frown, and I rubbed my chin whiskers. "Any reason to believe they worked together?"

Darrell checked his watch. "None, and nothing saying they didn't. Turned out to be a good investment for them."

I checked my information. "I have an address for Bilko on Third, near the courthouse on Fourth Avenue, Robbie gave me."

"Correct."

"How about Barnes?"

Darrell glanced at the door. He needed to go. "He works out of his house, but the company occupies a small office and a yard to store equipment on Potter Road. He's a gruff old buzzard, reminds me of LBJ, and might be as crooked. I'll give you his particulars before I leave."

A plane flew over, and I waited for the noise to pass before replying. "I haven't ever been a fan of politics, but Johnson was in the Senate when I left Texas with a reputation in Fort Worth."

Darrell shrugged it off. "The old codger Barnes is quite a business tycoon and has his fingers in a lot of people's pies and is friends with our State Representative in Congress. Bilko is buddies with city politicians, and as you know, Dot is affiliated with all the state politicians in Juneau. I recommend you take a crash course on politics because, one way or another, it's involved."

"I will need a cheap place to live over the winter and transportation."

Darrell thought for a moment. "A friend at Alaska Sales and Service has a fair selection of used cars. I saw a little grey Renault with excellent traction and hardly burns any gas. It's a sweet ride around town."

"Darrell, you sound like a salesman. I want something I can use up at the mine, a pickup and four-wheel drive."

He snapped his fingers. "I know an Air Force Tech-Sergeant fishing buddy. He is ready to rotate back to the States and has an old hunting buggy he might sell. In the meantime, see Chuck Harriman at Alaska Sales and Service. It's within walking distance of this place, and he can rent you something while I check around. If you don't mind the hike, walk through Mt. View. You rode past it when you came into town. Folks rent out rooms or apartments, occasionally a whole house but nothing big."

"Thanks. Where can I find your office?"

"Anchorage is a small place where I have a lot of clients with ties to Bilko, and I have worked for him in the past. It's better if we meet outside my office. Let's get together at Peggy's Airport Café. It's across the street from the flight training place and close enough to walk past Chuck's dealership about halfway to Mt. View. I'll be there at seven a.m."

"Tandeske pointed Peggy's out and said they serve delicious pie and sourdough pancakes. I'll be there."

Darrell split, and I went for a walk to familiarize myself with Anchorage. I found the local Safeway on Gamble Street, hooked a left towards the airport, and walked back to the hotel at dark. I saw the sign for the car dealer along the way. I checked in, but Chuck was out, but would be in about lunchtime tomorrow.

I ended my stroll back at the Mush Inn around dark. It stayed lighter longer in Anchorage than up north. From the payphone in the lobby, I called the number Amy gave me.

"Crockett residence."

"Mrs. Crockett, this is Wyatt Peoples and—"

A clanging came through on the phone, and the woman yelled, "Amy, your fiancé is calling.

"Sorry, Mr. Peoples, my daughter is upstairs helping her dad. I'm sure she will be right down."

"Hello?"

Amy's voice sounded different, breathy, and unlike the boss. I felt like a schoolboy calling his girlfriend.

"Howdy, you got home okay?"

"Dumb question, I'm on the phone. We unloaded the Cat and got done in time to eat supper. Did you pick up your building?"

Sure, it sounded dumb, but I had little practice speaking to anyone on the phone, let alone my future bride. "Yes, ma'am."

"Where are you staying? Robbie's or at the lodge?"

I watched a man checking in at the counter. "I'm in room eight of the Mush Inn."

"In Anchorage? Did you fly?"

She knew my feelings regarding airplanes.

"With the frost heaves and road construction, we were airborne from time to time, but I rode with the State Police. It's a long story."

"I want to hear it, but I need to settle Dad in bed. Mom and Dad can't wait to meet you."

In the background, Mrs. Crockett asked, "When are you planning to marry her?"

"Mom, I told you it depends, so hold on." She returned to tell me, "I need a bath and to shed these clothes."

I wanted to meet her folks too but it could wait. "I'm meeting Darrell at the Airport Café at seven in the morning."

"Okay, if I can force some help from my brothers to unpack everything, I'll try to meet you guys. I wanted to set eyes on the mysterious private detective cowboy."

"He sizes up more like a business owner than a cop, PI, or cowboy."

"I can't wait for tomorrow. Love you, bye."

"I love you too, bye."

I reached over and hung up the phone, holding it for a second or two. I felt odd saying those words out loud.

The lobby felt stuffy and too warm. Everything I owned was dirty, including me. I spotted the clerk who listened to the radio and heard the announcer say it was KFQD. I asked where to find a laundromat.

The desk lady, a native gal somewhere south of five feet tall, wore black-rimmed glasses with a little gold chain. Her raven black hair cut off at shoulder high, and she had a friendly smile.

"Down the hall, we have a washer and dryer, and I can sell you quarters, dimes, and detergent."

I bought a pocket full of change. Marti, the clerk, loaned me a robe so I could get all my clothes cleaned in one machine load.

While the clothes sloshed around, I went to my room and bathed. Running hot and cold water was a novelty after leaving Dawson. I remembered Mom's joy when my folks put in indoor plumbing at the ranch after the big war. I finished up laundry late and went to bed.

~~~

At about 6:00 a.m., I woke out of habit and slipped on a blue wool shirt with two button-down pockets and my best well-worn Sears jeans. Using a shoe brush, I cleaned up my hat, slipped on a fleece-lined denim jacket I picked up in Dawson after Shorty and Slim blew up my gear, and started walking to Peggy's.

The breeze blew in from the east, and the orange airport windsock flopped lazily, dangling barely more than straight down. The temperature in town registered in the high forties, so warm compared to Tok or Chicken. Light glowed above the mountains, but the sun wouldn't peek over for a while, and only if the sky cleared.

I spotted the flying service with a Piper Aircraft sign hanging off a large hangar-sized Quonset hut building. The red Hiller sat off to one side. Crossing the street, I dodged the potholes in the gravel parking lot and passed two Anchorage Police cruisers.

Darrell waved from a corner booth so I could recognize him. He sat at the next booth from the two officers, one with sergeant stripes on his sleeves. The PI wore lace-up engineering boots, jeans, a red lumberjack shirt, and no hat. His hair was thin and gray on top. He combed it straight back, and the sides trimmed short.

"What happened to the suit?"

Darrell said, "I told you; I had a meeting. You clean up well."

"Still scruffy. I ain't clipped my hair or shaved in three years. I reckon I'll meet Amy's folks soon, and I need to chop this stuff back."

"Yeah, I agree. I brought a map and marked some places to check for helicopters when you acquire wheels, which could be in an hour or so. I called the Tech-Sergeant, and he has quarters over on Government Hill north of here, as the crow flies, but we have to go across the rail yard and up the bluff."

"He's not working today?"

"He's on leave until next week when he catches a MAC flight to North Dakota and his new duty station."

"That's soon."

"Motivated seller. If he doesn't sell it, he will throw the title and keys to some airman when he gets on the plane."

"Might be in my price range."

"It will be, so once you are out of there and mobile, stop in and see Bill at his barbershop. It's on your way, in Eagle River, about ten miles up the Glenn Highway from here. I'll mark it on the map, but you can't miss it."

Darrell continued, "I made Bill's acquaintance before he arrived in Anchorage. He cut hair as a GI working on the Alcan Highway. When the war ended, he moved to Delta and decided to be closer to town and a liquor store. Now, Bill can walk home to his trailer, and the liquor store is on the way. He charges a fair price, does a good job, and talks race cars." Darrell explained.

Glancing up at the doorbell ringing, a man stepped in.

"You expect someone?" the PI asked.

"Yes."

The two cops got up to leave; the sergeant slapped Darrell's shoulder and told him to stay out of trouble.

"Not in my job description, Archie."

The officers left, and the waitress came over.

"I'll have coffee. I'm waiting for someone before ordering."

"Amy's coming?" he asked.

"I hope so."

"Well, let's talk business."

Darrell explained he had been too busy, and the state guys were too short-handed to do a comprehensive search for the helicopter north of Anchorage, considering all the possibilities. We suspected it came back in or near town as we hadn't spotted it anywhere along the route it likely traveled.

He brought out a map and showed me the public and private airstrips. They were the ones to check first. He suggested stopping at cafés or bars nearby where a friendly conversation might get me a lead on a helicopter.

"Folks like knowing things, and if you understand how to ask dumb questions, the local know-it-all will make you out as slow in the head. It is effortless if they think you're a dumb Texan."

"I can do that."

The doorbell jangled, and Amy stepped in.

Chapter 30

Amy's hair looked different. It hung loose and not tied in a ponytail. Her makeup was on, and she wore a blue dress that fit her just right with a wide, white belt, giving her a professional appearance. She never put on anything like it, even when we worked at Gertie's. She carried a pocketbook and stood two inches taller in white shoes with heels.

I caught my leg on the table trying to escape the booth, hobbled over, and accepted a kiss. I introduced Darrell and sat down to order breakfast. The smell of bacon, sausage, and pancakes had my stomach snarling.

"I'm sorry I'm late, but Dad had a fit and wanted to see you. I told him you were in town on business and might be a day or two. He wanted Mom to take him to the Mush Inn and hunt you down."

"We can go over after breakfast."

She put both hands up. "No, sir, and fair warning, that may be the last kiss you get until you clip back the brush on your face and head so you are presentable out of the wilderness."

I saluted. "Yes, ma'am."

"I'm not your boss anymore."

Darrell laughed and slapped the table to the glare of Amy's eyes. "Oh, you better believe she is, and don't ever forget it."

"Yes, sir, my daddy would walk into a cave barehanded, kick an old bobcat, and carry him out by the scruff of his neck before he told Mama no. I'm not saying Pa didn't say no a few times. I can tell you he didn't like it none."

"It isn't how it will be in our home."

"Yes, ma'am, if you say so."

Amy's eyes glared back at me. The PI ducked his head and chuckled at her. Then we all laughed.

After breakfast, she left to drop off some job applications and go home to help her mother. Darrell gave me a ride to Elmendorf AFB and met with the Tech-Sergeant. He took one hundred dollars cash for the truck and a few nuggets of gold to show off to friends.

The airman handed me the title and keys to a dark blue 1955 Ford 4x4 pickup.

Darrell had already visited all the airstrips in Anchorage and marked the ones on the map north and west, requiring attention. Tandeske checked in and near Palmer, so the map included airstrips as far north as Gunsight Mountain. Officer Tew scouted the area of Glennallen down to Eureka Lodge to include Lake Louise and the lodges along the Glenn. On the off chance there may be something there, he covered down around Copper Center on the Richardson Highway. Stuart and Robbie cleared everything north of Gakona.

~~~

Northbound from Anchorage, the road took me through Eagle River, a new community serving the local homesteaders and an expanding group of suburban commuters who worked jobs on the bases or in the city.

I spotted Bill's barber pole from the highway. His shop occupied a spot in the Eagle River Shopping Center, a one-story block construction building with a grocery store at the left end and his shop near the right side with other businesses or empty spaces in between.

The barber was in his sixties, like Darrell. His hair was still black and held in place with Brylcreem. Bill's eyes lit up when I walked in the door. An older gentleman sat reading the *Anchorage Times* and looked to be keeping the barber company.

"Well, now, I ain't seen a challenge like your head in all my days cutting hair. I can see teeth and eyeballs, so someone must be under it all."

"I've been mining gold in the Fortymile district and never saw a barber for the past three years."

The man with the paper glanced up and shook his head. "Nothing to be bragging on, son."

Bill asked, "You meet Dottie up there?"

"Is there anyone in Alaska she doesn't know?" I wondered.

"Might be a few recent arrivals. How much of your mange do you want me to chop off?"

"Darrell Johnson said to trust you. Give me a haircut that you think will please my bride-to-be. If you can find my face under these whiskers, I plumb forgot what I looked like. I haven't seen my chin since leaving Colorado. I might not know me."

"Texans, all full of crap and talk," the newspaper man said. He folded it up and sat it down. "I'll be back when it ain't so danged noisy in here."

With the clang of the doorbell, the oldster left with the rolling walk of a man with a stiff back.

"What's up with him?"

"McGregor has a low tolerance for people." The barber watched him hobble down the sidewalk. "Lifer in the Army. He joined after WWI. He made the landing in Africa and Normandy. Doc stayed in Europe until World War II ended. The ol' boy came stateside for a while, and Uncle Sam sent him to Korea. He retired as a Sergeant Major. They gave Doc a big ceremony out at Fort Richardson.

"Who is your bride-to-be, son?"

I sat in the chair, and Bill flung an apron around my neck and tied it. "Amy Croc—I mean, Banks."

"Tim's sister?"

My head twisted, and my gut turned like someone jabbed a bayonet in me and gave it a sharp twist. Regret for not finding Tim's killer? Maybe, but I hadn't given up hope yet. "Is anyone a stranger in this town?"

"You, and not many others. Everyone knew Tim. Damned shame what happened. I cut his hair a week or two before he went north."

"Anything bothering him?"

Bill didn't recall any concerns, and the conversation turned to race cars. He owned a Chrysler and ran it on the dirt oval up at Willow. He worked hard to earn his money. When I finally saw myself in the mirror, I honestly didn't recognize myself. After a few years of sobriety and living outdoors, I looked older, yet healthier. My only concern, I looked like a raccoon.

"That skin under the whiskers hasn't seen daylight for a long time. Fortunately for you, it's fall, and the tan around your eyes will fade fast unless you're headed back for Texas."

"No, I'm marrying the gold miner's daughter come spring, and we have a couple of mines to tend."

"Well, you look right handsome without all that—"

Bill pointed at the floor, covered seemingly with inches-deep clippings for about six feet around the chair.

I said, "She might have felt sorry for me, like an ugly lost dog."

"Well then, you will be a welcome surprise."

"What do you know about helicopters, Bill?" I asked.

He put his hands on the back of the chair, cocked his head to one side. Behind him, through the window, intermittent traffic passed in and out of the shopping center off and on the main road.

"I've seen one or two, but I don't think I would want to ride in one."

"Anyone talk about them in here?"

Bill grabbed a broom and started to sweep up the mess on the floor and to clear me a path to the door. "None I can recall."

"If you think of someone, could you call Darrell?"

Writing the PI's number down on a slip of paper, I handed it to the barber, who taped it to the mirror.

Outside, the chill on my face and neck made me happy that I wore a hat. In Texas, my head never got cold in the summer, and Mom used her clippers to give me and my brothers buzz cuts.

Once girls began to interest me, I let it grow long enough to part. A cowlick in the back always stuck out until my hat pressed it down. Wearing one became a habit for my entire life. I replaced the Stetson with a green cap or a helmet while in the Army.

My current head cover stretched some by all the hair and fit a bit loose, but it would shrink, or my hair would grow enough to snug it up. Looking around for a second, I forgot I owned a truck.

I drove north to Willow Airport. On the way back, I stopped at Wasilla Airport. Later, I took the cut-off road to Palmer. Turning north on the Glenn Highway, it wound along the Matanuska River, dividing the Chugach Range from the Talkeetna Mountains.

At my turnaround spot, my stomach growled at me, so I pulled into Gunsight Mountain Lodge. It took its name from the mountain, which looked like the rear sight of a rifle with a notch cut out of the middle. The last time I was here, I jumped out of Officer Tew's car and into Tandeske's on the fly.

Inside, I ordered a hamburger, potato chips, and a slice of rhubarb pie from a teenaged boy. I spotted some activity on the airstrip below the lodge from a window. A Piper Super Cub was undergoing some maintenance. The white with red trim Cub had one gentleman on the ground and another in the pilot's seat with several spectators standing around.

Curious, I took my meal and moseyed that way. "What's going on?" I asked after hiking down.

A young woman holding a baby on her hip said, "My crazy husband got some kind of Air Force rocket he is mounting on his plane."

"Why?" I watched with increased attention.

"Whitey says the thing is a one-hundred-horsepower rocket; his plane engine has a hundred and fifty horsepower. He needs to be able to load most of a buffalo and take off in about fifty to seventy-five feet." She said.

"Is that possible?"

"He's not sure, so he is testing it."

A chill breeze kicked up, and the clouds hung in the tops of the Chugach Mountains across the Matanuska Valley, all decked out in red and gold.

"How does it work?"

"Husband says the Air Force uses an electric switch, but he rigged it with primer and a cable in the cockpit. When he is set, he pulls the line and holds on."

I guessed it might be like riding a bull, and I couldn't miss it. Walking to where I judged a safe distance at the edge of the strip, I sat on the ground, finished the bag of chips, and waited. Finally, just before dark, they readied for a test flight. The jet assisted takeoff tube rocket, Whitey mounted between the wheel struts at a slightly downward angle, presumably so it wouldn't catch the fabric-covered plane on fire.

Whitey taxied onto the gravel runway, locked his brakes, and revved the engine until the tail lifted. He pulled down the flaps and gave a thumbs-up to the spectators. I'm not sure what I or the pilot expected, but it wasn't what happened.

A pop, then a reddish-blue flame blew out the back. His rocket had a burn time of only about twelve seconds but must have been an eternity for Whitey with his wife and kid watching.

I never saw the Cub go airborne. One second, it was on the ground, and the next, it was climbing nearly straight up. You could see Whitey bouncing in his seat. He retracted the flaps, and his left arm moved like a sewing machine. Someone yelled, "More trim down." Not that he could hear the advice, and the pilot looked plenty busy.

The tail elevator pushed down, but five seconds in, the rocket had sent him three hundred feet into the air and halfway through a loop, flying upside down. Once over the top, he began a rocket-assisted dive at the runway.

Inches from the gravel, he pulled parallel, the booster sputtered out, and the Cub slammed into the earth. The impact splayed the landing gear, ruined the prop, and skidded into a loop on one wheel, pirouetting around a grounded wing tip.

As the dust settled, Whitey, the owner of the lodge, stumbled out of the wreck and headed for the bar to get a drink. With mixed results from his experiment, he decided to call off any future testing. Following him to the bar, I ordered an Olympia beer and asked Whitey why he didn't use a helicopter.

"Fish and Game made it illegal to hunt with a chopper." Whitey lifted a shaky hand and swallowed a second shot of blackberry brandy.

"You know anyone with one around here?"

"No, but one flies over from time to time. A guide friend said he watched it land on the Knik River past Stephess's sawmill. Ain't much up there. Good sheep and goat hunting, but it's pack in and out area only. A strenuous climb through the brush to four thousand feet from practically sea level."

Whitey described the helicopter and matched the one sold in Canada. He had spotted the numbers but didn't remember them. After regaining his composure, Whitey grabbed a flashlight and went to survey the damage to his airplane.

A large map hung on the lodge wall near the door, and I found a gravel road not named on the map going up the Knik River, where the highway crossed the bridge. *Sawmill* was written in pencil and marked on the map.

~~~

Following a long but uneventful drive out of the mountains to town, I arrived at the Mush Inn near midnight. Amy had left a message with the clerk to call whenever I got in. We talked briefly and agreed to meet for breakfast at Peggy's. Now that I was groomed correctly, it was time to meet her parents.

Chapter 31

In the morning, we stood outside the door at Peggy's, and she held me at arm's length.

"Oh my gosh. What a change," Amy said.

I stood in the early morning drizzle typical to Anchorage in late August, under a cold, dreary, overcast sky with no sun visible.

"Wow, there's a man under there, maybe a better-looking one than I hoped."

"I guess so, if you're partial to raccoons." I turned, opened the door, and said, "Let's eat, but I'm not spoiling my appetite with breakfast. I'm going for coffee and pie."

The commuter traffic passed on the street, kicking up a spray and dimming the view of the airport. I spied the flight service business with the helicopter. After breakfast, I planned to stop in and talk to the owner and maybe get a close look at his helicopter. I followed Amy to a seat in a wooden booth with red upholstered benches.

When I sat, she reached for me with her finger and touched my cheek.

"I can't believe you're the same guy."

The waitress said, "Me neither, hun, if you are talking about the mountain man you sat with yesterday."

The waitress sported a name tag that said *Frieda*. She had a pretty face and a warm smile. She poured two coffees.

"Thanks, I deserved that, but if I hadn't worked for this young lady all summer, I might have waited another year or two to save money."

"He's a keeper, Amy. So, your usual?"

Amy said yes.

"What's the usual?" I asked.

Frieda said, "Well, you have only been here once so—"

"You remember?"

"Yes."

"I don't want the usual. I want hot rhubarb pie with a scoop of vanilla ice cream."

"Can do, and Peggy took it fresh out of the oven an hour ago."

Freida returned, refilled two cups, took orders from two other tables, and never wrote a note.

"I take it you have been here before?"

Amy put her coffee down and smiled. "I have, but not as regular as she made it sound. We eat here once every few months, and she remembers every meal I ordered. Freida knows how I like my eggs, what I want on my burger, and my preferred salad dressing."

"Where is she from? The southwest, I would guess, but not Texas."

"Arizona and New Mexico before coming to Alaska."

I nodded and changed the subject. "I'm on a scouting mission today."

"Can I come along?"

"I would love for you to, but I thought you would be with your dad."

"He likes his space, but we must be back by six. Mom is making a spaghetti feed tonight in your honor."

"The last time I ate spaghetti, it came out of a green K-ration can, and I warmed it under my coat to unthaw it enough to eat."

Freida brought biscuits and gravy for Amy. Then she sat two slices of pie and a scoop of ice cream in front of me. I pointed at the plate.

She smiled and winked. "You look like she hasn't been feeding you very well."

"I like her," I said, nodding at Frieda.

The food smelled wonderful, and the pie tasted as advertised. After a few bites of biscuits, Amy reached over and forked a bite of pie. It was a simple thing, yet it gave me a warm feeling all over.

She closed her eyes and chewed, savoring as if she hadn't eaten in a week. When her eyes opened, she frowned.

"Not the way you remembered?"

"No, it's not that. In all this time, you never talked much about yourself. There are things I worry about asking."

"Hard to get a word in edgewise while working for my slave driver boss, and when I had time, well, I couldn't make any sense." I smiled. "You can ask anything. With the catch, I won't sugarcoat things. Dad didn't for any of us, Mom respected it, and they are still married."

"The war, too?"

I looked down at my plate. My vision went blurry. My fork dangled between my fingers, and I rested my wrists on the table. When it cleared, I raised my eyes from a cold, dark, and frozen hell.

"You can ask, but be careful. There is a lot of it I can tell you I won't forget, and trust me, for anyone who wasn't there, they don't want to know."

"Sorry, but Robbie said the war did things to you."

"I understand. Can I hold up my end of this bargain? I left Texas and some demons behind. The man you met on Poker Creek is who I am today. My upbringing and my experiences since then are all part of me. I'll let you know right now, surprise parties and sudden loud noises behind me will likely receive negative responses. Saying so, I would endure Korea all over again to have you as my partner in life."

"I never read anything so romantic in a book."

I chuckled at her sarcasm. "Need to work on my sparking with a woman. I guess I'm better at reading poetry."

"Yes, and I'll save my questions. We have a lot of time ahead of us."

I thought of her last name. "I might have questions too."

"Maybe we can both wait a while and enjoy not working and getting to know each other a little at a time."

After telling her and laughing at Whitey's exploits, we walked across the two-lane road. The city planned to widen it to four lanes, and work had started.

The new international airport southwest of town replaced Merrill Field as the main commercial airport. Besides servicing and maintaining airplanes, the flight service business also did pilot training. The main entry door to the side of the hanger had an artic entry, an enclosed porch about four feet by four feet with a sign that said Office.

Out front, several small planes were lined up and tied to the ground. I wasn't fond of flying, but I recognized the Piper Cub since I had ridden one, and from Whitey's experiment. Next to it was a blue Taylor Craft, the name was printed on the cowling with yellow accent lines. A Cessna like the State Police used, painted white with blue accents, was parked near the gas pump. The Hiller helicopter sat off to one side and looked neglected.

A bell rang when I opened the door for Amy. Inside, a counter ran three-quarters along the back wall, and a door led into the hanger. Through the window behind the counter, I saw a skinny guy with red hair, a crooked nose, and blue coveralls, hustling to the hanger door.

A table with maps, pilot study guides, and three chairs occupied the outer wall. A small bookshelf hung from the wall near the table with magazines and other books relating to aviation and Alaska.

The door opened with a flourish, and the man stepped behind the counter.

"What can I teach you to fly today?"

"Not one single thing," I said.

"He's afraid of flying, but someday, I want a Cessna 170 to fly our kids out hunting and fishing."

"I can do that, and we have—"

"Not today, sir." I showed him the badge, a handy thing to have now and then. "I hope you can help me on a police matter."

"Chicken has a sheriff?"

Amy nodded. "They do now."

He shrugged. "My name is Fred Connoly; what can I do for you, Sheriff…"

"Wyatt Peoples, this Amy Croc—ah, Banks."

"If that's your ring on her finger, you better remember things like her name."

My face must have turned red, and there was more to see now.

"I called her boss and Amy for the whole summer and only learned her last— Well, forget it. A fellow named Bilko came in here for training on your helicopter sometime back."

"A private detective came in here asking about him and my trainer. It doesn't receive much use now, but I expect helicopters to become big business in the future up here."

Fred increased his volume as a ceiling-mounted furnace kicked on and blew hot air over my cowboy hat.

"I have that information, but I wondered if anyone else took lessons recently."

"I can't say recently, but two other fellows came back-to-back shortly after Bilko. He's an important lawyer, and I recognized him from the *Times* newspaper. The older one who trained on it said he owned a mine up on Poker Creek near the border." Fred dug through a file box. "The feller didn't know the least little thing about choppers. I had him checked out and flying fair after lessons."

Leaning over the counter, I watched the owner sort through the invoices. His paperwork wasn't very organized. He threw every invoice for maintenance, training, fuel, and parts in one box with the year marked on the front.

"Did he get a license?"

"Uh-uh, said he had a pilot and wanted to know what to do if something happened to him. Good thing to know."

"So, he owned a Hiller?

"He didn't say so, but it sounded like it, or at least he had use of one."

"You never saw it?"

"Nope, oh, here it is. Harold Barnes."

Amy said, "What?"

"That's the name he gave."

"Curly hair, going gray and bald spot in the back he combs over. About so tall." I held my hand a couple of inches higher than Amy.

"Sounds like him, alright."

"What about the other guy?"

He started flipping invoices on the counter. "They came in on different days but regular as clockwork. A younger fellow who drove a white truck with the new hardware store logo on the door."

Amy put her hand to her mouth. "Byron."

He looked up.

"You know him too?"

"My salesperson for our mine operation."

Fred nodded. "That reminds me. He said he had a lot of accounts up north, and a helicopter would make life easier for him for sales and deliveries. I'll tell you, one of these days, helicopters will be big business."

"Byron Lovell got murdered near Chicken last week. A helicopter was involved."

He stared at me. "So that's what this is about?"

Returning to Peggy's parking lot, we left Amy's Ford Fairlane and drove north to the Knik River Bridge. We turned off the highway past the Knik Drive Inn, and a sign saying: "Home of the Husky Burger." We took the gravel road that reminded me of the Taylor Highway, only, without the designation or even a sign.

The road existed to reach a sawmill and for logging operations. Past there, it petered out beyond Hunter Creek, where the logging ended, and a rock bluff ran out into the river.

We stopped and talked to the mill operator— a tall, lanky guy named Stephess. He said the helicopter we described flew by several times, headed for Palmer.

The mill operator thought it must be hangered at the airport. "It always comes by from over to Palmer or upriver around dark or early morning."

Not much we could do after we reached the end of the road other than turn around.

On the way back, we stopped at the Husky Burger, strategically located at the bridge's south end and east side. Handy for when the crowds came to watch when Lake George dumped, and the road closed. Amy said, "The flood is a regular event we miss each year while working in Chicken."

We ate burgers after Amy and the cook convinced me the meat was Alaskan-raised beef, and not huskies they grilled.

The whole business fit inside a twenty foot by twenty foot, barely one-story-high building. The ceiling, seven feet high or a little less, left scarcely enough room for me to wear my hat. Robbie would need to take his hat off. The outside of the place, someone had sheeted with unpainted plywood and lapboards.

Amy said, "Most bars and businesses here were built during the Eklutna Power Plant construction. They made the power building and footers from poured concrete, so most businesses along this road were cobbled from the old forms. Flat roofs and walls made from three-quarter inch plywood cut down to seven feet by the project contractor for making the footers. So, all the walls are that high and generally laid out in four-foot increments."

I mulled it over. "People don't like to waste things here."

My bride-to-be and a proud Alaskan said, "You mean, they are resourceful and broke, constructing communities from scratch using hard work and know-how."

"Yes, ma'am, that's what I meant. Changing the subject, Tandeske told me about the search around Palmer and sounded thorough. I'll talk to him and Robbie tomorrow and see if anyone searched past the end of this road."

"A great place to hide out, no road access and no cause for anyone to go up there. Boats are iffy in shallow water running with so much silt you can't spot sandbars. If you turn a boat over out there," Amy pointed her chin out the window at the water, "you drown. It moves too fast, and your clothes gain forty pounds of mud in seconds."

"Not to mention it is ice cold," I added, noticing the glacier coming down from the mountains. "Do people hunt up there?"

"Maybe, but much easier elsewhere."

Chapter 32

We left early enough for Amy to help with dinner and give me time to visit before we ate. I spent a wonderful evening with them. The sense of family and the welcome felt like home. Amy's dad spoke reverently about my time in service. Denied entry to the Army for problems with his feet, he had worked in a plant building parts for warships in Wichita, Kansas. Then, he moved to Seward, Alaska, after the war.

Dale told stories of working the docks in Seward, later working for the railroad, and moving to Anchorage. He repeated some of them. His kids and wife gave a sheepish smile at the repetition, and the family listened again to stories they heard hundreds of times.

Her father was not the man I briefly met almost two years ago. I made no impression on him he could remember. Amy's dad had been strong, vigorous, and commanding then. He appointed her as foreman, possibly realizing his decline before anyone. He aged ten years in less than two, a mere scarecrow image of his former self. My future father-in-law's health turned out to be the only sad part of the event.

~~~

The next day, Amy ran errands including a doctor's visit with her father, leaving me to search for a rental house in Mt. View. I found a log cabin with a basement apartment at the dead end of Flower Street. I paid rent for the month and moved out of the hotel.

Between Merrill Field and the Air Force base, it seemed like airplanes were everywhere, but no helicopters. I saw potential for them, but they weren't catching on very fast.

With a place to stay and nothing to do, I drove to Palmer and talked to Officer Tandeske, a wiry cop in his early thirties with dark hair and a dry sense of humor. Before leaving, I checked in with Robbie, who had nothing new but a weather report of a few inches of fresh snow. Freeze-up came right on time.

Neither officer gave me much chance to find a helicopter hidden at the end of the sawmill road. No place up there to hide it and no protection from the weather. Worth checking. Out of curiosity, I wanted to discover what they needed a helicopter for; as Whitey said, they were not for legal hunting.

I got up to leave the station.

"I'll see about having our pilot swing in low along that side of the river up to the glacier. There is nothing beyond there until the icefield, and for access to Chicken, it doesn't make much sense. Going over the glacier through Valdez and up the Richardson Highway is possible, but it requires covering a lot of ice and water with no road access. They would also have to refuel at Valdez," Tandeske said.

We consulted the map, and I didn't see any advantage, so I dismissed that route. Something else took them upriver. "I plan to hike up there tomorrow. I want to do something to find Tim's murderer." Maybe I procrastinated on getting a job, too. "Turns out police cases come together either immediately or in tiny pieces to the puzzle, in drips and drabs, as Mom would say."

The officer smiled. "Plan to get wet. Supposed to be another day of liquid sunshine."

Later, I met Amy at the Wishbone Café for supper. She wore slacks and a rain jacket over a sweatshirt. After hanging up her coat, she sat down, and the lines around her eyes spelled concern.

"What did the doctor say?"

Tears leaked out of her eyes, a more intense blue than her mother's, running down her freckled cheeks. She brushed the errant drips away with her sleeve.

"Bad news," her fist balled around a tissue and shook, "no, worse. The doctors tested Dad before we returned from Chicken. They had the results."

She stopped, staring at me as tears beaded and ran again. I waved the teenage girl waitress off, one of the owner's children who worked there.

"What?"

"The tests show his heart is weak, his liver is weaker, and his kidney function is terrible." She dropped the ruined tissue and picked up a paper napkin from the chrome holder on the table to catch the tears and blow her nose. "I'm sorry." She sniffed.

"Can they do anything?

I moved my arm around her shoulders, and Amy shuddered and began to cry in earnest. I assumed what it meant.

Signaling the girl in the white uniform with green trim, who watched with interest, I said, "We need some water."

Amy sniffed and added, "White meat chicken basket, too. We can split it."

I could down two of them by myself 'most any time, so she wasn't planning to eat much.

"To fully answer your question, the doctor said whatever they give him for his heart is hard on the kidneys and his liver. The meds for his liver are bad for his heart, and kidney medicine is bad for the liver and heart," she swallowed, "he's dying."

The waitress arrived with the water. Amy buried her face against my shoulder, sobbing until the food came. She drank water and picked at the fries but otherwise didn't eat. I felt guilty, but hungry. I ate.

We finished and drove the short distance to the new apartment. It was bigger than the hotel room I moved out of, but not by much. The sofa bed and armchair were covered in a rugged battleship gray plastic. A kitchen occupied one wall, with a white electric range, a counter with a sink, and some open shelves with plates and room for dry goods when I got around to buying some. The bathroom was similar in size to the one at the Mush Inn.

"Best place I've lived in since leaving the bunkhouse in Colorado."

Amy attempted to chuckle and started a run-on sentence regarding fixing it up, ending with saying, "You won't need it long."

"Why?"

"The doctor says Dad won't make it to Christmas without a miracle. He wants us to marry while he can still walk me down the aisle with the right man this time." She popped a grin. "Last time we walked, he said, 'This is the wrong one. You run, and I'll hold them off.' Turned out, he was correct."

"About the wrong man or the right one?"

"Both."

I didn't have sheets or a blanket, and Amy said she would take care of it in the morning from supplies at home. We slept sitting up on the couch.

I woke with a kink in my neck and the sound of her in the bathroom. "Wyatt, come here."

She called for my assistance with a bar of soap and a towel the landlord gave me. Helping her wash her back turned out to be the best decision of my adult life. Realizing her intent, it more than convinced me to get married sooner rather than later.

I asked because Tim told me she owned a house. "Where's your home?"

"Sold it last winter so I could help Mom out with Pop. I have an apartment in the basement of their place twice as big as this one."

"I guess I need a paying job and to start hunting for a home for us."

"You don't need a house."

"I can't live with your parents. It wouldn't be right for a man—"

"Dad needs help, or rather, Mom needs it with him, and he responds to me better than the boys. But I'll move in here with you. When I can."

"For how long?"

"My folks signed the house over to me back in December. I pay the utilities and the taxes. Mom stays as long as she lives. If I sell, the boys get a percentage. Dad's a planner. There was never a loan. He paid cash for it years ago. Took the hit on the taxes when we had a good year."

"I don't know."

She watched me. "Until you know, we can decide to leave her be, and I'll stay here. She planned to move to the apartment in the basement and give me the run of the house once." Her face scrunched, and she choked some. "Dad—" Amy paused, took a breath, and continued, "She decided that over a year ago when he started going downhill with the old timers."

The hurt look on her face tore a hole in my heart. Amy tugged on my sleeves, and I rested my hands on her hips. She stared through cloudy eyes and blinked back tears. "Aw, that ain't fair. Okay, we can talk about it, but I need a real job, or it won't feel right."

She left with a key to my place and intentions of buying groceries, and picking up pillows, sheets, and blankets from her mom's house.

~~~

I needed time to think and to cool off memories from our bath. Thinking more about Amy and her dad than where I drove, the twenty miles or so to the end of East Knik Road, which most folks call Sawmill Road, went by in no time.

The City of Palmer sat on the other side of the Butte, a massive rock structure left between the Knik and Matanuska Glaciers thousands of years ago. It stood nine hundred feet above the fertile farmland surrounding it. The government used the land as bait to colonize the area and create the town.

The river, a shiny gray mass, moved swiftly toward the Knik Arm. The weatherman predicted drizzle and got it half right for once. The sky was overcast and could rain, but for now, it held off.

Parking the truck, I followed the path into the woods. My jeans and jacket got soggy from dripping bushes after two minutes on the trail over the rocky ridge. A nearly vertical sheet of basalt formed a barricade to the upper river, but the climb kept me warm. I dodged Devil's Club, a thick-stemmed plant with huge leaves shaped like a maple, but larger than dinner plates. The undersides of the foliage and stems were covered in stickers. I learned the hard way in Canada the thorns break off under the skin and fester, thus, the name.

Wild rose bushes intertwined in the brush. The shoulder-high grass and other less painful weeds overhung the trail.

Topping the ridge, I noticed the tree leaves this far south and at low elevation remained thick and barely turning yellow. The path turned toward the mountain and then switched back to the river.

Fifty yards along, it looked like a dead end. I discovered it dropped four feet through the sagging underbrush and switched sharply toward the water. A steep, slippery incline slick as snot on glass and dangerous to walk on.

My foot slipped, and I grabbed a handful of Devil's Club. After that, I carefully held on to any available tree limb wherever possible. Doubling around again, I came to another four-foot drop to the sandbar below.

At the Husky Burger, I saw pictures of the annual floods hanging on the wall. They raised the river level twenty feet above the average high-water mark. The deluge resulted from the glacier butting against the mountain.

All winter, Lake George filled, and it melted through the ice dam each summer. The lake dumped millions of cubic feet of water and caused the annual event. I assumed water jammed with ice scrubbed the rock protrusion bare where the ridge extended into the flowing water.

From the sand bar, clear of the trees, I saw the glacier. Still miles away, a two-mile-wide, three-hundred-foot-thick layer of ice flowed from the mountains and disappeared into the overcast. *That much ice sure could cool a lot of beer.*

The Knik Glacier also chilled the air with a steady breeze I hadn't felt in the woods. Walking away from the brush and on a sandbar, it turned out to be more of a beach. Leftover flood waters pooled between the solid rock of the mountain and the wet black sand I stood on.

A hundred yards further, the mountain receded, and a steep gully appeared. Twisting my head, I saw a waterfall pouring from the typical U-shaped hanging valley shrouded in the clouds that obscured the peaks.

During the Ice Age, a smaller glacier fed into the Knik over a thousand feet thick and ran south past Anchorage. It merged with another river of ice coming from out of Turnagain Arm.

A clear-water stream coursed down the slope and dumped into the sand before twisting its way past me to the muddy waters of the Knik.

Recently, someone used a path on the other side of the little stream going up the bank and disappearing into the trees. I hopped across shallow creek channels to reach the path looping around a patch of trees — old alders, twenty feet high and as thick as my bicep at the bases, with a root system extensive enough to survive the annual flood.

I skirted the thicket and found another patch of beech half the size of a football field. The area was screened from a view other than from upslope or upriver.

In a trail used by black and brown bears searching for salmon, I made out recent boot tracks .

Multiple prints in different sizes, but one set stood out, a smaller boot, that had left a deeper imprint. Someone heavy with little feet or a small man carrying something heavy made it. Rain and wind removed any identifying characteristics. Following the boot prints, I found the marks where the helicopter landed multiple times. Just as Whitey and Stephess said.

Why come here? I slowly turned 360 degrees.

The answer, I suspected, would be at the other end of this trail. Walking back around the alders, following the path I saw going up the little valley, my hat flew off. I thought from the wind, but the whir of a bullet passed nearby, smacking off the rock outcrop, said otherwise.

Instinct ingrained from being shot at thousands of times, I dove left and rolled to the edge of the alders. It wouldn't stop a bullet, but it would make it harder to see me. Reaching back, I pulled the Colt Gail had given me. I brushed the sand off it, checked the round in the chamber, and full-cocked the pistol.

Turning my head, I looked at my hat sixteen feet away and saw the hole in the crown.

Someone owes me a new hat.

I gave a swipe across my head—no blood. With my face on the sand, the trail I followed was barely out of sight, and the cover of the alders made seeing the attacker impossible. Whoever fired held the high ground, hidden in a jungle of weeds and trees. Probably, they had a rock to hide behind. These alders looked thin.

Dirt kicked up inches from my toes, and the sound marked it as another rifle. A smaller caliber than the first shot, the difference in sound between, say, the M1 Garand and the M1 Carbine. Two shooters fired at me, one in front and another circling behind me over where the chopper landed.

Pushing up, I ran forward two steps—a person's average reaction time— to give the guy coming around a lousy angle. Hopefully it was not in the direction the big gun expected me to jump. Falling right, I rolled and heard the zip of a bullet, followed by a big boom from the tree line.

Firing twice at the last shooter and a puff of smoke, I grabbed my hat and ran for the rock ridge trail. Bullets zinged, ricocheting off the stone, and forced me to veer right.

The smaller rifle, semi-automatic, peppered bullets into the ground by my feet and near my head, pinging off the rocks. I ran full speed to stay ahead of them. I wanted to turn the bend, putting the basalt ridge between me and the shooters.

Reaching the apex, I realize their plan. Another bullet whipped past my ear and into the murky waters of the Knik River, foaming against the solid rock jetty. Trapped, I could turn into the rifles, or swim.

Amy's words came to me. *Clothes gain forty pounds in seconds, and it's ice water.* "Shit!"

I never stopped running, flung my hat into the current, dropped the . 45 into the drink by the protruding bedrock, unbuttoned my jacket, dropped it in the water, and somersaulted into the river. Figuring to drown, I survived human wave attacks while assuming I would die.

Adrenaline was my friend, and I hardly noticed the cold as the current slammed my back into the smooth rock wall. Water on my right swirled into an eddy by the sandbar I jumped from. To the left, it rolled and curled along the rock into the river's main channel.

I stood in a watery death trap five to eight feet deep with nothing to grab on to. For now, the current pinned me stationary on the cliff with my face out of the river. My rubber boots and clothes began to fill with mud and drag me down. I kicked the footwear off underwater while pulling my shirt and T-shirt over my head.

A bullet pinged off the rock near me and smacked into the water. With the sting of shrapnel on my face, I ducked into an undertow. The current dragged me along the rocks, slick with slime and polished by water. Helpful since it didn't hang me up, but it didn't slow me either.

Shedding the pants and boxers, holding my breath, I clutched the one thing I couldn't throw away: the sheriff's gold star. Bumping past the ridge point, I learned firsthand the feeling of being keel-hauled. I tumbled in a big circle, twisting in the eddy. I became disoriented until my foot hit the sand-clay bottom. Up must be the other direction.

Breaking the surface, I sucked in a big breath and paddled ninety degrees from the current, afraid of stiffening up before reaching the shore. The muddy water clouded my eyes, but the dark green of the mountain soared above me, and the ridge I climbed over twenty yards upstream faded in the distance.

It gave me hope. Less than a minute after entering the river, I hit the sand with my toes and pushed onto the shore. The air felt warm, crawling out from the river, not yet cold to the core, but my knees and elbows would barely bend. I kept moving and used a drift log's roots to pull and push me to my feet.

The adrenaline surge waned, and I shivered violently as my body fought to generate heat. Cold, thanks to the war, I understood intimately. I stumbled toward the trees and road. Stilt walking on feet as useful as wooden stumps.

I waved my arms, slapping them against my ribs and alternating while I stumbled forward onto the road. The truck keys were in the river. I stopped and considered. I had nothing to build a fire with other than the truck itself. If the shooters came to look for me, safety was a mile in the other direction at the sawmill.

On the road, I turned toward the mill not far on the other side of Hunter Creek. The stream wasn't much of an obstacle driving in, but fast-moving, knee-deep cold water and slick rocks didn't sound fun now. My legs started to function better, warming from exercise. Pain surged from my feet. I saw blood oozing from cuts on sharp shards of shale. Through blurry eyes, I kept moving forward in a hypothermic stupor. Finally, I stopped and stared at the frigid stream.

Placing one foot in, I cringed at the pain, then heard and spotted a green Chevy pickup rounding the bend. Covering myself with one hand, I waved the badge with my other hand.

Chapter 33

The Shetzle brothers had planned to hike up Hunter Creek to do some Dall sheep hunting. Unable to talk through chattering teeth and my dulled motor function, they wrapped me in a sleeping bag, picked me up, and shoved me in the middle. They cranked the heat on high and drove to the Palmer Alaska State Police Office. They started to go to the hospital, but after I gained some vocal ability, I insisted on the police station.

At the station, officers wrapped my feet in gauze and slapped a wad on my cheek. They dressed me in undersized insulated coveralls someone found while I told my story. I ended with, "Don't call Amy. I'll get home and get the spare keys. Tomorrow, I will pick up my truck."

Tandeske said, "Not a great idea. I think you are hurt worse than you realize."

He and his partner half carried me to a patrol car and drove to the hospital.

Amy stopped by the apartment, grabbed my spare truck keys and warm clothes, then drove to the hospital. Tandeske called the Anchorage office and sent someone to contact her since he promised me not to call her.

Hours of warming later and after a final tetanus shot, we walked out of the hospital at two in the morning. The predicted rain finally arrived and dropped like a blanket of cold mist.

Standing under the awning at the Emergency Room entrance, Amy pulled my arm. "Let's go home."

"No, I need my truck. We can pick it up and head home afterward."

"Damned hardheaded Texan I up and decided to marry. We can get it tomorrow."

I stepped carefully on bandaged feet covered in plastic wrap to keep them dry and clean. "You forgot, handsome." I ignored the tomorrow comment as I struggled with crutches.

My face twinged as the anesthetic wore off. The doctor stitched cuts from pieces of rock and bullet fragments he dug out. He cleaned, stitched, and treated the cuts from walking and jogging across broken shale with feet so numb I couldn't feel them. Bruises ran across my back from bouncing off rocks, and several bumps on my head I couldn't account for added to the discomfort.

The worst irritation turned out to be the dad-blamed Devil's Club stickers. Infection swelled the palm of my hand and fingers.

"I ought to make you walk."

A flash of endless days of fighting chilled my soul, a vision of slogging through snow-covered tundra marching out of the Chosen Valley. I stared into the drizzling darkness, my teeth grinding loud enough to hear. My voice came out like a first cousin to the Grim Reaper. "I've walked further and under worse conditions."

Startled, Amy stared, then dipped her head. "I suppose you have. Let's go get your danged truck."

We rode in silence since Amy already heard the story, and I tried to force thoughts of drowning and never seeing her again out of my mind. My Ford hurt my feet operating the pedals, but I insisted, so I couldn't complain.

Amy went home, and I drove to the apartment, hobbled on crutches inside, and crashed on the couch.

~~~

The knock on my door around 9:00 a.m. forced me off the sofa. I opened the door to State Police Officer Turner and a dull gray overcast. With one look, I decided Stuart was the only short state cop in Alaska. This one came to take me to the scene to help with the search. Only my feet were so swollen and tender that after watching me struggle to the couch, Turner decided I couldn't hike over the trail.

In lieu of escorting them to the scene, I dictated everything about where I got shot at, dropped my gun, and came out of the river in as much detail as I could remember. Turner took notes and made sketches before he left.

~~~

That afternoon, Darrell Johnson came over, and Amy brought sheets, blankets, and groceries. She beat the PI by a few minutes and made us peanut butter and jelly sandwiches, and we drank coffee as I retold the story.

Darrell said, "A chance there's a cabin or cave nearby. A friend of mine who works for Rutherford Engineering, a geologist, found a couple

236

of caves in the Eklutna Lake area, but around the turn of the century, prospectors crawled all over the area hunting gold. They built shelters and rode out winters to get an early jump on prospecting in the spring. Resourceful ones ran traplines for furs while they waited."

I wondered aloud, "What would be there to attract someone with a helicopter, and is worth shooting me over?"

Amy munched on potato chips and shifted her attention to Darrell.

"The location is for secrecy, a place to meet or hideout, with limited access to a road from Anchorage. Our suspect doesn't want to be seen with someone and associated with the helicopter. My theory is only a guess."

She asked me, "Did you tell him about the pilot training place?"

"I forgot. Would you believe, besides Bilko, Barnes and Byron took lessons flying the Hiller during the same time frame on different days?"

Darrell said, "Now, there's something to consider. Three possible pilots. Maybe a way for one to be gone to Chicken long enough to kill Tim and not be missed or reported out of town."

I held my sandwich short of taking a bite. "I thought so, and something else. Where would Barnes run into killers like Skinny and his pal? They might have been job hunting, but Robarts said Barnes hired the felons. It sounded like he hadn't consulted his foreman."

Darrell said, "I suppose it is possible, but more likely, a lawyer referred them. One with leverage to motivate felons to work for the old goat."

"Yesterday, I didn't find the helicopter, but after talking to the mill operator, the feeling I got from a short look around, it must be close, but we know, not at the airport in Palmer."

Darrell's brow wrinkled as he wiped some jelly off his lips with a paper towel, then took a sip of coffee. "It's possible. The state boys checked the area well, but some homesteads have barns big enough to hide one."

"Barnes is into real estate speculation. What's the chance he owns property up there?" I asked.

"I'll look into it. Bilko is a real estate speculator too and buying up land on the hillside here in Anchorage."

Darrell gestured to the east, and Amy nodded, understanding, but confused me. "What hillside? This place is covered with hills."

Amy said, "South and east of Anchorage, Rabbit Creek and O'Malley Road. Not much up there other than deep wells and a view. Guessing the view is the primary selling point."

"I don't know either of those places, but you're saying the mountainside rather than the hills."

Darrell said, "You two can discuss geography. I have a job, and it includes a stop at the land office to search titles for property around Palmer. Might be a two-day project unless I get lucky."

Amy left to check on her dad. Once they departed, I pulled an ice tray from the fridge, broke out the cubes into a bowl, and stuck my sore hand in it.

Bored, I hobbled to the truck and drove ten blocks to Brewster's Department Store. I made my grand entrance on crutches. They carried a bit of everything, but also Western wear. I bought a pair of rubber boots you can pull over shoes, with the metal clasp to snap them closed. They would slip over my bandage-wrapped feet. I picked out a new fleece-lined jacket, two pairs of jeans, and two wool shirts. Considering winter approached, I bought a cap with ear flaps like the one Robbie had worn during the blizzard.

I cussed about burning through my funds while driving home on North Flower Street. I passed Parsons Street and saw the Government Hill Power Plant and the Air Force north-south runway. Also, I spotted trouble —an Alaska State Police car and Amy's red and white Fairlane parked on the curb in front of the house.

Standing near a small spruce tree next to the wooden walkway to the cabin, Officer Tandeske spoke to Amy.

"Where did you go barefoot?" she asked.

"Well, I wasn't barefoot. I pulled some wool socks over the bandages. I bought some boots I can slip on, decent in-town clothes, and this jacket."

Her lower lip still stuck out, and she shook her head.

I turned to Bill. "You have questions?"

Tandeske said, "I might have a few, but I brought you some things also. Go in and let this gal fix us some coffee. I'll be right there."

"I can fix it."

He spoke over his shoulder on the way to his car. "That's not what Robbie says."

"I warned him."

Amy prepared the percolator. Bill walked in carrying my hat and the Colt 1911.

"One of our guys used a rope and a magnet big enough to tow a car to find the gun about where you said to look. It is scratched some and full of sand and mud. Mountain View Sporting Goods is on the main drag. You can get some cleaner and oil there."

Amy said, "I have everything at my place. Gail taught me to shoot that one, so I bought a government surplus 1911 to practice with. I keep it at home. We can go there for dinner, and I'll show you," she tipped her head toward me, "my apartment."

She started the coffee heating and came to the table. The soggy hat weighed three times its dry weight. Amy took it and swung it around, examining the entrance and exit holes. "Lucky he was a lousy shot."

"I'm lucky he was an excellent shot. They both were." I stuck a finger in the hole. "I figure they wanted me to drown and never expected me to make it out alive. I remembered what you said about the silt and started ripping clothes off before I hit the water."

"Fewer questions if anyone ever found your body with no holes in it," Bill said.

Amy nodded her agreement.

"Where did you find my hat?"

"A hundred yards downstream, half submerged on the far side of the channel. Fish and Feathers brought their riverboat from the bridge and searched both banks. The pistol and the hat are all we recovered. It backs up your story. We found pockmarks in the rock, left by two different angles and guns. But no bullets were recovered. My shift partner owns a metal detector and plans to take you up there to show him where to look."

"You located where they shot from?"

"Hard to say exactly where, no brass casings, so they picked them up. We found a dug-out cabin with a sod roof on a bench above the high-water mark. Invisible from the water or the air because of the overgrowth. It's old, with no windows, and a newer cast iron Franklin wood stove and stovepipe, indicating someone fixed it up. They either burned everything in the stove or cleared out with it."

We drank up the coffee and talked over the case. Barnes was connected to Skinny and Shorty and, therefore, to the F& F Mine murders.

"Byron links to Bilko and Barnes, and all three to helicopter lessons at nearly the same time. In my opinion, a circumstantial case for criminal conspiracy and felony murder charges."

Only Bill pointed out, "We have no solid evidence of a conspiracy or a way to connect any of them with Tim's murder, let alone recently trying to kill you. The mysterious helicopter is key and putting someone in it at the time Tim and when the salesman got killed."

I said, "According to Darrell, Barnes and Bilko were in their offices when I got shot at, and Byron is dead. But the helicopter is still missing."

Tandeske stood to leave. "One other matter." He reached into his pocket and handed me an envelope from the State of Alaska. "You've been served and must appear next Friday for a coroner's inquest in Fairbanks regarding Skinny's untimely passing. Officer Turner served Doug already. The State will pay your airfare—"

"Do I have to fly?"

"Quickest, but you could drive. If you break down and don't show, the court may find you in contempt since they offered you a ticket. Just saying, I've seen your truck."

"Can he take the train?" Amy asked. "I'm sure my brother will because he can ride for free. He started work again for them down in Seward."

"I don't see why not as long as he is in court and on time."

An hour later, I sat at the table alone with orders from my future bride to heal. Mom used to say— generally after I got hurt forcing something— that patience was a virtue I lacked. I felt plumb short of it and wanted to make things happen. Then I shoved my hand in the ice again, a reminder of my last try.

Chapter 34

When it came time to travel to Fairbanks, my feet healed enough to get winter snow boots on, and it would not be too warm there. The ground there would be frozen, and sunny midday temps barely cleared the freezing mark. Doug rode the train with me. Amy planned to come along but canceled when her dad suffered an episode.

A scenic trip, but views of the mountains were shrouded in clouds. The overnight ride took all of twelve hours.

After deboarding in Fairbanks, we caught a cab downtown to a hotel and stayed overnight. We chose a place close enough to walk to the Third Avenue and Cushman Street courthouse after morning coffee.

Robbie met us at the courthouse with his map. He said, "Darrell found a homestead at the northern end of Wolverine Road, north of Palmer. If you look up remote homesteads in the dictionary, they probably have a picture of it."

"Bilko acquired the property through settlement of debt for legal fees. The family moved off the place back in '57. A gate blocked access, and weeds were growing on the road, indicating no one lived there for years. The main road ends at Wolverine Lake on the map, but land office records show it runs to the property." Robbie jabbed the location with his finger. "Tandeske confirmed it reaches the gate and assumes it goes on to the house. It looks like an occasional moose hunter or someone checking on the property goes up there, but very infrequently."

I studied it. "This is the Matanuska River," I poked it, "and the Glenn Highway route to Gunsight Mountain over Eureka Pass to Glennallen."

"Yes, and to the cutoff road to Gakona and Tok. The way you took to Anchorage," Robbie said.

"Judging from the scale, it would be possible to fly to Gakona non-stop from there."

"You're sharper than the average Texan." Robbie said.

"Not necessarily. I'm just thinking out loud. So, he must refuel somewhere around Palmer when he gets back. If so, why haven't your guys found the pilot and chopper?"

"I guess the people in Texas never lie to the police."

"You know they do. Generally, lawmen know the most likely to fib and why." I replied.

"You talk to Bill Tandeske and tell him what you are thinking. He might suggest places fitting that description. Somewhere, a guy out of work could go undercover and talk to folks about winter employment."

"Lodges with gas stations?" I asked.

Robbie shook his head. "No, more likely, construction companies with bulk fuel trucks and large farms, too. When I worked around Palmer, there was a mine that supplied coal to the military bases. The Army ran a railroad spur line to Sutton and into the mine."

Doug said, "Still do. We did some track repair up there about this time last year." He added, "Most of them won't be hiring this late. Easier to find a job at the airport. If you know someone, the railroad has some decent winter jobs."

"Who did you know?" I asked, and Robbie looked interested.

"Dad, he worked for them when he came to Alaska and before he started teaching. He knows the old timers who are in charge these days."

"I didn't know he was a—"

A court officer cut me off. "Wyatt Peoples?" I nodded. "You're up." I followed the young guy into the courtroom.

~~~

After court, I kept the map on a promise to return it since Robbie used it for hunting in the Chugach Mountains. The jury found Doug not guilty by self-defense, and the consensus was he saved the taxpayers money. With no death penalty and a likely life sentence for double homicide, he would have cost the state plenty.

The following day, we caught the Moose Gooser to Anchorage. The train got its nickname from the number of moose chased or knocked off the tracks.

I left the train at Anchorage, and Doug stayed on to Seward, where he worked at the rail yard this year.

Riding the rails beat flying, and I liked it. The communities along the route became places I longed to explore. The weather ruined the stop at McKinley Park. Clouds so thick you couldn't locate any mountains, let alone the tallest mountain in North America.

The conductor said the views of McKinley on a clear day sealed his career on the rails. He talked a lot about the railroad's origin, but being the only federally owned railway in the USA struck a chord.

I picked up my truck from the parking lot. Labor Day was only three days away. A stiff wind blew out of the northwest against the Ford, giving the air a chill. Sailing foliage filled the air and skidded down Fourth Avenue, drifting against the curb by Woolworths and down past the movie theater. I intended to meet Amy somewhere for dinner but drove to her house instead of waiting.

At Amy's, birch trees on either side of the driveway sprinkled autumn gold across what passed for a lawn. If green and mowed, it was a lawn, grass or no grass. The two-story wood-sided house looked fit for a suburban home in Fort Worth, only newer. An older house in Anchorage was anything more than twenty years old.

I shoved the truck door closed, and Amy ran from the house in tears.

"What happened?"

"Dad got disoriented last night and fell on the stairs to the first landing." She wrapped her arms around my waist. "He's at Providence Hospital. He broke some ribs and bruised his arms."

"It's okay. Your pa will get better."

She went quiet. Looking at my chest, her hands tightened around two fists full of my jacket. "No, Wyatt," her voice lowered and steadied, "he won't. Doctors are afraid he will only mentally deteriorate faster." She took a deep breath. "They say he might be able to walk in a couple of weeks."

"That's good."

"Yes," I waited a while before she continued, "but soon after, he may forget who we are, or his heart could stop or kidneys or anything. He told me today that his dream is to walk me down the aisle."

I didn't think about or hunt for words. "You tell me when, and I'll be there." I let her go and punched my fist into my other hand. "But I need to find a job. Now."

"Well dear, with or without a job, on September twenty-fifth, we stand before Mom and Dad's preacher. I booked the church today."

I blinked. I'm going to be married. It triggered a thought. I wrote home to my mother a half dozen times in four years. Her last letter came to Chicken before the road opened, and it had gotten blown up. I hadn't responded yet.

"I have to call home and explain. It's a long story for the short notice." I gulped. "They don't know for sure I'm alive, and I have to tell them I'm getting married."

"You call your momma on our phone. For now, come in and eat something. You look like you are starving without all that hair to cover it up."

"I'm marrying an angel, but I need a job."

"One track mind." She wiped her eyes, took a deep breath, and shoved me toward the door. "Go in the house."

~~~

Mom had mixed emotions after my calling her long distance and explaining the circumstances. Likely, they couldn't afford the trip, but she made us promise to come home to Texas soon. Her next question was, "What kind of work are you doing?"

Rather than say none, I said, "Got a temporary slot as sheriff and investigating a murder."

Mom said, "I'm happy you are working, but I worry about the *temporary* part. You have responsibilities, you know."

"Trust me, I know it."

We hung up, and my gut hadn't been right since Amy said yes. Someone tried to kill me twice, then the trip to Fairbanks. Job hunting was always on my mind, but hunting for one was different.

I could easily get a construction job come springtime, but then I couldn't work the claim. I didn't want to lose my mine based on the gold I found so far. Pa and Ma both warned me love was complicated, but it slipped my mind. *What next?*

~~~

Early the following day, I woke on the Crocketts' couch. Amy came upstairs and fixed coffee. "What's your plans today?"

Yawning, I rubbed my face stubble, and it felt funny without the beard. "I have exploring to do around Palmer."

"Fantastic, I'm bored with Dad in the hospital."

The coffee perked and smelled good. I braced myself. "I meant to go it alone."

"No, sir, last time you went snooping, you ended up half-frozen naked as a jaybird." She turned back downstairs. "I'll get my gun and be right back."

I guess I got used to taking orders from Amy as my boss. I realized I enjoyed it. Smiling, I stepped out to go to the truck. Her mom caught my sleeve as I hit the stoop.

"Wyatt, you're a good man. All my kids say so, but you'll have to learn to put your foot down when she needs to be told no. And I never said so, you understand?"

"Yes, ma'am. If that time comes."

"If the time comes for what?" Amy asked as she topped the stairs.

"That's between Wyatt and me, and you better quit bossing him around so much. If you ask nice—"

"Saves us both time if I tell him what he wants to do."

Her mom said, "Get you a Thermos of coffee, take off out of here, and don't shoot yourself with that hog leg."

Amy's pistol sat in a well-worn, custom-made holster, snugly on her hip and sexier than any negligee she could have put on.

"What are you packing?" I asked.

"Smith and Wesson .357 Magnum. Two-legged varmint gun, Daddy calls it. He gave it to me after I married Banks. I never shot him, but I considered the idea a few times." The devil twinkled in her eyes.

~~~

We drove north of Palmer and got lost a couple of times. The roads didn't have signs, and the map didn't show names, but we found the landmarks we needed at Wolverine Lake. Wolverine Mountain was the only identifiable location we could see over the trees, but it looked much closer than on the map.

We drove to a gate fitting Bill's description. Fifty feet on the other side of the barbed wire, a bull moose grazed. The velvet covered forked horns were not big, but the animal was huge.

Amy said, "Dang it, I should have brought my rifle."

"Why?"

"Hunting season, I've got a license."

I shook my head no. "I'm on duty and have a job to do." Opening the door, the moose took off, high stepping for the woods.

Amy said, "Young bull, the best eating. The ones with big racks are tough, mostly suitable for sausage."

Was there any way she could be more perfect?

"Wait here."

"No. I'll follow along close enough to keep you in sight so no one sneaks up on you again." We started hiking. "Didn't the Army teach you anything about walking quietly?"

"Yes, but I'm out of practice with people shooting at me, and the Army went out of their way to make loud noises and ruin my ears. If things go sideways, you run back to the truck, turn it around, and if I don't show up in a hurry, go find Bill Tandeske and drag him back up here."

"Why isn't he out here right now?"

A fair question, and although I wasn't sure I wanted to be a lawman, I wanted to solve Tim's murder. Trying to drown me made it personal. "Well…"

"Well, why?"

"Because I, ah, technically, we are trespassing, and he needs a warrant to do that legally." As a semi-sort-of State Investigator, I did also. Robbie said they took that back even though the paperwork he kept sat somewhere in the mail system. The State would happily deny any part of my actions.

I heard a shot in the distance behind us and turned. Amy gave me a shove. "Go on, it's hunting season. You might get hit with a bullet by accident this time of year."

The reports from Bill looked to be correct. Willows and alders grew in small patches in the drive about as high as my shoulders. The ditches were soft enough that the moose feet left holes four inches deep. Glancing back, Amy rested against the fence.

Ducking low, I used the new brush for cover. Peeking over my shoulder, I couldn't see Amy, but then I spotted her hand waving me on.

Glad those Chinamen weren't as good at hiding as my fiancée.

The road drifted left, and ruts filled with muddy water. The breeze picked up straight from the North Pole. Most of the trees were spruce and dark green, nearly black. Patches of undergrowth with berries and Devil's Club made my hand itch thinking about it.

Sneaking through the weeds, I caught the scent of wood smoke, the wind in my face coming down the valley. Smoke meant fire, and out here — people. From habit, I raised my arm and closed my fist. In Ranger School, a signal for those following to stop and find cover. I hoped Amy knew from watching war movies.

Chapter 35

The building wind whispered through the limbs of the tall spruce, some higher than fifty feet tall. I heard nothing else. Easing ahead, pressure against my leg stopped me. Looking down, I saw a single strand of clear monofilament fishing line pulled taunt against my knee.

In Korea, I would expect a booby trap like I nailed Skinny with. Here, it was probably an alarm system. Line was tied to cans with rocks. Moose, foxes, wild dogs, and bears likely provided many false alarms, but if I tripped it, someone would check.

I wanted more information, but also not to engage with shooters with only a pistol. It hadn't worked out well last time. Discretion being the better part of valor, I backed away and felt a hand.

I jumped and turned slowly, not wanting to be shot—Amy. My heart sounded loud in my ears, and she scared the crap out of me. Pointing two fingers at her eyes and then up ahead. Using the same fingers, she walked them across her hand and followed with a question mark in the air.

She wanted to know where to go next. I gestured to a line near the ground, pretending to pull an imaginary line ringing a bell. I pointed to the truck.

Once in the Ford, I explained someone lived there, and the alarm system meant they didn't want guests. Enough information, I thought, for now. Later, we might go out hunting and claim we discovered a helicopter there, accidentally— of course. We might get enough for a warrant if other evidence points to this location.

On our way back, we stopped at the ASP office in Palmer. Tandeske was out, so we walked downtown. We passed the Koslosky department store, locally famous for its big African lion in the window. Locals referred to it as "Cost-a-lots-ski's."

On the next block was a café with a view of the water tower and Pioneer Peak. About halfway across the valley to Pioneer Peak was the Butte. The Knik River ran on the far side, and the Matanuska on the close side.

We finished our burgers and fries and talked some about the wedding.

Tandeske came in, and the kid behind the counter said, "Your favorite? We picked the berries up by Long Lake last weekend."

"Yes, sir, with coffee."

Amy yelled, "Make that three."

The kid gave her a thumbs-up.

"What did we order?"

Amy smiled, bounced her eyebrows, and said, "Yum, the berries up there this time of year are blueberries, and his mom bakes the best pies. He plays forward on the Palmer Moose High School basketball team. His father is the coach."

"You know more people than Dottie."

"Dad taught school at Anchorage High before they built the new one called West. They built a newer one at Bragaw and Northern Lights called East High. He also coached basketball."

Bill said, "You were a cheerleader and sang in the choir."

I looked at Bill, then back to Amy.

She answered the question in my expression. "Bill went to Anchorage, too; it was a small school back then."

The pie met expectations and then some, and so did the coffee. The officer said, "Because of the proximity and travel distance to and from Chicken, I suspect Sutton to be a refueling source. It's a likely place to take another peek at."

Bill continued, "The area is not exactly crime-riddled, but the citizens are clannish and used to handling their disputes. They didn't care for oversight by the State Police or the Territorial cops before them. They tend to be suspicious of strangers. Many outsiders come looking for work at the mine, but generally, the owners hire locals or face strikes and shutdowns. A big strike would bring in the National Guard because the coal they produce supplies the power and heat on the bases along the railroad."

"Better to appear curious and ignorant. Sometimes, that works. People everywhere want to sound smart and important," Bill said.

"I've used the dumb Texan act before with reasonable luck."

She smiled and nodded. "Wyatt's been pulling it off for years."

Bill grinned. "Happy hunting."

"Bill, we're having a wedding on September twenty-fifth, and there's no time for fancy invites. You and Debbie come to town and help us celebrate."

"Yes, ma'am. We wouldn't miss it. You broke my heart last time, but now I have Deb, and life is full. Congrats." Tandeske departed.

"Was there more—?"

"No, I hardly knew him, but I was the coach's daughter and a cheerleader. Everyone knew me, and a lot of boys had crushes. You should get used to it."

"I'm feeling lucky. Let's go hunting helicopters."

~~~

We took a short drive along the west bank of the Matanuska River through the woodlands to Sutton. Besides being a gas station, our first stop was a commercial truck and tire repair shop. Pulling in, we parked in front of a long wooden building. Painted white and green, it had seen better days. There were three bays with doors that swung open tall and wide enough to pull semi-tractors inside and a small office door near the two gas pumps.

Coming through the door, I saw a kid behind the counter, no older than the one who served us lunch. He wore grey pinstriped coveralls smudged with oil and grease. He wasn't tall but looked hard as nails, and the name tag said, appropriately enough, *Stubby*.

I said, "While in Anchorage, I heard about a coal mine out here, and a guy could find some fossils there."

The boy picked at a scab on his chin. "You sound like a Texan. What happened to your eyes?"

"You have an ear for accents. I shaved my beard recently, and the tan...never mind."

"No, sir, just you all sound alike. You see here, that's this place." He pointed to a blank spot on the counter. "Out here is the main highway." Stubby ran his finger along the lip of the counter.

"Over there, out the window, is the road what runs to the coal mine, but it doesn't go straight. Some turn-offs put you on dead-ends." Referring to his imaginary map, he drew a dirty finger across ninety degrees to the edge. "There's a big silver tank here, and you don't go straight, you turn left..."

After ten minutes of describing broken-down road graders, big rocks, and other landmarks, I determined I would never find the mine. I admired the kid for his work ethic and efforts to give directions in a place where it appeared to me the government passed some ordinance against putting up street signs.

The second thing I learned from him was that a bulk gas station serviced the trucks and heavy equipment for the mine on that road. The railroad delivered the fuel, and the little depot had a helicopter pad the Army used when they inspected the mines.

"Other helicopters buy gas there, too, sometimes." Stubby was seriously proud he knew the difference between civilian and military choppers. "I seen a gray-colored one not long ago, a day or two, maybe a week at most. No others for at least a month."

Apparently, a helicopter in Sutton wasn't as unusual as in Chicken, but still rare. Staking it out would be impossible. In a community of this kind, word got around.

According to Stubby, lost tourists were a common problem. One you could be sure the young mechanic made worse. Without much effort, I managed to get lost on purpose since the boy's directions were perfectly clear to Amy. We stopped at the fuel depot for directions on the pretense of being lost.

A union rep in a yellow hard hat came out waving his arms and said, "This isn't a public gas station."

"I see. Hey, is that a helicopter pad?" I asked.

"What, did the big H on the ground give it away?"

After some talk about helicopters, I asked for and got directions back to the highway.

Driving south toward Palmer, the sun burned through the clouds, changing the dull, wet, yellow coating on the mountain slopes into sparkling gold with a fresh snow cap. It contrasted with the gray, soupy river coursing along the highway. On my first ride with Tandeske, he had described the Matanuska as too thick to drink and too thin to plow.

Thinking out loud about what we learned, I said, "What do you make of that? Stubby seemed adamant there's a civilian helicopter filling up there, but the guy said they only pumped gas for the mine."

Amy said, "Either the chopper's owner holds a legal interest in the mine, or an employee is selling their fuel on the side." I gave her idea credence.

I nodded. "I have more research for Darrell to do, and I have a sneaking suspicion Bilko or Barnes, and maybe both, have part ownership in coal mining. I don't see the operators or the government auditors overlooking a few hundred gallons of gasoline yearly." I recalled that even in a war zone, keeping track of gas was a priority for many reasons.

"Don't airplanes and helicopters use a different kind of fuel than cars and trucks?"

"Maybe…" I thought about it. "Bill and Robbie indicated the Hiller could fuel up almost anywhere along the highway. I'll call and ask Darrell when we're back in town and not long distance."

On the drive home, my mind tried to connect the dots. I half listened as Amy talked about what preparations were needed and her concerns about her father being able to walk before the service. I nodded absently and kept the truck in my lane.

In a criminal case, as Robbie reminded me, it wasn't a matter of convincing myself what the evidence showed. As an investigator, I needed to persuade ordinary citizens beyond the shadow of a doubt who killed Tim.

On the other team, Bilko was a recognized expert in creating doubt from his imagination, if not from facts.

Glancing at the multi-span girder bridge across the Knik River, I shivered. Had I drowned and washed downstream, caught in the constant backwash of tides up the arm, rising and falling over twenty feet twice a day, likely as not, no trace of me would have ever been found.

Due to the mine, Amy studied engineering as a hobby and told me the mud flats in the arm measured over three hundred feet deep. Lord only knew what sins lie buried there. The Matanuska and Knik Rivers dumped millions of cubic feet of suspended silt into the Knik Arm every year since the end of the last ice age. They built the miles of mudflats between the bridges near Palmer to Anchorage and beyond.

~~~

An hour later, I dropped Amy at home. We called Darrell from her house, and he agreed to meet at the Bone, as locals called it. The

Wishbone Café became a central meeting place. Amy drove to the hospital and checked on her father.

Traffic was light, and Anchorage didn't suffer from the rush hour jams that plagued Fort Worth in the evening. The sun burned off the clouds overhead that still shrouded the Alaska range in the distance. It would be daylight for another hour, and the sunset's orange and reds only accentuated the fall colors.

I arrived first, and Darrell entered with the doorbell clanging. The fragrance of fried chicken, burgers, and onions filled the room. We ordered burgers and fries with milkshakes.

I asked, "What can you learn about the coal mine owners?"

"Incorporated, it should be a public record. If Barnes is involved, it will likely be easy to trace. Bilko holds a lot of real estate and small companies. They don't show much activity, and he uses them to make investments that are not in his name. Slimier than a slug but still legal."

"The hallmark of a successful lawyer."

Darrell said, "You chased the guys out of the cabin on the Knik, and fresh tracks indicated the helicopter made multiple trips removing the shooters and the evidence that might tell the police who was there. The state boys got some fingerprints, but without a person to compare them to, it's a slow process."

"Check with the Army; Skinny was in prison in Leavenworth. Maybe he had friends."

Darrell sucked hard on the straw, gave up, and spooned out a mouthful of his milkshake before responding. "Jail and prison prints are a slow slog without any names to look for. They flew multiple trips and stayed hidden for the most part. Their destination must be someplace close by. Like the homestead on Wolverine Road."

I nodded in agreement. "I thought so, and not wanting to get us shot when I found the tripwire, I got us out of there. It made me think I missed one tramping through the weeds and underbrush up at their cabin on the Knik."

"It also puts them within spitting distance of Sutton. After all that flying, they probably needed gas. I see your face is healing some."

I touched the stitches in two places on my cheek. The shattered rock fragment left tiny glass-like cuts by my ear, and pieces of the bullet jacket the doctor dug out and stitched over.

"Yeah, reckon I'll have Amy snip the threads and pull them out. I can't see in the mirror up close well enough to do it myself."

After eating my last fry, I sucked the bottom dredges of the tall glass with a straw to get the last drop of strawberry shake and sat the heavy glass down with a solid clunk. "Darrell, I'm getting tired of pussyfooting around with this bunch."

Darrell sat back and put both hands on the table. "Okay?"

"Thinking it is time to rattle the tree and find who falls out."

"What did you have in mind? More important, is it legal? Robbie will be fit to be tied if you mess up his case doing something illegal."

"I want to stay legal, but I also want to wrap this up before the twenty-fifth."

He cocked his head. "Why the rush?"

I rolled the bottom of my glass between my fingers and tipped my head toward Amy's house. "Her dad got hurt, and doctors are saying he doesn't have long. She wants him to have a chance to walk her down the aisle."

"You could have said you were getting married."

"Yeah, well, it puts the rush on this investigation and finding a job. You know anyone on the railroad?"

Darrell tilted his head to the right. "I might. Are you thinking of working for them?"

"Crossed my mind, Doug says they pay fair wages and federal benefits. It would count with my service time toward a retirement someday."

"Give me a chance to connect either of our suspects to the coal mine. Hold off on anything brash. I'll check with someone at the railroad I know and see who can hire a body."

~~~

We parted in the parking lot, and I crossed Fifth Avenue and headed for my apartment. When I pulled out, a man in a blue parka with a hood stood in the shadows at the Mush Inn. The guy gave me— or my truck—a lot of attention.

After a quick check in the review mirror, I saw he stayed put, but it didn't feel right. Better keep a sharper eye out. Life in Anchorage might be as dangerous as it is in the bush.

Chapter 36

Labor Day came and went. Amy cared for her father when he came home from the hospital. Her past employer at the Anchorage Westward Hotel called wanting her to do back-office work for them. She explained she wouldn't be available until October and would need flexibility to deal with her dad. They negotiated while she arranged the wedding, adding more to her full plate.

Ricky worked at the Anchorage schools doing maintenance, and one evening, after dinner with the family, he took me aside. "Mom says Amy is running this place like a prison warden and keeps it humming, but she barely holds herself together. My sister acts calm on the surface but is set on a high simmer and could boil over in an instant."

"I had a feeling, so why mention it."

"Amy has this way of asking if something is okay when she means it is for her. Mom says, in this mode, if Amy suggests something, the answer is okay, especially regarding the wedding."

"Got it. The answer is 'yes, dear.'"

He shook his head at me. "It's easy to tell you were never married. You might not want to use those exact words, but going along to get along is an excellent policy."

Later, Amy asked about postponing a honeymoon, which I hoped for because it's hard to get a job and leave immediately. I acted disappointed but agreed it would be best. She let out a long breath and gave a tight smile of relief.

Determined to be gainfully employed, the next day, I went to the railroad office near Ship Creek and filled out an application. When completed, I handed it to a bored man who lifted a stack of other older applications and dropped mine on the bottom.

~~~

Leaving the rail yard, I drove up C Street. On my way out of town, I stopped and called Darrell for an update on the payphone in Peggy's.

The PI answered. "Sorry, I'm working on a paying gig for a civil suit, and it goes to trial next week. I researched the Sutton mine, and

Barnes has an interest in the mine. Bilko doesn't have any direct connection I could find."

I listened as he went on. "On another note, court records show, last February, Skinny was looking at twenty years hard time for an assault and robbery. Bilko took the case pro bono and made a plea deal for misdemeanor assault with three months for time served."

"Three months later, Skinny or Slim and an ex-cellmate you call Shorty went to work for Barnes. Shorty did six months for a bar fight where he busted up a bouncer and left him with a permanently bad knee."

I said, "Talk about karma."

Darrell coughed. "What?"

The PI couldn't see my grin. "Nothing. Anything else?"

"Nope, other than the obvious, all circumstantial evidence. Nothing to connect the old miner or Bilko to Tim's murder or a helicopter."

"What's your read on Robarts?" I asked.

"Funny you asked. Robbie wanted me to look at him, too. No criminal record but was arrested for fighting. Charges were either deferred or dropped. Not overly intelligent but can move heavy objects and ride herd on a crew of rough men."

"Think he could have killed Tim?"

"With the chopper available, I guess it's possible, but the people I talked to said he enjoyed a good fight but wasn't a killer." Darrell replied.

I hung up. With two hours to kill before going to Amy's for supper, Barnes had his office on Potter Road, east of Arctic, and I had a question or two.

Sitting in the truck, I studied the city map to decide the best route to get there. Looking in the mirror while backing out, I saw the guy in the blue hooded parka. Once, it was weird—twice, a coincidence, and I'm not fond of them. The man stood next to the flight service hangar.

Instead of lining up to merge onto Fifth Avenue to town, I waited for traffic to clear. Then I popped the clutch and backed across the street through the open gate as fast as the Ford would go in reverse. The feller took off running around the flight service hangar.

Run, fatso. You will talk while hot and tired instead of cool and relaxed. Skidding to stop, I jammed the truck in gear and surged forward, my bumper inches from his lard ass. When we reached the corner of the building, Tubby threw up his arms in surrender, and I slowed to a stop.

Slamming the door, I walked up to him. "Take your hands out of your pockets."

"Why?"

The smirk on his face didn't help his situation. "Because I asked nicely and only ask once. Then I assume you have a weapon, and I start breaking arms."

In his thirties, he didn't look like a thug—chubby, five eight, with three days of whiskers growing on his pudgy face.

The man pulled his hands out slowly, and his right hand fit into a set of brass knuckles.

"Put the knucks back in your pocket and keep your grubby paws where I can see them. Do you have a gun? And before you ask why, expect I'm willing to shoot you because I do have one."

"Yes, but I have a city carry permit." He got brave. "Do you have one?"

"I'm a cop." It surprised him. "I don't need one, so why do you?"

He sneered. "Private detective." He shifted on his feet, nervous, unsure.

"Who are you, and why are you watching me?"

"I don't have to say."

The left jab hit him square in the jaw. When Fatso landed flat on his back, I dropped a knee into his soft belly. It knocked the remaining wind out of him. His face turned purple, but he carefully kept his hands away and opened.

"I thought we talked about asking nicely once. Now, don't make me ask again because you won't like it."

"My client is a lawyer and wanted to know what you were doing."

"His name?" I drew my fist back when he hesitated.

The PI turned his face away. "Bilko."

"How long?"

"A few days."

After some follow-up questions, the honest answer was the day after I nearly drowned. I let the guy go.

"You didn't ask my name."

"I don't need it. If I catch you following me again, I will read your name in the *Times* when they find your body floating in Ship Creek. I suggest you see or call Bilko and quit this job. Do we understand each other?"

He nodded, turned, and walked away. I planned to talk to Barnes, but decided the old miner could wait. Instead, I went to Bilko's office. It was a short drive for me down Fifth Avenue, jogging north at C Street to Third. The business overlooked the dock and rail yard and occupied a two-story house. Someone gutted it and turned it into an office two blocks from the Federal Building and Territorial, now State, Court House.

Bilko's place was clad in blue clapboard siding with white trim. Amy told me once it was one of the homes built for executives while the railroad was under construction. I stepped into a foyer with a reception desk. Behind the twenty-something blonde with glasses and a knit sweater, I spied a mahogany door with a brass plate that said Bilko.

Reading my intent, she jumped up.

"Mr. Bilko is busy with a client—"

Driving my shoulder past her, I opened the door. Not exactly the guy I pictured. The suit and tie, sure, but a bigger and older man than I imagined. The lawyer didn't seem the least bit intimidated. He recognized me, which meant someone fed him a description or he had pictures. Probably from the guy I punched.

A gray-haired woman dressed in black sat across from the lawyer, but she stood and walked past me in a hurry, eyeing me over her shoulder until out of my reach.

Bilko said, "Widow, discussing her late husband's estate before you interrupted."

"Yeah, well, I was enjoying a perfectly ordinary life minding my own business when someone murdered a friend and tried to frame me for it."

"Sounds distressing, but how may I help you? Do you need an attorney?" He sat, leaning back in his chair, behind a sturdy, dark walnut desk, undisturbed by my— I hoped— threatening stance.

"Like a hole in my head. Explain why a guy who tried to blow me up went from being a client of yours to a killer for hire. One who killed two, possibly three men who did nothing to deserve it beyond turning down offers to sell their claims to you."

"I don't buy mining claims. I send out offers for clients who pay for my services as an attorney. I have no further obligation to speak on the matter. Is there anything else?"

"Yes, your private eye quit."

Bilko blinked and looked past me at the receptionist. I turned in time to catch her nod yes.

"A shame. He has been useful in the past."

"I'm asking this once and only once. Why, the day after someone shot at me, did you sic your PI on me?"

"Attorney-client privilege is my answer. Close the door on your way out."

The front door jerked open in the foyer, and booted feet approached rapidly. I glanced around at two city officers. The larger one with shoulder stripes said, "It's time to go, mister."

Escorted to my truck, the officer, a sergeant named Walker, asked for ID. I gave him the badge and the letter I kept in the glove box, thankful that I didn't have it on me in the river.

Walker laughed. "Chicken-Sheriff."

"They elected me. I didn't name the town."

It took time to explain my license and wallet had sunk in Knik Arm. Despite the badge and letter, the concealed weapon the cops objected to until they called the State Police. Then, according to Walker, the Police Chief called long-distance to the Attorney General in Juneau, who backed my story.

Walker said, "I guess you're free to go."

"Thanks, guys. My next stop is down on Potter Road. Care to join me?"

"Potter Road is in state jurisdiction. You need a replacement driver's license ASAP. The Department of Motor Vehicles is about twelve blocks east, next to the Army recruiter's office."

"I needed a new one anyway. Texas issued my old one."

They gave me the address for the DMV and said they were keeping an eye out for me.

~~~

Twenty minutes later, I drove into the parking lot at Barnes's office. The door was locked, the office closed, and no lights on inside. The yard gate was closed and locked. No parked cars. Bilko must have dropped Barnes a heads-up call when I went on the warpath. The old miner not being there made all the connection I needed for now.

Calling Bilko out alerted Barnes I was on to them. It might not be how Robbie would have handled it. Pa would have liked it.

I remembered the day I wanted to see how popcorn worked. I hoped this case didn't burn me as badly as that popcorn did.

Chapter 37

Arriving for supper at the last minute, I walked into a quiet house; everyone was seated around the table and not talking. I took a chair, and Amy came from the kitchen with burnt dinner. She glared and set the lasagna on the table as a dare, and we ate without comment. Everyone took some, but quietly. The garlic bread fared better, so it and the salad went fast, but most of the main dish remained. Dessert wasn't offered.

Tension remained high around the dining room throughout the meal. After eating, Amy disappeared downstairs. Ricky excused himself, took his plate through the door to the kitchen, and headed home.

I helped Amy's mom clear and do dishes after her daughter disappeared. I volunteered to wash them because I didn't know where to put everything after drying them. I started wiping down the table when Amy came up from downstairs.

Her hair tangled, and her eyes red-rimmed from crying. Creases on her cheeks made her look vulnerable, and I surmised she recently removed her face from a pillow.

"I'm sorry the food was burnt. Dad called for help pulling himself out of bed to go to the bathroom. Between Mom and I, we had a time. His ribs are so sore."

"It's okay. Your pa took the biggest serving and ate it with a smile."

She asked, "Did you help him upstairs?"

"Yes, he's back in bed and praying he can walk by the twenty-fifth."

She curled her fingers into a ball and said, "He better, or I'm going to drag him to the altar with me," sounding more like herself.

"Take a breath and sit."

I handed the dishrag to her mom, who smiled and whispered, "You'll make a fine husband."

I nodded, walked to the table, and sat beside Amy.

She said, "Tell me something funny."

I thought for a second and shrugged. "I punched a private detective in the face, threatened a prominent lawyer, and got detained by the Anchorage Police."

She blinked with her mouth open, jaw moving up and down, but no sound came out.

"Close your mouth. It looks funny with your—"

"Bullshit— oops— horse hockey. Sorry, Mom."

"You've had a hard day, dear." She shook her head and put a glass away in the cabinet.

"No, really—I stopped to use the phone at Peggy's to call Darrell…"

When I finished, she said, "I thought my day was bad."

"I didn't mind because it accomplished what I wanted. I'm tired of playing around, waiting months for evidence to be processed, and getting shot at twice. I have a concussion from getting blown up. Stitches in my face and feet, lost most of my spending money in the river, and when I saw that bastard—sorry, Mom."

"You had a hard day, too, but you guys should clean up your language before having kids."

Kids? My head turned, eyebrows raised a hair, and after thinking too long, Amy said, "She wants grandbabies to spoil. We're a big family."

"What do you want?" I asked.

"To make you happy and fill a house with children."

"Me too. By Texas standards, we had a small clan of six."

Amy smiled, genuinely happy.

"Will six be enough? Oh, and Mom has a twin sister. They run in her family."

Things were finally moving on Tim's case, but the expectations of a future family and the two-week wedding deadline all came at once and hit me square in the heart.

"I need a job."

~~~

We talked a bit about family planning before I drove home. Living at the dead-end of the street made spotting strange cars easy. Not seeing any odd ones, I went in and to bed. I slept, dreaming about a house full of kids.

In the morning, I stopped at the licensing place next door to the State Police office. Officer Turner came over and vouched for me. I took the written test and missed some questions about stopping on ice, but otherwise, I aced it. Turner made me drive around the block and park. He signed off on the driving test. I officially became a licensed driver and a citizen of the State of Alaska.

In truth, when I took the job for Barnes in '59, I became a citizen, but I never went to town to get a license and didn't have a car. With a new license, I needed a wallet, so I stopped by Woolworths to look at billfolds. Then, I walked past the movie theater to the National Bank of Alaska. Darrell took me there before I got the truck to set up an account and sell enough gold to put cash in the bank.

My old wallet and temporary checkbook lay at the bottom of the Knik River. I withdrew cash and got some new temporary checks. I bought a new wallet at Woolworths and saw a couple of walking sticks for sale I'm sure Boyd carved. I decided driving in town on paved roads without potholes was spoiling me as I headed south on Arctic Boulevard through a blizzard of yellow leaves.

The wind blew in gusts out of the north. The air promised winter sometime soon. Once across Northern Lights Boulevard, the road resembled the highways around Tok, rough with frost heaves and potholes. Turning onto Potter Road and into Barnes's parking lot, the sign said open.

Robarts and a young college-aged kid stood behind a counter.

The young man asked, "May I help—"

Chet cut him off. "There is no helping this guy. How are you, Wyatt?"

"Chet, I'm looking for old man Barnes."

"He's out of town on business."

I leaned an arm on the counter, and the kid eyed Robarts and stepped back.

"Coward, as I expected from a man who hires out his killing to an amateur."

"Mr. Barnes is a tough old bastard and smart. If he wanted someone dead, he's capable of doing it himself."

Staring unblinking into Chet's eyes, I tried to read him. The foreman wasn't afraid, but unsure. Maybe he wondered if his boss really could kill or hire killers. "He cleared out of here mighty fast after Bilko called him yesterday."

The kid nodded, but the foreman said, "Nothing of the kind."

The clerk's eyes got big, and his jaw dropped. That made me smile. "Chet, step outside."

"You want to fight? I'm your man."

"I want to talk. If I came here hunting a fight, I'd have shot you in the knee by now."

Chet started to shed his jacket. He held it for a second or two and then pulled it back over those massive shoulders.

Outdoors, I leaned on the truck. "I don't like what's going on and haven't since someone— Byron— tried to frame me for Tim's murder. Skinny and Shorty are dead, Byron is too, and the court said Byron was murdered and not a suicide the way they made it look." I watched for Chet's reaction.

"Frick and Frack got murdered for their claim. Byron was pals with your boss, and the kid screwed something up. Bilko and your boss had him killed to give them cover and tried to kill me twice. I'm tired of it, and I'm coming for them. Prison is their only chance to grow old."

"What's all your tough talk got to do with me?"

"Some folks I know think you aren't a killer. Maybe you aren't." I grinned but with no humor in it. "The only reason you're still breathing is because I'm not sure. I'm sure about the codger who runs this place and his shyster lawyer pal. I'll nail them soon. Don't put yourself between them and me."

"You could have said that—"

"In there? Yeah, but in there, you had a witness. Bilko wants witnesses. If you're not dirty, tell Barnes his lawyer plans to leave all this on him when you quit Barnes. Bilko may already have the suicide note drafted out for Barnes to sign."

"You think they killed Byron."

I nodded. "I'm certain."

"Why?"

I put a hand on Chet's shoulder, and his muscles twinged. "I know they did and only need the evidence to convince a jury. Byron didn't get the job done they sent him to do. They needed a patsy to take the fall. Someone talked nicely to him— someone he trusted. They got close and blew his brains out."

~~~

It occurred to me that's not how the Anchorage or the State Police would have handled it. If I worked for either department, I would be obligated to make a legal case and take them to court.

My father retired, and my uncle still served as a Texas Ranger. The stories I grew up with leaned heavily on extracting justice as needed. If this case was going to be solved by the twenty-fifth, it required putting a goat head bur between the two old crooks and their easy chairs. I intended to cause them enough pain to make mistakes.

On Potter Road, I tooled eastbound to Lake Ottis, taking a different route back to Peggy's. I needed a bite to eat and to call Darrell. All the eating out started to add up. *I need a job.*

The PI could catch Robbie up on my theory about the case. Much of what I told Chet came to me while talking. Byron, plain and simple, amounted to a clean-up murder.

Bilko and Barnes were behind it, but it didn't mean they pulled the trigger on Tim or Byron, and I didn't have proof to take it to court.

In the parking lot phone booth by the café, I listened as a Cessna powered up and taxied away from the air service hanger.

Talking to Darrell, I said, "Those three have access to a helicopter. With one of those, you can fly in and murder Tim and drop his body in the woods and his gear along the road. Never leave a track."

Darrell sighed. "I wished you would have talked to me first. You left them no choice. They will kill you, and no one will buy an accident or suicide. You'll go out to start your truck and get blown up. It's happened here before."

"Those two old crooks may shoot each other first. Trying to off me brings them out and gives us evidence."

"They tried before. Not so long ago, someone killed the Chief of Police here, and it is still unsolved. Sure, it brings them out in the open and leaves Amy with a dead fiancé."

"Half a million dead Chinese soldiers can tell you killing an Army Ranger is tougher than it may appear."

"You are still healing from the last try, troop, and I think the one before with the dynamite is messing with your little pea brain. What do you think will happen now?"

"I never mentioned a helicopter, or we know anything about one. Guessing, Bilko will stay in town. He's slime, and if cornered, he'll make a deal and sell Barnes out faster than you can say Jack Sprat. That's if he can't kill Barnes and frame him for the works."

"The old miner is as dangerous as a cornered mountain lion, and according to you, Chet feels sure Barnes could murder to save his hide. The old goat has no hole card." Darrell took a breath. I heard it over the phone.

"Bilko was in town the night you got shot at and went swimming. Meaning, he didn't fly. Whoever shot at you, someone flew them out of their cabin and probably to the Wolverine Lake property. Byron is indisposed, leaving Barnes or possibly another pilot we don't know yet. The miner was in the office the day you were swimming and is not around now, staying away from you. So, he might be with his boys at the homestead with the chopper."

Traffic drove steadily on the road. Another small plane revved up the engine and took off toward the mountains. I asked, "Can Tandeske get a warrant?"

The PI didn't hesitate. "No, sir. Not on what we have so far."

"That cuts it for me. I'm going out to the Wolverine homestead tonight."

"Why, what's your hurry, son?"

My rush, well, getting married, solving Tim's murder, and finding a steady job. "I need to clear this off my dinner plate so I can do other things. I must take care of this now."

"What time? I'll put on my war paint and join you."

"Darrell, this isn't in your job description, especially on what I'm not paying you."

"I'm Texan by birth, and there's a war on, so naturally, I must be there."

I couldn't argue. "Naturally. Okay, meet me at the café in Palmer, about six, the one with the blueberry pie."

Digging out another dime, I looked across the street for the pudgy PI but didn't spot anyone. Calling Amy, I told her I planned to work on a lead with Darrell, wouldn't be over for supper, and most likely would be home late.

Always perceptive, she said, "You're not lying, but you are leaving something out."

"I sorta lit a fire under Barnes, and Darrell thinks being around me is dangerous for you. I'm going to stay scarce until the state boys have their stuff together and file arrest warrants. My hope is this will end in the next day or two."

"Doug's coming home tomorrow on the train and will be here in time for supper. So, be careful and bring one of those blueberry pies home for dinner tomorrow."

"Okay." *Oh hell.* "We will be fine. I love you."

"Call me when you get home, please." She hung up.

Hopefully, Barnes isn't as sharp. Otherwise, I'm leading Darrell into a trap.

Chapter 38

Amy's request for pie upset me because she guessed where I planned to go. Worse, I unintentionally confirmed it. I hoped she would not turn up at the homestead.

Her father mentioned Amy worked as a family friend's assistant guide for a few years after high school. My future bride spent time hunting and camping in the wilderness, besides mining. I still didn't know a lot about her. Asking about her life gave me a sense she didn't want to discuss it. In turn, she asked very little about my past, and we shared a silent understanding past trauma should remain out of our future.

I drove north and glanced at the murky water as I crossed the Knik River Bridge. A couple of miles further, I pulled off at the Matanuska River near Palmer Airport. Stepping out behind my truck, I gazed southeast up the Knik Valley at the mountain past Hunter Creek and the ridge I climbed over. An easy flight from there to the Wolverine homestead: five minutes, maybe ten in the air.

The Knik looked soupy but almost transparent compared to the water I watched flowing under the bridge. Finding a discarded Coke bottle, I decided to test how much of what I watched was water and how much silt. At the river's edge, the closer I came, the scarier it looked. I dipped the bottle in and filled it to the top.

Darrell wasn't due in Palmer for forty-five minutes, and the cool, stiff breeze blowing up dust on the flats felt good. I stepped up on the bridge and placed the bottle on a steel girder.

A blue and gray Nash four-door stopped, and the driver opened his window. "You broke down?"

I guess the appearance of my truck caused his concern. "No, sir, I'm sightseeing."

The guy waved and drove on toward Knik. After a quarter-hour, the silt had not settled enough to see through the neck. I tipped it, letting the water dribble out on the ground. Turning the bottle upright, I saw mud filled more than half of it.

Like Darrell said. *Too thin to plow*. The river flowed like my life this year, caught in the current, weighed down by circumstances, and I can't see through to an end. Maybe we'll get closer tonight.

<center>~~~</center>

In Palmer, I parked by the café. Darrell arrived a little before six. We ate, and I ordered a pie to go before traveling to the homestead. The trip in the dark went quicker since I remembered the way and never missed a turn. Past the last homestead on the lake and a quarter mile from the gate, I pulled off in the last wide place in the road and stopped.

After dark, the wind died to light gusts, just enough to rattle the dead leaves clinging to branches. Leaves carpeted the ground everywhere, and the mountain's shape rose black in the fading twilight. The path we drove was easy to pick out by the scattered leaves, and I surmised no one traveled the road ahead recently.

Taking his time, Darrell strolled up and said, "What's the layout?"

Pointing, I said, "The gate is up ahead; a four-wire fence runs off left and right to dead ends. It's a recent addition and looks to be there to keep people from driving around the gate. The driveway makes a sweeping curve where anyone in the house could spot someone coming fifty yards away."

I continued. "Last time here, I cut across the bend yonder and found a trip wire. I guess it's an alarm system and likely gives plenty of false alarms from wildlife. If we happen to set one off, step away quietly and find cover. If they check it, no one will likely look too hard in the dark."

"I know you're fond of kicking hornet nests, but what's your goal here?"

Kicking I found made things happen, but it was not always what you hoped for. "Finding evidence of who killed Tim and Byron."

"Okay, say, as a police officer, I buy that. What's your excuse for being here?"

I grinned. "I went hiking with my Texan friend who has been here awhile, but we got off course coming down off the mountain. We wandered onto the property in the dark by accident, looking for a road."

He coughed, pretending to choke. "You're giving us Texans a bad name, and it's rough enough."

"Well, shucks, I just plain got myself turned around—"

Darrell shoved me down the road. "Enough of Li'l Abner, let's go."

"I'm going to circle wide to the south and around to the mountainside where cops would be less likely to approach and may not be trip-wired."

He nodded in the dark. "Keep in mind, moose and bears of the black and brown variety are out here with us and might be more dangerous than Barnes and his crew."

"Duly noted."

Ten minutes later, scouting by moonlight, I tried to avoid dead falls and sticker bushes. The going turned out rougher and more time-consuming than I anticipated. After a stinging switch swept across my face from a spruce limb, I felt like a dumb Texan lost in the woods.

Darrell tapped on my shoulder and pointed to his ear. Listening carefully, I turned, looking back toward Palmer's lights. My partner must have spent less time around noisy ordinance and picked up the sound of an approaching helicopter.

The mechanical beast had no navigation lights on and impossible to see even in the moonlight until it thundered above us. The chopper hooked around, slowed to a hover, turned on a spot, and landed a short distance away. When the engine died, we heard voices grunting and groaning.

Darrell cupped his hands over my ear and said, "They're moving their bird into cover. I heard at least two voices."

I spoke into Darrell's ear. "Could two people move it by themselves?"

Darrell shook his head and showed three fingers, then four.

Having seen the one at Merrill Field, I guessed three men only if one happened to be Chet Robarts. That chopper had wheels on the skids and allowed lifting it by the tail to push it around. Still, it's a big job, with one lifting, two pushing— three men minimum, possibly more.

Finding a place to observe the house took another thirty minutes of skulking through the weeds. A larger home than I expected, it was a one-story home with a high-pitched roof. A loft over the first level, and the whole building sat near a circle drive.

The house front faced toward the road with at least five acres of cleared yard. Someone had logged off the tall spruce, probably to construct the home. Someone had chopped away the underbrush on the sides and back. It left several large stumps visible. The open area made for a good field of fire from the house.

With light from the window and the moon, I couldn't see the Hiller. Painted gray, it blended into the shadows.

Moving around to the rear of the house, I made out windows and a stove pipe. The pipe protruded through a corrugated metal roof. Fireplaces weren't common in homesteads and were inefficient compared to a wood stove for heating. It reduced the fuel required to heat the home through a long winter. A large stack of freshly cut firewood sat under the window near the back door and stood ready for winter use.

The only light besides the moon came from inside a window. Oil lanterns, likely, as I saw no power poles past Wolverine Lake.

I couldn't see the helicopter. It wouldn't fit in the one outbuilding slightly bigger than a detached single-car garage. The outhouse sat at the edge of the woods at the back of the house to the left of our observation post. One other dark window and a back door were visible through the trees.

Darrell tapped my arm, then whispered, "No sign of a hound dog."

I nodded, pointed at my chest, walked my fingers in a big circle, and pointed at the ground. The detective gave me the thumb, forefinger circled for okay and positioned himself behind a tree to wait.

Reaching in front of my legs, I swept my hands slowly up and down, feeling for fishing line until reaching the clearing behind the house. The back door swung open. I stepped into the clearing, and I sprinted for the cover of the outhouse.

A man stepped down, holding the door with his trailing hand, and let it close. Not slamming it, but it made a racket and slapped shut, breaking the stillness. He clomped down two steps before hitting the path to the privy.

Little chance walking from the light into the dark, he could make me out. So, I kept one eye on the feller until he entered the outhouse. The door opened with a screech of rusted hinges and the *sproong* sound of a coiled spring that closed the door with a smack.

"Damn," the man said and pulled out a flashlight. He slapped it in his hand before it put out a feeble light I saw through an open knothole.

The guy on the can was unarmed and easy pickings. I wanted Barnes, not an unarmed semi-bald guy with a scraggly beard. The man in the crapper may have shot at me. No way for me to know for sure.

Dropping his bib overalls, he took a seat, letting out a loud fart before grunting, constipated from the sounds of it and the time involved. After a minute or two, he wiped his pimpled ass, pulled his overalls on, and stepped out. The door slapped shut, and a match flared as he lit a cigarette.

Out of patience, I stepped out, and when the man turned, I put the barrel of Gail's Colt right in his gut and a finger to my lips. Pointing my prisoner, I pushed him in the direction of the woods. The smoker puffed hard on the cigarette, keeping his hands and shoulders high and walking quietly. Darrell came down and met us halfway.

Darrell whispered, "What are we doing with this one?"

I winked at the PI, hoping he saw it in the dark. "Bilko said to kill them all, but he didn't know this one. If he tells me what we need to know, I guess he can walk away and leave Alaska." Turning to the guy, I asked, "You planned on leaving, right?"

The man's head bobbed up and down.

"We're going to move carefully into the woods, don't trip, don't make any loud noises, or I'll gut shoot your ass and leave you for the bears to eat alive."

Out of view from the house, we sat him down, pulled his bootlaces, and tied his hands and feet with them.

I asked, "Who is at the house?"

"James, Terry, and Mister Barnes."

"What are you doing here?"

"I live here."

I pointed. "This is your house?"

"No, sir, Barnes hired me to take care of this place and the helicopter."

"Who flew in the helicopter tonight?"

"Barnes and James."

"Were you on the river the other day?"

My tone must have worried him because he flinched. "No, Terry and James. Barnes radioed me to go get them."

"You drove? There's no car. No phone lines."

"I flew, and we have a truck in the shed yonder with a radio in it. The boss called the mine. I call them twice a day. They told me to head over and pick those two up. It took several trips, and I made a gas run in the middle and picked Barnes up. I don't know where he went today, but he probably went to his house. He has a big backyard."

"How did you know to call?"

"I call at seven in the morning and six at night to check for messages."

"How long have you worked for Barnes?"

"Awhile. I saw him land the helicopter at the Flight Service place across from Peggy's. I was fixin' to sign out of the Army and thought I might find a job at the training center flying the guy's Hiller. Barnes was there and followed me out. We went to Peggy's. He told me to come to his office. Later, we went to Sutton. There's a big metal building where he kept the chopper. Next thing I know, I'm his pilot, mechanic, and caretaker for this place."

"I have a silly question. Do you need special airplane gas?"

"No, and that's why the Army likes them. Eighty-seven octane or above, up to a hundred, will burn in that engine." He grimaced. "These strings are making my hands hurt."

"It's better than being dead, right?"

Darrell pulled me back and spoke in my ear. "You have a chopper, a witness who says Barnes hired him to fly it. Barnes ordered him to pick up the two men who shot at you. All three are in the house. Robbie says you are a state-certified investigator."

"So?"

"You have probable cause to arrest all three and a witness who saw them in the house. You don't need a warrant because, if you leave, Barnes will probably get in that bird and fly away."

A male voice called out the back door. "Yo, Wade, did yous fall in?"

Chapter 39

"That's Terry. He's a mean SOB, and I'm familiar with a few. He thinks he's a New York gangster or something," Wade said.

"Stay here." I pulled a greasy rag out of Wade's coveralls, gagged him, and waved for Darrell to follow.

The thug at the door wore a red shirt, a wool vest, and dark, long pants. He started marching for the outhouse, threw open the door, and began looking around the backyard. Aside from a blocky build and dark hair, it was hard to make him out.

I eased behind the outhouse, stepped around it, and turned on Wade's flashlight.

Terry swung around. "Get that light out of my eyes before I stomp your scrawny ass into a mudhole."

I remembered a friend in boot camp who grew up in Brooklyn, and the accent was unmistakable. The light died.

"You're not—"

I owed the bastard a few stitches minimum. I walloped Terry on the chin with the flashlight, which came back on. The man backed up two steps but didn't go down.

"We've got company!" he yelled through bloody lips, spat, and stepped forward, fist-drawn back for a haymaker.

Darrell ran for the back door. The hired muscle glanced at him. Dropping the light, I punched his chin with all my might this time. His head snapped back, but he stood his ground and stayed standing. I struck the brute in the neck across his Adam's apple with the Colt. Terry grabbed his throat with both hands, and I backhanded the gagging crook across the temple with the gun. Darrell yelled, "Halt," and I heard three shots behind me.

Terry dropped, choking and bloody, but not out. So I took Ricky's advice and kicked him in the forehead. Glancing back, I saw the PI holding a gun on a man on the ground.

"Barnes is running," Darrell said. "This one is down for the count."

Terry's only inclination to fight was for air. I rolled the choking goon on his face, stripped his belt out, and used it to hogtie his hands and feet.

Running to the door, I saw a baseball sized chunk of the back of a man's head on the step, which I assumed belonged to James.

"I told him to halt, and he shot at me. I shot back and with greater accuracy." Darrell nodded toward the door. "We have to clear it before hunting Barnes down."

Then we heard a truck start on the other side of the house, and the shed door shattered. We caught a glimpse of an old Army five-quarter-ton like Gene's, only on the original-size wheels, headed out of the driveway.

In the little time it took us to make sure no more possible shooters were inside, the truck's taillights disappeared around the corner, and we heard a loud crash at the gate. He hadn't stopped to open it. Two more crashes followed a short time later.

"He didn't slow down to open the gate," I said.

At the sound of the second and third collision, Darrell said, "Damn, I liked my new Jimmy." Referring to his green and white GMC 4x4.

Barnes's getaway vehicle was a later model of Gene's old swamp buggy, but with street-legal semi-truck-sized tires and the same eight-inch-wide steel bumper, I watched the mayor mow down trees with barely a scratch.

We walked back to Terry, who was breathing better but still choking and spitting blood.

"I'll check on Wade." Darrell jogged into the weeds.

"Yous better hurry and," Terry coughed and spat, "snag him."

"We know who he is and have enough to charge him with murder."

The thug shook his head. "Old Barnesy is a vengeful a-hole."

I said, "He won't make it too far."

Terry gagged, choked, and hocked out a gob of snot and blood. "He planned on killing you at your girlfriend's house tonight. They're waiting for ya to show up before they firebombed it to kill them Crocketts, too. If you aren't there when the lights go out, they'll burn it anyway."

Darrell walked out from the brush with Wade in tow.

"Holy shit!" Wade said, looking at the dead man.

The PI said, "Could have been you."

"I have to run to the truck, make sure it's usable, and drive back to town. Barnes plans to burn Amy's house with everyone inside."

"What?" Darrell processed it. "Go."

Terry yelled, "Too late. What time is it?"

I checked my watch: 9:45. Amy's family would be in bed in the next thirty minutes.

Wade said, "I didn't know any of that. I swear. I probably can't take you to Anchorage. Barnes burned up too much fuel, but I can drop you in Palmer near the police station."

I turned on him. "How?"

"In the Hiller."

Untied, he led us past the shattered door and the garage. Barnes had chopped a hole through the branches of four good-sized spruce trees, creating ample space for the helicopter. He covered it with a tarp as a makeshift hangar.

The old miner cabled the tops of the trees together, bending them so the limbs were too thick to see through from the air. He embedded two timbers into the ground that acted as rails to roll the bird uphill.

Wade explained, "I can move it out alone, but I use the four-by and a pully to drag it in when I'm alone."

We jerked the tarp off, and in five minutes, the Hiller was ready to fly.

Wade said, "Climb aboard."

"I hate flying."

Darrell said, "You love Amy and are the legal authority here. Now, jump in."

Wade cranked the engine, and the blades started turning.

With Darrell shoving me, I climbed into the seat as the blades came up on full power. Wade lifted off. The doors were missing, and I frantically searched for the safety harness and struggled to figure out how to hook it up. The pilot had both hands full but yelled instructions.

By the time I fastened my belt, I saw the water tower and the lights of Palmer. It looked all different from the air, and I contemplated being violently ill.

Wade blew through town across the flats, cutting off miles of road travel. We spotted Barnes's taillights on the narrow road running through the trees down the highway near the Eklutna Power Plant trail race. He swung the chopper around in a steep arc.

"We don't have enough time, gas, or a landing spot to catch him." He nodded at the gas gauge. "We have to get back to Palmer and a phone." He looked at me. "There's a bag under the seat. Where's the police station?"

Finding the bag, I puked my guts up and wiped my mouth on a sleeve. Supper came up, which reminded me the station was a block behind the café. As Wade flew us over Palmer, I spotted the patrol cars in the parking lot and pointed. "There. Where can we set this thing down?"

Wade tipped his head. "Right there?"

"There's no room!"

Wade ignored my concerns. The chopper settled in as Tandeske and another officer came out and drew their weapons. A power pole with a guy wire stood at one side of the lot. A porch roof came off a building across the lot from the pole. The police cruisers parked at an angle by the porch.

"You're going to hit the car."

"No, the blades are too high if I hold power and keep them up. You take off out here, and I'll land at the airport and wait for you."

"You're not on the ground."

"It's only a couple of feet, jump."

My desire to be out almost equaled my fear of unsnapping the harness. I stepped out on the strut, the pilot jostled it, and I jumped. The chopper roared off into the dark. I never expected to see Wade again.

Stumbling over on my hands and knees, Tandeske pulled me to my feet and demanded to know, "What was going on?"

"Call APD for assistance, and they are planning to burn the Crocketts' house with them in it."

After further clarification and a quick call, the Anchorage Police reported they dispatched two officers. The other city cops were tied up at a fire only a few blocks away from the courthouse.

Tandeske tuned the Anchorage PD radio frequency in on their radio, and we listened. The arriving policemen at Crocketts' house spotted a two-tone '57 Chevy fleeing as they drove up with lights and sirens. The cops went in pursuit. Miscalculating a curve, the suspects drove into a utility pole. The car burst into a ball of flames. APD officer requested the fire department.

Tandeske waited for confirmation that everyone at the Crocketts' house was okay before going to the airport. Wade landed and waited for them. Bill arrested the pilot and charged him as an accessory to murder. I figured to testify for Wade and didn't think the State's charge would stick. The other state policeman went to the Wolverine homestead and took over the scene until another backup arrived to help.

~~~

Barnes disappeared, and APD found no sign of him. Tandeske gave me a ride out to my vehicle and planned to transport Terry to a hospital and then a judge before going to jail.

Darrell stayed with our trucks. Barnes sideswiped both our vehicles. My old Ford sustained the least damage but sat high centered at the road's edge. Darrell's GMC rested in the same situation, with the front fender pinned against the tire.

A tow truck pulled our vehicles from the ditch. My Ford remained drivable, with a bent left front wheel and no spare. The wrecker hauled Darrell's to a yard in Palmer. The PI rode with me back to Anchorage.

Darrell said, "What the hell are you doing running around without a spare?"

"I never checked for one until today."

Driving it above forty would shake any loose fillings from our teeth.

I dropped Darrell at his office downtown. He said, "I'll meet you at the State Police office after a few hours of sleep."

"Yeah, I'm headed home to catch a wink too. Amy and the family are bound to be asleep. After all the excitement, they need the rest."

We said goodnight even though light started to show over the mountains.

~~~

The city went silent with no traffic, taking a breather after back-to-back emergencies. Turning onto North Flower Street, I spotted Amy's Fairlane from two blocks away and smiled. *I could use a bath.* I pulled behind her car, half expecting her to come out and meet me. Eight hours since the police chased off the bombers, she had probably fallen asleep waiting.

As a kid, I grew up without locked doors. In Chicken, they mostly didn't have doors you could lock or any reason to need them. Amy had a key. I lost mine in the mud in Knik Arm. I balanced a slightly misused pie and shut the truck door, which popped loudly against the bent fender.

Kicking the crud off my boots, mud I picked up from the ditch helping push the old Ford onto the road, I walked the length of a wooden sidewalk to the basement door under a shed roof covering a stairwell.

I opened the door quietly, in case Amy slept on the sofa so I wouldn't wake her. Only, she sat up awake on the sofa bed, fully dressed in the dark. I flipped on the light.

"We've been waiting for you, Wyatt. Keep your hands out. If you reach for your gun, I'll shoot you first and Miss Crockett next."

"Banks," we said together.

"Who cares? Sit."

I put the pie on the table, raised my hands shoulder high, turned, and sat as far away from Amy as possible. I glanced over, and she wasn't a cowering, frightened woman. She was mad— I knew the look.

"Sorry," she said, "he came in, and I thought it was you."

"She's my bonus. Chet told me before he quit, you doubted my willingness to kill. Tim didn't think I would kill him either." Amy's body jerked like he hit her with a club. "Tim didn't know how I got there ahead of him. I parked the bird right in the middle of your claim." He nodded at Amy. She went ghostly pale. "I told him to sell his interest in your claim at Bilko's office. He refused and laughed when I said I would take it."

"Why did you want their claim?" I asked.

"That whole area will be worth more than a billion dollars. We think by sixty-five. We needed to control it while the prices stayed reasonable, but that sniveling Rosenberg brushed off our offer and then walked away from his claim."

"Must be hard being so disliked."

Barnes reached with his left hand, pulled a kitchen chair out, and sat while holding the gun steady on my chest. He ignored my remark.

"When I found out he left the claim, I flew to Fairbanks to file, and it was already gone. One of my employees stole it out from under me."

"I had no idea."

Amy asked through clenched teeth, "Why kill Tim? The mine is in a trust, and he couldn't make a deal. None of us can unless we all do."

"He should have said so, but by then, Byron had run his yap and told Tim our plan to try and bring him in on the deal. I had no choice."

Amy sat, shocked. "Byron was in on it?"

Barnes flipped the gun around casually, then locked it back on me.

"Well, he knew all the miners and was friendly with most, especially you Crocketts. I've always wanted your mine and Rosenburg's upstream from ours. We showed plenty of potential and expected the claims upstream would be rich, but the Davis Creek crowd never knew what they were doing."

Barnes continued. "Frick and Frack, I thought the same, inept brothers playing at mining, but the Walker Creek Mine produced well, and we planned to make them a deal. Byron made the offer for the F & F when we didn't get a call from our letter. Slim and Byron sewed up a deal with the widow, I thought. Until you found their cache."

"Where did he hide before—"

Amy interrupted my question. "You killed him and put him in the truck."

Barnes looked at Amy, dismissed her, and said, "Byron hid out in a cabin on the other side of the border until they killed the brothers. Then Shorty got shot, and your brother," he swung the gun on Amy, "offed Slim. I didn't have anyone I could depend on, so I flew up to take care of things with Terry."

"Who's Slim?" Amy asked.

"The guy Doug shot; we called him Skinny," I said.

"I could have handled it. Only the Chicken's sheriff snooped around and nearly walked into our camp. One of the other miners sent him away. I didn't want anything to do with bringing the Mounties down on us." Barnes said, "Bilko organized the investors, suggested letting Byron take the fall for Frick and Frack, Tim, and how to set it up. Your suggestion to Chet, the shyster might want a new fall guy, worried me."

"Bilko doesn't look like much of a threat."

"He isn't, personally, but he knows people, and he's where I find talent for the dirty work."

"Chet, too?" I asked.

"No, he's a good foreman, dependable and loyal, or was. I'll see him next."

"So, what about your old partner?" I didn't care about the lawyer but suspected I didn't want this conversation to end.

"You haven't heard. The old bastard died in an arson fire at his offices. Killed by the very guys he sent me to replace Shorty and Slim."

"The two who got cooked on the telephone pole leaving Crocketts' place?"

He nodded at me. "One of the hazards of driving around with gasoline firebombs in your backseat. Amy told me about them."

Barnes launched to his feet faster than I believed a man his age and size could move.

"Time for me to go. I have business to tend to and a plane to catch."

Turning a bit, I raised my hands high, pulling up the jacket above my waist and exposing the gun behind my back. I glanced at Amy. She nodded and scooted across the couch toward me.

Barnes smiled. "Aw, she still loves you. Now she gets to watch you die."

Amy screamed, "No!" and threw her arm as if she had a baseball in her hand rather than a Kleenex tissue.

Barnes swung the five-shot Detective Special at her and jumped back as she dove behind me. I jumped up and stepped toward Barnes to draw his fire, twisted my hips and shoulders, throwing a punch with no possibility of hitting Barnes. The move turned me sideways, and made a smaller target, knowing Barnes wouldn't miss at such a close range.

My turning gave Amy a chance by making the pistol behind my belt more accessible. I felt the Colt slip out and heard the hammer click on full cock. After cringing at my swinging fist, Barnes's eyes flared wide. He took half a step back and turned the gun, aiming for me. Flame belched, the sound thundered, he over-corrected, and the bullet punched my chest at an angle. It rotated me further, and I stepped closer and shoved my fist at Barnes's head.

The miner sidestepped, dodging the blow. His eyes showed glee, and he grinned. Using two hands, Barnes steadied the gun pointed at my head. Falling to my left, I ducked. Three shots boomed evenly spaced but close together as I hit the floor.

Landing hard, I glanced up, looking for Barnes, and spotted him on the floor. My first employer in Alaska laid out there next to me with blood pouring from his mouth and two front teeth missing.

I closed my eyes, and Amy screamed, "Wyatt!"

Chapter 40

I learned from the firemen my landlord upstairs called the police. Three Anchorage cops surrounded the house, and I heard them demanding Amy come out. She held a pillowcase on my chest, trying to stop the bleeding. Mr. Simpson, the landlord, came down the stairwell. He saw her, waved to the officers, and yelled for an ambulance.

When firemen and an ambulance crew arrived, they started an IV, patched my chest with gauze, and wrapped it tight. The rescuers struggled with the stretcher to get me up the narrow stairs and into the ambulance. I saw no foaming blood, so I guessed it missed my lung.

Awake, I rode to the hospital. One officer detained Amy and kept her at the scene. At Providence Hospital, they took my clothes and then took X-rays. The doctor, a short, skinny blonde guy with glasses and one of those surgeon outfits, stopped in to check me over.

"Well, sir, you're a lucky man."

I sat up on the exam table with one of those hospital gowns on. "I know. I'm getting married in a couple of weeks."

He put his hands on his hips and leaned over. "I meant because you aren't dead. The medic found this in your shirt pocket."

He reached into his jacket and tossed the gold star on my lap.

I picked it up with my right hand. The other one didn't work too well. I twisted the badge in the bluish fluorescent light. The doctor watched from inside a curtain wrapped around the table in the ER.

One point remained attached by a sliver of gold. Barnes's bullet hit the center of the badge at an angle, punching an oblong hole through the star open between the top and side points. The shot all but obliterated SHERIFF etched across the shiny star.

"Well, one way or another, this case is closed, and I can marry my angel." It struck me, then—the resemblance to the Texas Ranger's star my father took so much pride in wearing. Not a badge or a job I wanted. In fact, I ran from that responsibility all the way to Chicken. Well, I've earned some pride in it.

Doc Hudson interrupted my musings, partially induced by drugs. "We must get the bullet out. It flattened from hitting your badge. Made a ragged hole that carried gold, fleece, and cotton into the wound and stopped close to an artery under your shoulder. A wrong move may cut the vessel, and you will see angels differently."

"Trying to scare me, Doc?"

He gave a little smirk. "Nope, I'm trying to keep things truthful."

Right then, State Police Officer Turner came in with an APD Detective. He said his name was Gentile, a big guy, well fed. He combed his hair back like Gene's but much thicker on top. The detective smiled like something struck him as perpetually funny. He wore a rumpled suit.

Turner said, "You're looking better than I expected."

The doctor said, "The medics controlled the bleeding and started an IV, so his blood pressure is better. I'm leaving to wash up for surgery to remove the bullet. In five minutes, the nurses will push him to the OR. Any questions after surgery will be tomorrow if his luck holds out."

Turner said, "Talk to Father John here and make it quick."

"I need you to run me through what happened at your apartment," Gentile said.

I wondered at the Father John reference, explained what I recalled, and ended as the nurses arrived.

Gentile said, "It sounds okay and squares with what the other witness said, but Barnes was a prominent community member, and his lawyer is toast, in the literal sense, also."

"Yeah, and Barnes had him cooked. Detective," I said, "there are many pieces to the puzzle, but Darrell Johnson and Robbie Robertson are the best sources if I don't make it out of surgery. Where's Amy?"

The nurses released the brakes on the gurney.

"She is giving her statement at the city station, and we will transport her to the hospital as soon as we can," he said, as they pushed me out of the ER. She killed a man. He needed it, but taking a life changes you, and I learned firsthand what that was like.

~~~

Clear weather turned cold while I recovered in the hospital. After being released two days before our Sunday wedding, I sat in my basement apartment, contemplating if it was over. I wanted to ask Darrell if Barnes and Bilko had the funds to buy up all those claims. Barnes mentioned investors.

A knock on the door. Robbie took a room at the Mush Inn before the wedding and called my landlord. He told me Robbie planned to check on how I held up. The tall cop pushed the door open and peeked around before coming in. He looked unofficial in his jeans; a dark-blue, long-sleeved shirt; and a light jacket.

"You still have your left wing in a sling," he said.

The plaid wool shirt I pulled on my right arm, the buttons undone, and the left side I hung over my other shoulder.

"They say I'll be able to go without it to get married. It hurt less getting shot than cutting the bullet out. Doc said the slug had a death grip on my innards. Funny, I went through Korea and came all this way to Anchorage to stop a bullet."

"Probably not as scary as getting married."

"You speak from experience?"

Robbie reached to his left hand. "We had a good run. She got pneumonia. It's been a few years now."

"Sorry for your loss. The only thing scaring me about marrying Amy is not having a job. Tim's case is solved. So, the State's check is not coming in anymore."

"On the bright side, since you were working the case and wounded by one of the perpetrators, the State is self-insured and picking up your substantial hospital bills."

Robbie grabbed a seat at the table and turned it to face me like Barnes did. The floor, Amy had stripped to bare concrete. The carpet, she ripped up, and Amy scrubbed the slab by hand with bleach. "It's great news because my bride said she would pay the bill. I didn't need to owe the Crocketts any more than my life. Turns out my soon-to-be wife is a hell of a shot."

"It still smells like bleach in here," Robbie said. "Turner told me about the bills, and Gail claims credit for her shooting lessons. Amy fired the pistol you carried with Gail out at Chicken and understood the safety and the half-cocked hammer."

"If Barnes had gotten off a second round, neither of us would be here."

Robbie said admiringly, "She stitched him up the middle. One in the breadbasket, one through the heart, and for good measure, one more in the mouth. How did you know she could handle a pistol?"

"Everyone carries a gun in the bush for protection, but on the first trip to the homestead on Wolverine Road, I knew she hunted and handled a gun like it was part of her."

"The State District Attorney ruled the shooting as self-defense and isn't bringing any charges."

I held up a hand. In Robbie's mind, it was over. It would be a long road for Amy. "Let's talk about something else."

"Okay," Robbie patted the table with his hand, "I've been nominated for Public Safety Commissioner."

"Hey, that's great. I could use a good job."

"I have been told no, at least for you. The AG didn't like being put on the spot with APD. I tried. Dottie too, but her influence goes only so far, and I suspect my appointment, if approved in Juneau, is her doing."

"Well, I plan on finding employment—"

Amy knocked twice and walked in. "I thought I saw your old truck out front. How are you?"

"You look beautiful, dressed like a city girl in a pretty dress instead of a mine foreman's getup," Robbie said.

It might be true, and she worked to sound lighthearted, but Amy aged remarkably in less than a week.

"Thanks, but I'm more comfortable at the mine."

I looked away from the lines creasing her face. "Robbie is getting promoted to Commissioner."

He stood and offered her a chair, but she hugged the tall cop and sat with me.

"It isn't carved in stone. I planned to give you your present at the wedding, but your husband-to-be has his guts all tied up in knots. So, I need to give you two this present early; it is also from Darrell and Dottie."

"When will you and Dottie admit you're a couple?" Amy asked.

Robbie's face turned a little red, and he slowly tipped his head back and forth, holding his chin in one hand. "It's a complicated thing. There needs to be time. Dot's a powerful, independent woman and a bit older than me."

"She's been waiting for you to say it's time. Maybe the next wedding will be yours."

"Well, this one is for you two, and I have something to make it easier on your fella, but I hope you both like it."

"I'm curious, what's up your sleeve?" I asked.

"A friend of mine is the Railroad Agent for the Alaska Railroad. He is quitting, and on our say, he recommended you for the job."

My face went blank. I felt like a kid holding a stocking full of coal on Christmas Day.

"That's wonderful," she said.

I looked at Amy and then back to Robbie. "What's so great about selling tickets to ride the train?"

Amy bumped into my least injured arm, and the state cop nearly fell out of his chair laughing.

"I don't see what's so funny." I swiveled from watching Robbie and Amy, confused.

When he quit laughing and rubbed tears from his eyes, he said, "It's an appointed office, Wyatt. Like the US Marshals, officially at the designation of the President of the United States, but he signs the paper the Railroad Administrator sends him."

"Any crimes on railroad properties or the train is up to the Railroad Agent to investigate, and you have some fellows working for you who are the train police." He explained.

Amy hugged me, careful not to hurt my left side.

"Well, I never heard of such a thing. Does it come with a badge? My old one is ruined."

"There is only one badge of that kind in America, here in Alaska. Other railroads hire their detectives, but this is the only Federal Railroad in the country, and it will be yours to protect. Like being the sheriff of Chicken, it's unique."

Grinning, I said, "Thank God it isn't an airline."

The End

www.ingramcontent.com/pod-product-compliance
Lightning Source LLC
Chambersburg PA
CBHW051102030726
47504CB00006B/1752